Emmanuel Guibert

Marc Boutavant

ARIOL

The Little Rats of the Opera

PAPERCUTZ™
New York

ARiOL Graphic Novels available from PAPERCUTZ™

ARiOL graphic novels are also available digitally wherever e-books are sold.

ARiOL
Just a Donkey Like You and Me
PAPERCUTZ

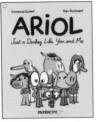

Graphic Novel #1
"Just a Donkey Like You and Me"

ARiOL
Thunder Horse
PAPERCUTZ

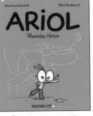

Graphic Novel #2
"Thunder Horse"

ARiOL
Happy as a Pig...
PAPERCUTZ

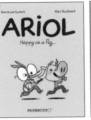

Graphic Novel #3
"Happy as a Pig..."

ARiOL
A Beautiful Cow
PAPERCUTZ

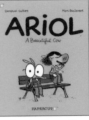

Graphic Novel #4
"A Beautiful Cow"

ARiOL
Bizzbilla Hits the Bullseye
PAPERCUTZ

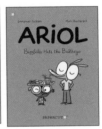

Graphic Novel #5
"Bizzbilla Hits the Bullseye"

ARiOL
A Nasty Cat
PAPERCUTZ

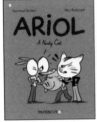

Graphic Novel #6
"A Nasty Cat"

ARiOL
Top Dog
PAPERCUTZ

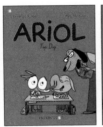

Graphic Novel #7
"Top Dog"

ARiOL
The Three Donkeys
PAPERCUTZ

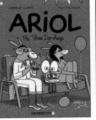

Graphic Novel #8
"The Three Donkeys"

ARiOL
The Teeth of the Rabbit
PAPERCUTZ

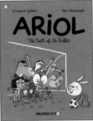

Graphic Novel #9
"The Teeth of the Rabbit"

ARiOL
The Little Rats of the Opera
PAPERCUTZ

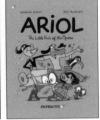

Graphic Novel #10
"The Little Rats of the Opera"

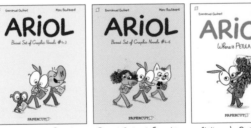

ARiOL
Boxed Set of Graphic Novels #1-3
PAPERCUTZ

Boxed Set of Graphic Novels #1-3

ARiOL
Boxed Set of Graphic Novels #4-6
PAPERCUTZ

Boxed Set of Graphic Novels #4-6

ARiOL
Where's PETULA?
PAPERCUTZ

"Where's Petula?" Graphic Novel

ARiOL graphic novels are available for $12.99 only in paperback, except for "Where's Petula?" which is $9.99. The ARiOL Boxed Sets are $38.99 each. Available from booksellers everywhere. You can also order online from papercutz.com. Or call 1-800-886-1223, Monday through Friday, 9 – 5 EST. MC, Visa, and AmEx accepted. To order by mail, please add $4.00 for postage and handling for first book ordered, $1.00 for each additional book and make check payable to NBM Publishing. Send to: Papercutz, 160 Broadway, Suite 700, East Wing, New York, NY 10038.

papercutz.com

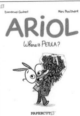

The Little Rats of the Opera

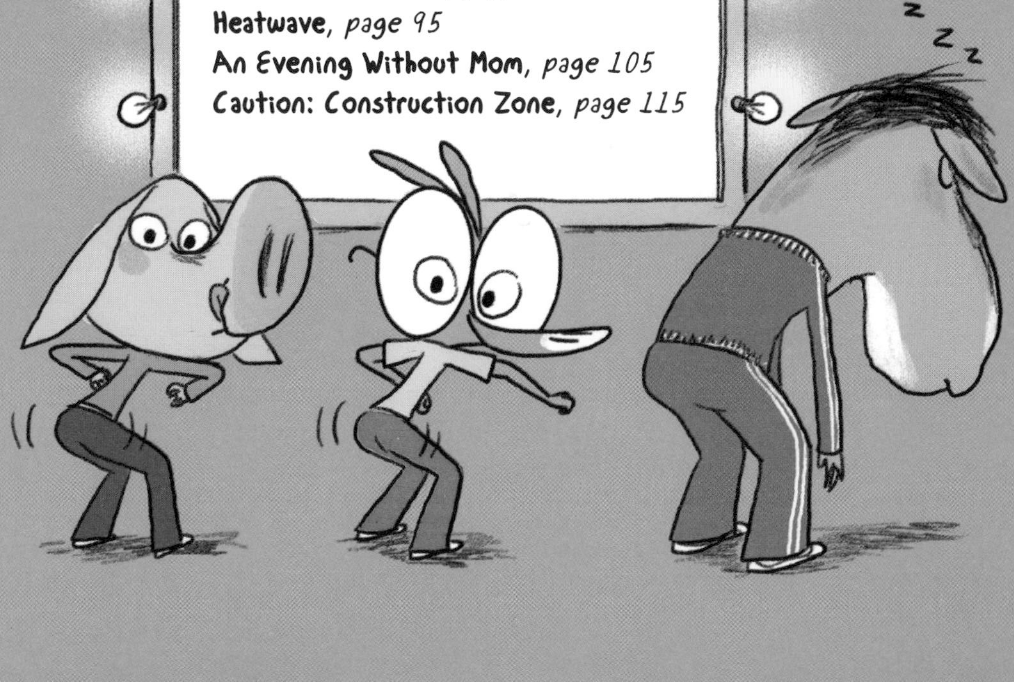
z
z
z

To Madame Tyrode.
— Emmanuel Guibert

ARIOL

#10 The Little Rats of the Opera

Emmanuel Guibert — Writer
Marc Boutavant — Artist
Rémi Chaurand — Colorist
Joe Johnson — Translation
Bryan Senka — Lettering
Dawn Guzzo — Production/Production Coordinator
Jeff Whitman — Assistant Managing Editor
Jim Salicrup
Editor-in-Chief

Volume 10: Les petits rats de l'opera© Bayard Editions, 2015

ISBN: 978-1-62991-736-8

Printed in China
Printed June 2017

Papercutz books may be purchased for business or promotional use.
For information on bulk purchases please contact Macmillan Corporate and Premium Sales Department at
(800) 221-7945 x5442.

Distributed by Macmillan
First Papercutz Printing

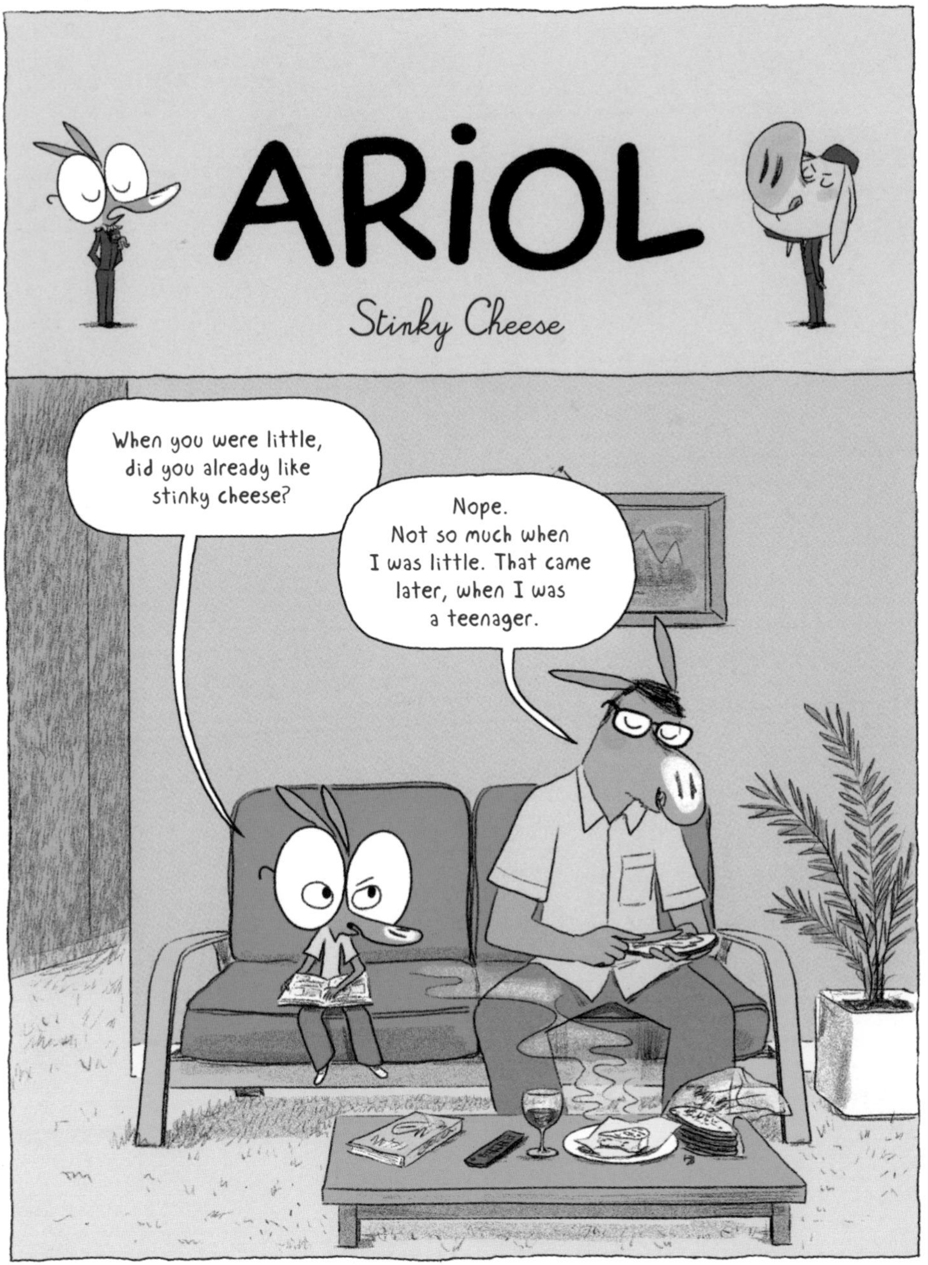
ARiOL
Stinky Cheese
When you were little, did you already like stinky cheese?
Nope. Not so much when I was little. That came later, when I was a teenager.

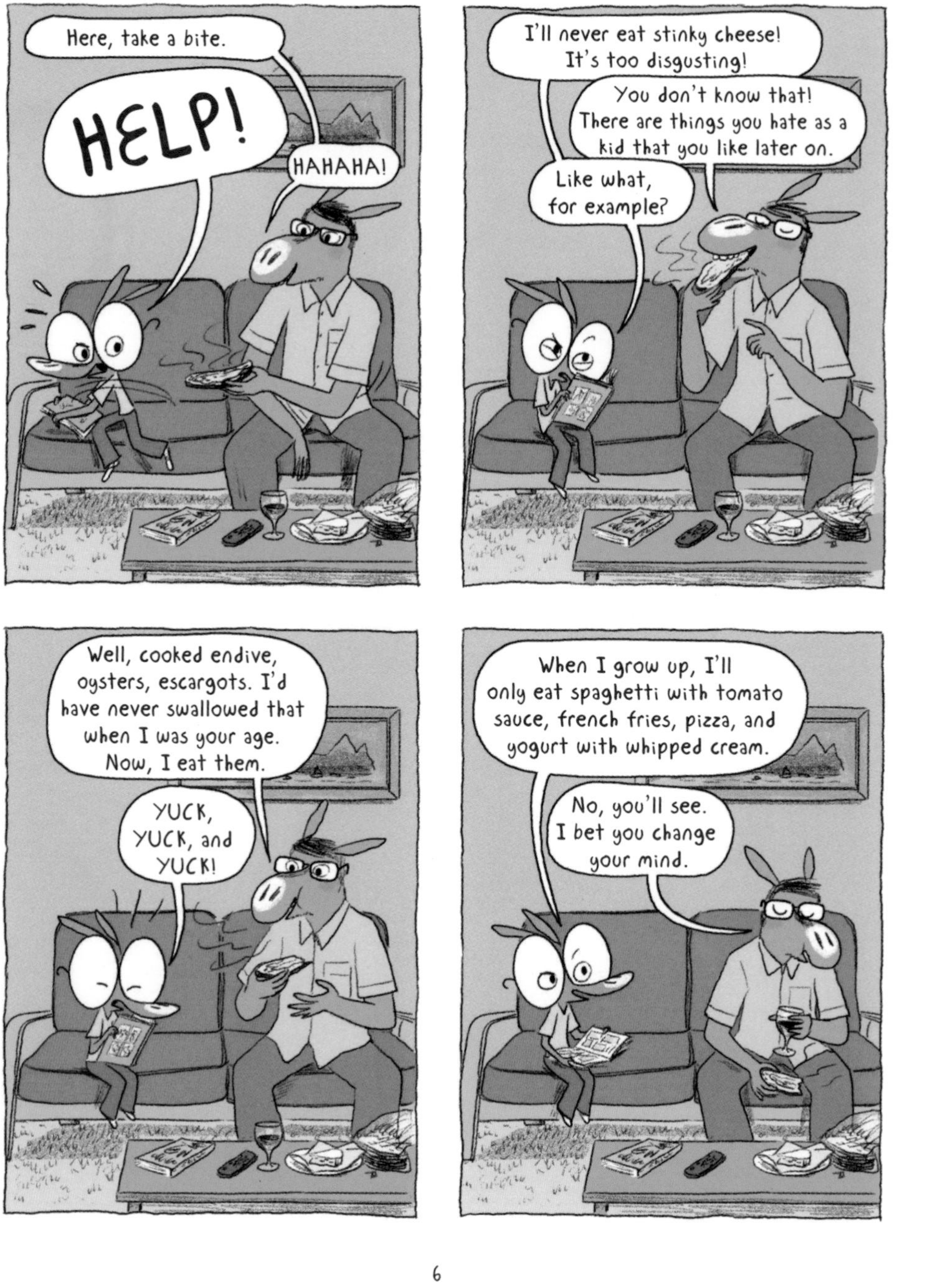
Here, take a bite.
HELP!
HAHAHA!
I'll never eat stinky cheese! It's too disgusting!
You don't know that! There are things you hate as a kid that you like later on.
Like what, for example?
Well, cooked endive, oysters, escargots. I'd have never swallowed that when I was your age. Now, I eat them.
YUCK, YUCK, and YUCK!
When I grow up, I'll only eat spaghetti with tomato sauce, french fries, pizza, and yogurt with whipped cream.
No, you'll see. I bet you change your mind.

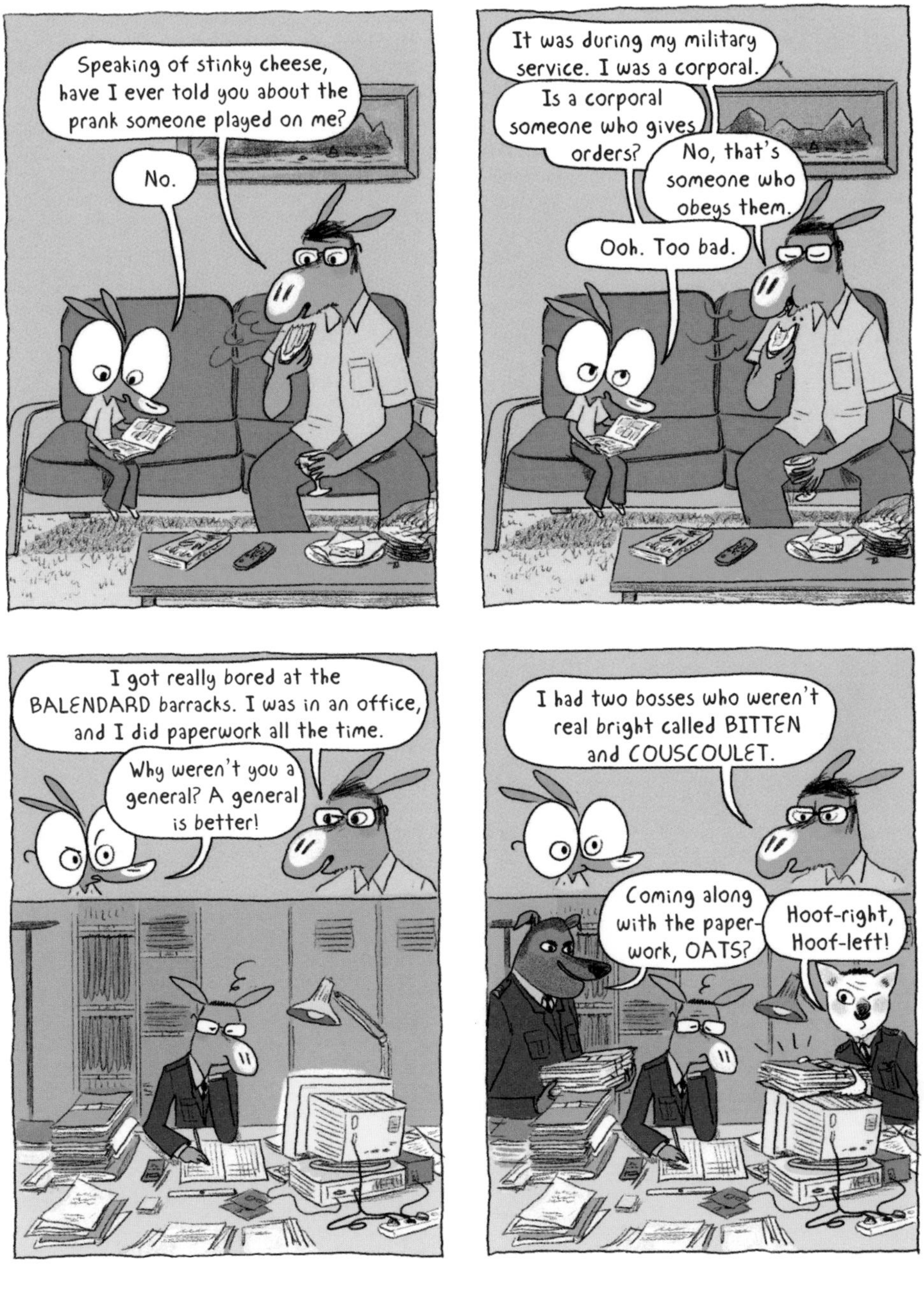

Speaking of stinky cheese, have I ever told you about the prank someone played on me?
No.
It was during my military service. I was a corporal.
Is a corporal someone who gives orders?
No, that's someone who obeys them.
Ooh. Too bad.
I got really bored at the BALENDARD barracks. I was in an office, and I did paperwork all the time.
Why weren't you a general? A general is better!
I had two bosses who weren't real bright called BITTEN and COUSCOULET.
Coming along with the paper-work, OATS?
Hoof-right, Hoof-left!

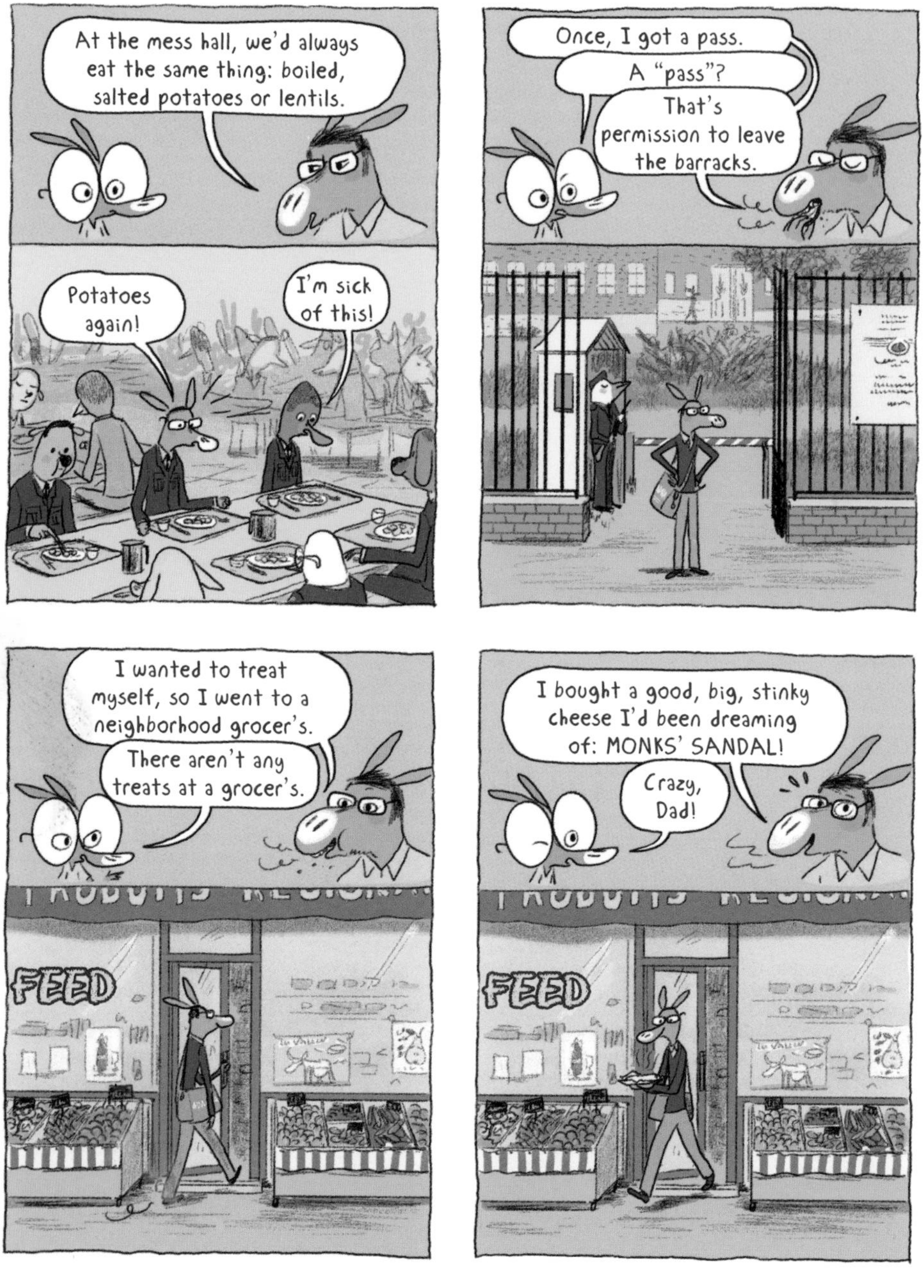
At the mess hall, we'd always eat the same thing: boiled, salted potatoes or lentils.
Potatoes again!
I'm sick of this!
Once, I got a pass.
A "pass"?
That's permission to leave the barracks.
I wanted to treat myself, so I went to a neighborhood grocer's.
There aren't any treats at a grocer's.
FEED
I bought a good, big, stinky cheese I'd been dreaming of: MONKS' SANDAL!
Crazy, Dad!
FEED

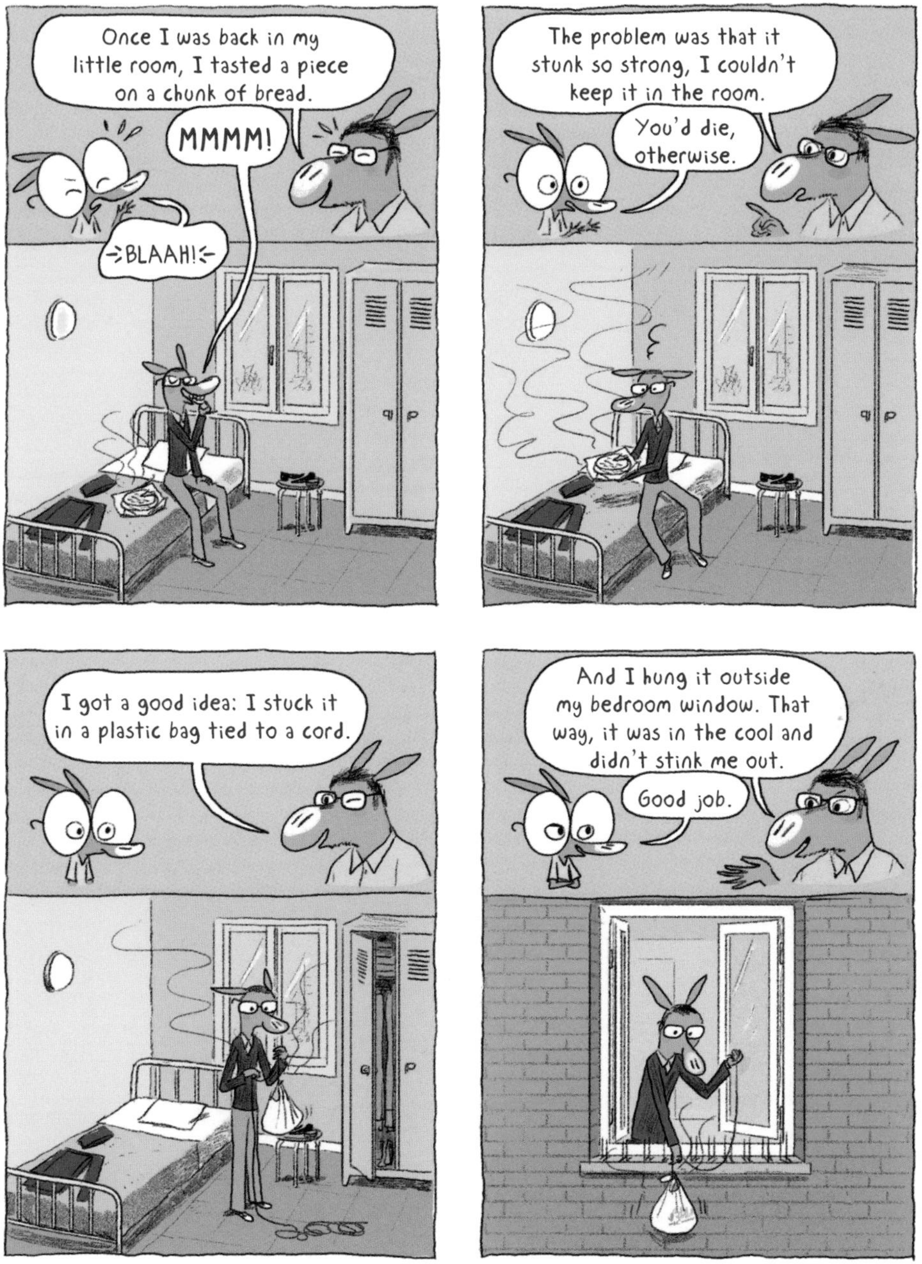
Once I was back in my little room, I tasted a piece on a chunk of bread.
MMMM!
BLAAH!
The problem was that it stunk so strong, I couldn't keep it in the room.
You'd die, otherwise.
I got a good idea: I stuck it in a plastic bag tied to a cord.
And I hung it outside my bedroom window. That way, it was in the cool and didn't stink me out.
Good job.

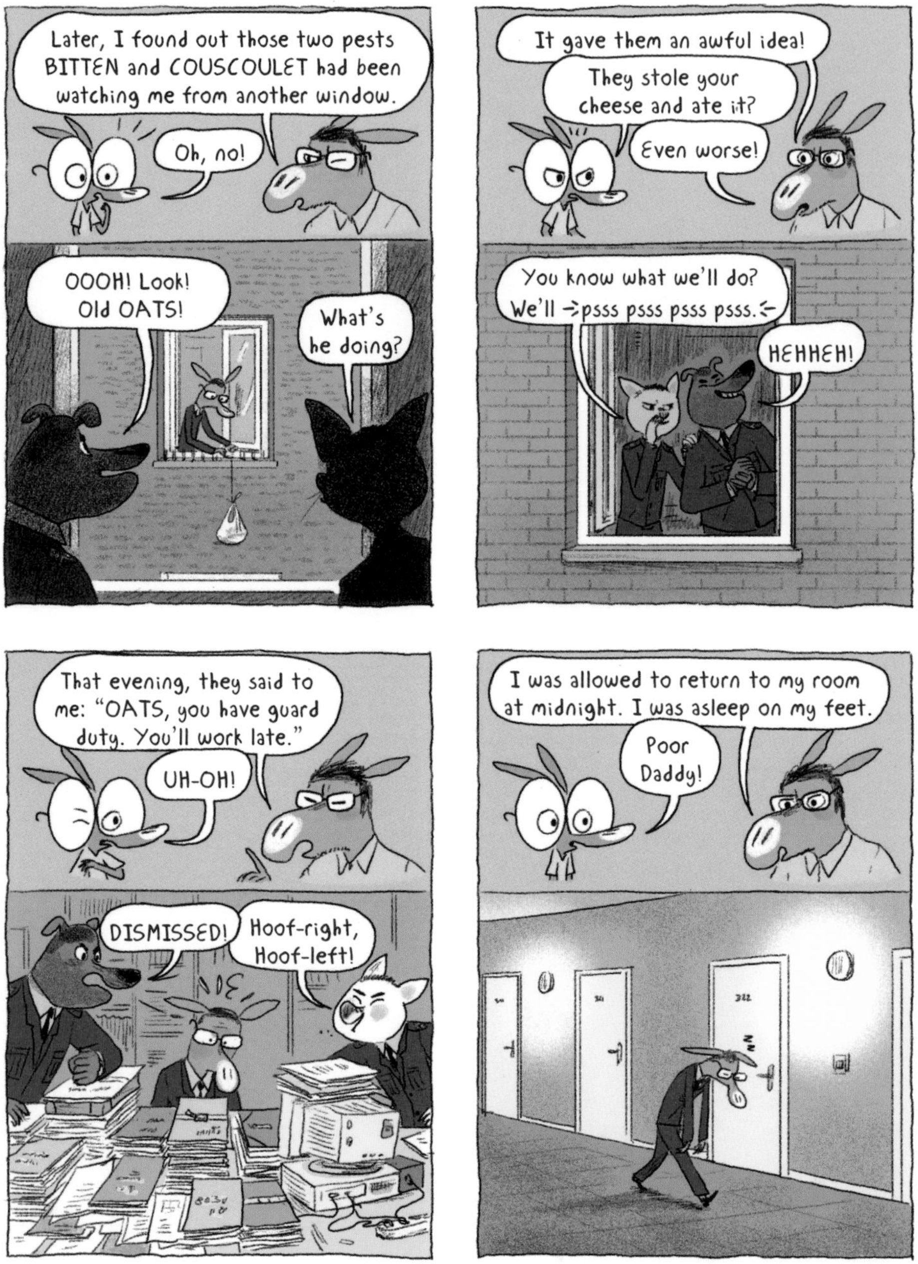
Later, I found out those two pests BITTEN and COUSCOULET had been watching me from another window.
Oh, no!
It gave them an awful idea!
They stole your cheese and ate it?
Even worse!
OOOH! Look! Old OATS!
What's he doing?
You know what we'll do? We'll →psss psss psss psss.←
HEHHEH!
That evening, they said to me: "OATS, you have guard duty. You'll work late."
UH-OH!
I was allowed to return to my room at midnight. I was asleep on my feet.
Poor Daddy!
DISMISSED!
Hoof-right, Hoof-left!

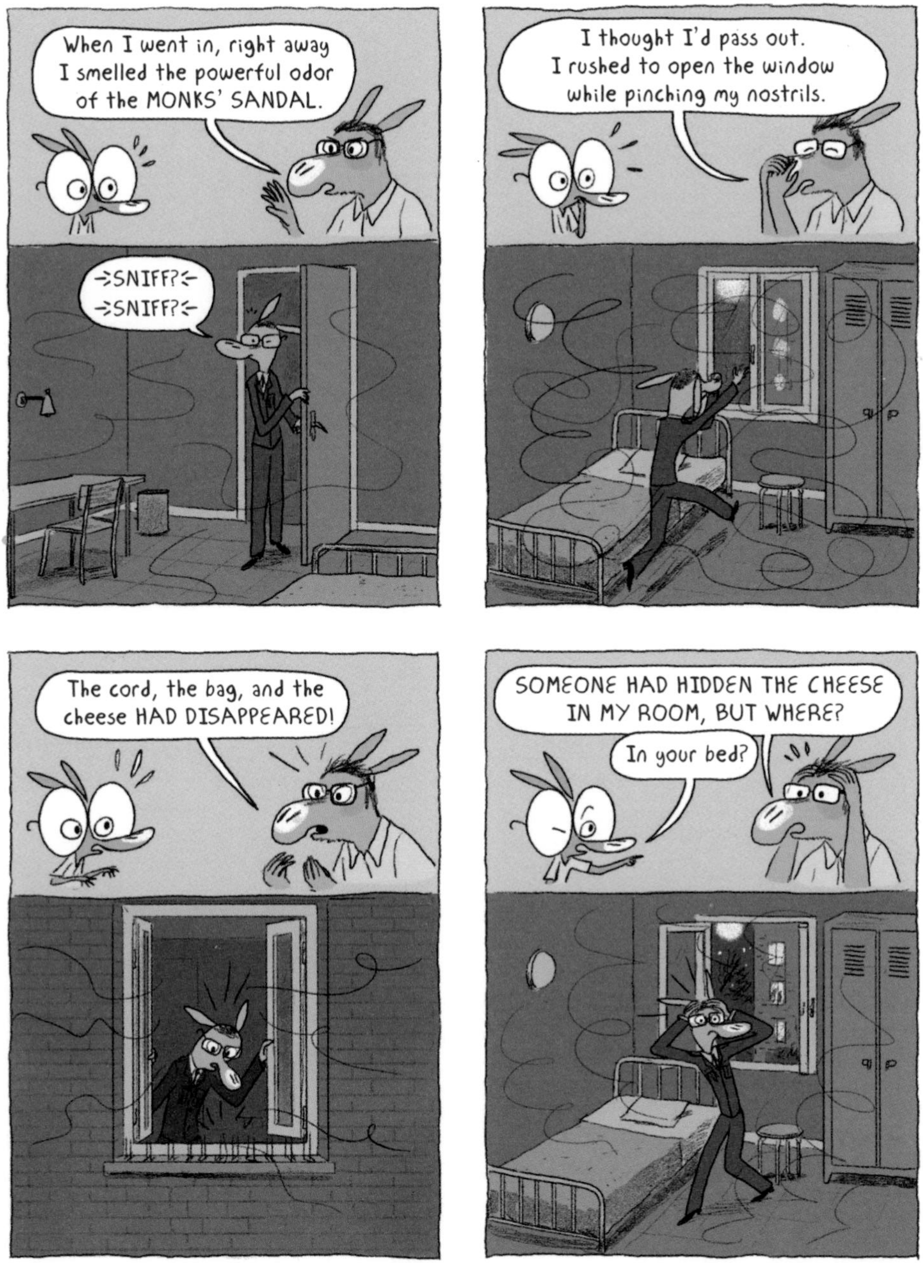
When I went in, right away I smelled the powerful odor of the MONKS' SANDAL.
SNIFF? SNIFF?
I thought I'd pass out. I rushed to open the window while pinching my nostrils.
The cord, the bag, and the cheese HAD DISAPPEARED!
SOMEONE HAD HIDDEN THE CHEESE IN MY ROOM, BUT WHERE?
In your bed?

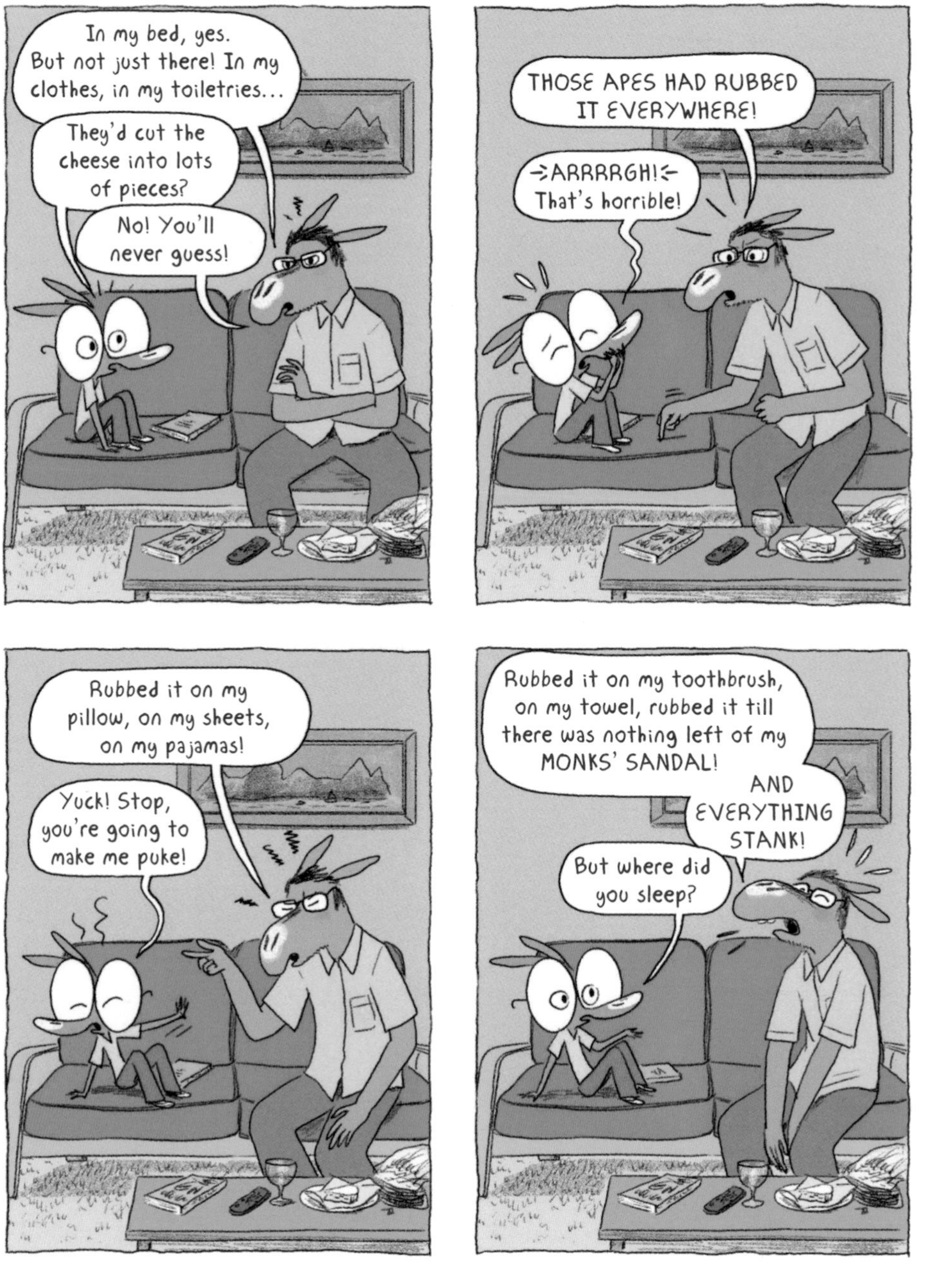

In my bed, yes. But not just there! In my clothes, in my toiletries...
They'd cut the cheese into lots of pieces?
No! You'll never guess!
THOSE APES HAD RUBBED IT EVERYWHERE!
ARRRRGH! That's horrible!
Rubbed it on my pillow, on my sheets, on my pajamas!
Yuck! Stop, you're going to make me puke!
Rubbed it on my toothbrush, on my towel, rubbed it till there was nothing left of my MONKS' SANDAL!
AND EVERYTHING STANK!
But where did you sleep?

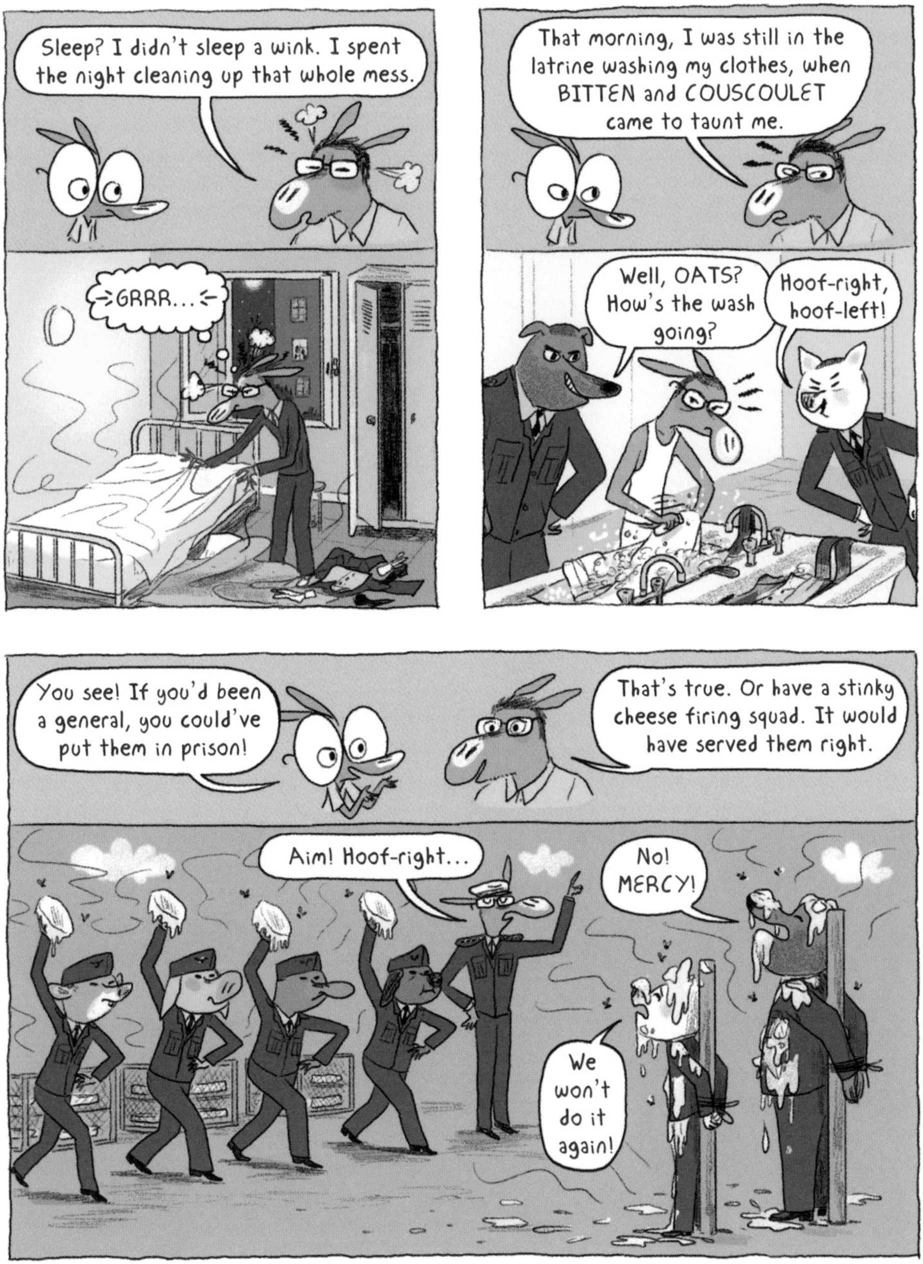

Sleep? I didn't sleep a wink. I spent the night cleaning up that whole mess.
That morning, I was still in the latrine washing my clothes, when BITTEN and COUSCOULET came to taunt me.
GRRR...
Well, OATS? How's the wash going?
Hoof-right, hoof-left!
You see! If you'd been a general, you could've put them in prison!
That's true. Or have a stinky cheese firing squad. It would have served them right.
Aim! Hoof-right...
No! MERCY!
We won't do it again!

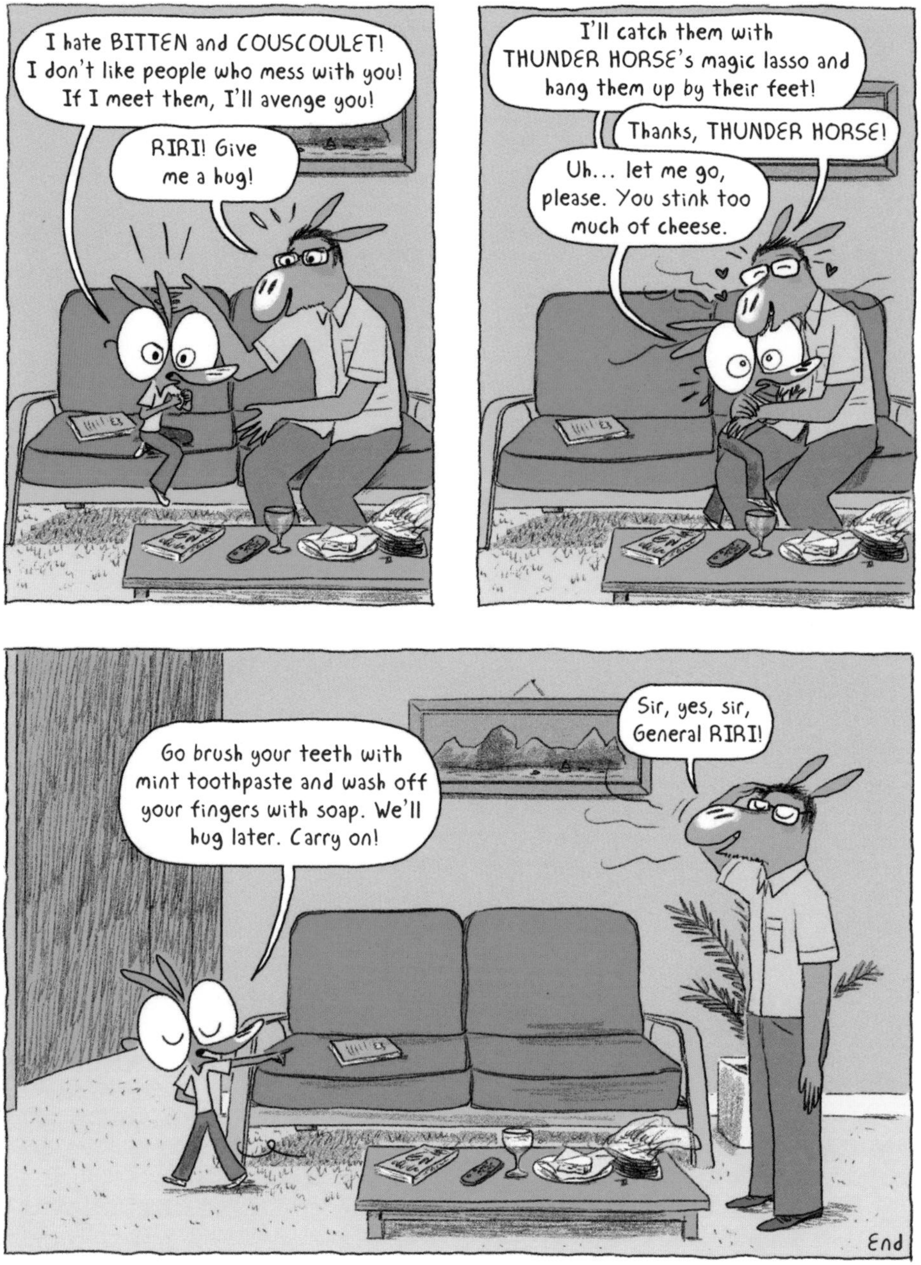
I hate BITTEN and COUSCOULET! I don't like people who mess with you! If I meet them, I'll avenge you!
RIRI! Give me a hug!
I'll catch them with THUNDER HORSE's magic lasso and hang them up by their feet!
Thanks, THUNDER HORSE!
Uh... let me go, please. You stink too much of cheese.
Go brush your teeth with mint toothpaste and wash off your fingers with soap. We'll hug later. Carry on!
Sir, yes, sir, General RIRI!
End

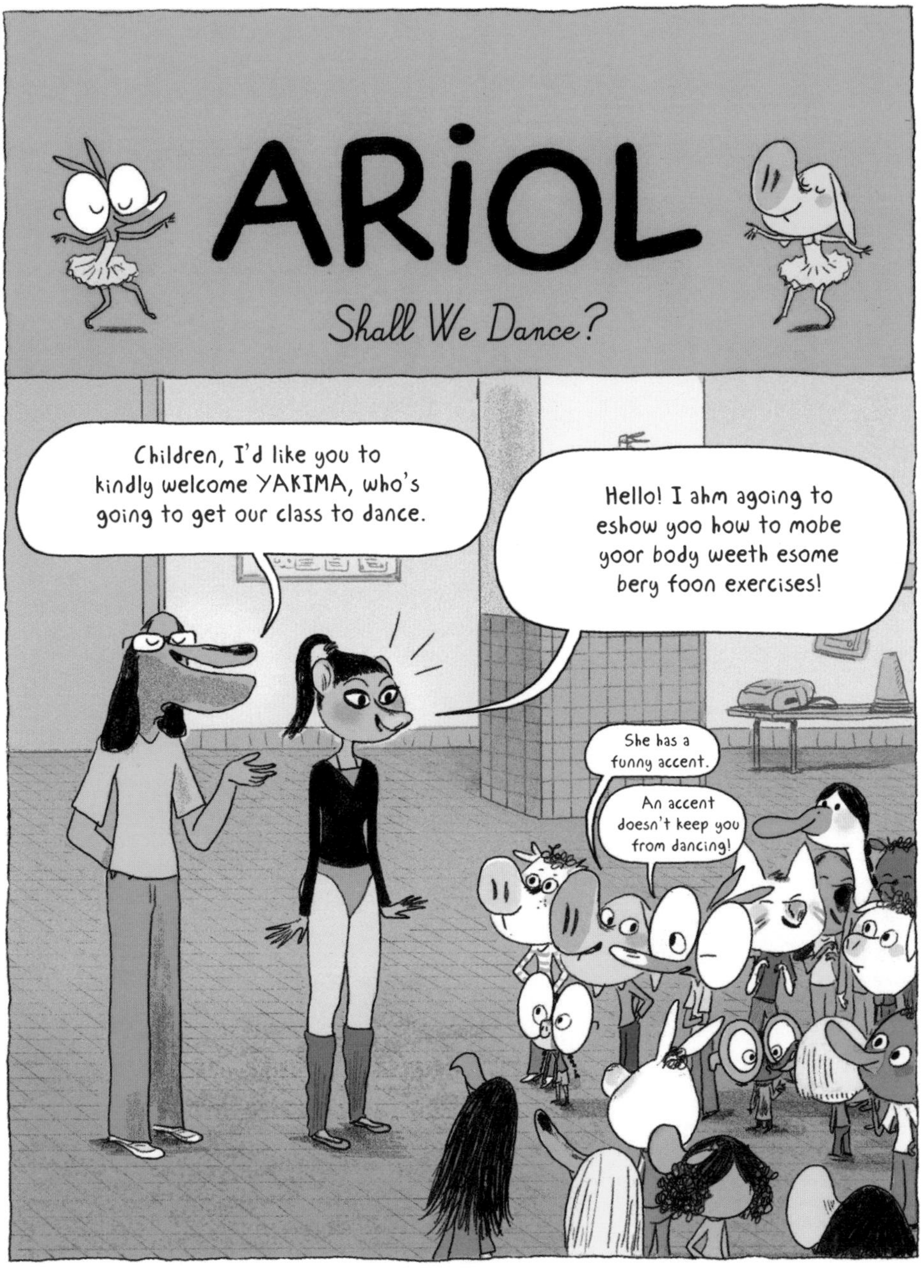

ARiOL
Shall We Dance?
Children, I'd like you to kindly welcome YAKIMA, who's going to get our class to dance.
Hello! I ahm agoing to eshow yoo how to mobe yoor body weeth esome bery foon exercises!
She has a funny accent.
An accent doesn't keep you from dancing!

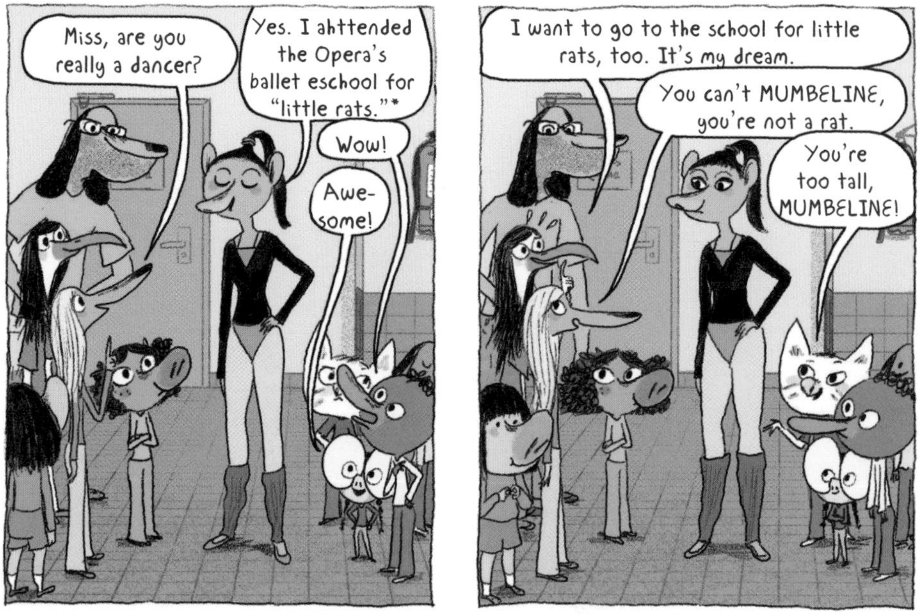
Miss, are you really a dancer?
Yes. I ahttended the Opera's ballet eschool for "little rats."*
Wow!
Awe-some!
I want to go to the school for little rats, too. It's my dream.
You can't MUMBELINE, you're not a rat.
You're too tall, MUMBELINE!

*In France, the student dancers at the Paris Opera are called "little rats."

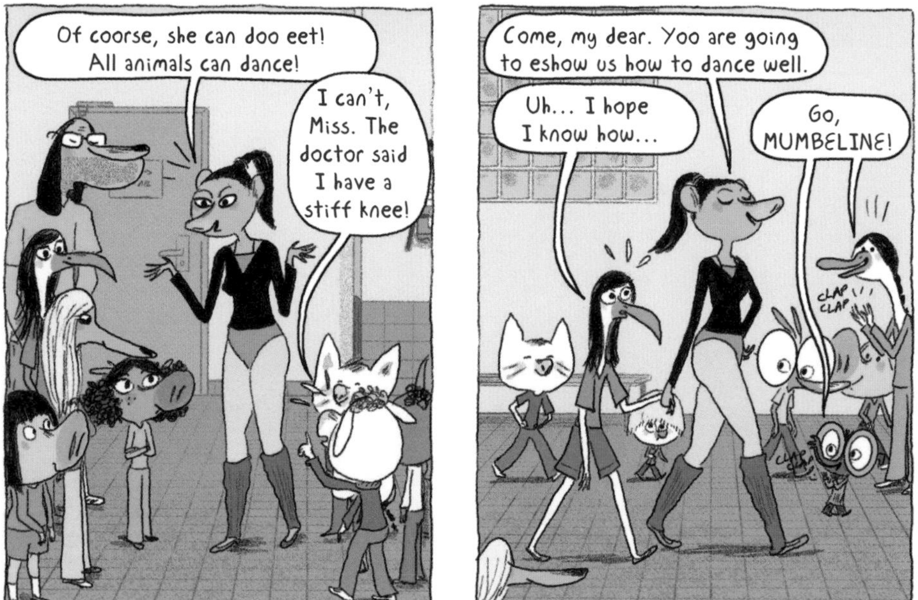
Of coorse, she can doo eet! All animals can dance!
I can't, Miss. The doctor said I have a stiff knee!
Come, my dear. Yoo are going to eshow us how to dance well.
Uh... I hope I know how...
Go, MUMBELINE!
CLAP CLAP
CLAP CLAP

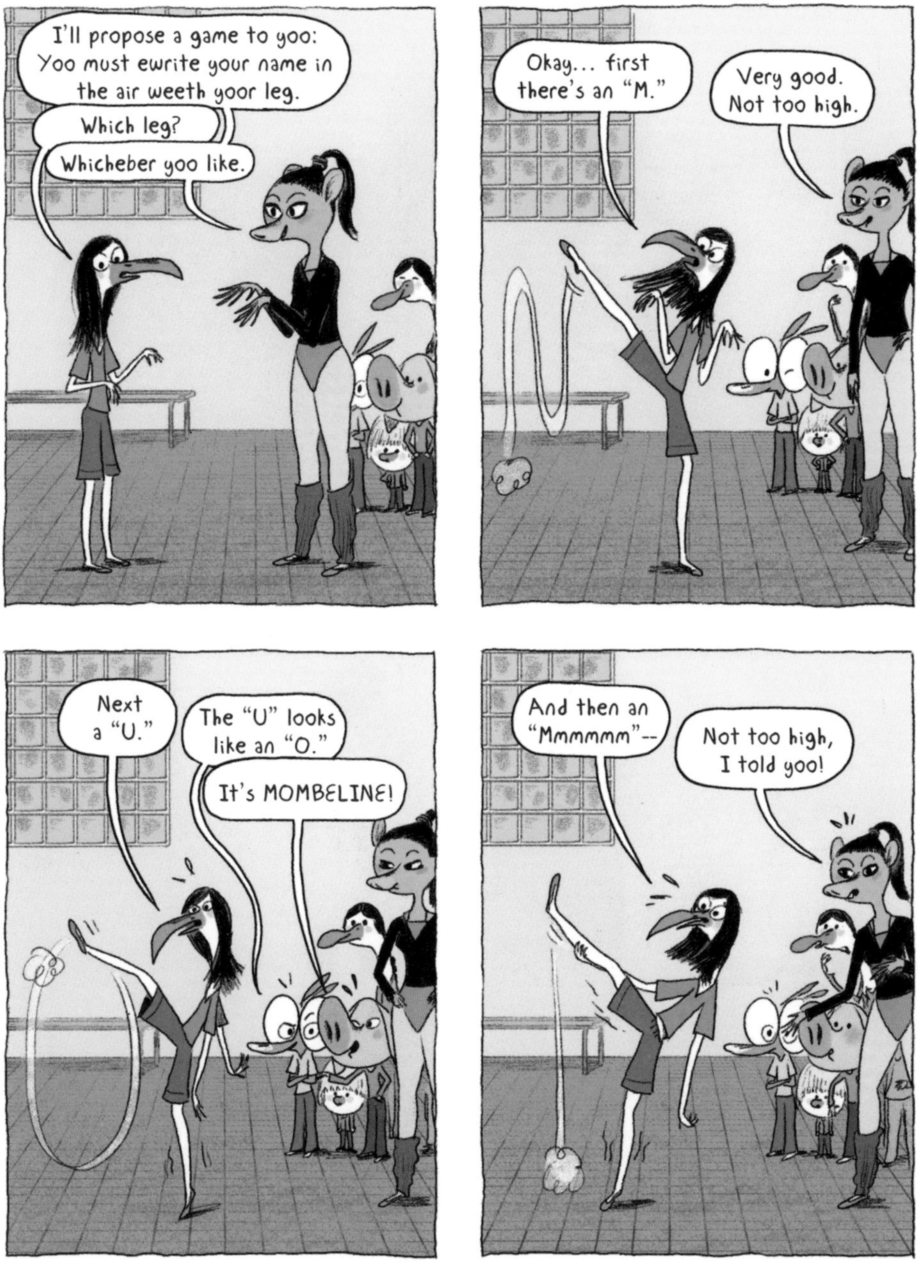

I'll propose a game to yoo: Yoo must ewrite your name in the air weeth yoor leg.
Which leg?
Whicheber yoo like.
Okay... first there's an "M."
Very good. Not too high.
Next a "U."
The "U" looks like an "O."
It's MOMBELINE!
And then an "Mmmmmm"--
Not too high, I told yoo!

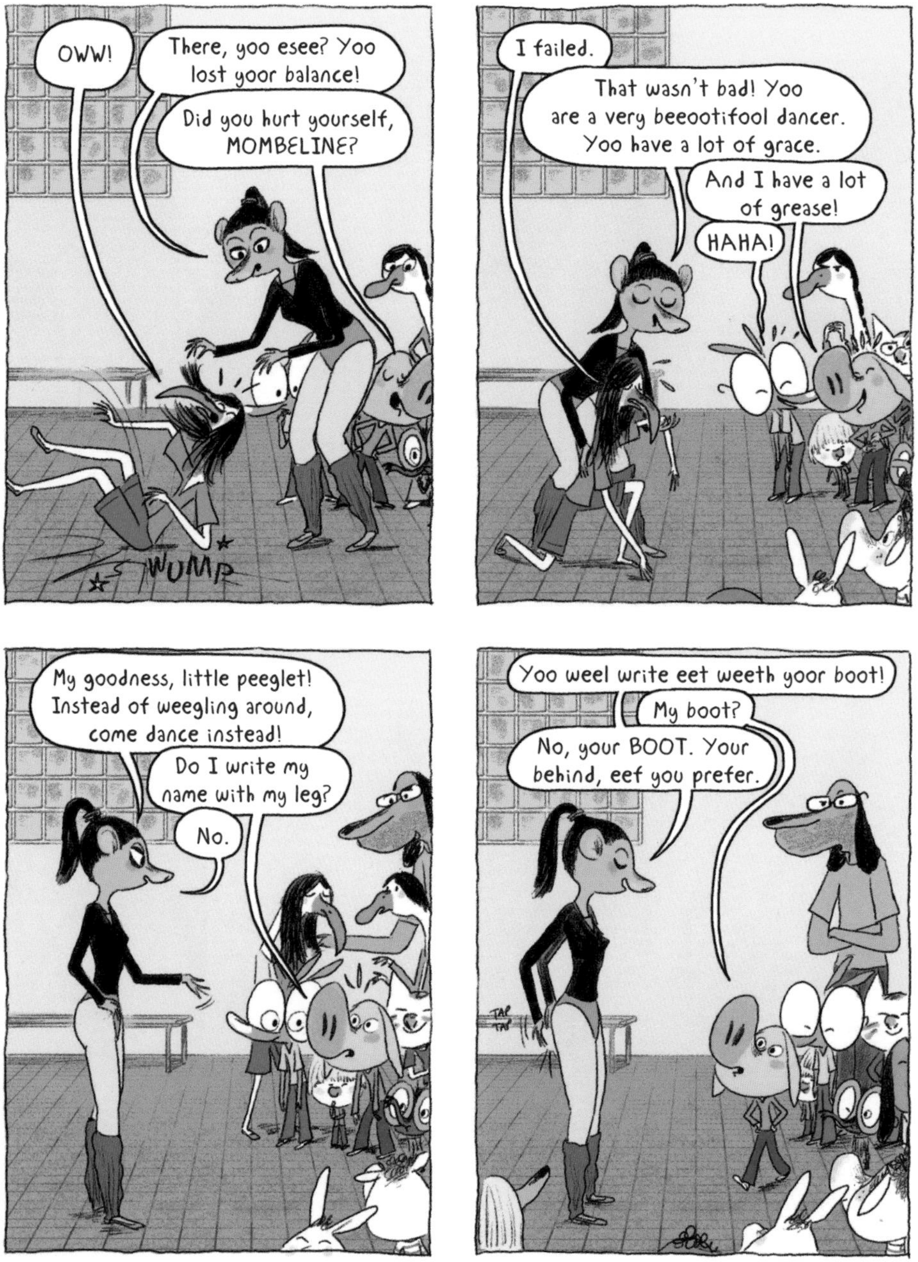
OWW!
There, yoo esee? Yoo lost yoor balance!
Did you hurt yourself, MOMBELINE?
WUMP
I failed.
That wasn't bad! Yoo are a very beeootifool dancer. Yoo have a lot of grace.
And I have a lot of grease!
HAHA!
My goodness, little peeglet! Instead of weegling around, come dance instead!
Do I write my name with my leg?
No.
Yoo weel write eet weeth yoor boot!
My boot?
No, your BOOT. Your behind, eef you prefer.

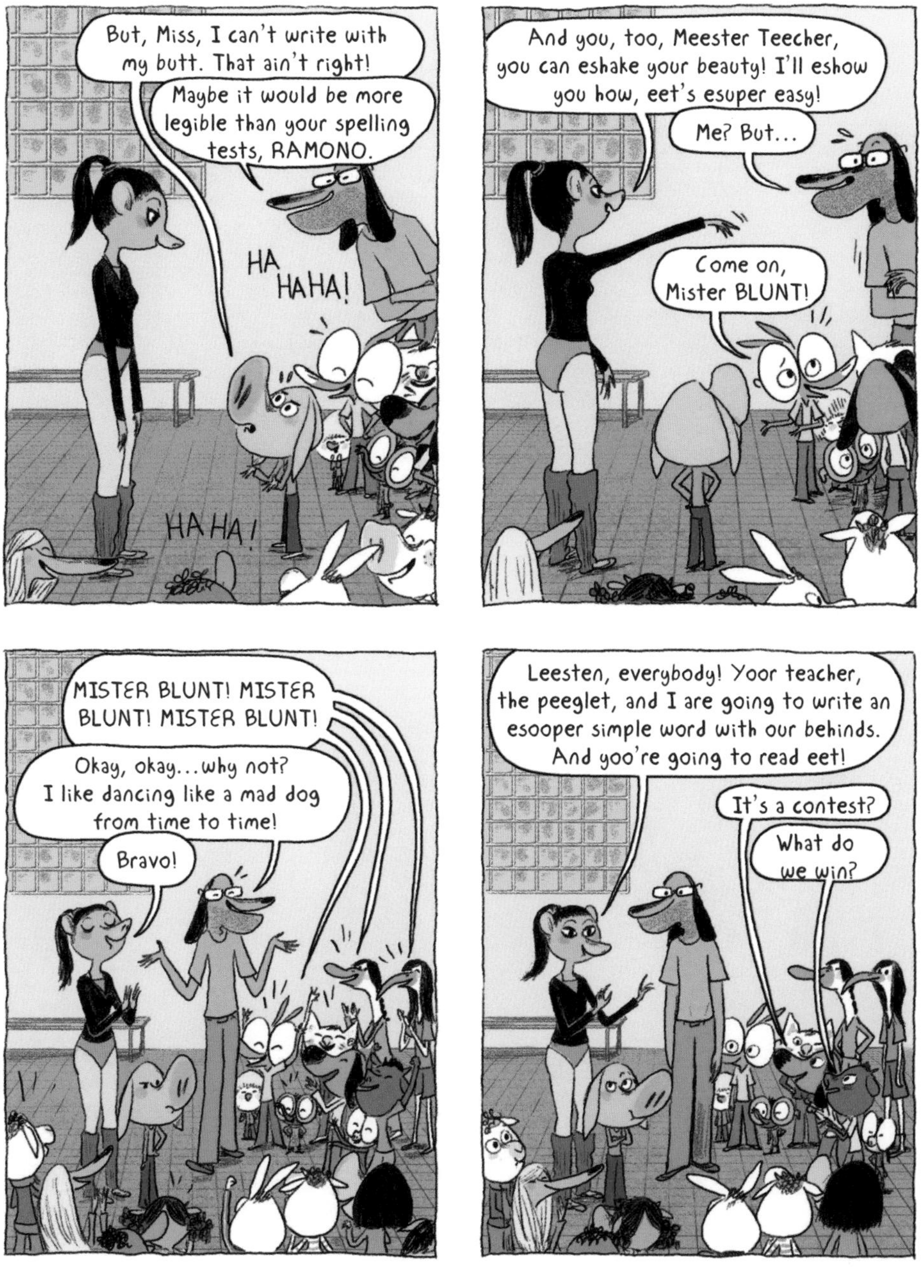

But, Miss, I can't write with my butt. That ain't right!
Maybe it would be more legible than your spelling tests, RAMONO.
HA HAHA!
HA HA!
And you, too, Meester Teecher, you can eshake your beauty! I'll eshow you how, eet's esuper easy!
Me? But...
Come on, Mister BLUNT!
MISTER BLUNT! MISTER BLUNT! MISTER BLUNT!
Okay, okay...why not? I like dancing like a mad dog from time to time!
Bravo!
Leesten, everybody! Yoor teacher, the peeglet, and I are going to write an esooper simple word with our behinds. And yoo're going to read eet!
It's a contest?
What do we win?

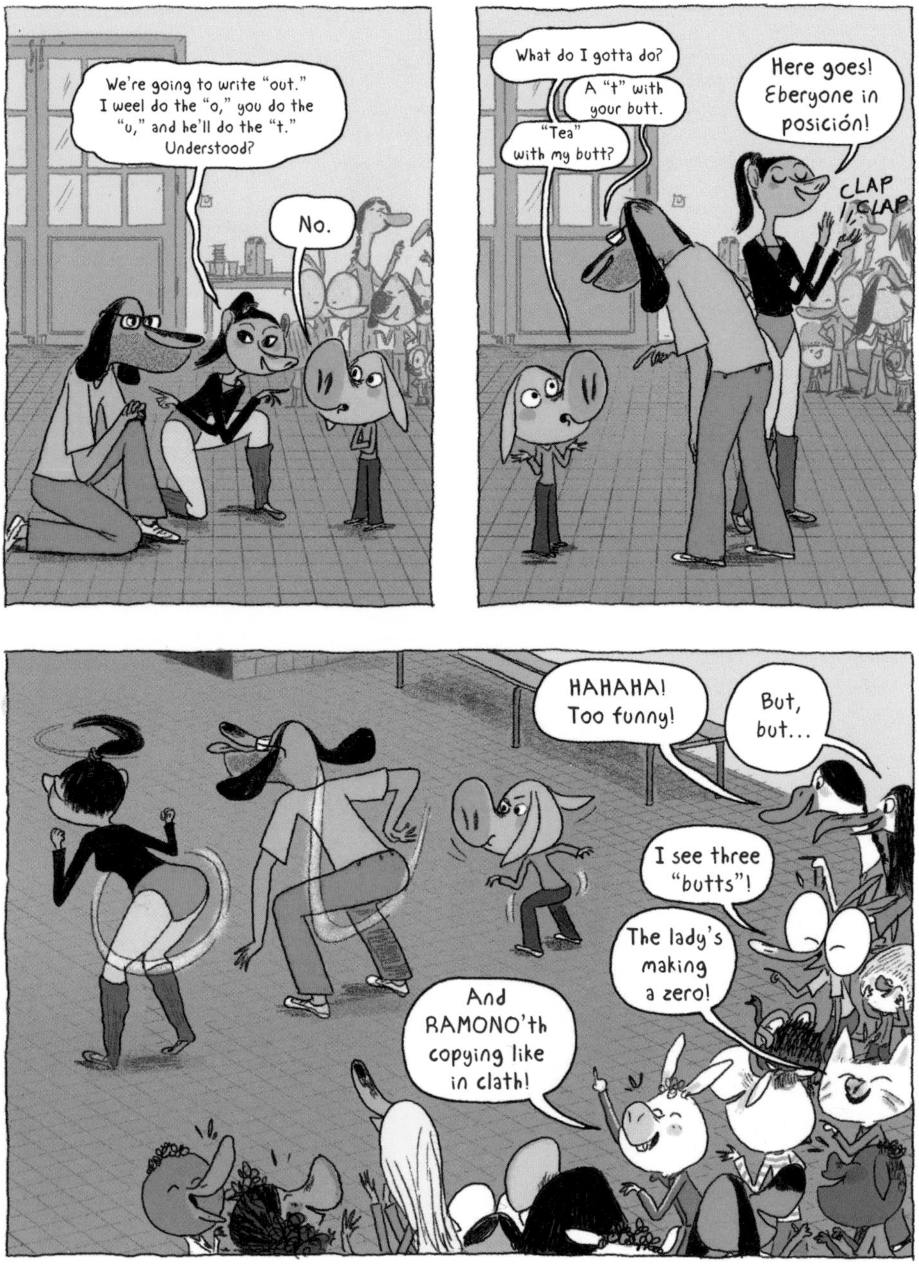
We're going to write "out." I weel do the "o," you do the "u," and he'll do the "t." Understood?
No.
What do I gotta do?
A "t" with your butt.
"Tea" with my butt?
Here goes! Eberyone in posición!
CLAP CLAP
HAHAHA! Too funny!
But, but...
I see three "butts"!
The lady's making a zero!
And RAMONO'th copying like in clath!

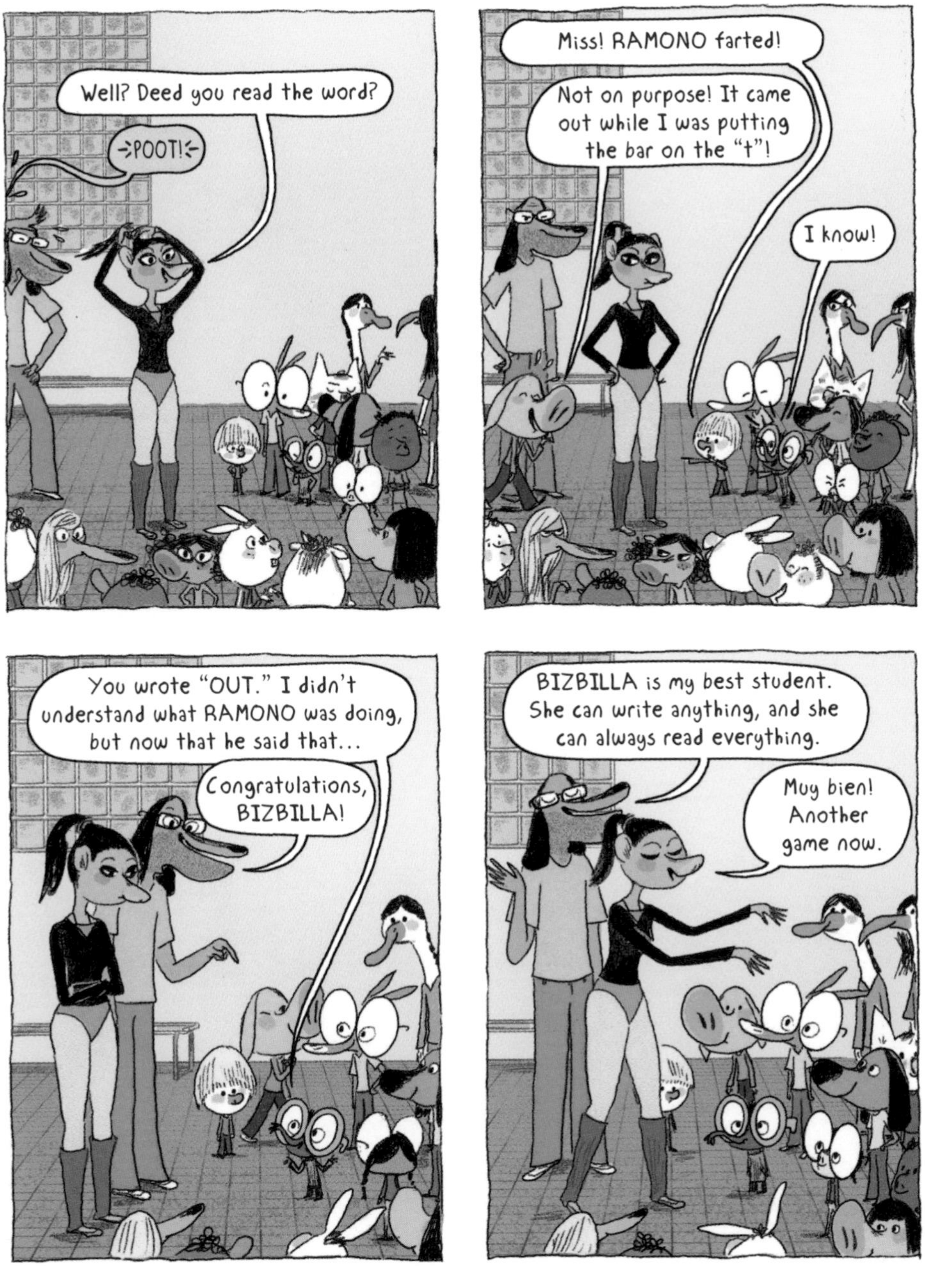
Well? Deed you read the word?
POOT!
Miss! RAMONO farted!
Not on purpose! It came out while I was putting the bar on the "t"!
I know!
You wrote "OUT." I didn't understand what RAMONO was doing, but now that he said that...
Congratulations, BIZBILLA!
BIZBILLA is my best student. She can write anything, and she can always read everything.
Muy bien! Another game now.

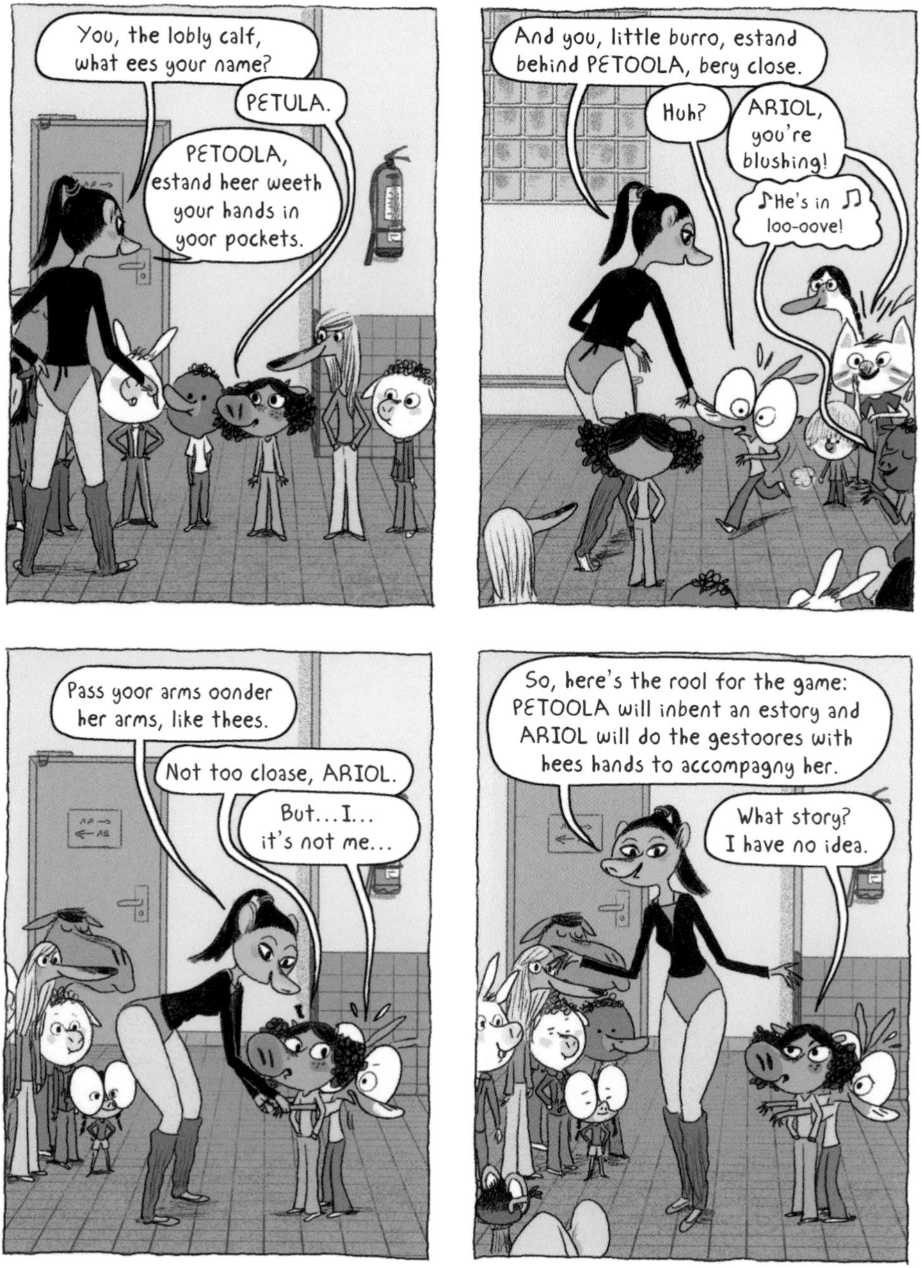
You, the lobly calf, what ees your name?
PETULA.
PETOOLA, estand heer weeth your hands in yoor pockets.
And you, little burro, estand behind PETOOLA, bery close.
Huh?
ARIOL, you're blushing!
♪He's in ♫ loo-oove!
Pass yoor arms oonder her arms, like thees.
Not too closse, ARIOL.
But... I... it's not me...
So, here's the rool for the game: PETOOLA will inbent an estory and ARIOL will do the gestoores with hees hands to accompagny her.
What story? I have no idea.

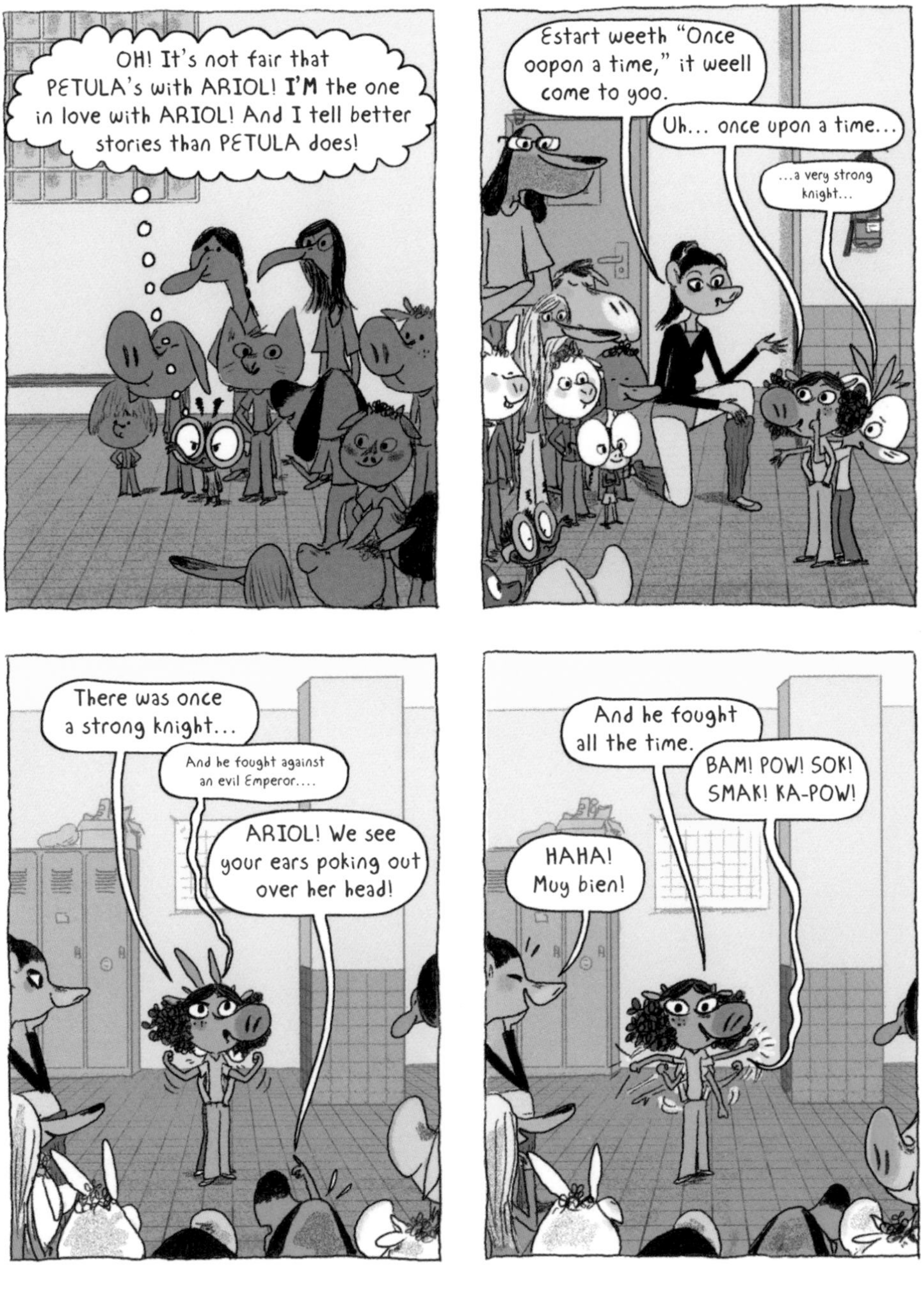
OH! It's not fair that PETULA's with ARIOL! **I'M** the one in love with ARIOL! And I tell better stories than PETULA does!
Estart weeth "Once oopon a time," it weell come to yoo.
Uh... once upon a time...
...a very strong knight...
There was once a strong knight...
And he fought against an evil Emperor....
ARIOL! We see your ears poking out over her head!
And he fought all the time.
BAM! POW! SOK! SMAK! KA-POW!
HAHA! Muy bien!

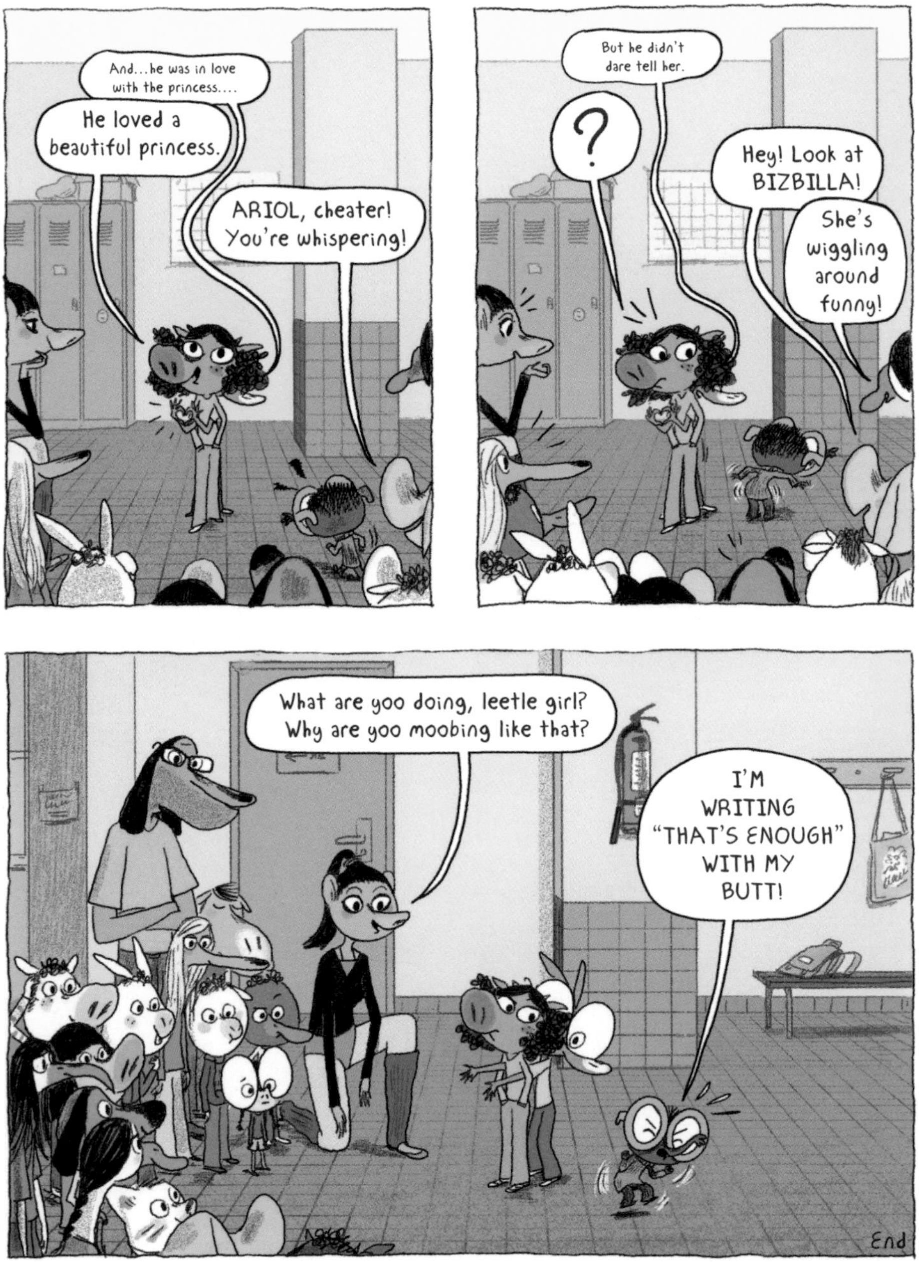

And...he was in love with the princess....
He loved a beautiful princess.
ARIOL, cheater! You're whispering!
But he didn't dare tell her.
?
Hey! Look at BIZBILLA!
She's wiggling around funny!
What are yoo doing, leetle girl? Why are yoo moobing like that?
I'M WRITING "THAT'S ENOUGH" WITH MY BUTT!
End

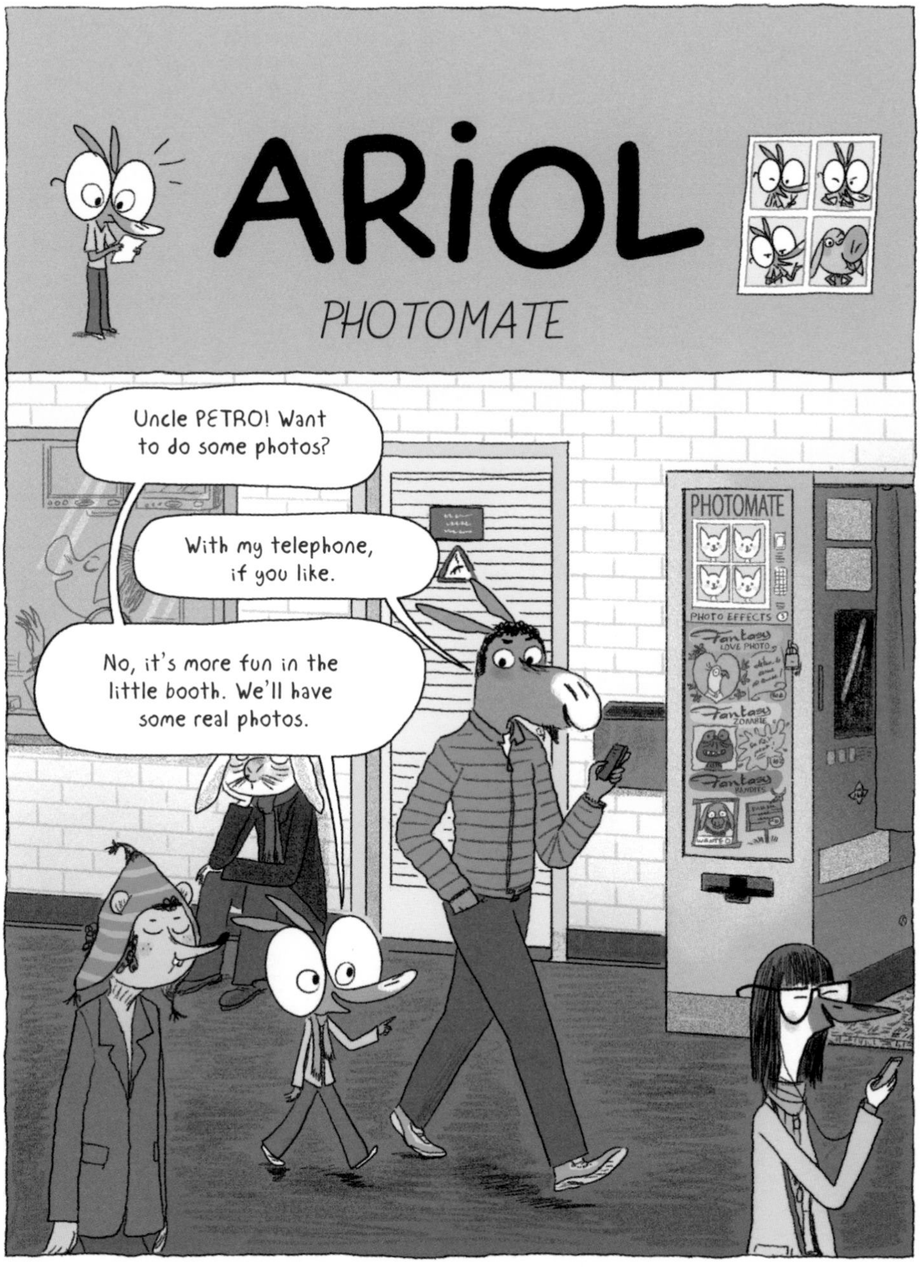
ARIOL
PHOTOMATE
Uncle PETRO! Want to do some photos?
With my telephone, if you like.
No, it's more fun in the little booth. We'll have some real photos.
PHOTOMATE
PHOTO EFFECTS
Fantasy
LOVE PHOTO
Fantasy
ZOMBIE
Fantasy
BANDITS
WANTED

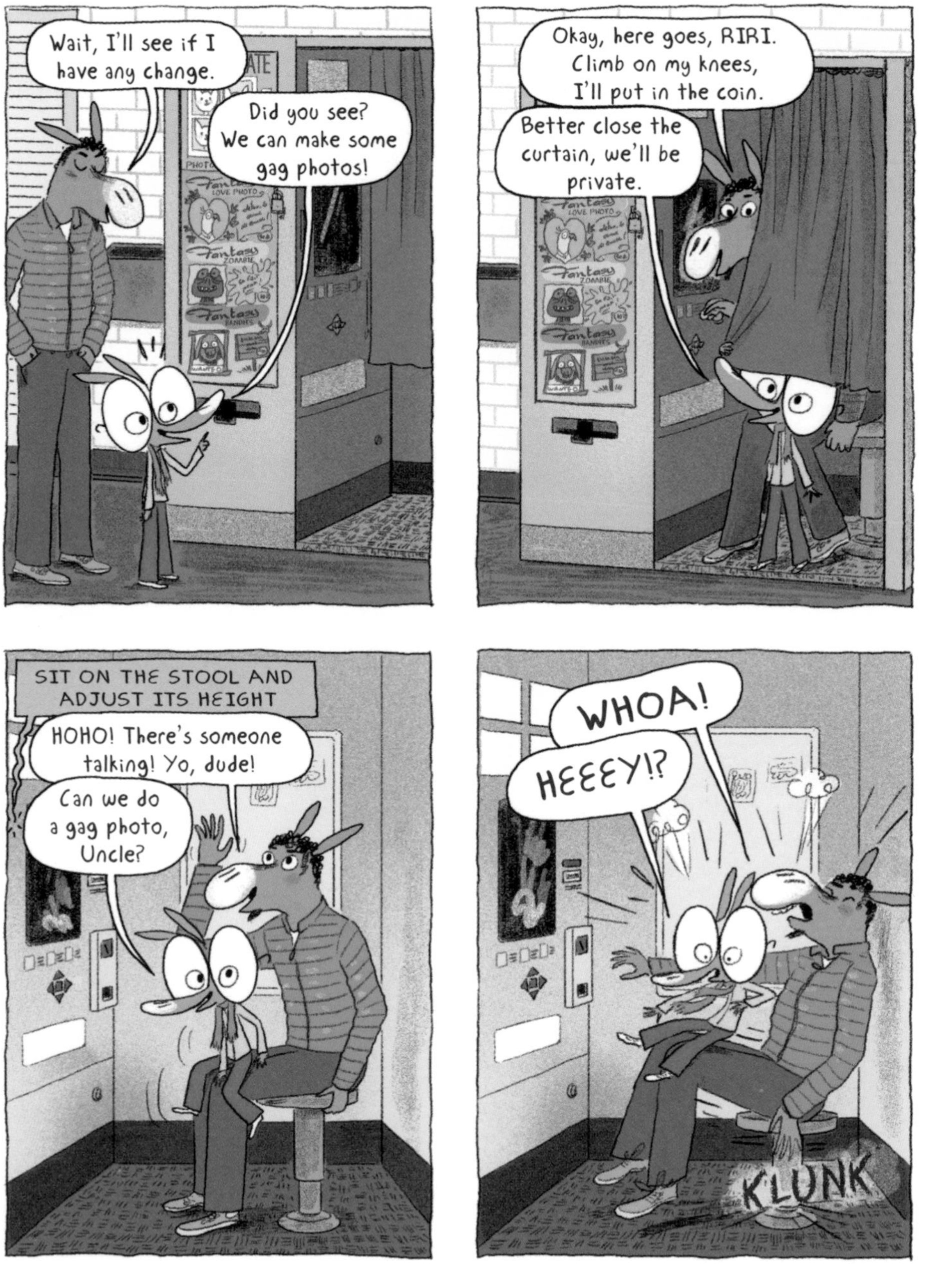
Wait, I'll see if I have any change.
Did you see? We can make some gag photos!
Okay, here goes, RIRI. Climb on my knees, I'll put in the coin.
Better close the curtain, we'll be private.
SIT ON THE STOOL AND ADJUST ITS HEIGHT
HOHO! There's someone talking! Yo, dude!
Can we do a gag photo, Uncle?
WHOA!
HEEEY!?
KLUNK

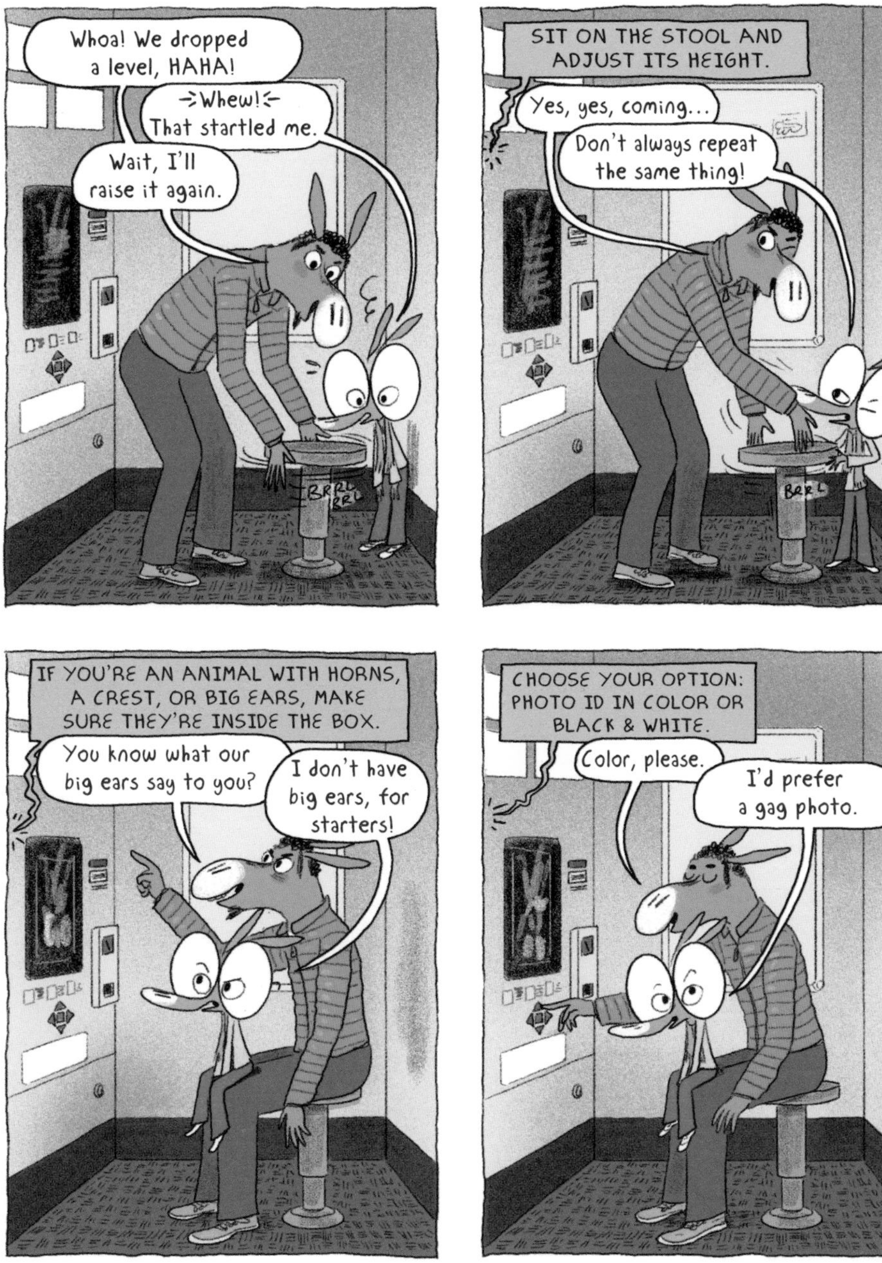
Whoa! We dropped a level, HAHA!
Whew! That startled me.
Wait, I'll raise it again.
BRRL BRRL
SIT ON THE STOOL AND ADJUST ITS HEIGHT.
Yes, yes, coming...
Don't always repeat the same thing!
BRRL
IF YOU'RE AN ANIMAL WITH HORNS, A CREST, OR BIG EARS, MAKE SURE THEY'RE INSIDE THE BOX.
You know what our big ears say to you?
I don't have big ears, for starters!
CHOOSE YOUR OPTION: PHOTO ID IN COLOR OR BLACK & WHITE.
Color, please.
I'd prefer a gag photo.

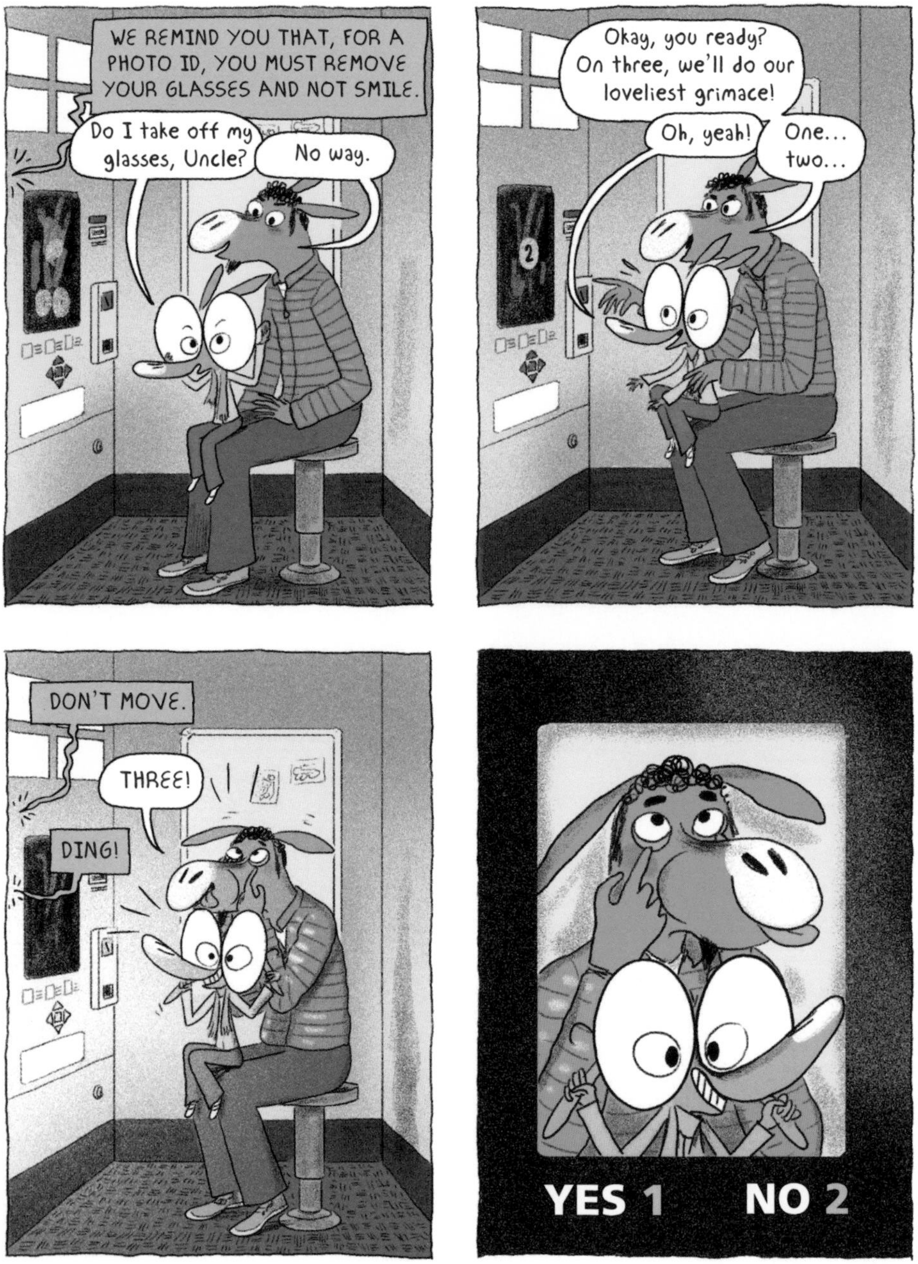

WE REMIND YOU THAT, FOR A PHOTO ID, YOU MUST REMOVE YOUR GLASSES AND NOT SMILE.
Do I take off my glasses, Uncle?
No way.
Okay, you ready? On three, we'll do our loveliest grimace!
Oh, yeah!
One... two...
DON'T MOVE.
THREE!
DING!
YES 1
NO 2

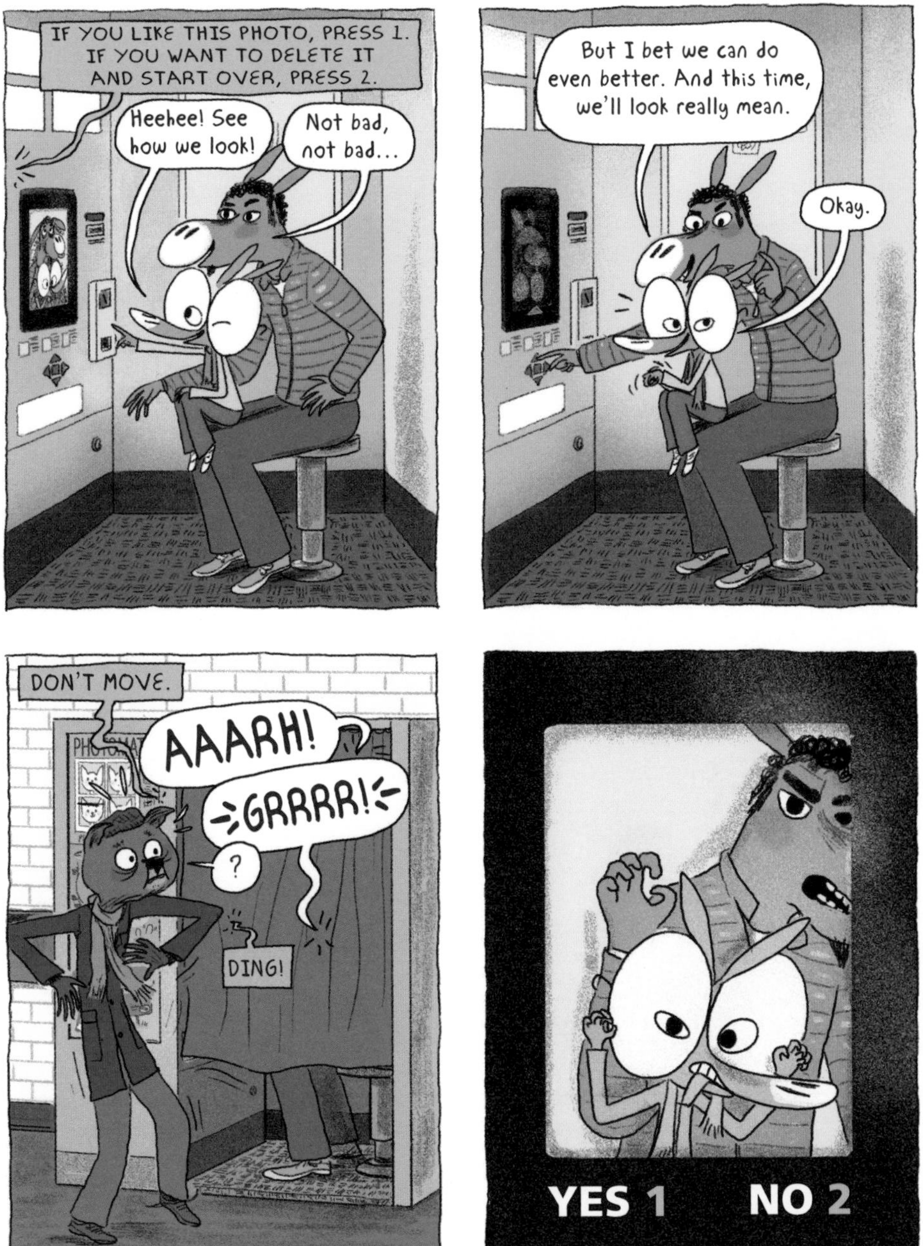
IF YOU LIKE THIS PHOTO, PRESS 1. IF YOU WANT TO DELETE IT AND START OVER, PRESS 2.
Heehee! See how we look!
Not bad, not bad...
But I bet we can do even better. And this time, we'll look really mean.
Okay.
DON'T MOVE.
AAARH!
GRRRR!
?
DING!
YES 1
NO 2

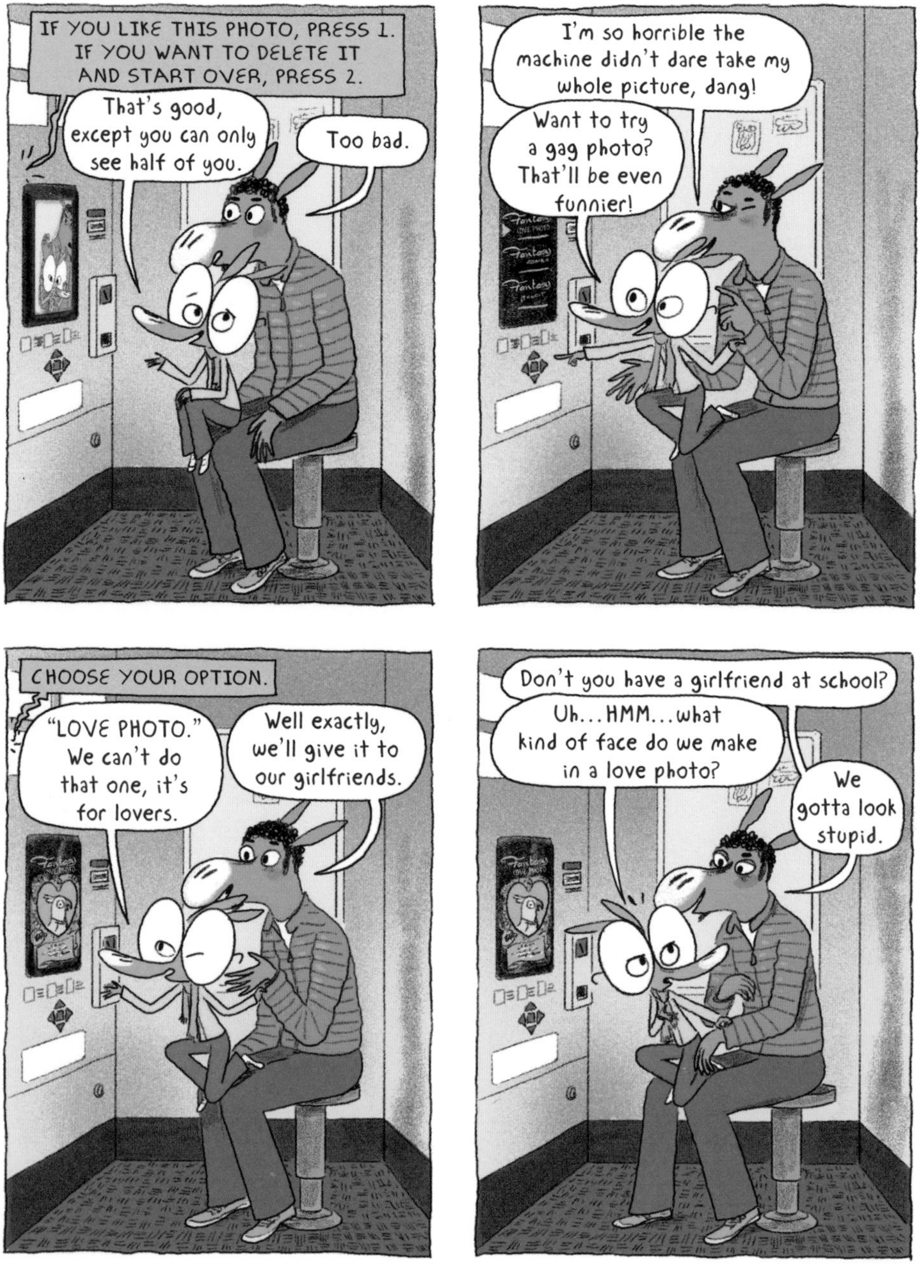
IF YOU LIKE THIS PHOTO, PRESS 1. IF YOU WANT TO DELETE IT AND START OVER, PRESS 2.
That's good, except you can only see half of you.
Too bad.
I'm so horrible the machine didn't dare take my whole picture, dang!
Want to try a gag photo? That'll be even funnier!
CHOOSE YOUR OPTION.
"LOVE PHOTO." We can't do that one, it's for lovers.
Well exactly, we'll give it to our girlfriends.
Don't you have a girlfriend at school?
Uh...HMM...what kind of face do we make in a love photo?
We gotta look stupid.

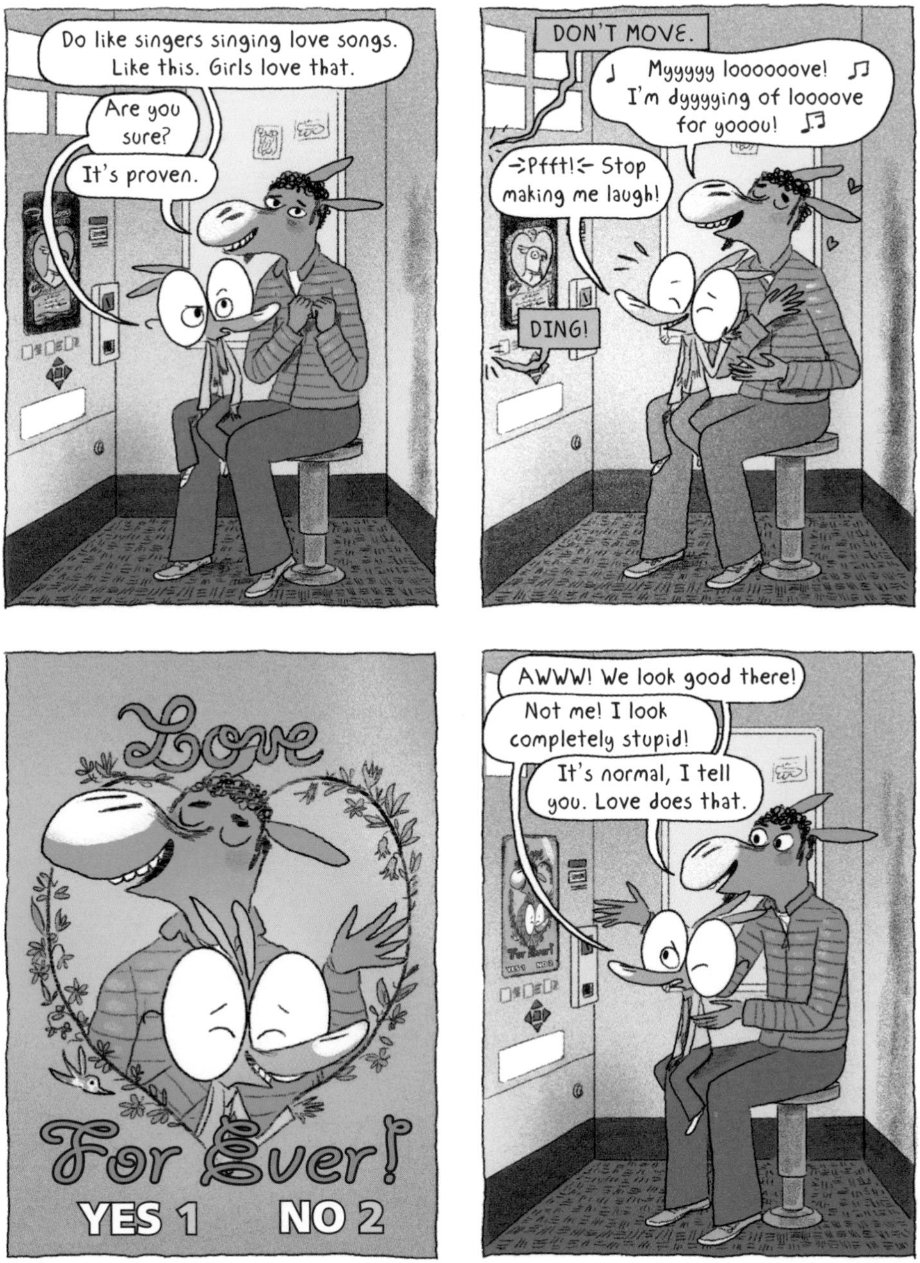
Do like singers singing love songs. Like this. Girls love that.
Are you sure?
It's proven.
DON'T MOVE.
Myyyyy loooooove! I'm dyyyying of loooove for yooou!
Pfft! Stop making me laugh!
DING!
Love
For Ever!
YES 1
NO 2
AWWW! We look good there!
Not me! I look completely stupid!
It's normal, I tell you. Love does that.

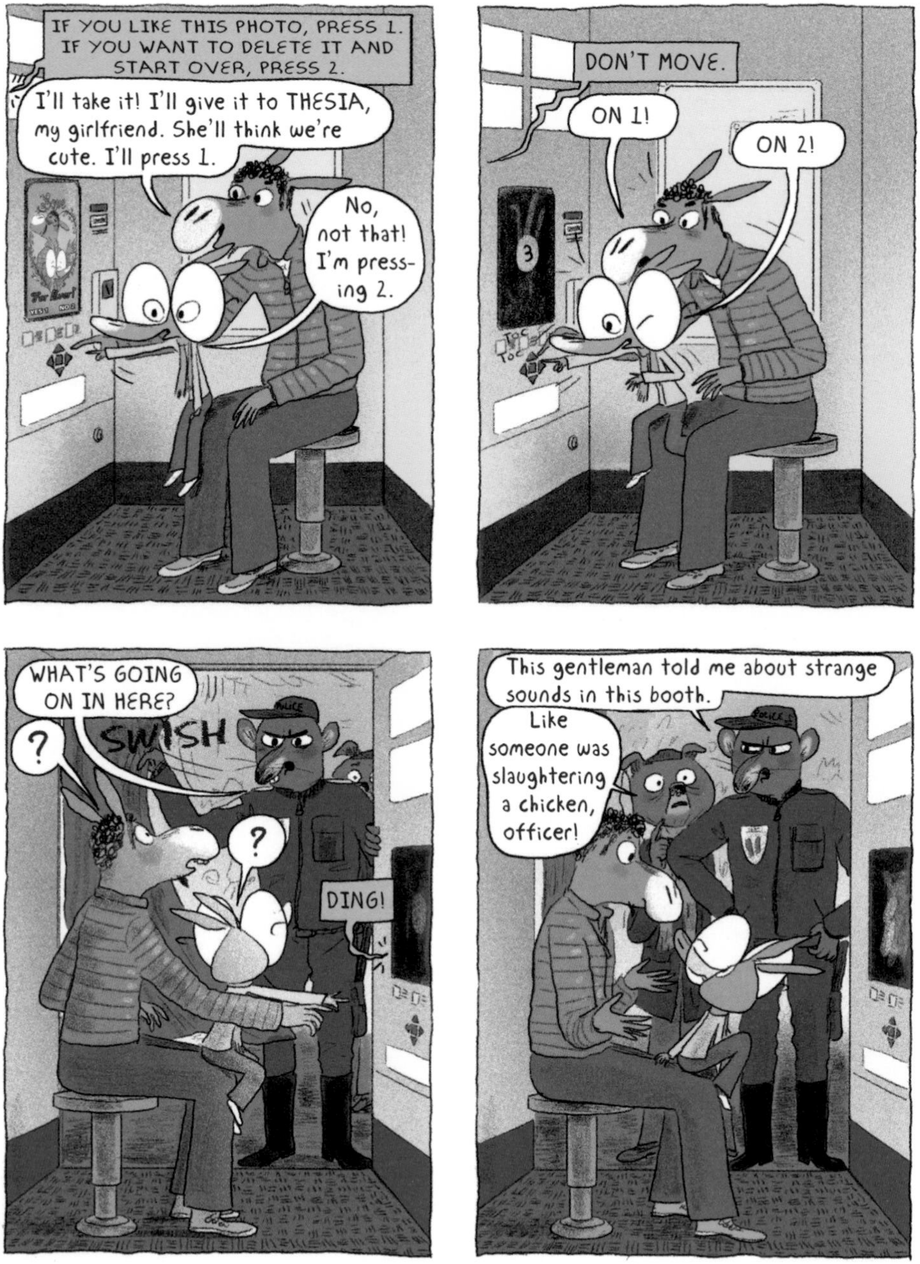
IF YOU LIKE THIS PHOTO, PRESS 1. IF YOU WANT TO DELETE IT AND START OVER, PRESS 2.
I'll take it! I'll give it to THESIA, my girlfriend. She'll think we're cute. I'll press 1.
No, not that! I'm pressing 2.
DON'T MOVE.
ON 1!
ON 2!
TOC TOC TOC
WHAT'S GOING ON IN HERE?
?
SWISH
?
DING!
This gentleman told me about strange sounds in this booth.
Like someone was slaughtering a chicken, officer!

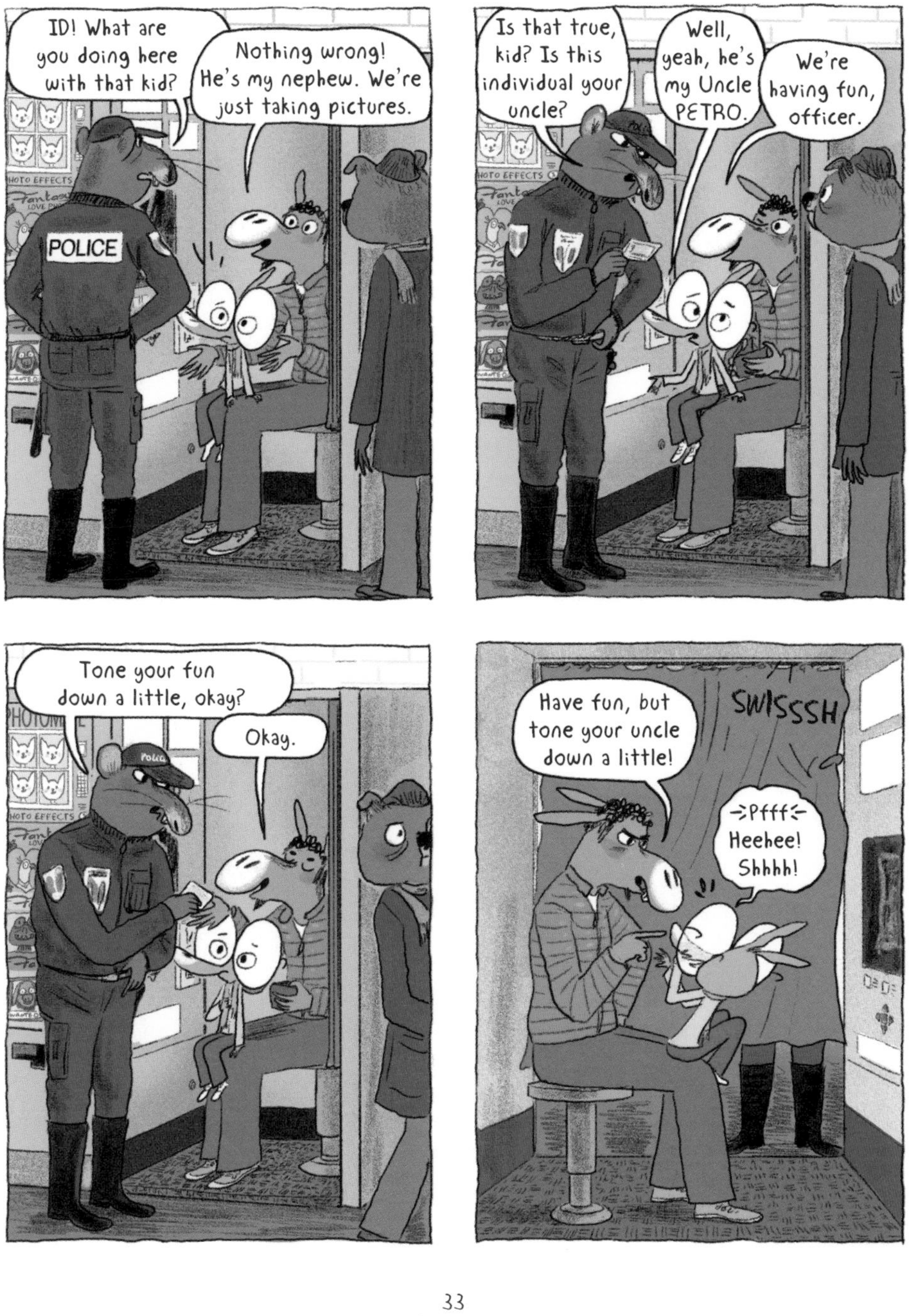
ID! What are you doing here with that kid?
Nothing wrong! He's my nephew. We're just taking pictures.
POLICE
Is that true, kid? Is this individual your uncle?
Well, yeah, he's my Uncle PETRO.
We're having fun, officer.
Tone your fun down a little, okay?
Okay.
Have fun, but tone your uncle down a little!
SWISSSH
Pfff Heehee! Shhhh!

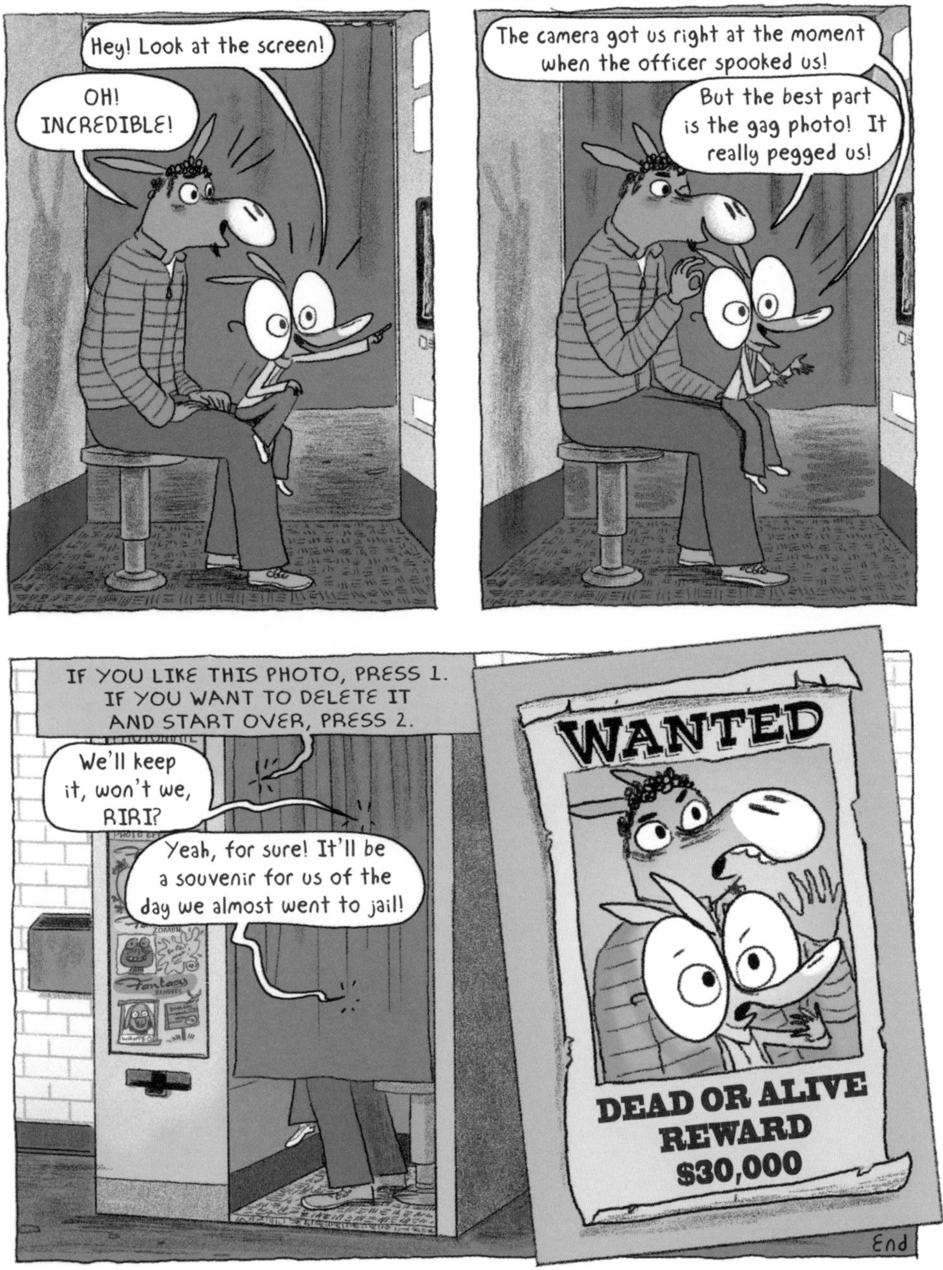
Hey! Look at the screen!
OH! INCREDIBLE!
The camera got us right at the moment when the officer spooked us!
But the best part is the gag photo! It really pegged us!
IF YOU LIKE THIS PHOTO, PRESS 1. IF YOU WANT TO DELETE IT AND START OVER, PRESS 2.
We'll keep it, won't we, RIRI?
Yeah, for sure! It'll be a souvenir for us of the day we almost went to jail!
WANTED
DEAD OR ALIVE
REWARD
$30,000
End

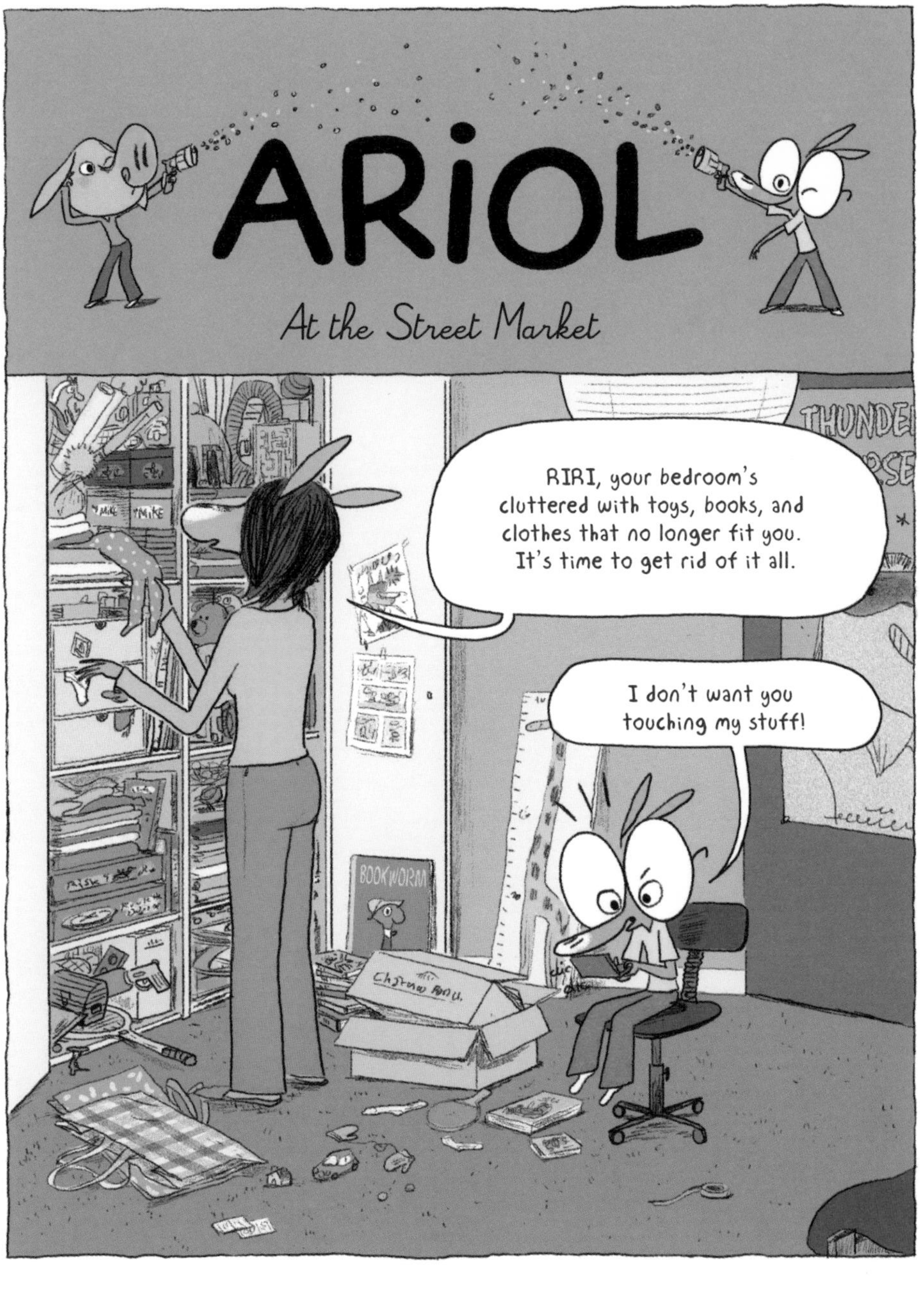
ARiOL
At the Street Market
THUNDE
BOOKWORM
RIRI, your bedroom's cluttered with toys, books, and clothes that no longer fit you. It's time to get rid of it all.
I don't want you touching my stuff!

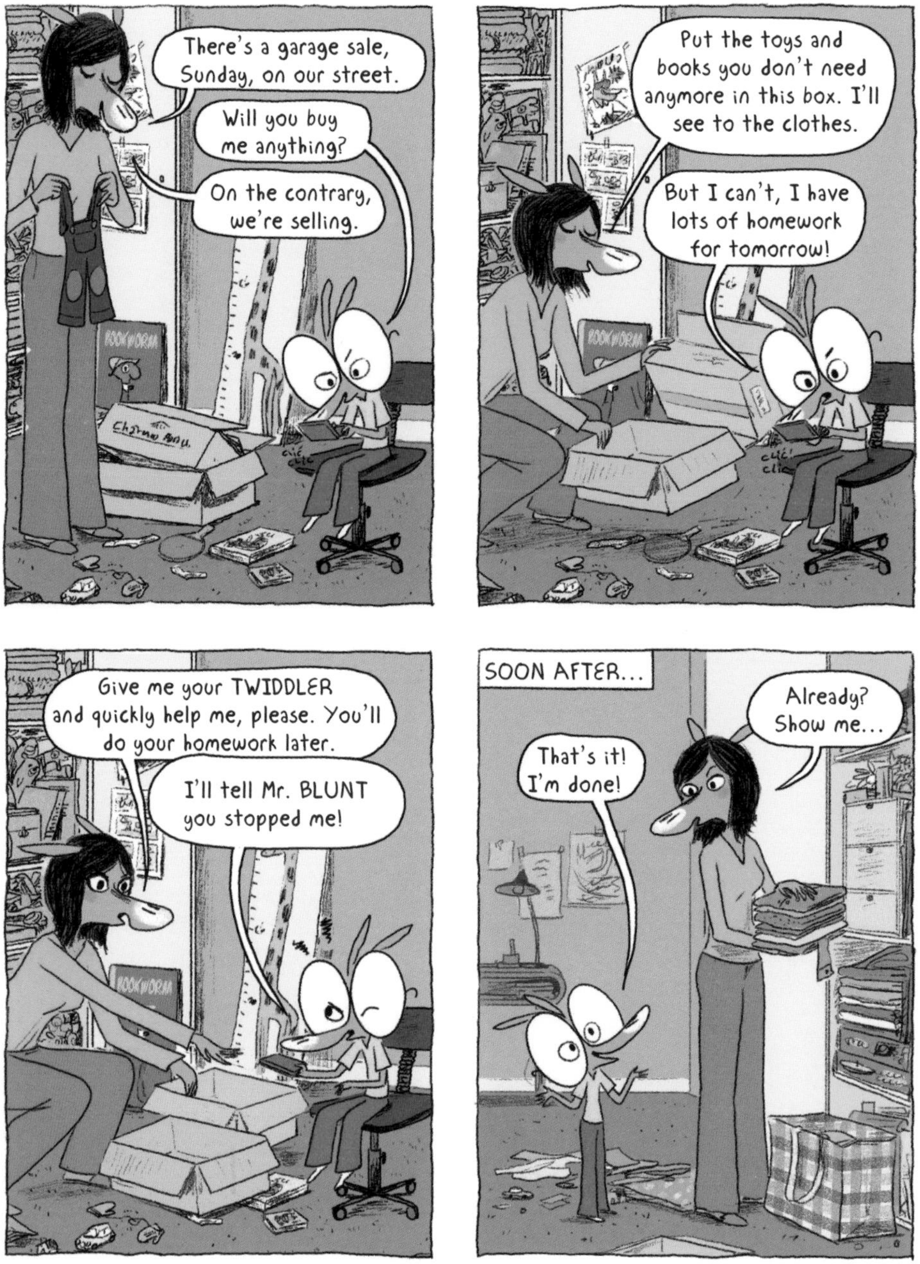
There's a garage sale, Sunday, on our street.
Will you buy me anything?
On the contrary, we're selling.
Put the toys and books you don't need anymore in this box. I'll see to the clothes.
But I can't, I have lots of homework for tomorrow!
Give me your TWIDDLER and quickly help me, please. You'll do your homework later.
I'll tell Mr. BLUNT you stopped me!
SOON AFTER...
That's it! I'm done!
Already? Show me...

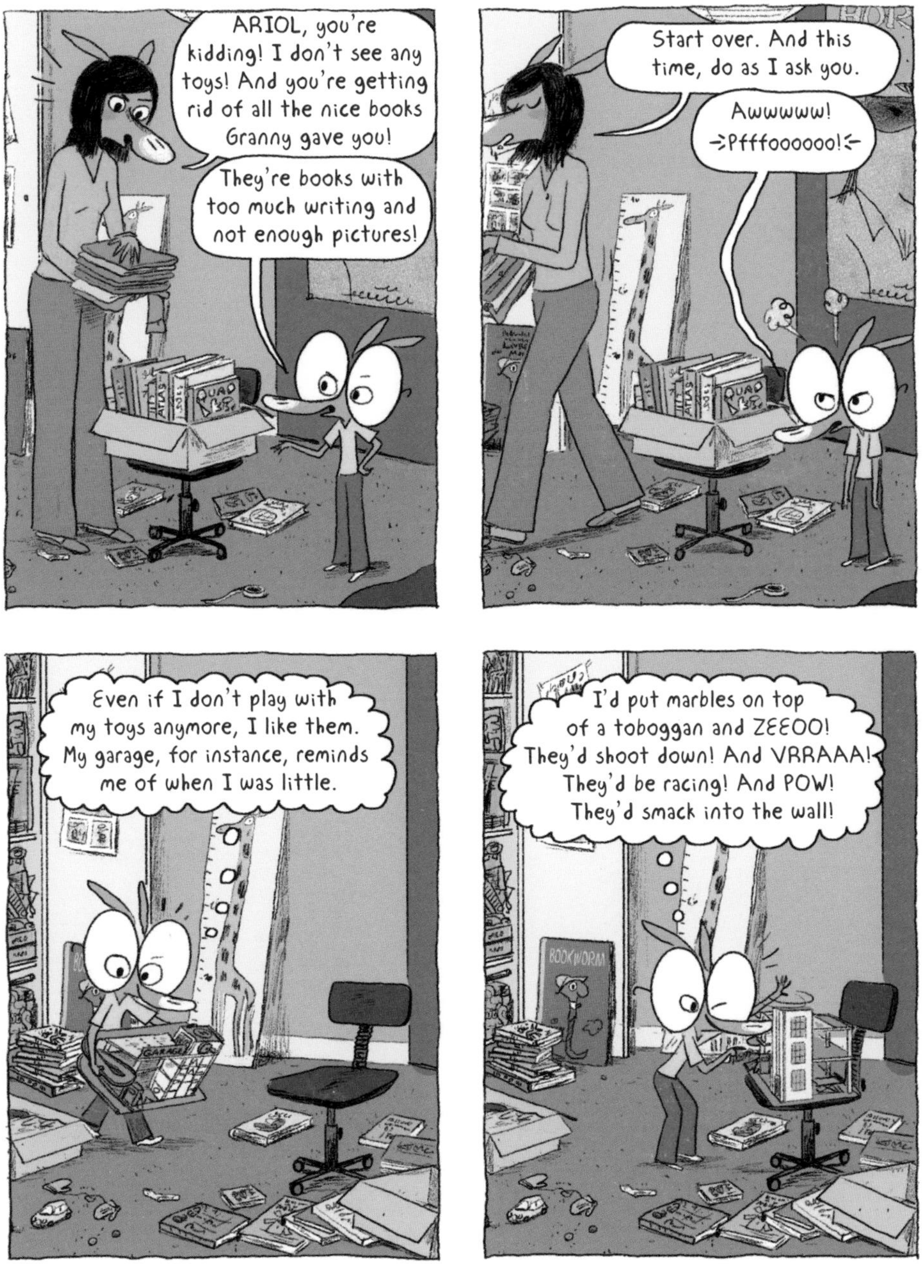
ARIOL, you're kidding! I don't see any toys! And you're getting rid of all the nice books Granny gave you!
They're books with too much writing and not enough pictures!
Start over. And this time, do as I ask you.
Awwwww! Pfffoooooo!
Even if I don't play with my toys anymore, I like them. My garage, for instance, reminds me of when I was little.
I'd put marbles on top of a toboggan and ZEEOO! They'd shoot down! And VRRAAA! They'd be racing! And POW! They'd smack into the wall!

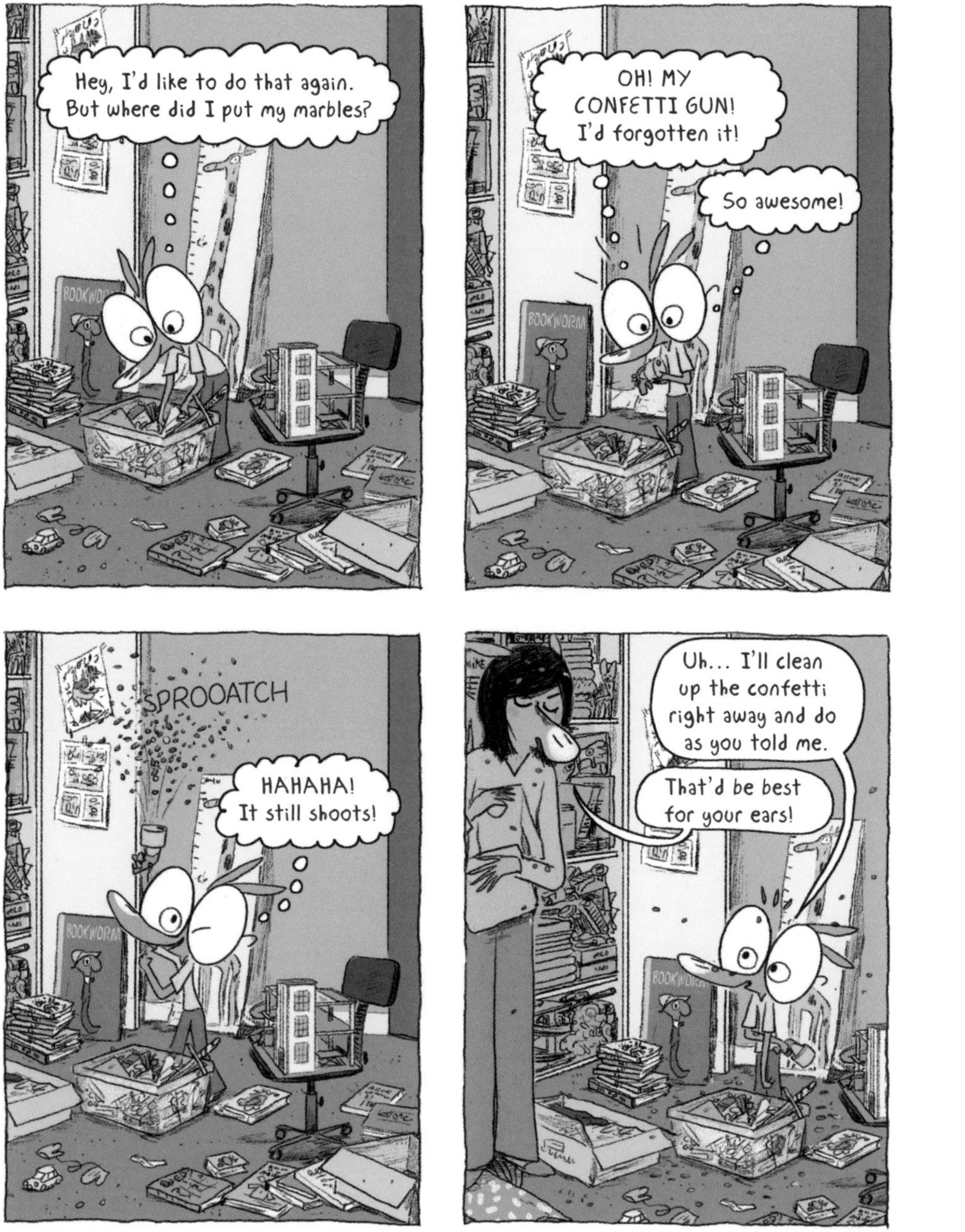
Hey, I'd like to do that again. But where did I put my marbles?
BOOKWORM
OH! MY CONFETTI GUN! I'd forgotten it!
So awesome!
BOOKWORM
SPROOATCH
HAHAHA! It still shoots!
BOOKWORM
Uh... I'll clean up the confetti right away and do as you told me.
That'd be best for your ears!
BOOKWORM

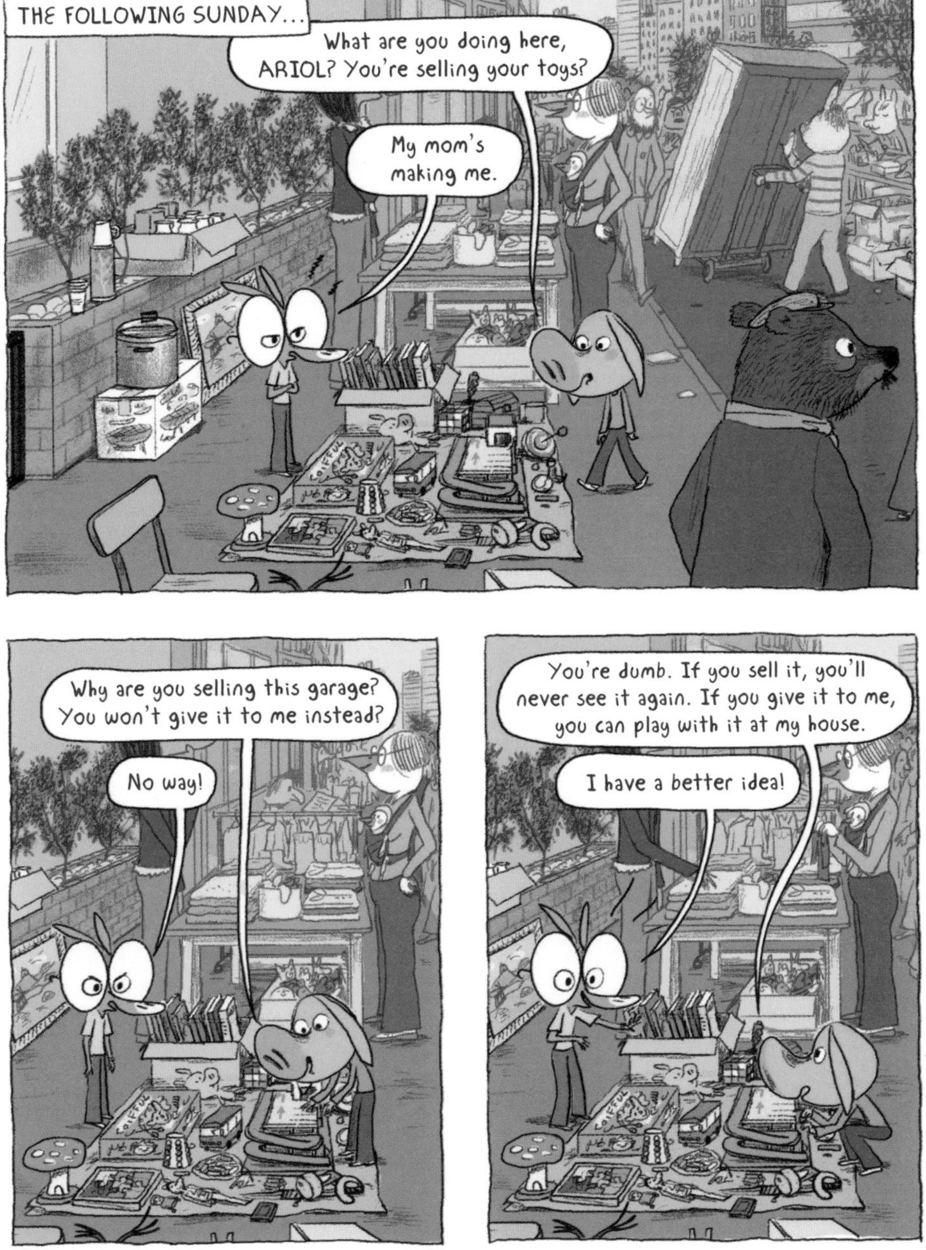
THE FOLLOWING SUNDAY...
What are you doing here, ARIOL? You're selling your toys?
My mom's making me.
Why are you selling this garage? You won't give it to me instead?
No way!
You're dumb. If you sell it, you'll never see it again. If you give it to me, you can play with it at my house.
I have a better idea!

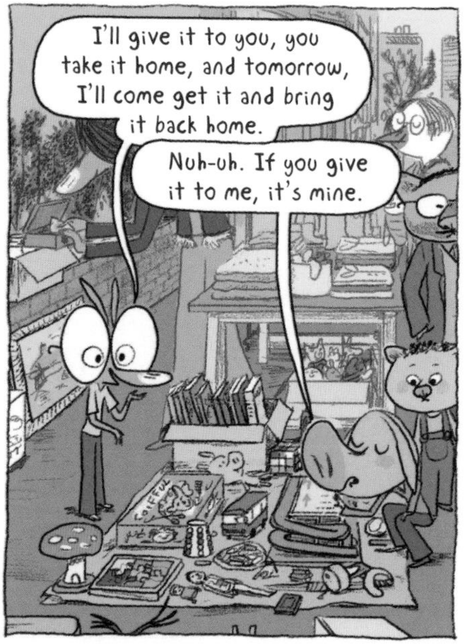
I'll give it to you, you take it home, and tomorrow, I'll come get it and bring it back home.
Nuh-uh. If you give it to me, it's mine.

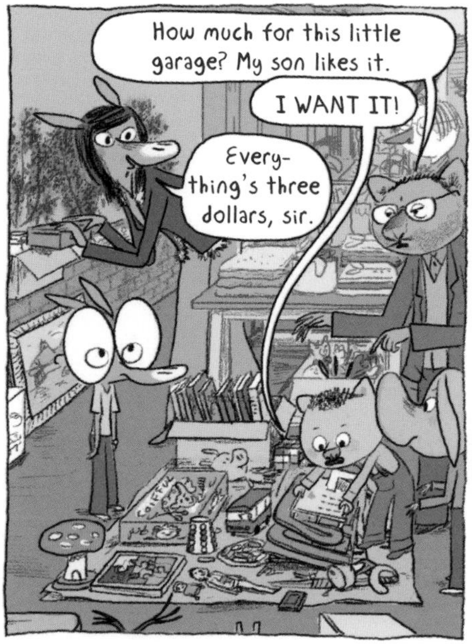
How much for this little garage? My son likes it.
I WANT IT!
Every-thing's three dollars, sir.

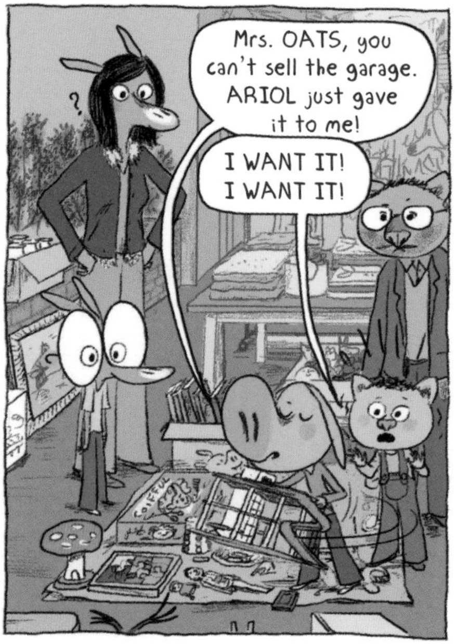
?
Mrs. OATS, you can't sell the garage. ARIOL just gave it to me!
I WANT IT! I WANT IT!

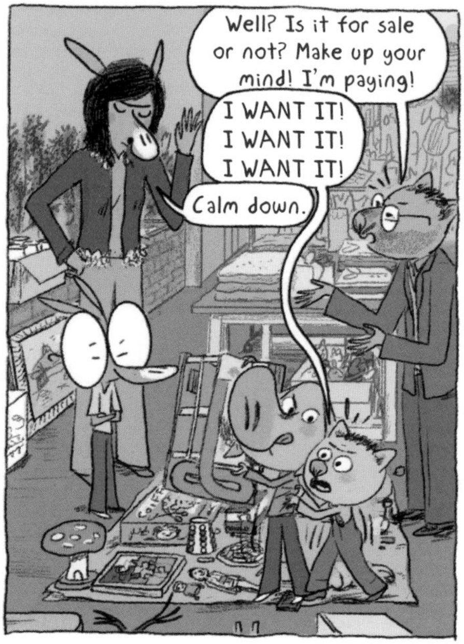
Well? Is it for sale or not? Make up your mind! I'm paying!
I WANT IT! I WANT IT! I WANT IT!
Calm down.

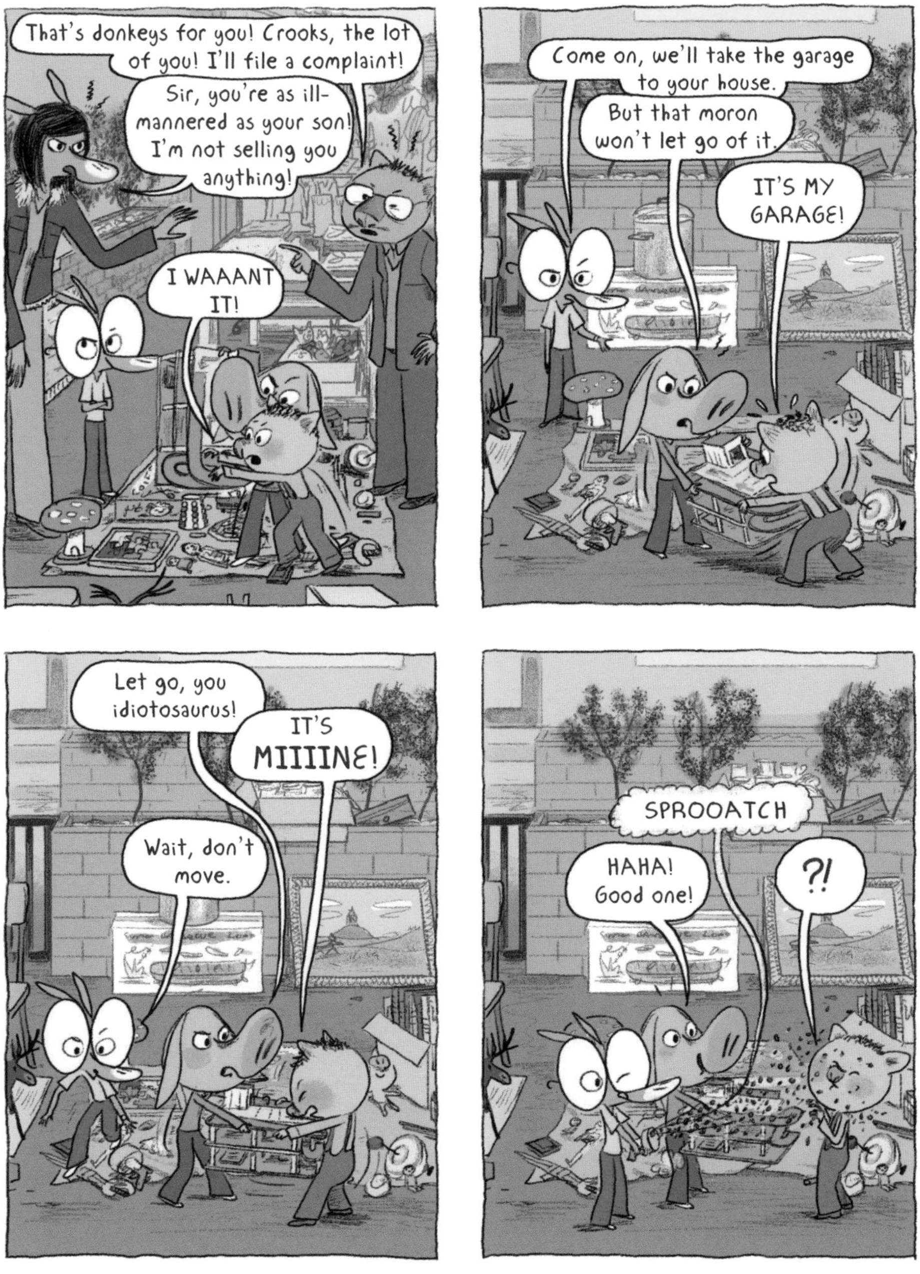
That's donkeys for you! Crooks, the lot of you! I'll file a complaint!
Sir, you're as ill-mannered as your son! I'm not selling you anything!
I WAAANT IT!
Come on, we'll take the garage to your house.
But that moron won't let go of it.
IT'S MY GARAGE!
Let go, you idiotosaurus!
IT'S MIIIINE!
Wait, don't move.
SPROOATCH
HAHA! Good one!
?!

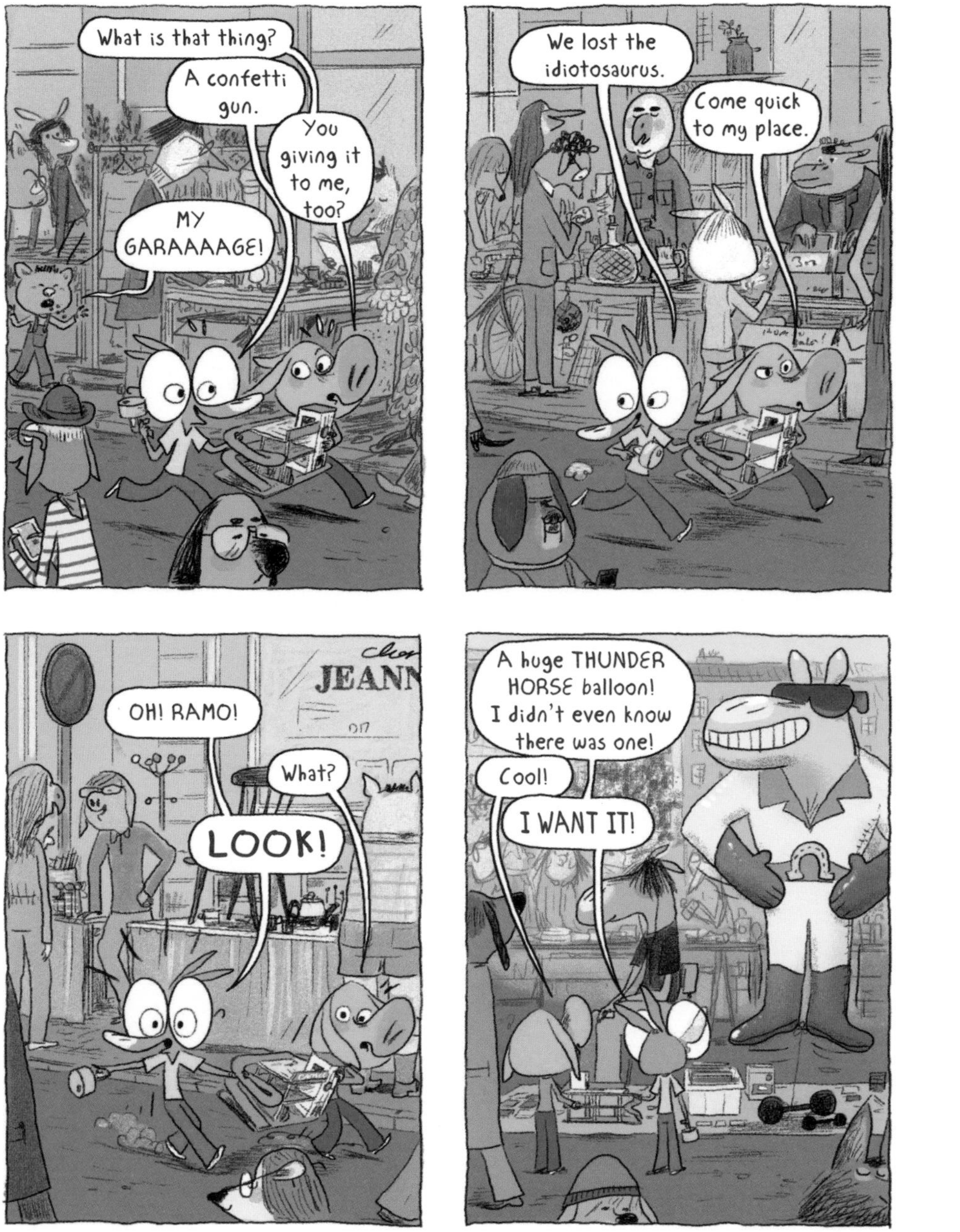
What is that thing?
A confetti gun.
You giving it to me, too?
MY GARAAAAGE!
We lost the idiotosaurus.
Come quick to my place.
JEANN
OH! RAMO!
What?
LOOK!
A huge THUNDER HORSE balloon! I didn't even know there was one!
Cool!
I WANT IT!

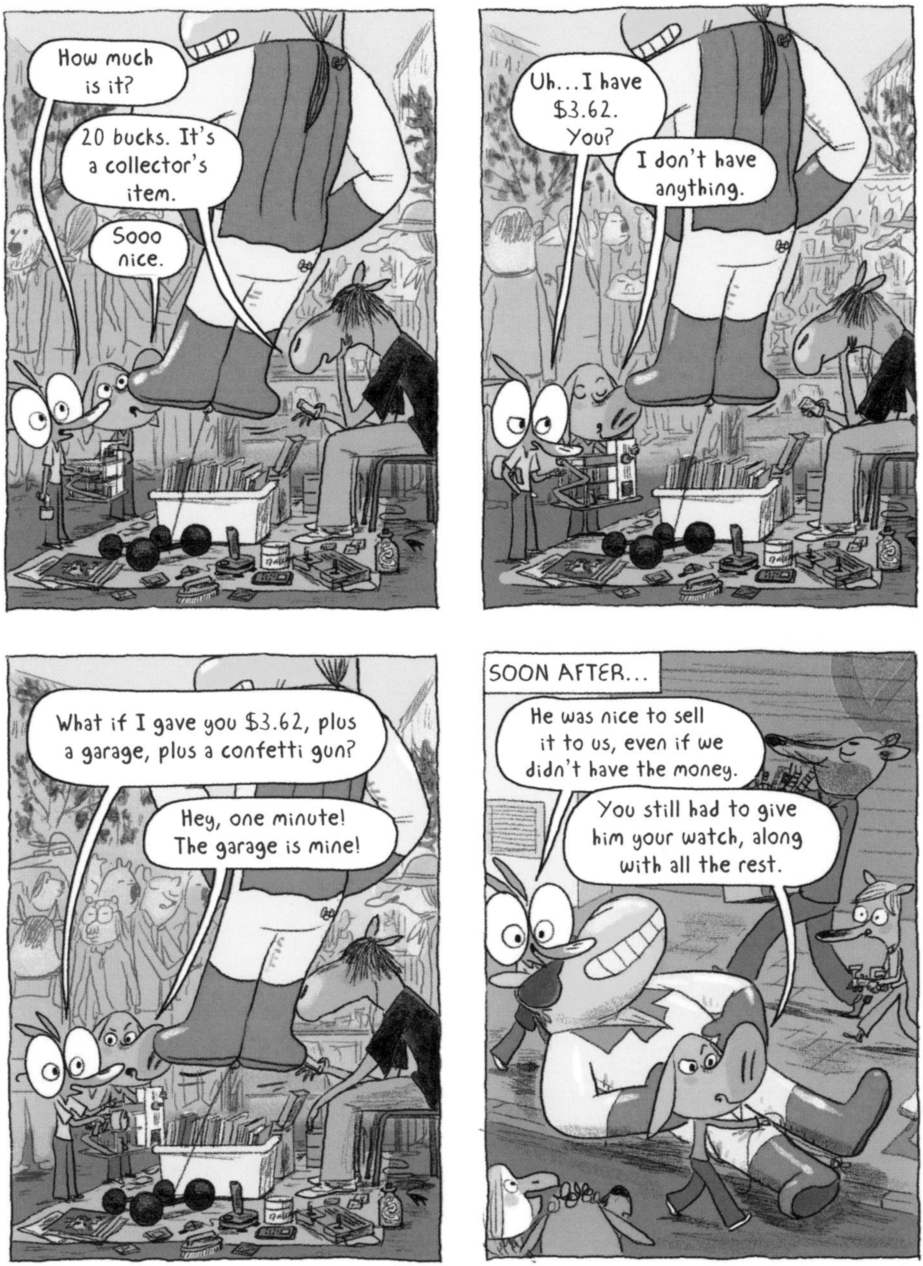
How much is it?
20 bucks. It's a collector's item.
Sooo nice.
Uh...I have $3.62. You?
I don't have anything.
What if I gave you $3.62, plus a garage, plus a confetti gun?
Hey, one minute! The garage is mine!
SOON AFTER...
He was nice to sell it to us, even if we didn't have the money.
You still had to give him your watch, along with all the rest.

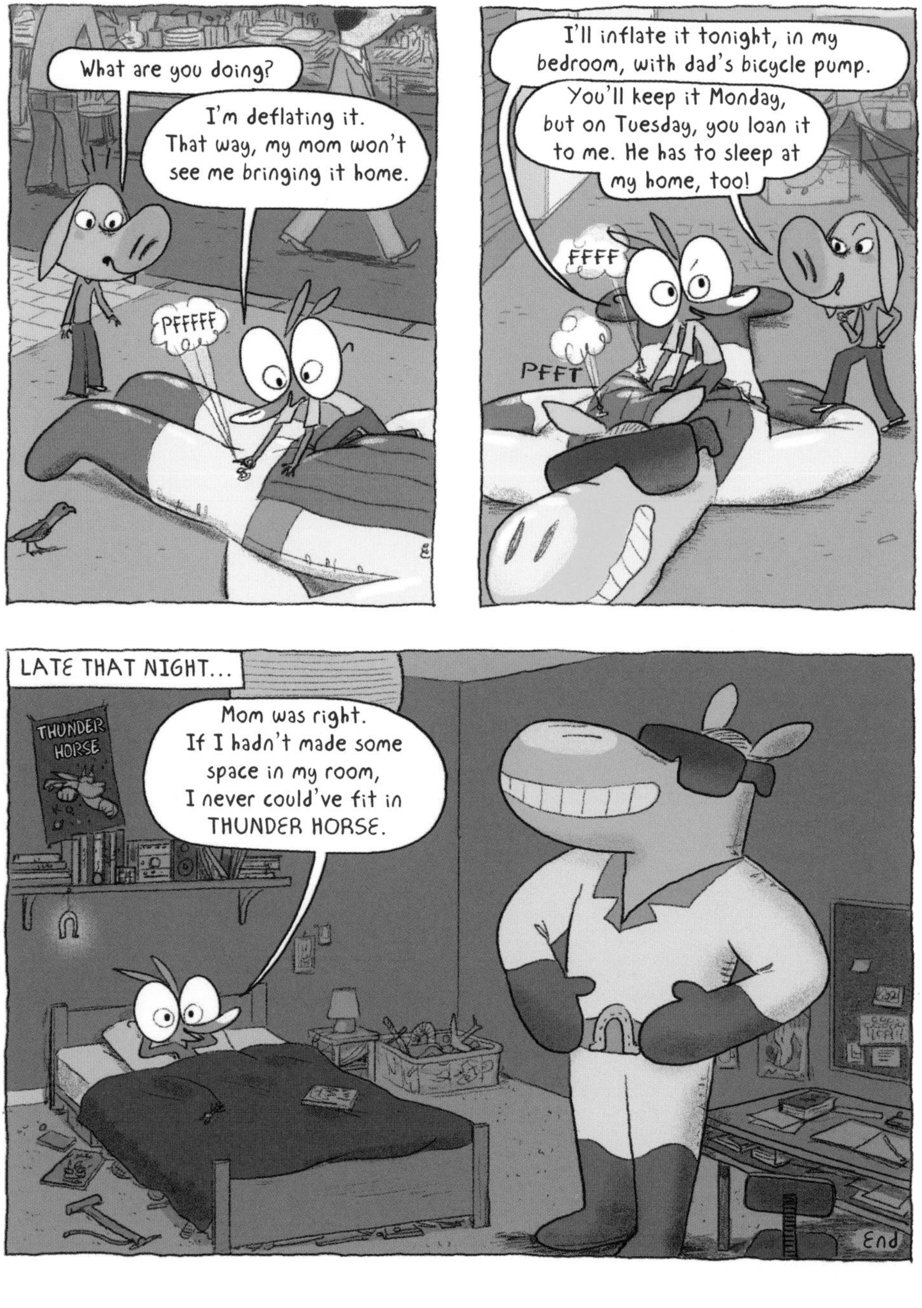
What are you doing?
I'm deflating it. That way, my mom won't see me bringing it home.
PFFFFF
I'll inflate it tonight, in my bedroom, with dad's bicycle pump.
FFFF
PFFT
You'll keep it Monday, but on Tuesday, you loan it to me. He has to sleep at my home, too!
LATE THAT NIGHT...
THUNDER HORSE
Mom was right. If I hadn't made some space in my room, I never could've fit in THUNDER HORSE.
End

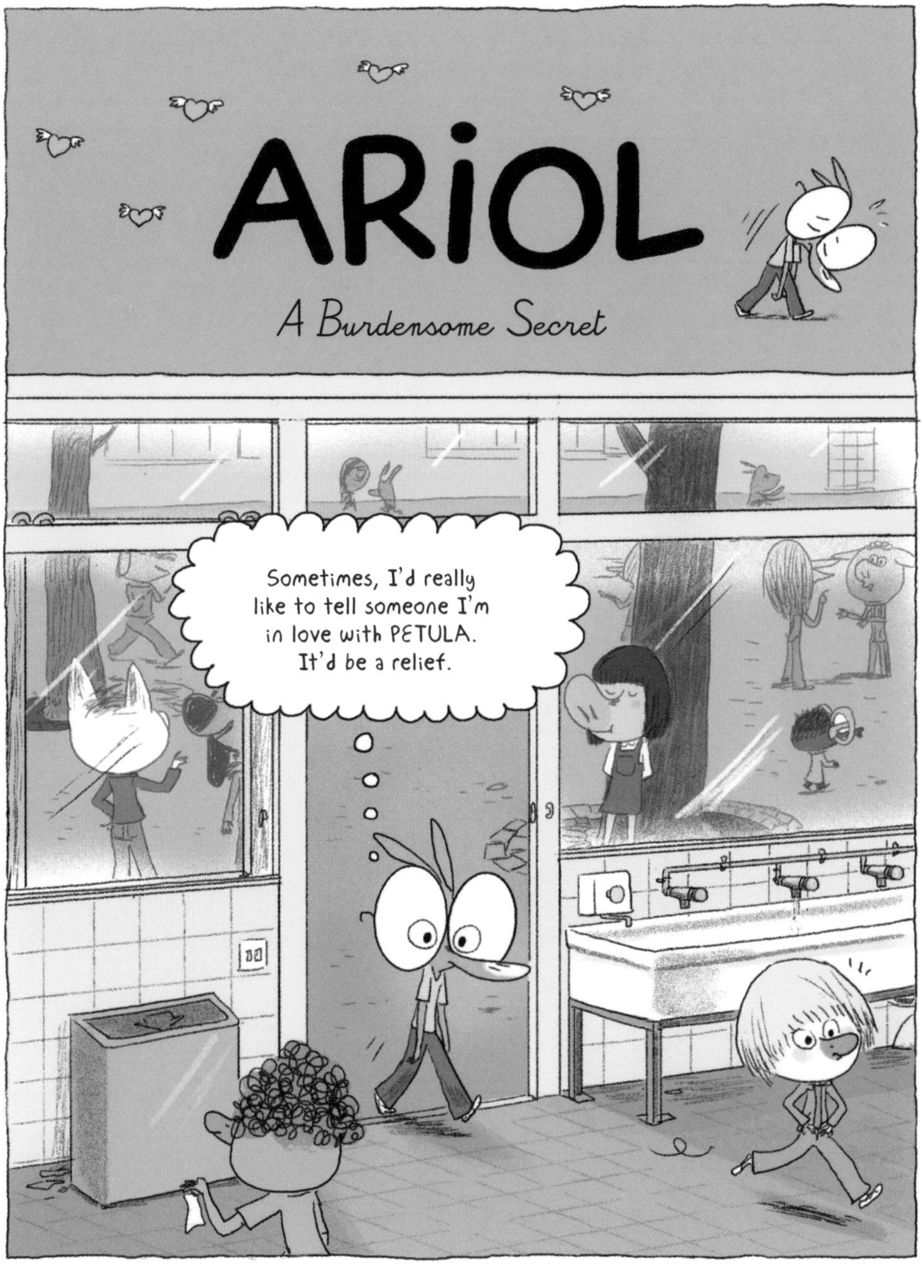
ARiOL
A Burdensome Secret
Sometimes, I'd really like to tell someone I'm in love with PETULA. It'd be a relief.

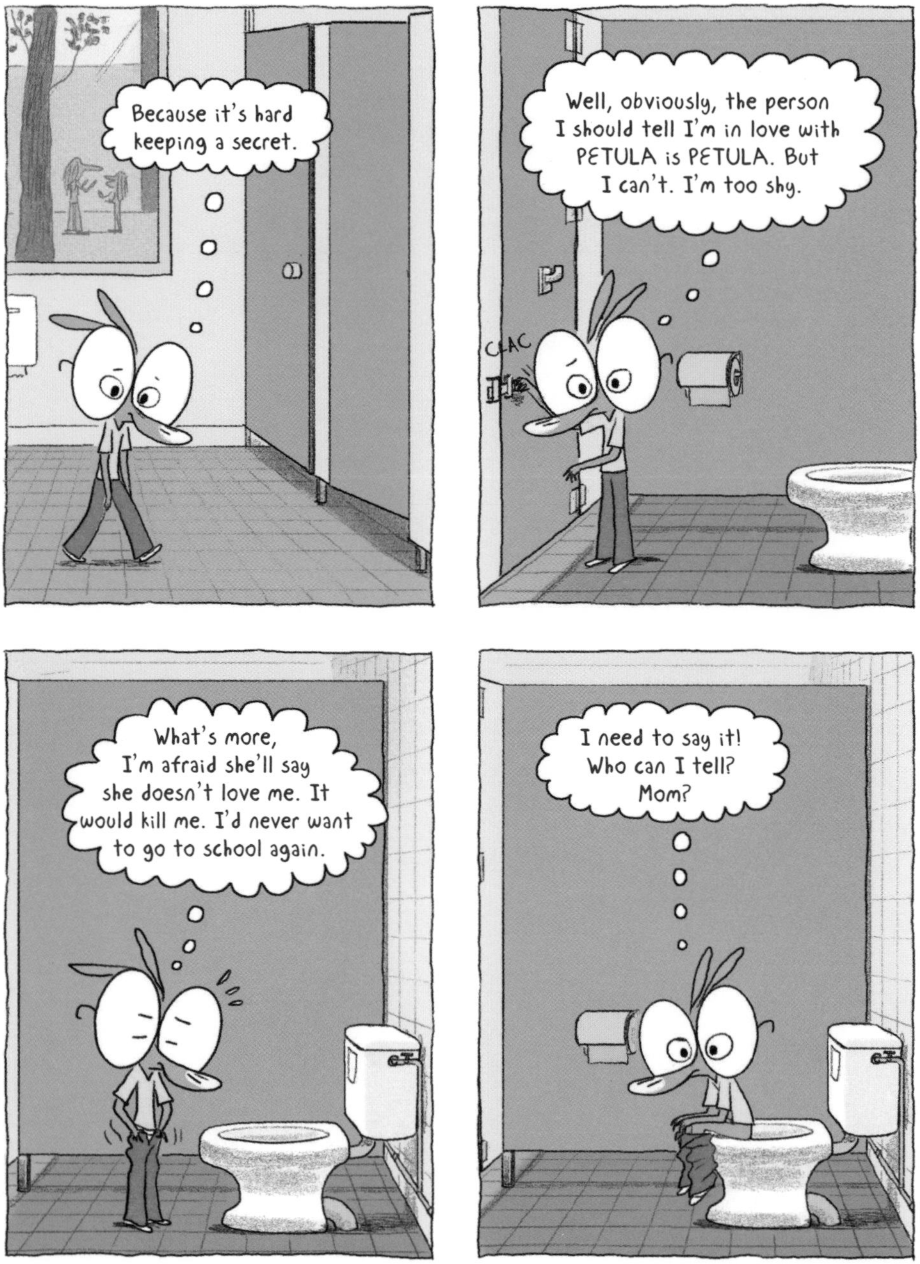
Because it's hard keeping a secret.
Well, obviously, the person I should tell I'm in love with PETULA is PETULA. But I can't. I'm too shy.
CLAC
What's more, I'm afraid she'll say she doesn't love me. It would kill me. I'd never want to go to school again.
I need to say it! Who can I tell? Mom?

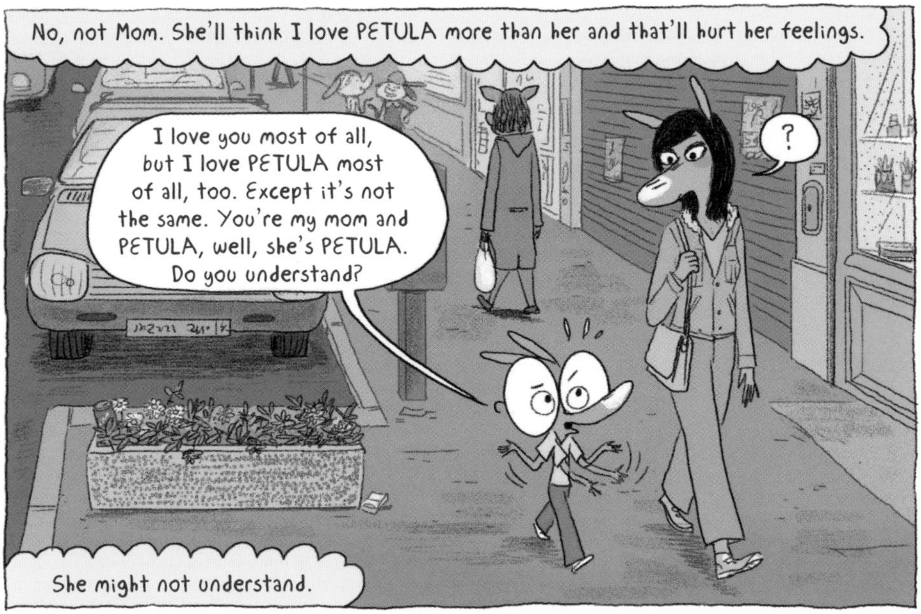
No, not Mom. She'll think I love PETULA more than her and that'll hurt her feelings.
I love you most of all, but I love PETULA most of all, too. Except it's not the same. You're my mom and PETULA, well, she's PETULA. Do you understand?
?
She might not understand.

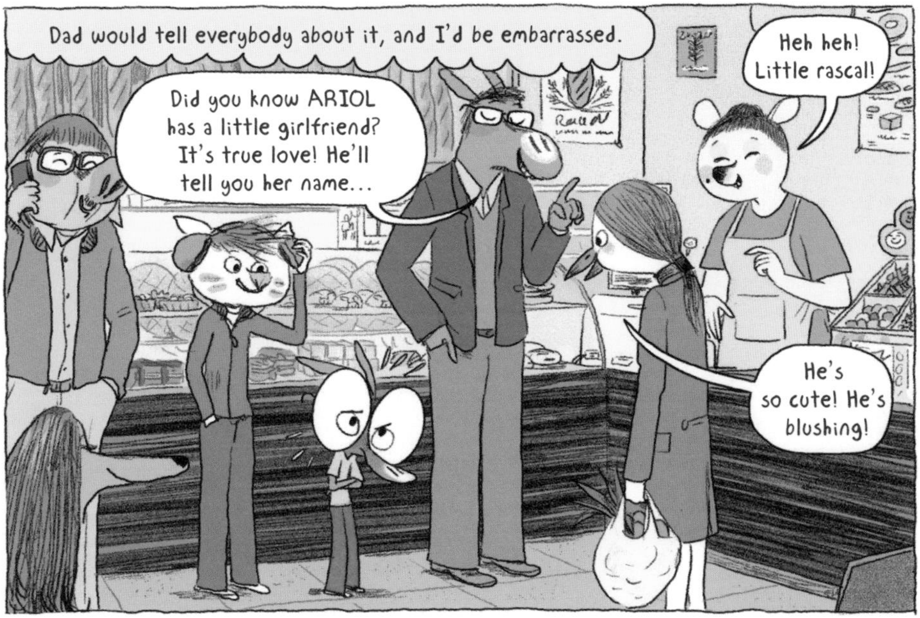
Dad would tell everybody about it, and I'd be embarrassed.
Did you know ARIOL has a little girlfriend? It's true love! He'll tell you her name...
Heh heh! Little rascal!
He's so cute! He's blushing!

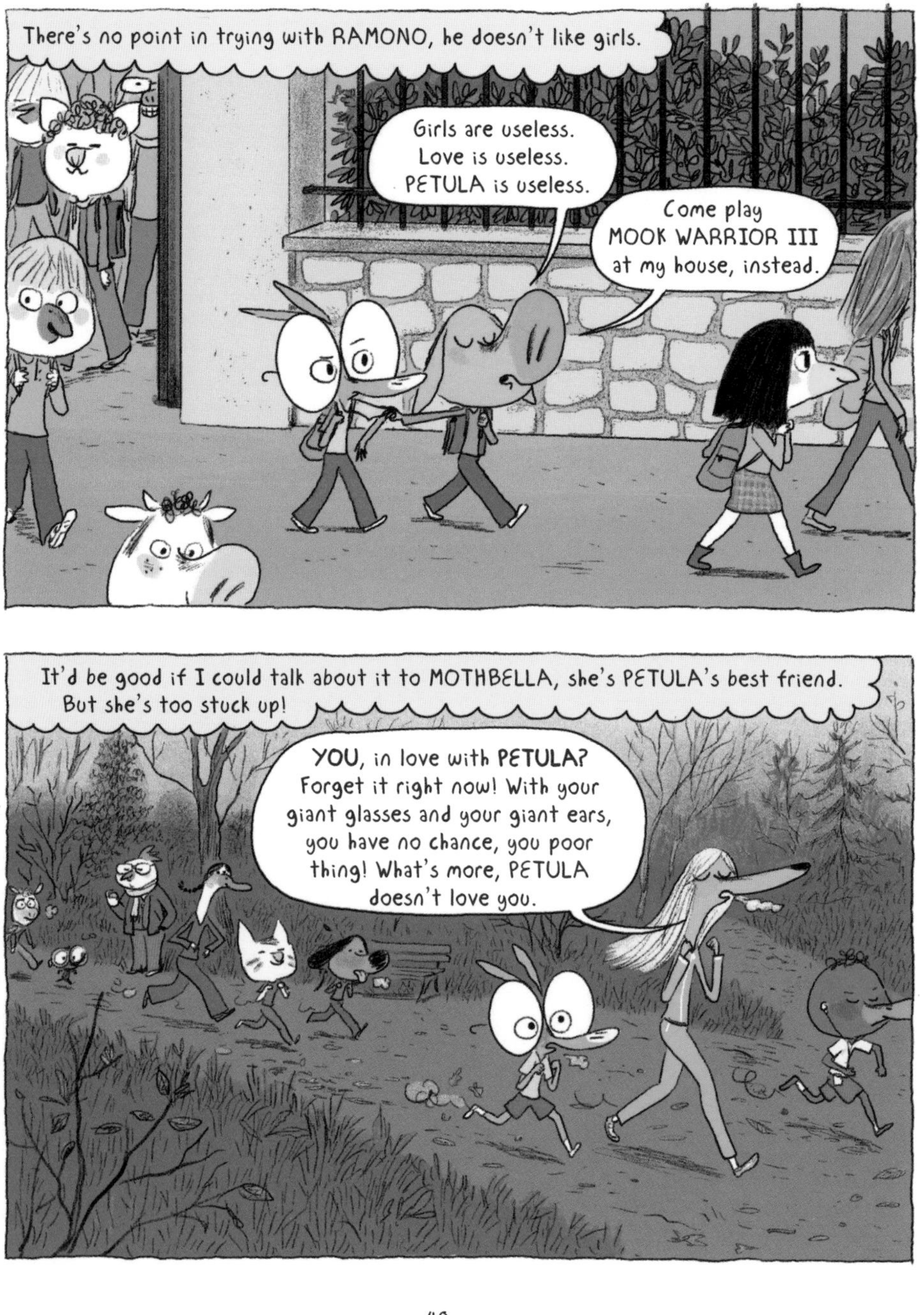
There's no point in trying with RAMONO, he doesn't like girls.
Girls are useless. Love is useless. PETULA is useless.
Come play MOOK WARRIOR III at my house, instead.
It'd be good if I could talk about it to MOTHBELLA, she's PETULA's best friend. But she's too stuck up!
YOU, in love with PETULA? Forget it right now! With your giant glasses and your giant ears, you have no chance, you poor thing! What's more, PETULA doesn't love you.

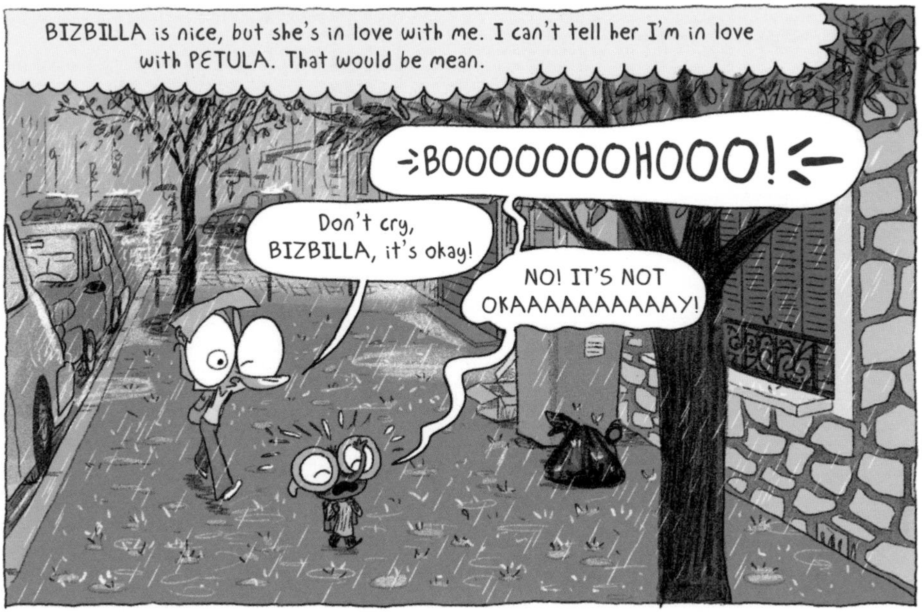
BIZBILLA is nice, but she's in love with me. I can't tell her I'm in love with PETULA. That would be mean.
BOOOOOOOHOOO!
Don't cry, BIZBILLA, it's okay!
NO! IT'S NOT OKAAAAAAAAAAY!

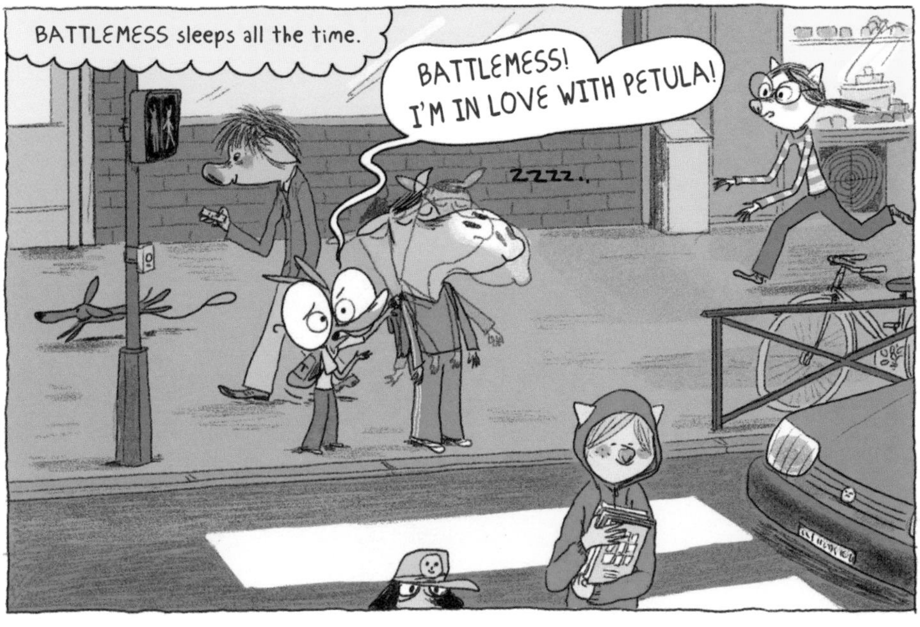
BATTLEMESS sleeps all the time.
BATTLEMESS! I'M IN LOVE WITH PETULA!
ZZZZ..

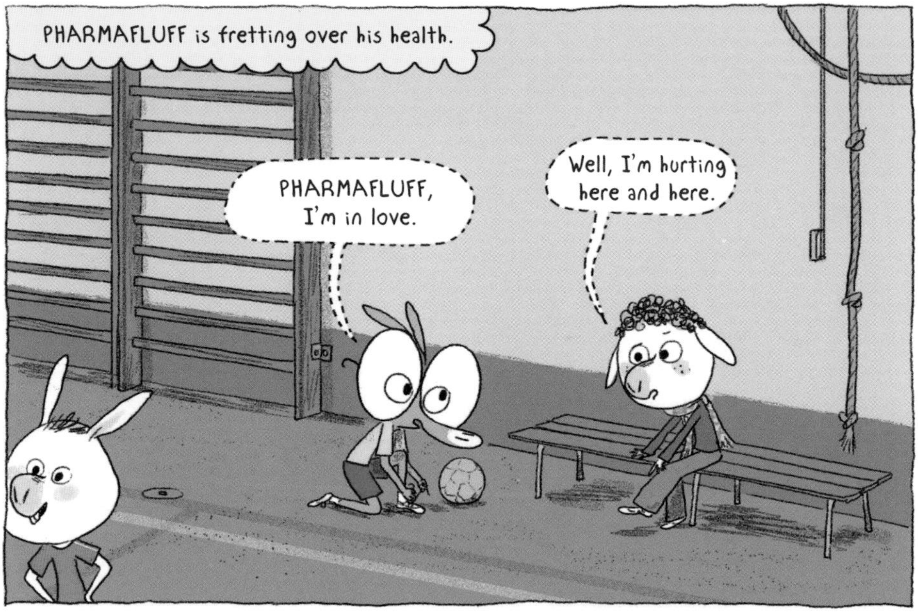
PHARMAFLUFF is fretting over his health.
PHARMAFLUFF, I'm in love.
Well, I'm hurting here and here.

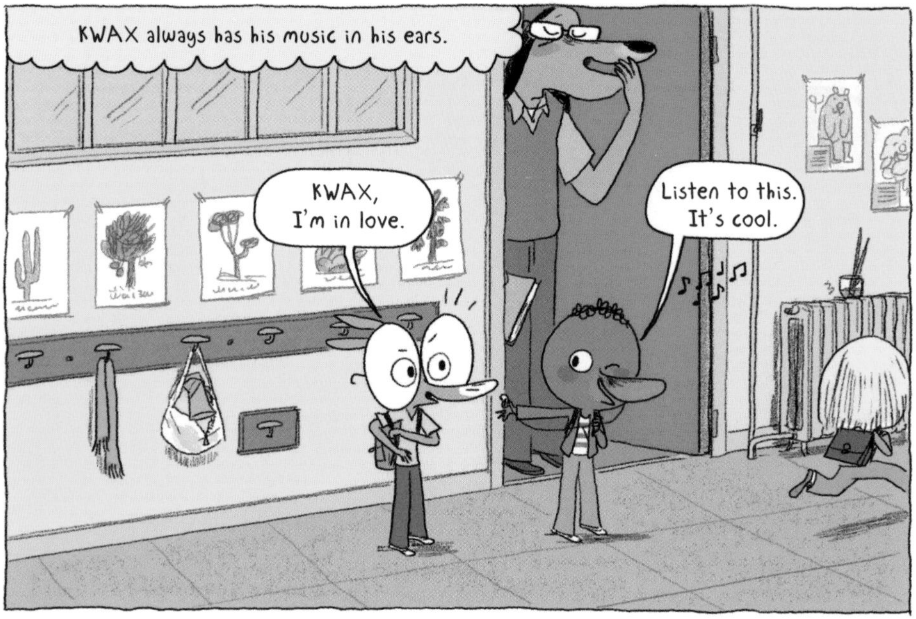
KWAX always has his music in his ears.
KWAX, I'm in love.
Listen to this. It's cool.

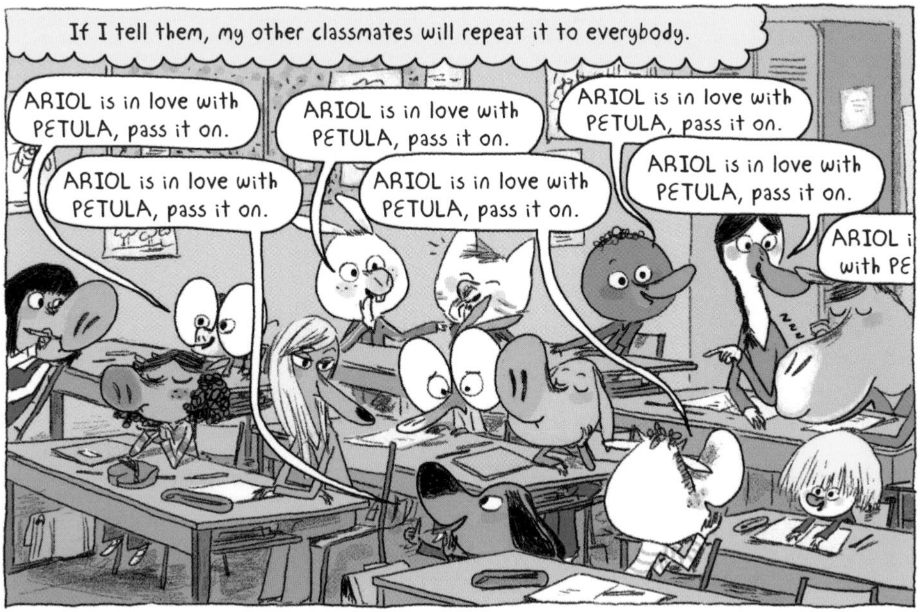
If I tell them, my other classmates will repeat it to everybody.
ARIOL is in love with PETULA, pass it on.
ARIOL is in love with PETULA, pass it on.
ARIOL is in love with PETULA, pass it on.
ARIOL is in love with PETULA, pass it on.
ARIOL is in love with PETULA, pass it on.
ARIOL is in love with PETULA, pass it on.

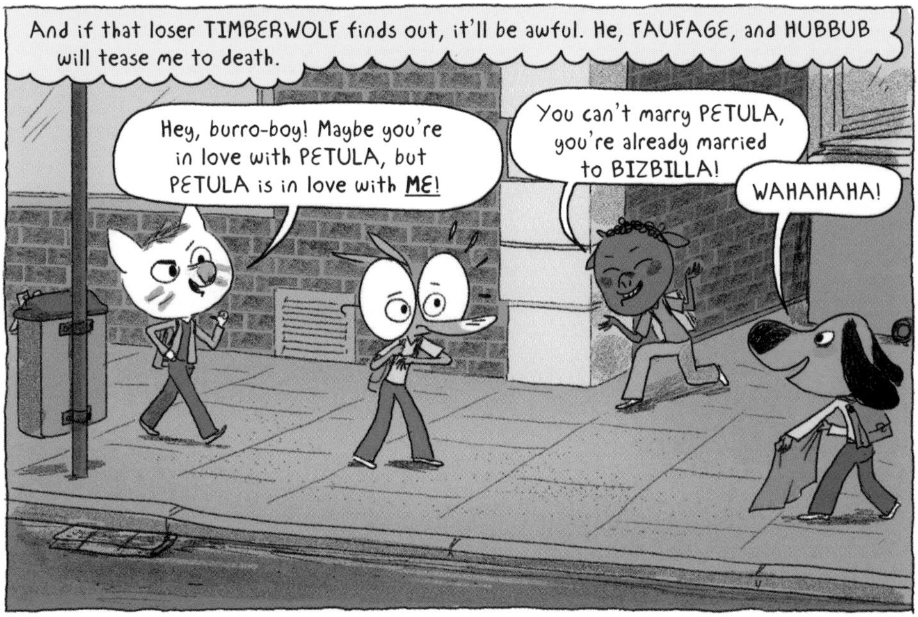
And if that loser TIMBERWOLF finds out, it'll be awful. He, FAUFAGE, and HUBBUB will tease me to death.
Hey, burro-boy! Maybe you're in love with PETULA, but PETULA is in love with ME!
You can't marry PETULA, you're already married to BIZBILLA!
WAHAHAHA!

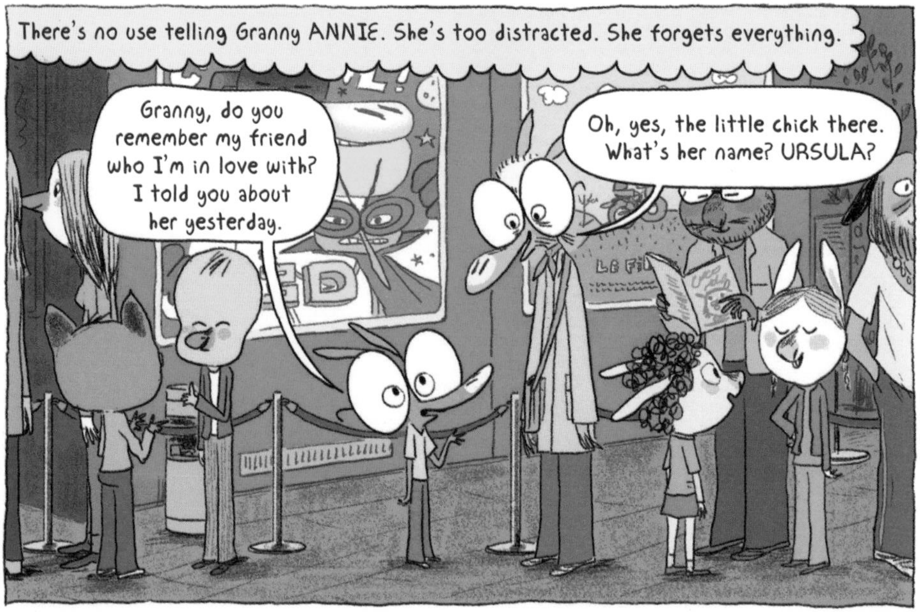
There's no use telling Granny ANNIE. She's too distracted. She forgets everything.
Granny, do you remember my friend who I'm in love with? I told you about her yesterday.
Oh, yes, the little chick there. What's her name? URSULA?

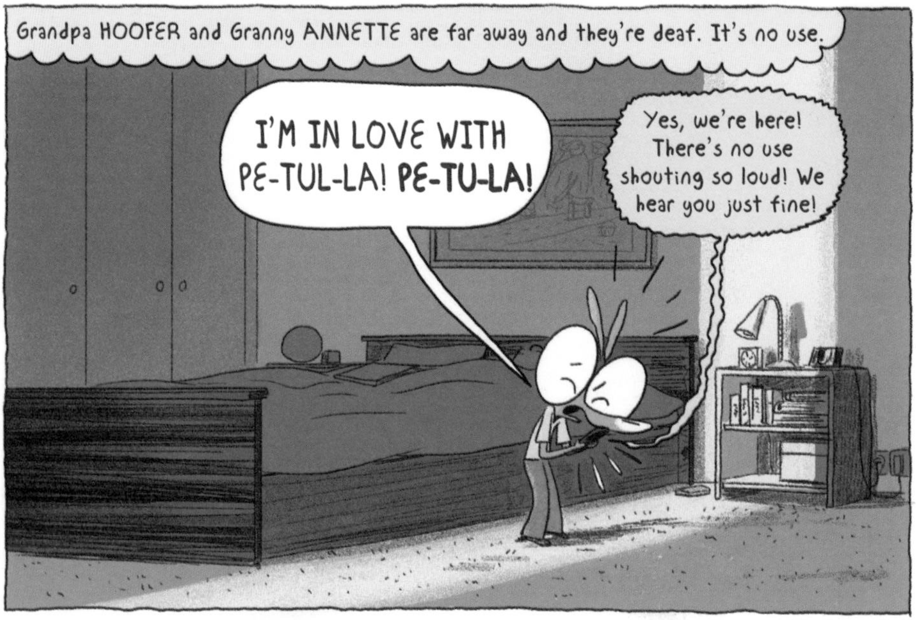
Grandpa HOOFER and Granny ANNETTE are far away and they're deaf. It's no use.
I'M IN LOVE WITH PE-TUL-LA! PE-TU-LA!
Yes, we're here! There's no use shouting so loud! We hear you just fine!

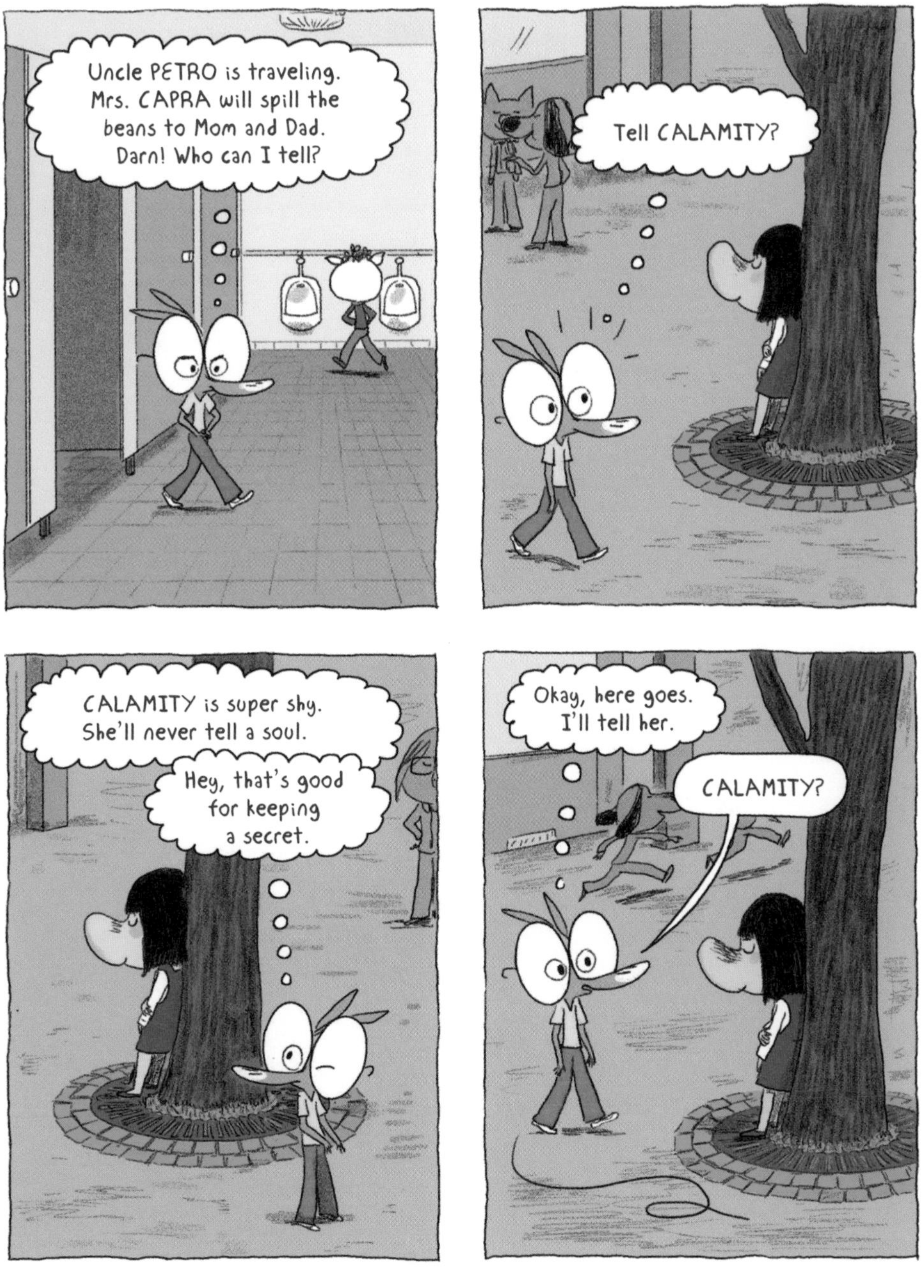
Uncle PETRO is traveling. Mrs. CAPRA will spill the beans to Mom and Dad. Darn! Who can I tell?
Tell CALAMITY?
CALAMITY is super shy. She'll never tell a soul.
Hey, that's good for keeping a secret.
Okay, here goes. I'll tell her.
CALAMITY?

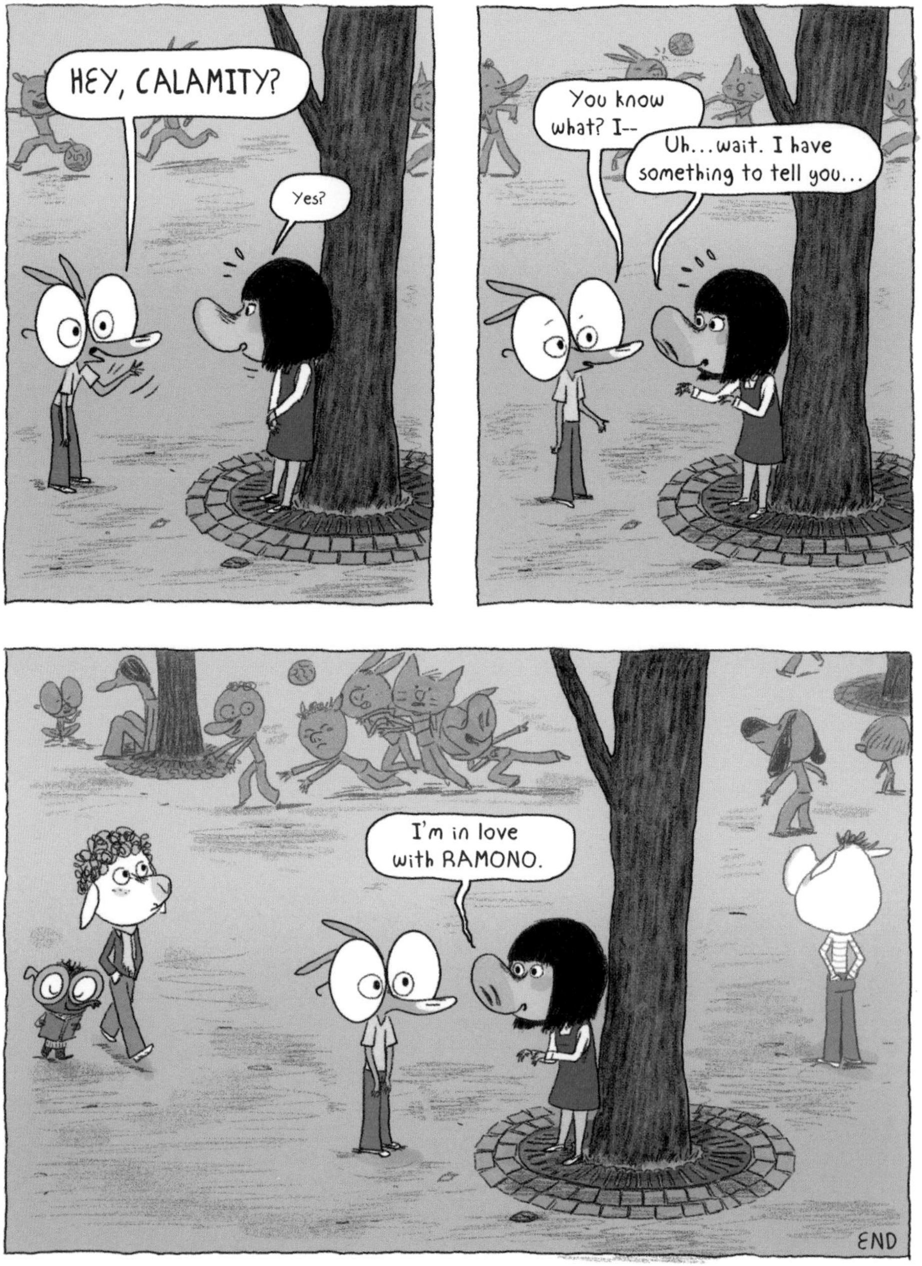
HEY, CALAMITY?
Yes?
You know what? I--
Uh...wait. I have something to tell you...
I'm in love with RAMONO.
END

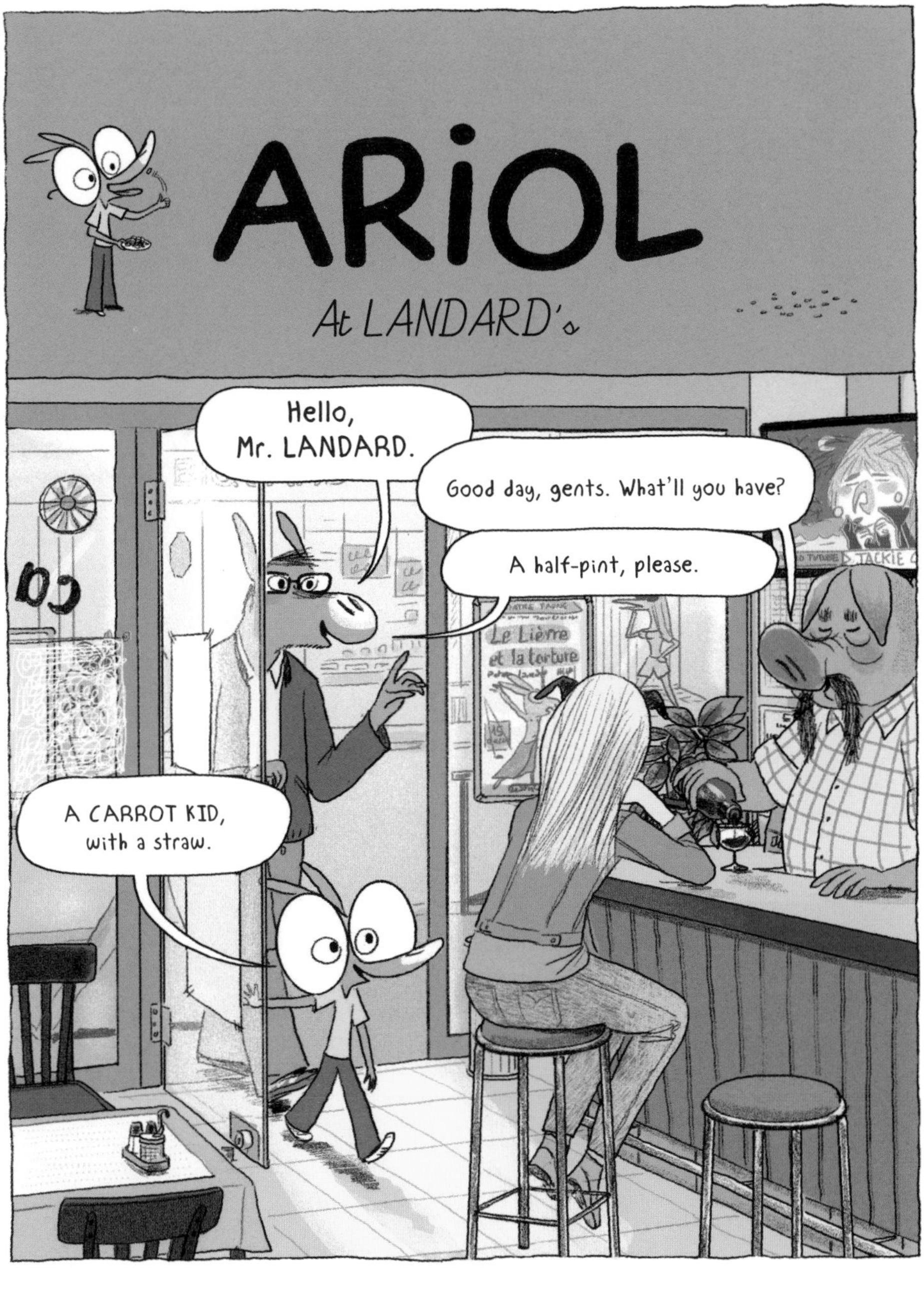
ARiOL
At LANDARD's
Hello, Mr. LANDARD.
Good day, gents. What'll you have?
A half-pint, please.
A CARROT KID, with a straw.
Le Lièvre et la torture

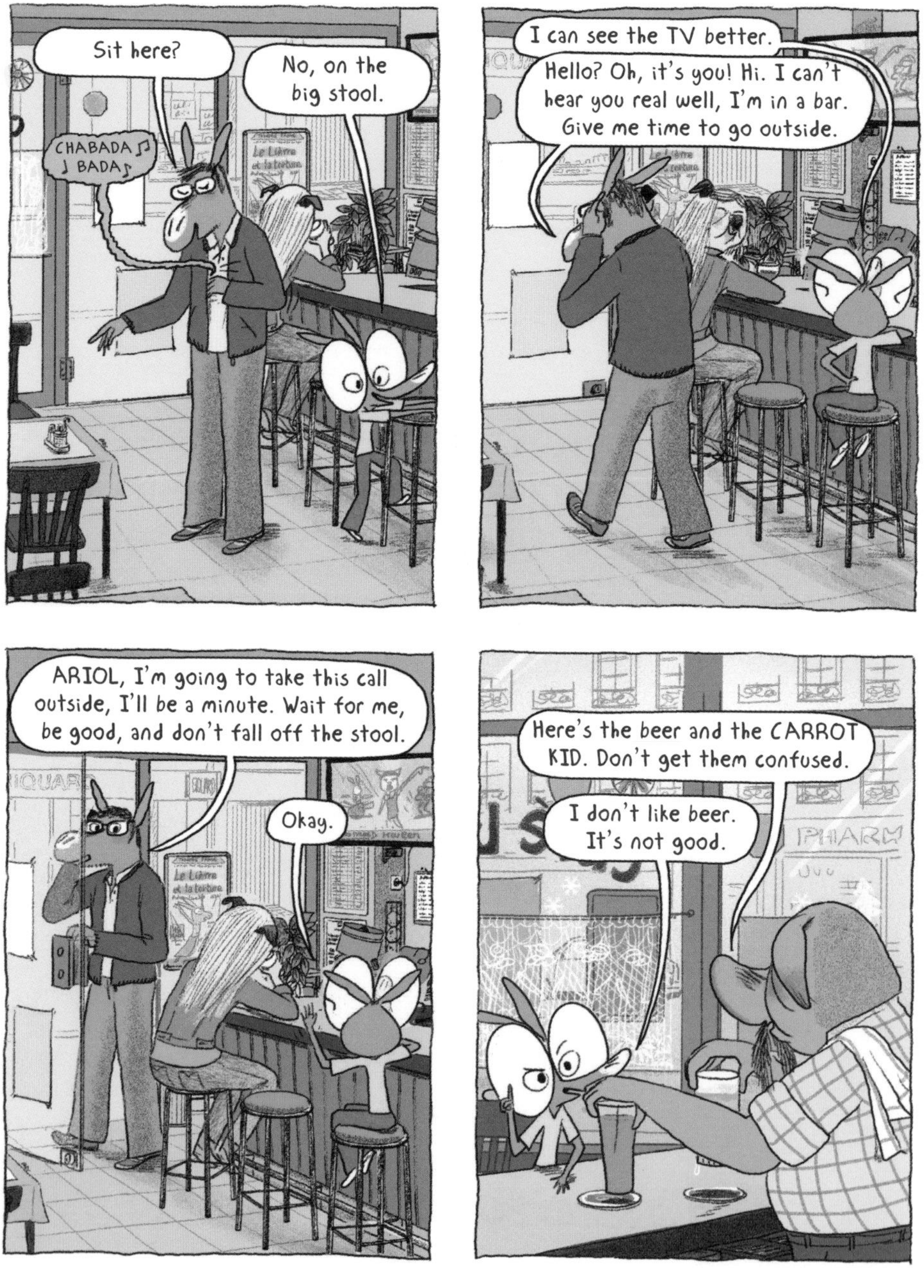
Sit here?
CHABADA BADA
No, on the big stool.
I can see the TV better.
Hello? Oh, it's you! Hi. I can't hear you real well, I'm in a bar. Give me time to go outside.
ARIOL, I'm going to take this call outside, I'll be a minute. Wait for me, be good, and don't fall off the stool.
Okay.
Here's the beer and the CARROT KID. Don't get them confused.
I don't like beer. It's not good.
PHARM

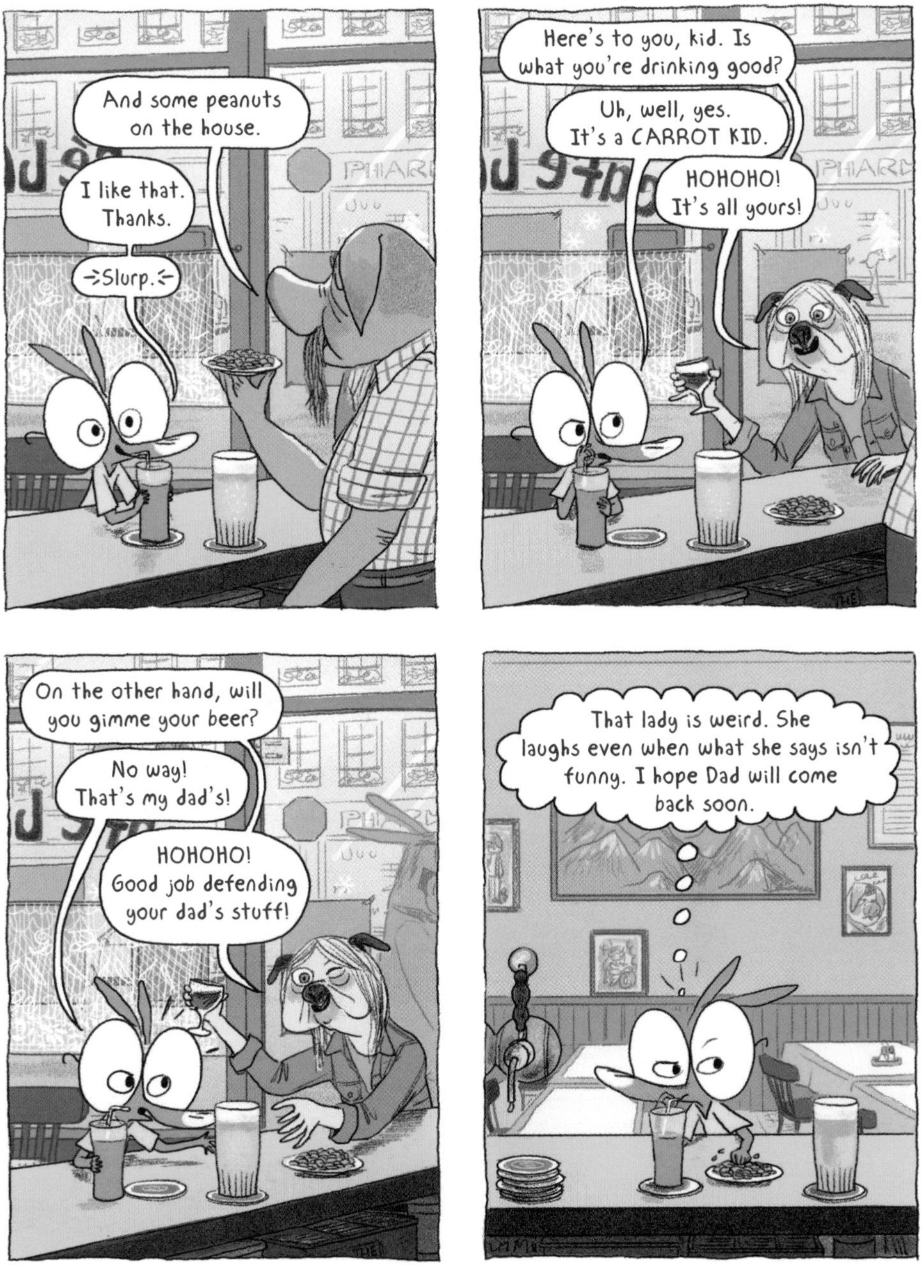
And some peanuts on the house.
I like that. Thanks.
Slurp.
Here's to you, kid. Is what you're drinking good?
Uh, well, yes. It's a CARROT KID.
HOHOHO! It's all yours!
On the other hand, will you gimme your beer?
No way! That's my dad's!
HOHOHO! Good job defending your dad's stuff!
That lady is weird. She laughs even when what she says isn't funny. I hope Dad will come back soon.

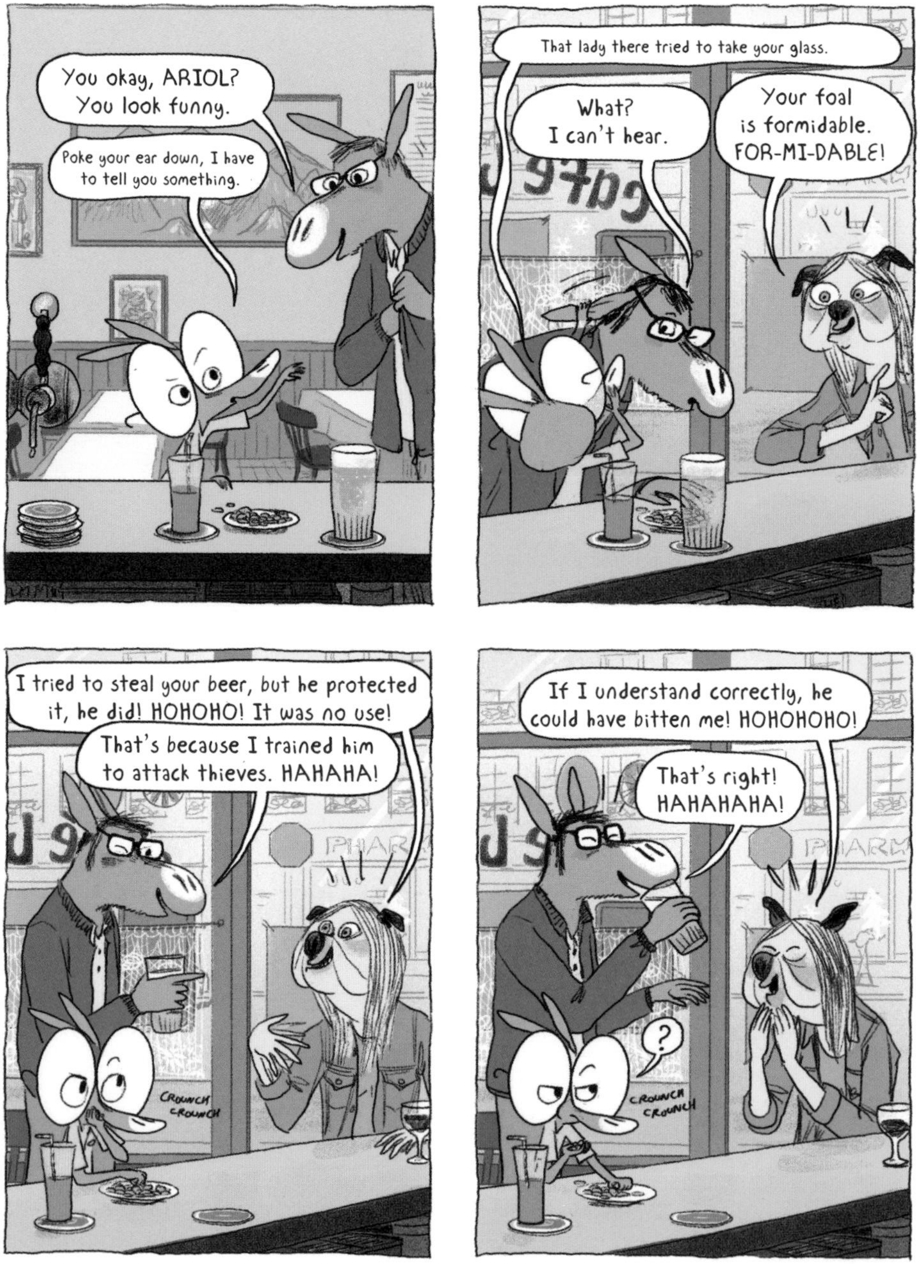
You okay, ARIOL? You look funny.
Poke your ear down, I have to tell you something.
That lady there tried to take your glass.
What? I can't hear.
Your foal is formidable. FOR-MI-DABLE!
I tried to steal your beer, but he protected it, he did! HOHOHO! It was no use!
That's because I trained him to attack thieves. HAHAHA!
CROUNCH CROUNCH
If I understand correctly, he could have bitten me! HOHOHOHO!
That's right! HAHAHAHA!
?
CROUNCH CROUNCH

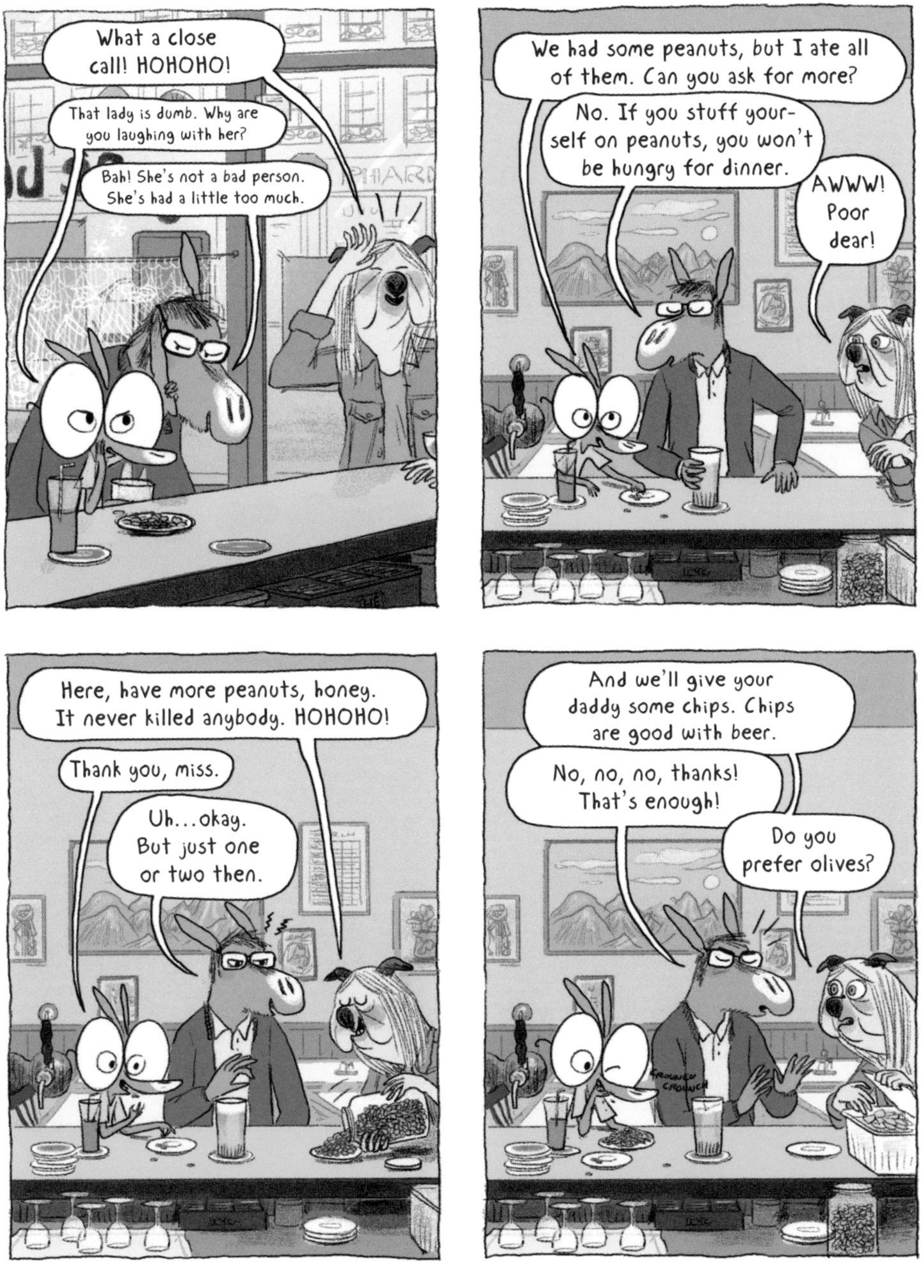
What a close call! HOHOHO!
That lady is dumb. Why are you laughing with her?
Bah! She's not a bad person. She's had a little too much.
We had some peanuts, but I ate all of them. Can you ask for more?
No. If you stuff yourself on peanuts, you won't be hungry for dinner.
AWWW! Poor dear!
Here, have more peanuts, honey. It never killed anybody. HOHOHO!
Thank you, miss.
Uh...okay. But just one or two then.
And we'll give your daddy some chips. Chips are good with beer.
No, no, no, thanks! That's enough!
Do you prefer olives?

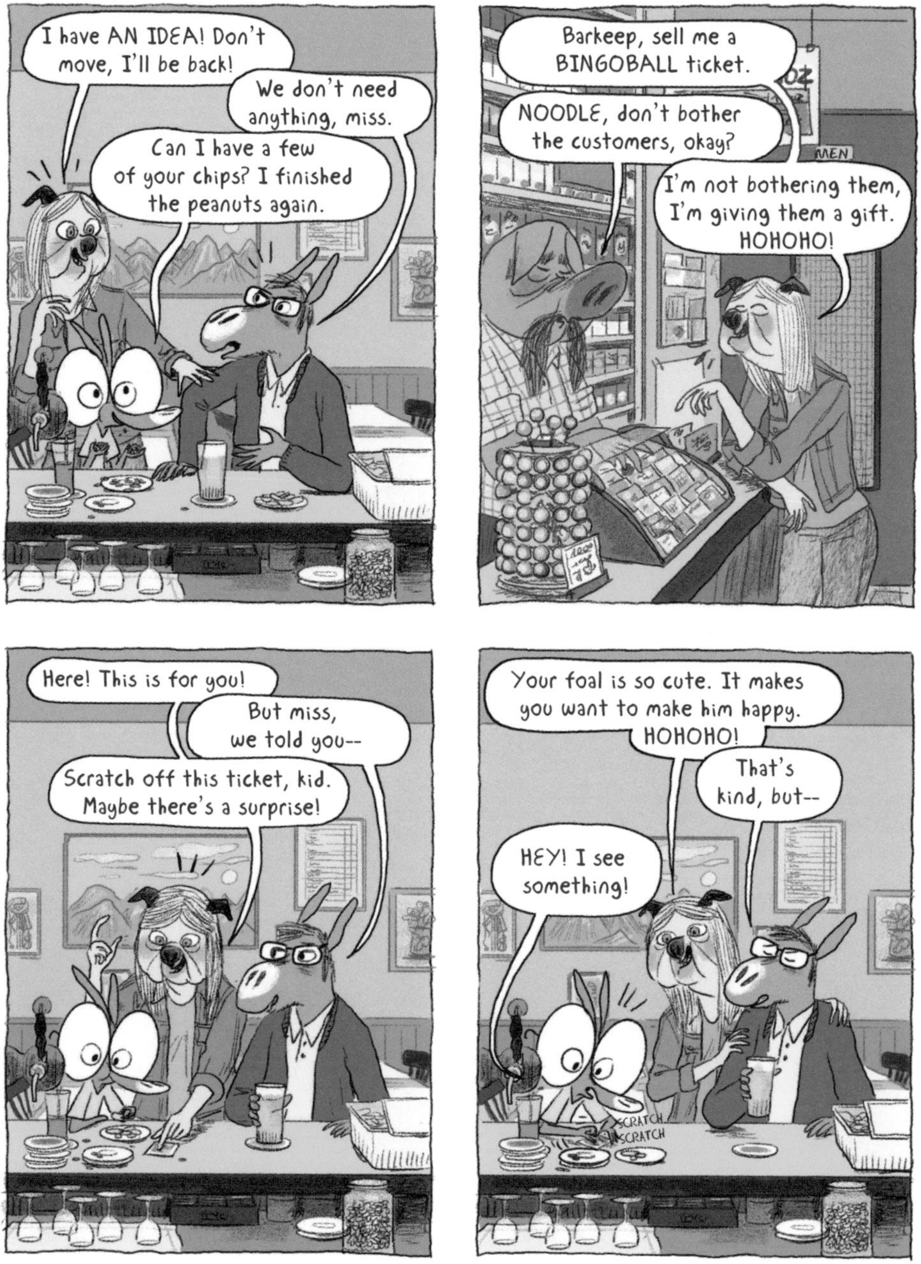
I have AN IDEA! Don't move, I'll be back!
We don't need anything, miss.
Can I have a few of your chips? I finished the peanuts again.
Barkeep, sell me a BINGOBALL ticket.
NOODLE, don't bother the customers, okay?
MEN
I'm not bothering them, I'm giving them a gift. HOHOHO!
Here! This is for you!
But miss, we told you--
Scratch off this ticket, kid. Maybe there's a surprise!
Your foal is so cute. It makes you want to make him happy. HOHOHO!
That's kind, but--
HEY! I see something!
SCRATCH SCRATCH

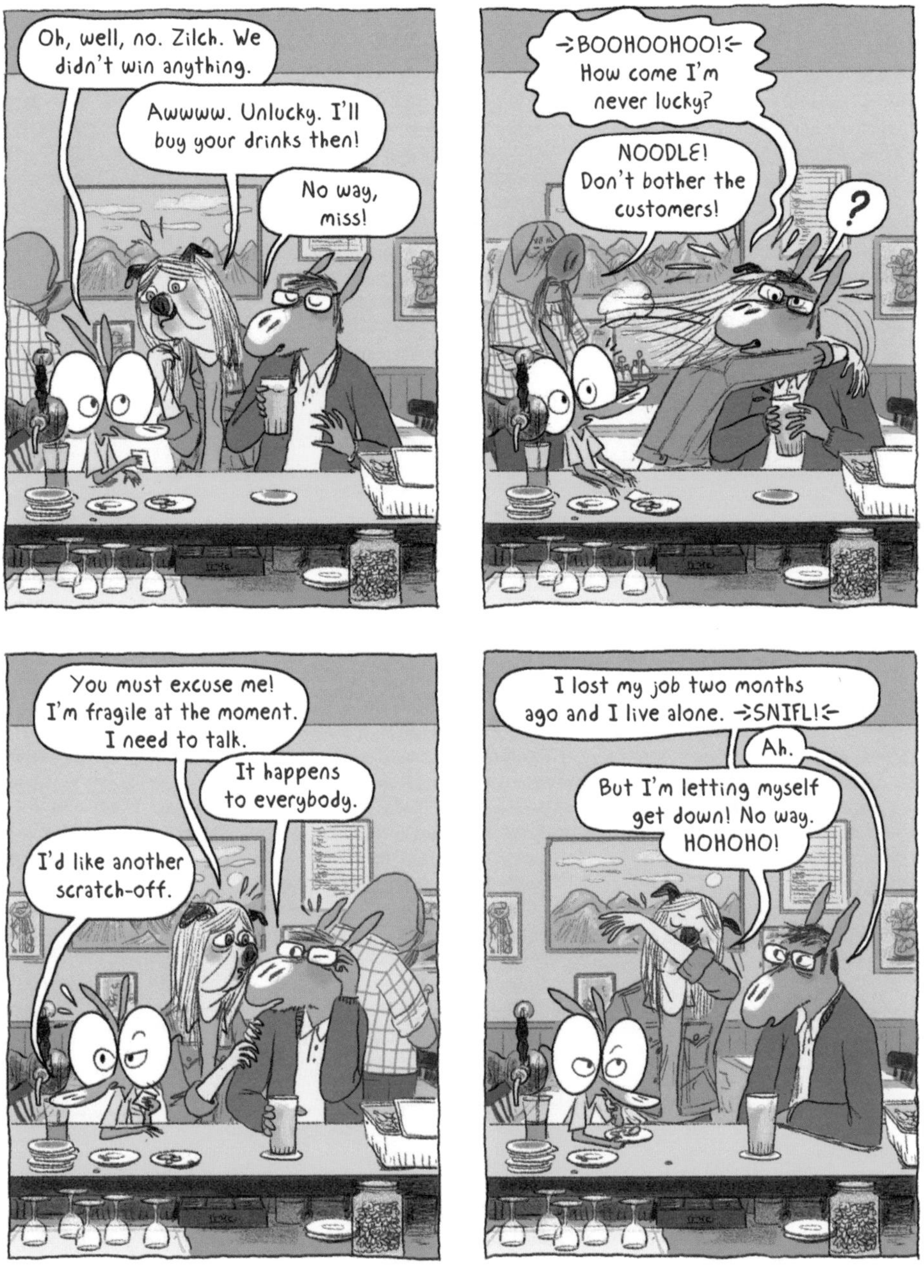
Oh, well, no. Zilch. We didn't win anything.
Awwww. Unlucky. I'll buy your drinks then!
No way, miss!
→BOOHOOHOO!← How come I'm never lucky?
NOODLE! Don't bother the customers!
?
You must excuse me! I'm fragile at the moment. I need to talk.
It happens to everybody.
I'd like another scratch-off.
I lost my job two months ago and I live alone. →SNIFL!←
Ah.
But I'm letting myself get down! No way. HOHOHO!

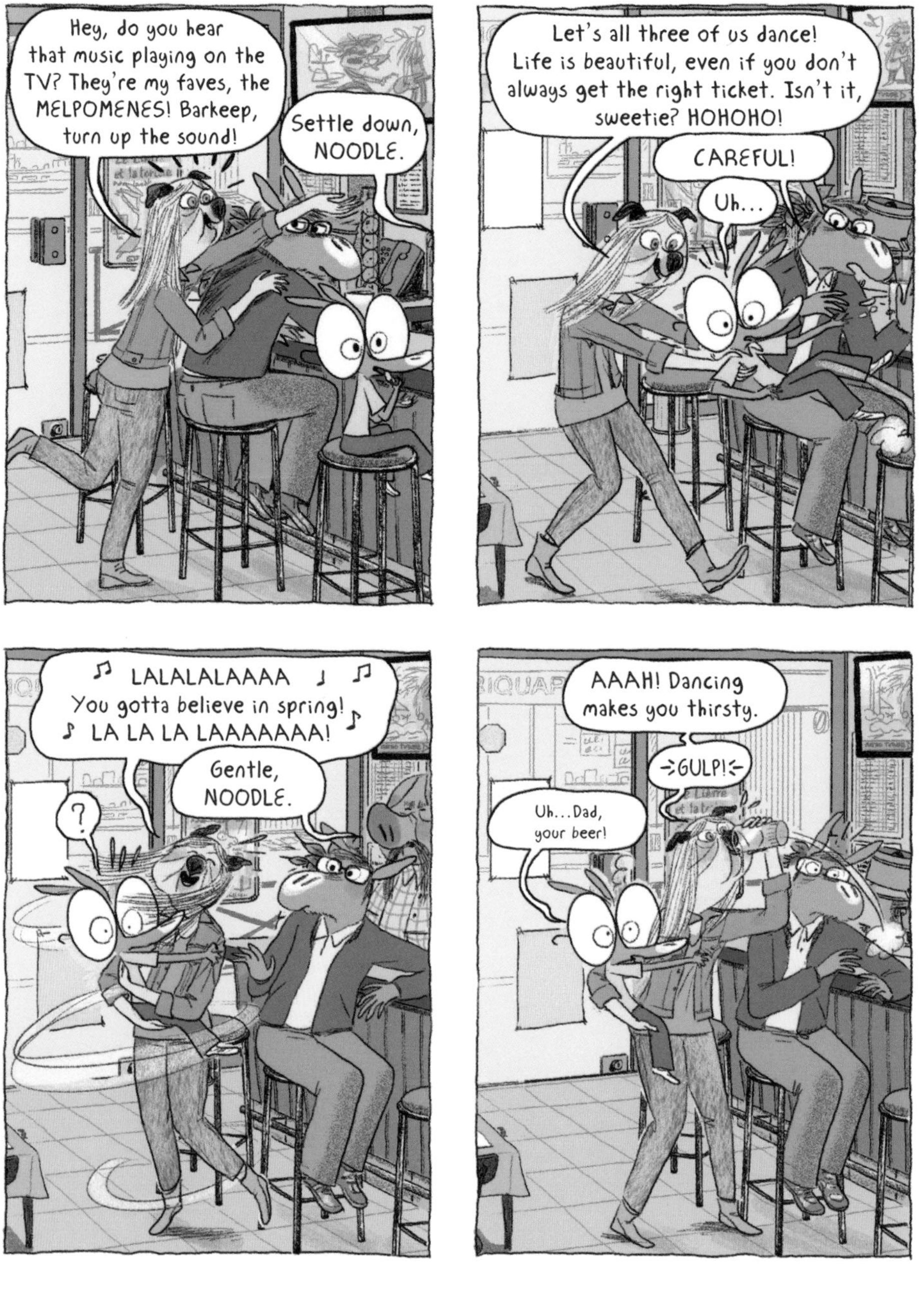
Hey, do you hear that music playing on the TV? They're my faves, the MELPOMENES! Barkeep, turn up the sound!
Settle down, NOODLE.
Let's all three of us dance! Life is beautiful, even if you don't always get the right ticket. Isn't it, sweetie? HOHOHO!
CAREFUL!
Uh...
♫ LALALALAAAA ♩ ♫ You gotta believe in spring! ♪ ♪ LA LA LA LAAAAAAA!
?
Gentle, NOODLE.
AAAH! Dancing makes you thirsty.
GULP!
Uh...Dad, your beer!

Panel 1:
Come to think of it, what if we played some pinball? Would you like that?

Uh...well, yeah!

Come this way.

Miss!

Panel 2:
Miss, I'm sorry, but we absolutely have to go. My wife's waiting for us.

Oh, I understand! A mom is sacred.

Just one game, Dad!

Panel 3:
Let's hug, okay? You did me good. HOHOHO!

That's good. HAHAHA!

There's no ball in the pinball machine! How do I play?

Panel 4:
Come on, ARIOL. Tell the lady and Mr. LANDARD goodbye.

Farewell, sweetie. Kiss your mama for me.

Okay.

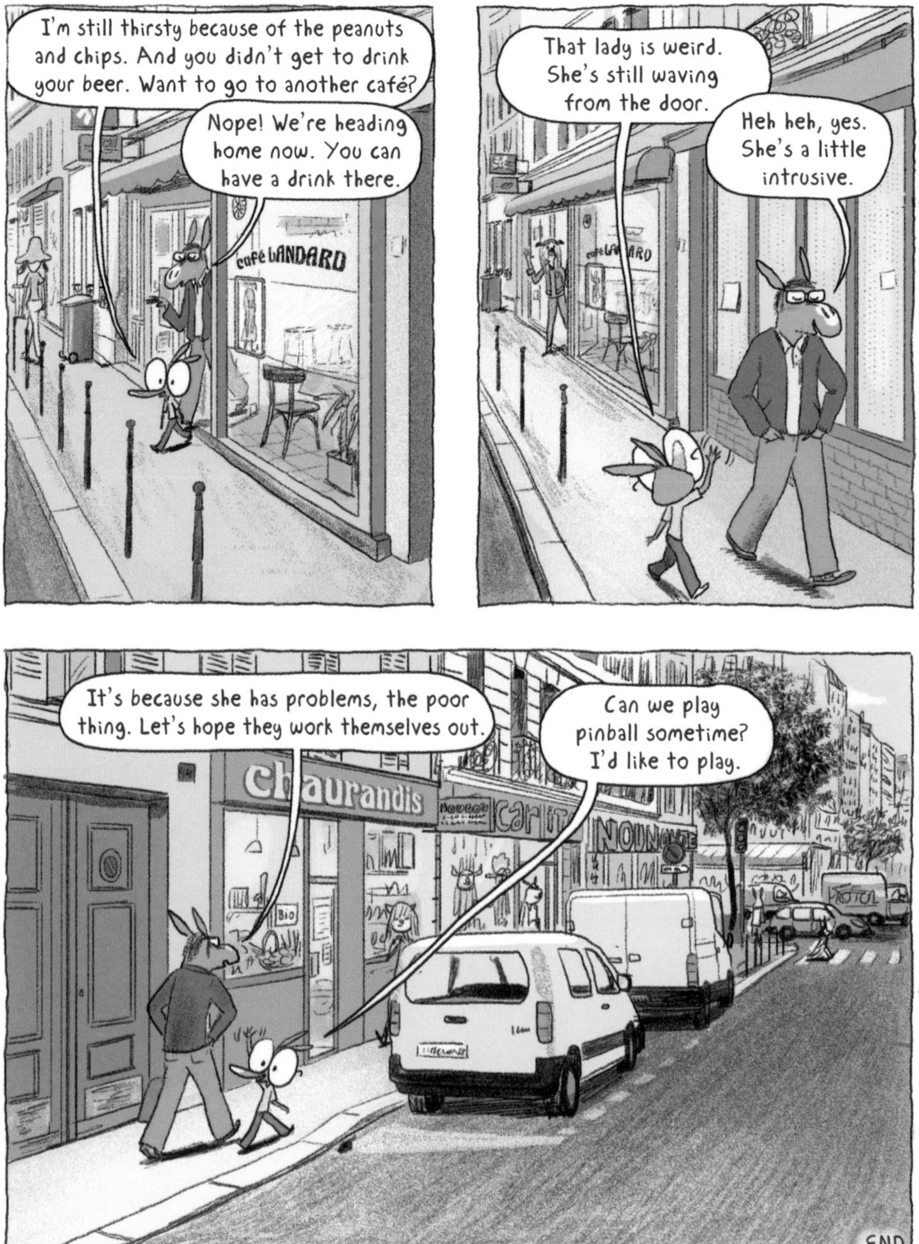
I'm still thirsty because of the peanuts and chips. And you didn't get to drink your beer. Want to go to another café?
Nope! We're heading home now. You can have a drink there.
café LANDARD
That lady is weird. She's still waving from the door.
Heh heh, yes. She's a little intrusive.
It's because she has problems, the poor thing. Let's hope they work themselves out.
Can we play pinball sometime? I'd like to play.
chaurandis
BIO
END

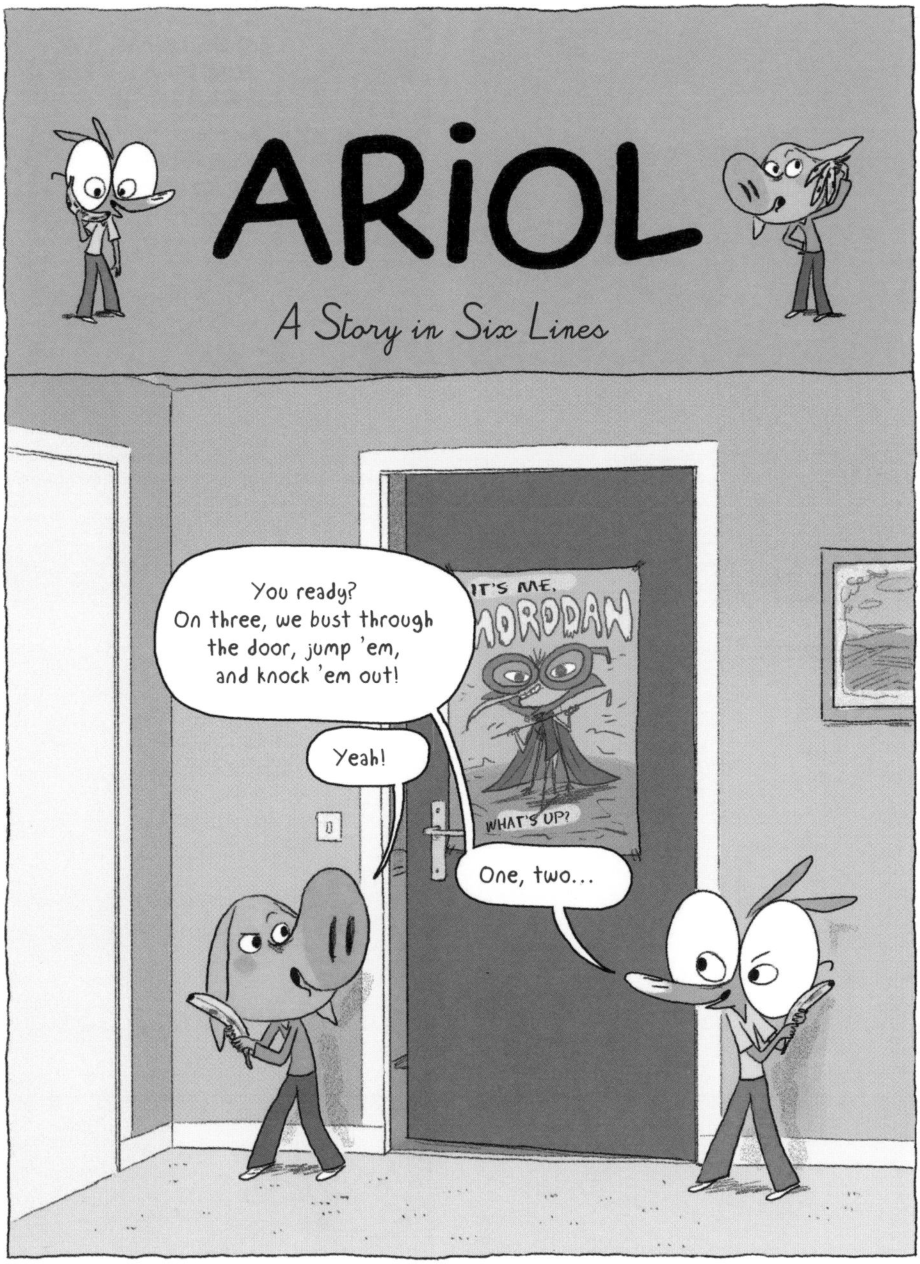
ARiOL
A Story in Six Lines
You ready? On three, we bust through the door, jump 'em, and knock 'em out!
Yeah!
IT'S ME,
WHAT'S UP?
One, two...

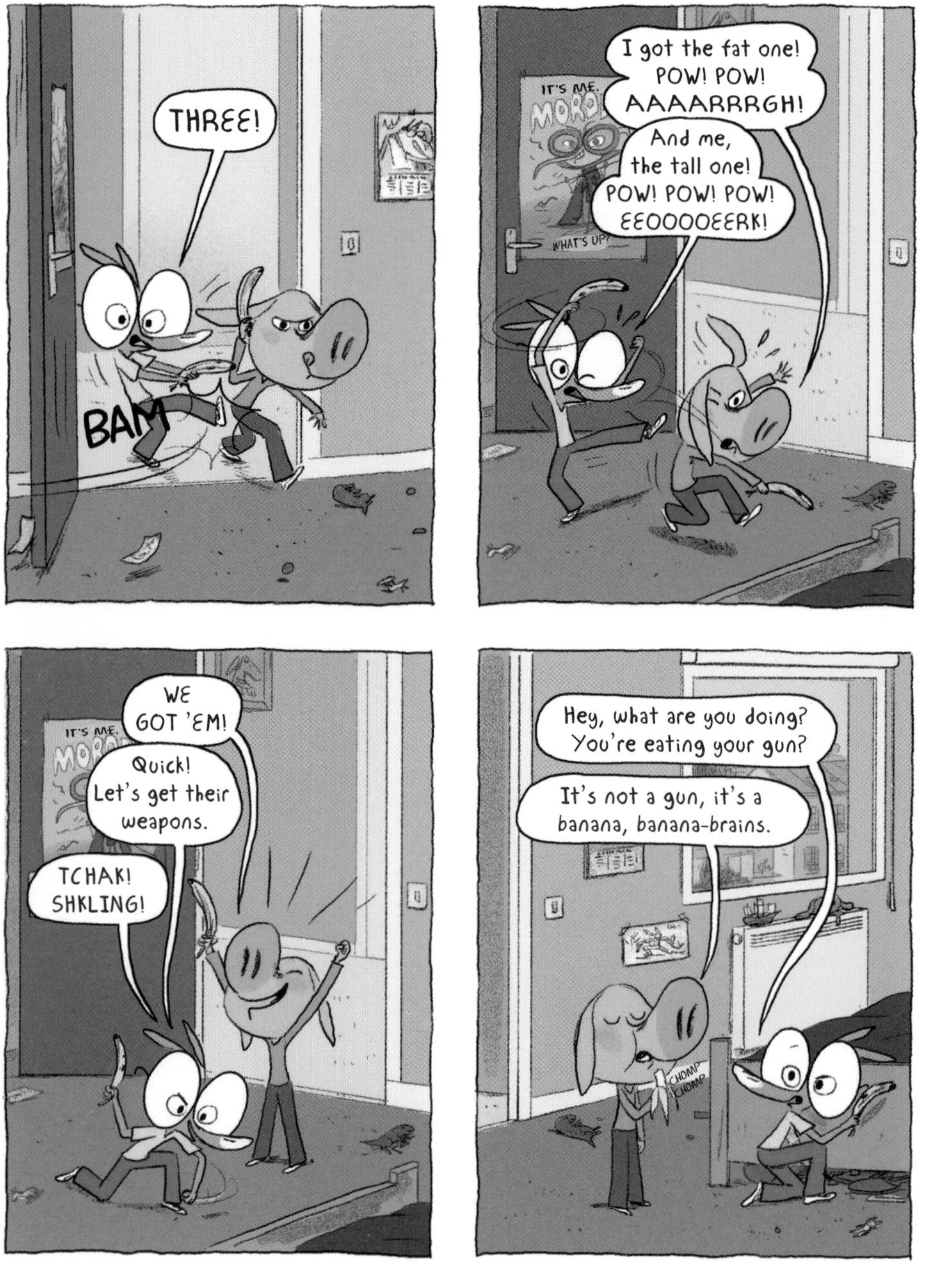
THREE!
BAM
IT'S ME, MORO
WHAT'S UP?
I got the fat one! POW! POW! AAAARRRGH!
And me, the tall one! POW! POW! POW! EEOOOOEERK!
WE GOT 'EM!
Quick! Let's get their weapons.
TCHAK! SHKLING!
Hey, what are you doing? You're eating your gun?
It's not a gun, it's a banana, banana-brains.
CHOMP CHOMP

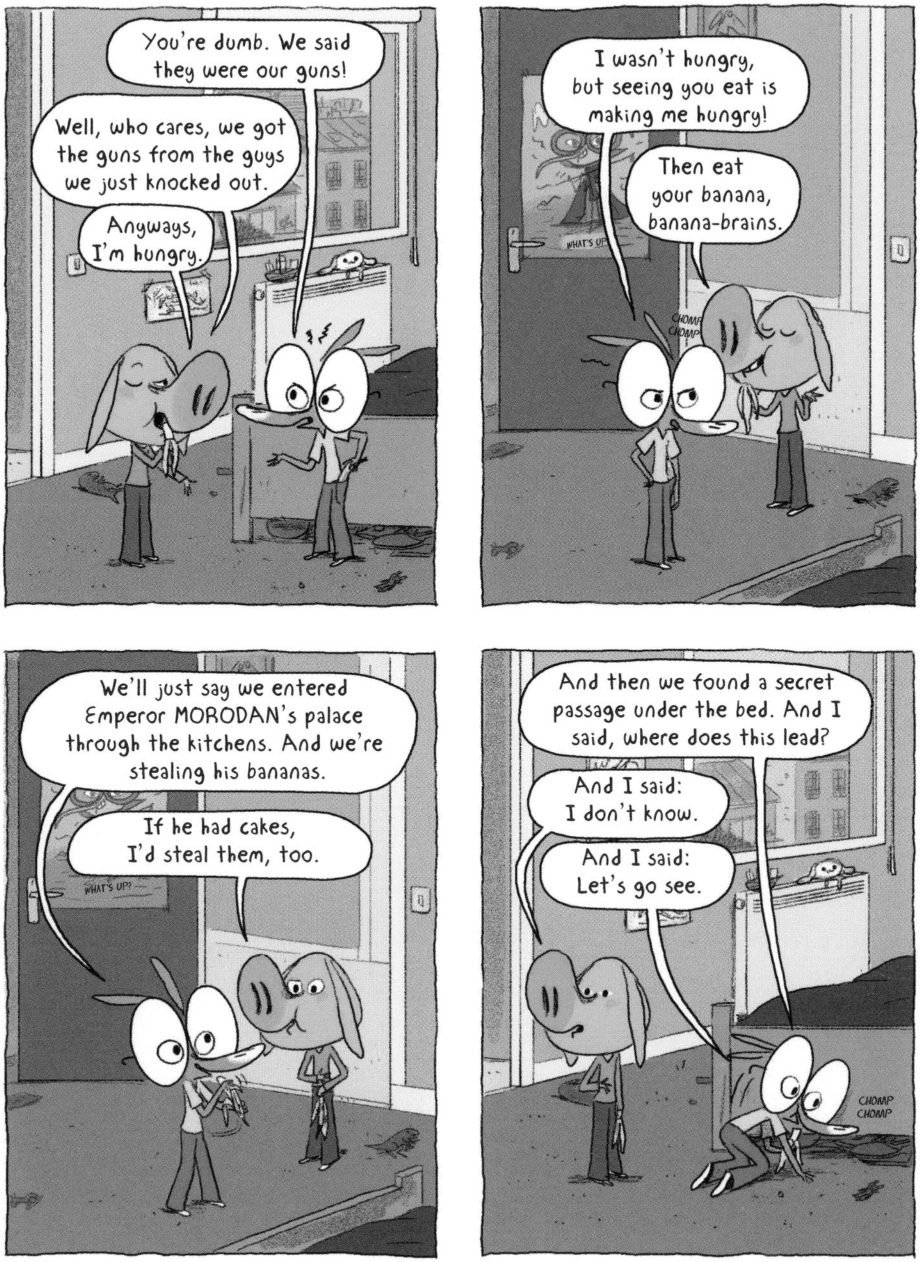

Well, who cares, we got the guns from the guys we just knocked out.
You're dumb. We said they were our guns!
Anyways, I'm hungry.
I wasn't hungry, but seeing you eat is making me hungry!
Then eat your banana, banana-brains.
CHOMP CHOMP
WHAT'S UP
We'll just say we entered Emperor MORODAN's palace through the kitchens. And we're stealing his bananas.
If he had cakes, I'd steal them, too.
WHAT'S UP?
And then we found a secret passage under the bed. And I said, where does this lead?
And I said: I don't know.
And I said: Let's go see.
CHOMP CHOMP

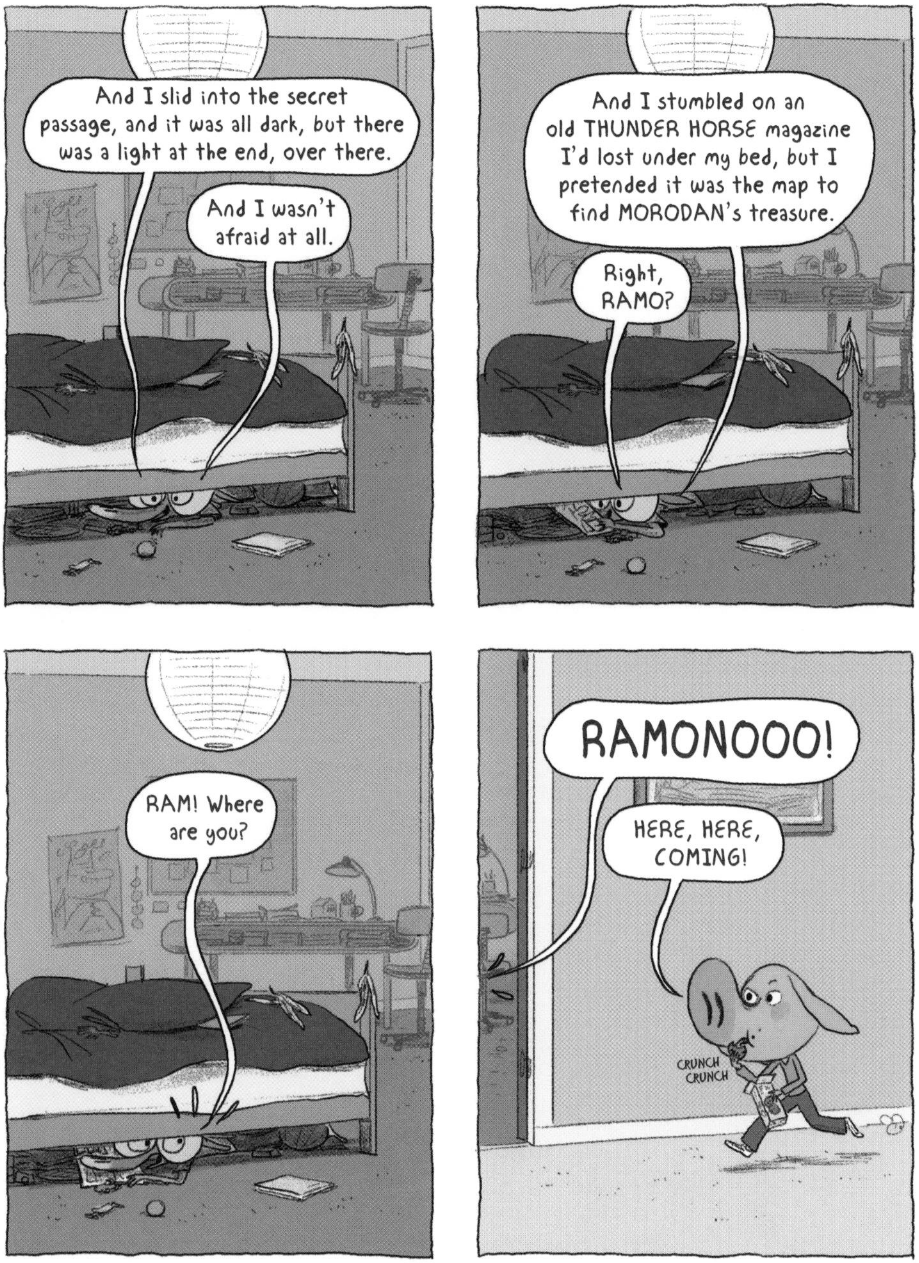
And I slid into the secret passage, and it was all dark, but there was a light at the end, over there.
And I wasn't afraid at all.
And I stumbled on an old THUNDER HORSE magazine I'd lost under my bed, but I pretended it was the map to find MORODAN's treasure.
Right, RAMO?
RAM! Where are you?
RAMONOOO!
HERE, HERE, COMING!
CRUNCH CRUNCH

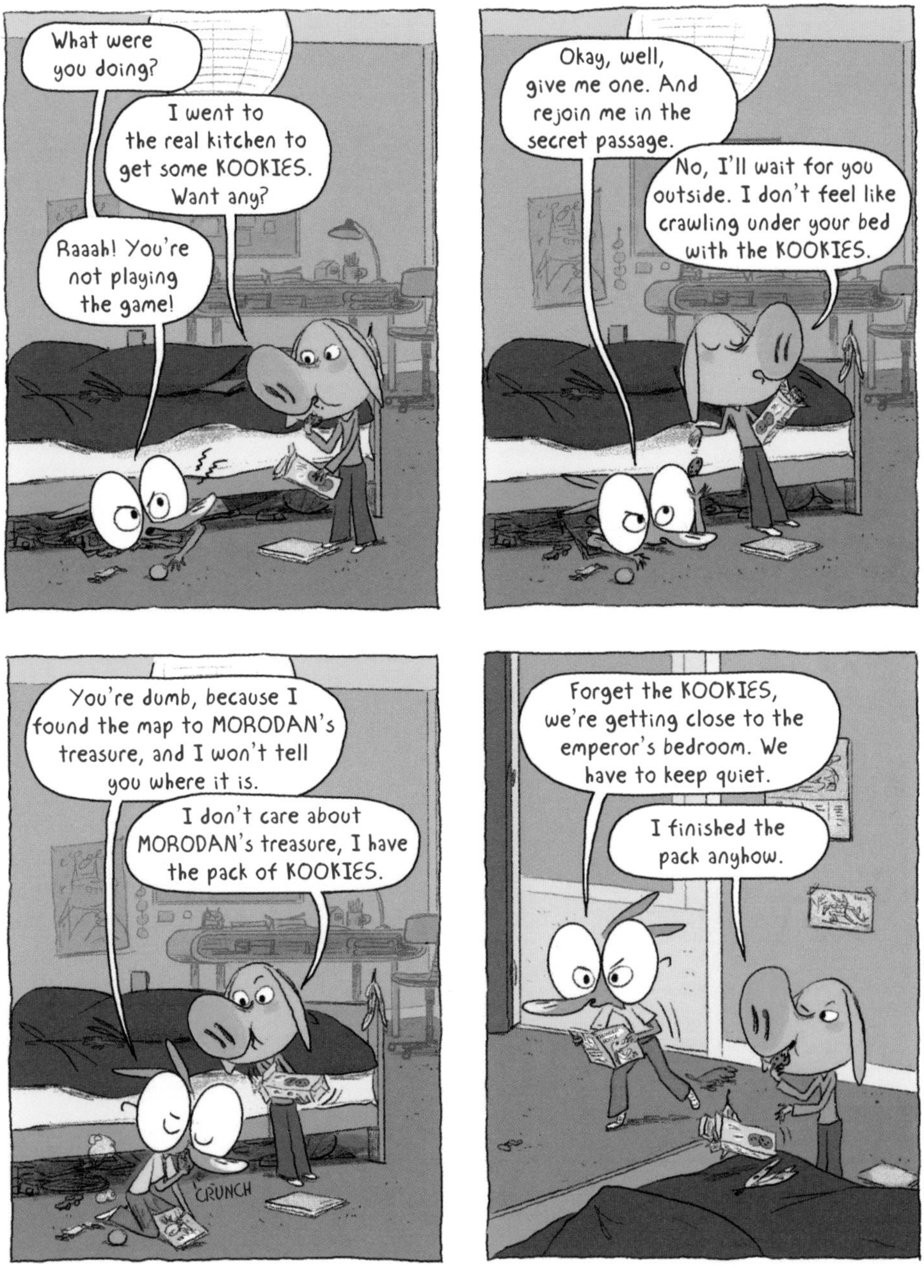
What were you doing?
I went to the real kitchen to get some KOOKIES. Want any?
Raaah! You're not playing the game!
Okay, well, give me one. And rejoin me in the secret passage.
No, I'll wait for you outside. I don't feel like crawling under your bed with the KOOKIES.
You're dumb, because I found the map to MORODAN's treasure, and I won't tell you where it is.
I don't care about MORODAN's treasure, I have the pack of KOOKIES.
CRUNCH
Forget the KOOKIES, we're getting close to the emperor's bedroom. We have to keep quiet.
I finished the pack anyhow.

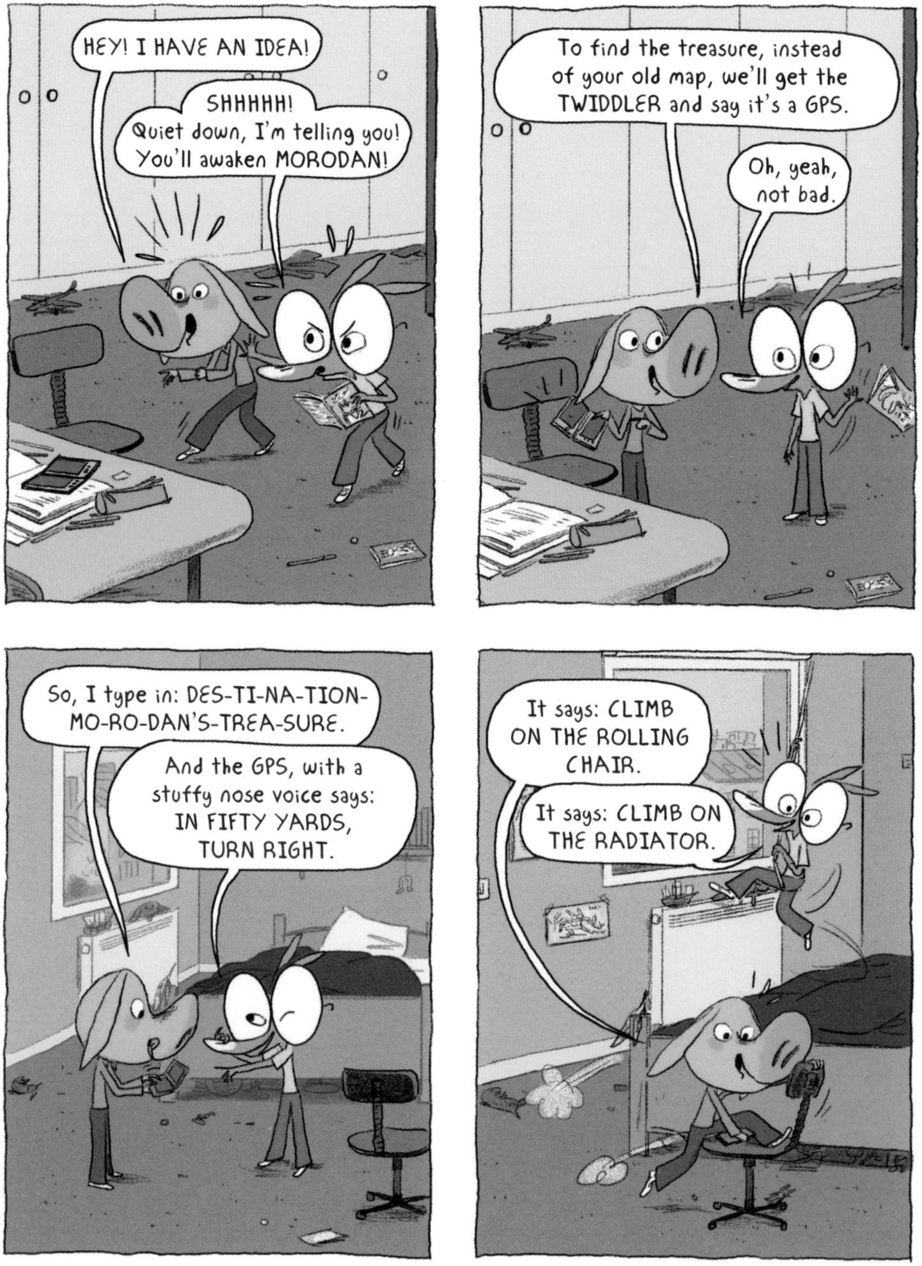
HEY! I HAVE AN IDEA!
SHHHHH! Quiet down, I'm telling you! You'll awaken MORODAN!
To find the treasure, instead of your old map, we'll get the TWIDDLER and say it's a GPS.
Oh, yeah, not bad.
So, I type in: DES-TI-NA-TION-MO-RO-DAN'S-TREA-SURE.
And the GPS, with a stuffy nose voice says: IN FIFTY YARDS, TURN RIGHT.
It says: CLIMB ON THE ROLLING CHAIR.
It says: CLIMB ON THE RADIATOR.

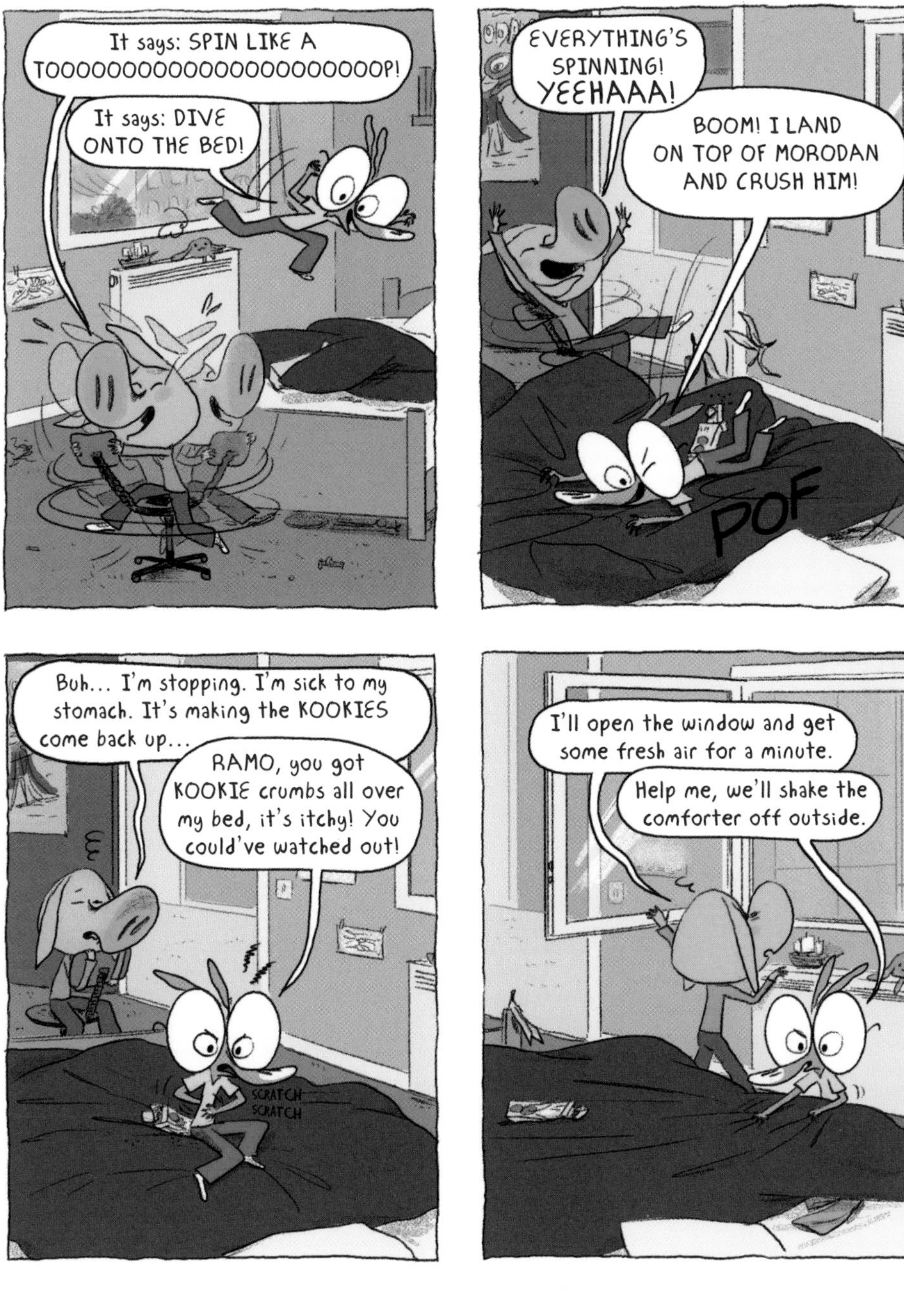
It says: SPIN LIKE A TOOOOOOOOOOOOOOOOOOOOOOOP!
It says: DIVE ONTO THE BED!
EVERYTHING'S SPINNING! YEEHAAA!
BOOM! I LAND ON TOP OF MORODAN AND CRUSH HIM!
POF
Buh... I'm stopping. I'm sick to my stomach. It's making the KOOKIES come back up...
RAMO, you got KOOKIE crumbs all over my bed, it's itchy! You could've watched out!
SCRATCH SCRATCH
I'll open the window and get some fresh air for a minute.
Help me, we'll shake the comforter off outside.

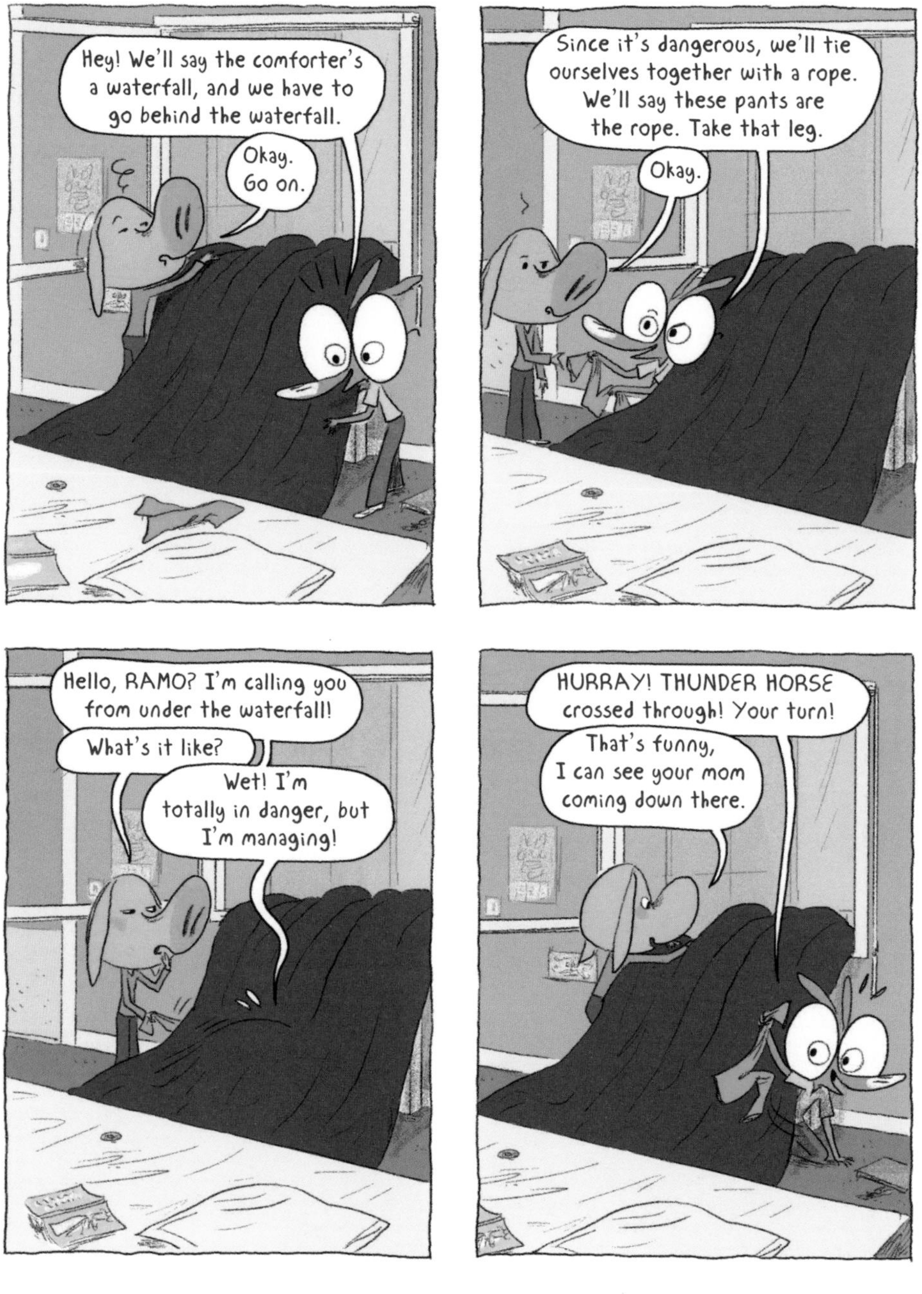
Hey! We'll say the comforter's a waterfall, and we have to go behind the waterfall.
Okay. Go on.
Since it's dangerous, we'll tie ourselves together with a rope. We'll say these pants are the rope. Take that leg.
Okay.
Hello, RAMO? I'm calling you from under the waterfall!
What's it like?
Wet! I'm totally in danger, but I'm managing!
HURRAY! THUNDER HORSE crossed through! Your turn!
That's funny, I can see your mom coming down there.

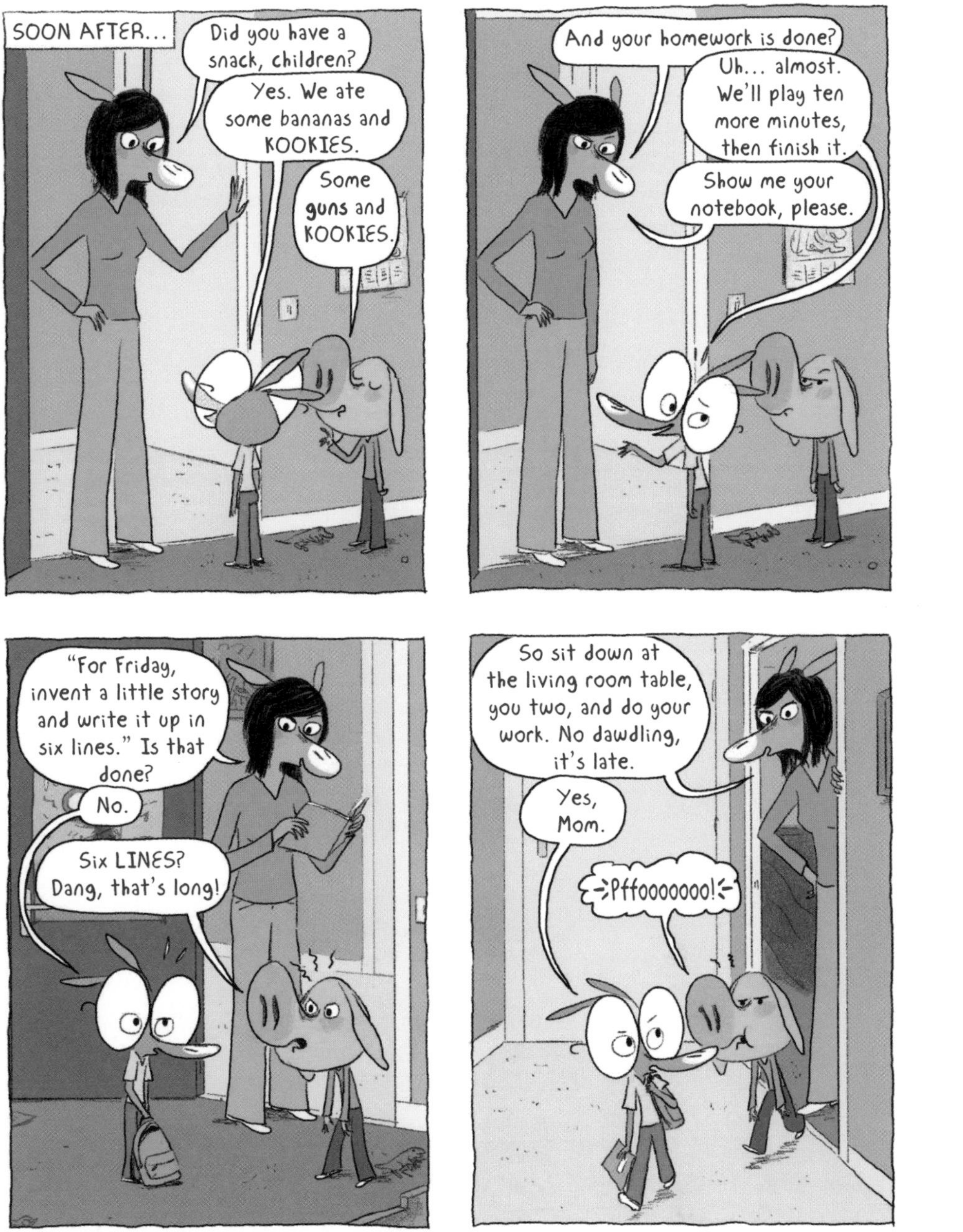
SOON AFTER...
Did you have a snack, children?
Yes. We ate some bananas and KOOKIES.
Some guns and KOOKIES.
And your homework is done?
Uh... almost. We'll play ten more minutes, then finish it.
Show me your notebook, please.
"For Friday, invent a little story and write it up in six lines." Is that done?
No.
Six LINES? Dang, that's long!
So sit down at the living room table, you two, and do your work. No dawdling, it's late.
Yes, Mom.
Pffooooooo!

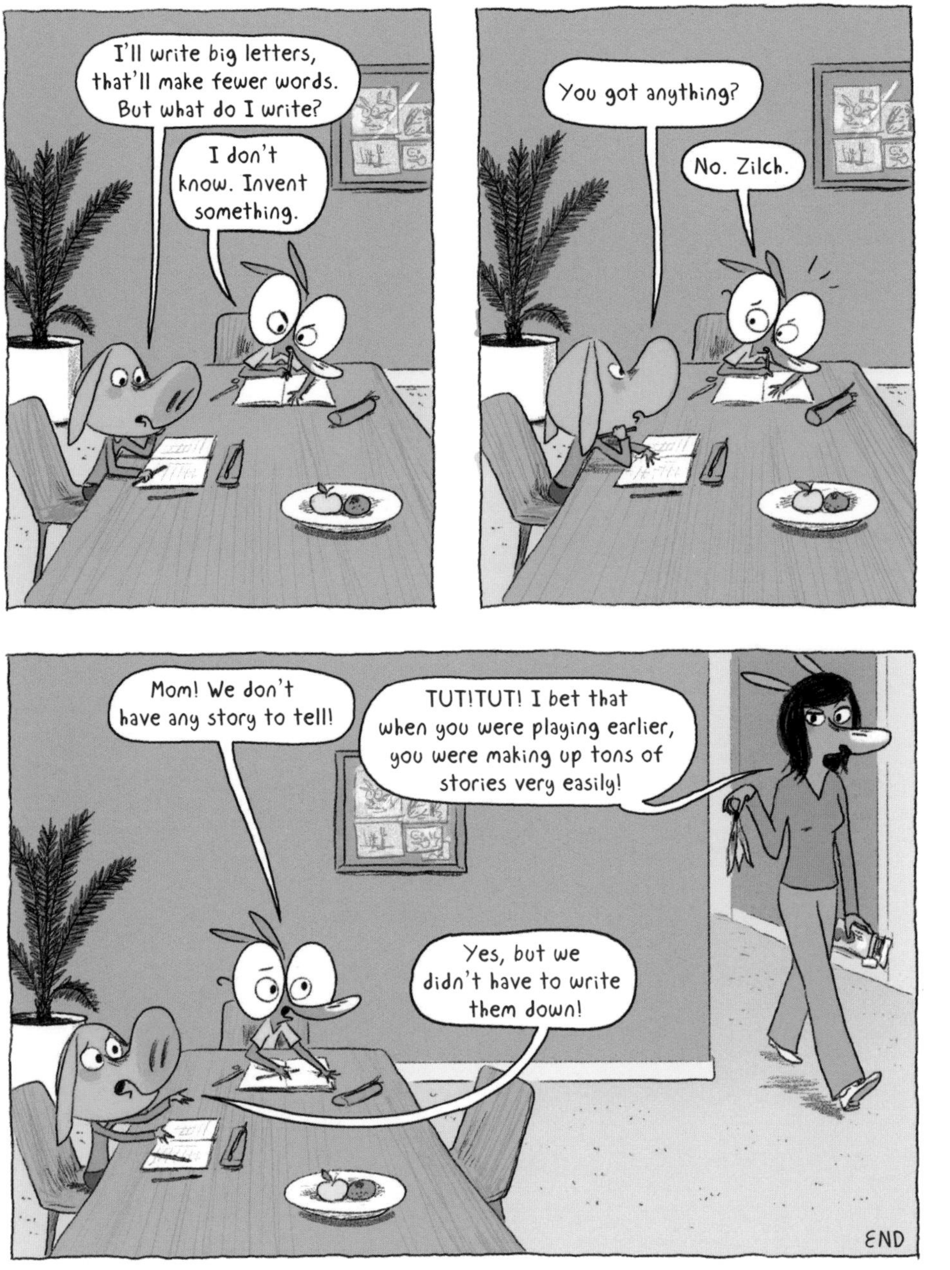
I'll write big letters, that'll make fewer words. But what do I write?
I don't know. Invent something.
You got anything?
No. Zilch.
Mom! We don't have any story to tell!
TUT!TUT! I bet that when you were playing earlier, you were making up tons of stories very easily!
Yes, but we didn't have to write them down!
END

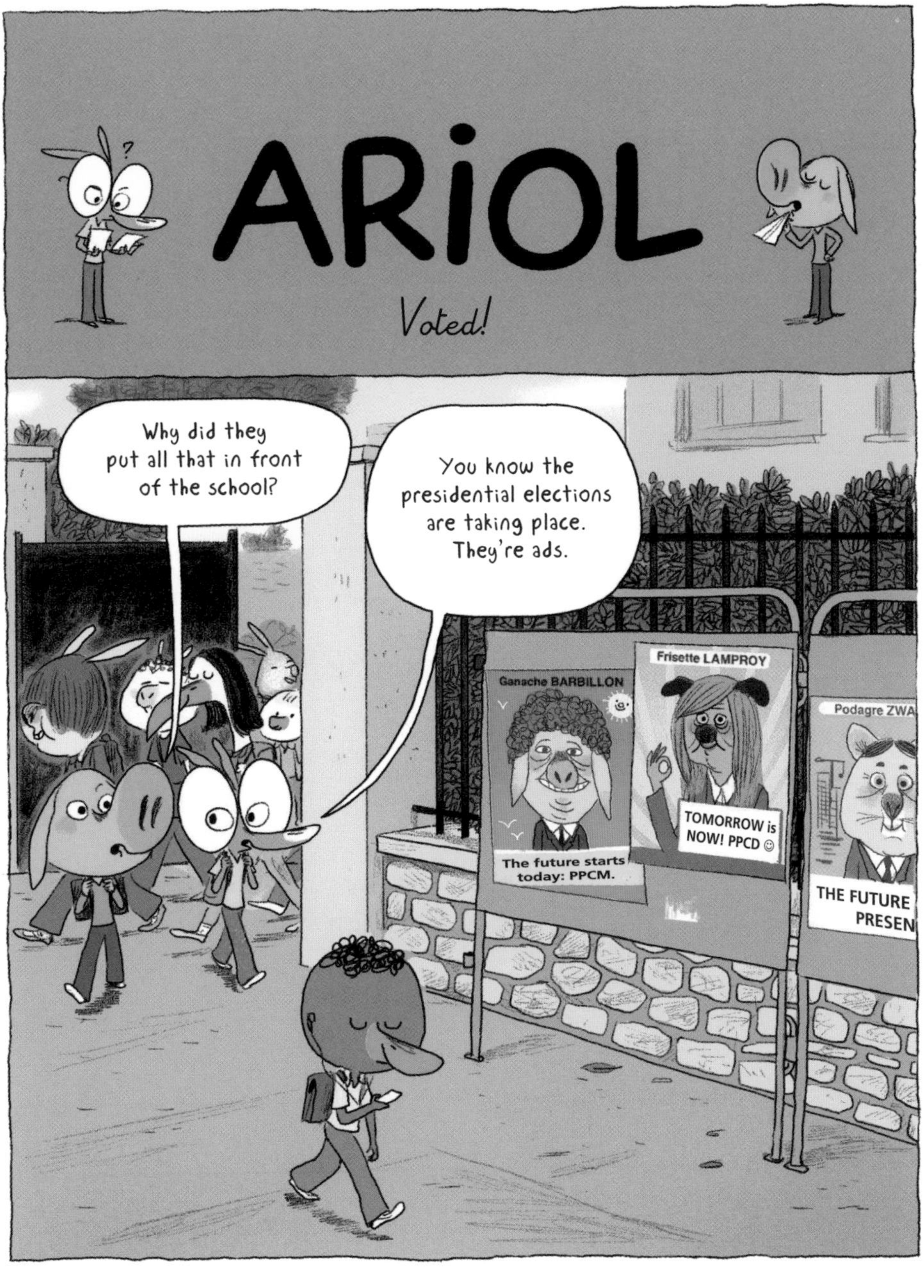
ARIOL
Voted!
Why did they put all that in front of the school?
You know the presidential elections are taking place. They're ads.
Ganache BARBILLON
The future starts today: PPCM.
Frisette LAMPROY
TOMORROW is NOW! PPCD ☺
Podagre ZWA
THE FUTURE
PRESEN

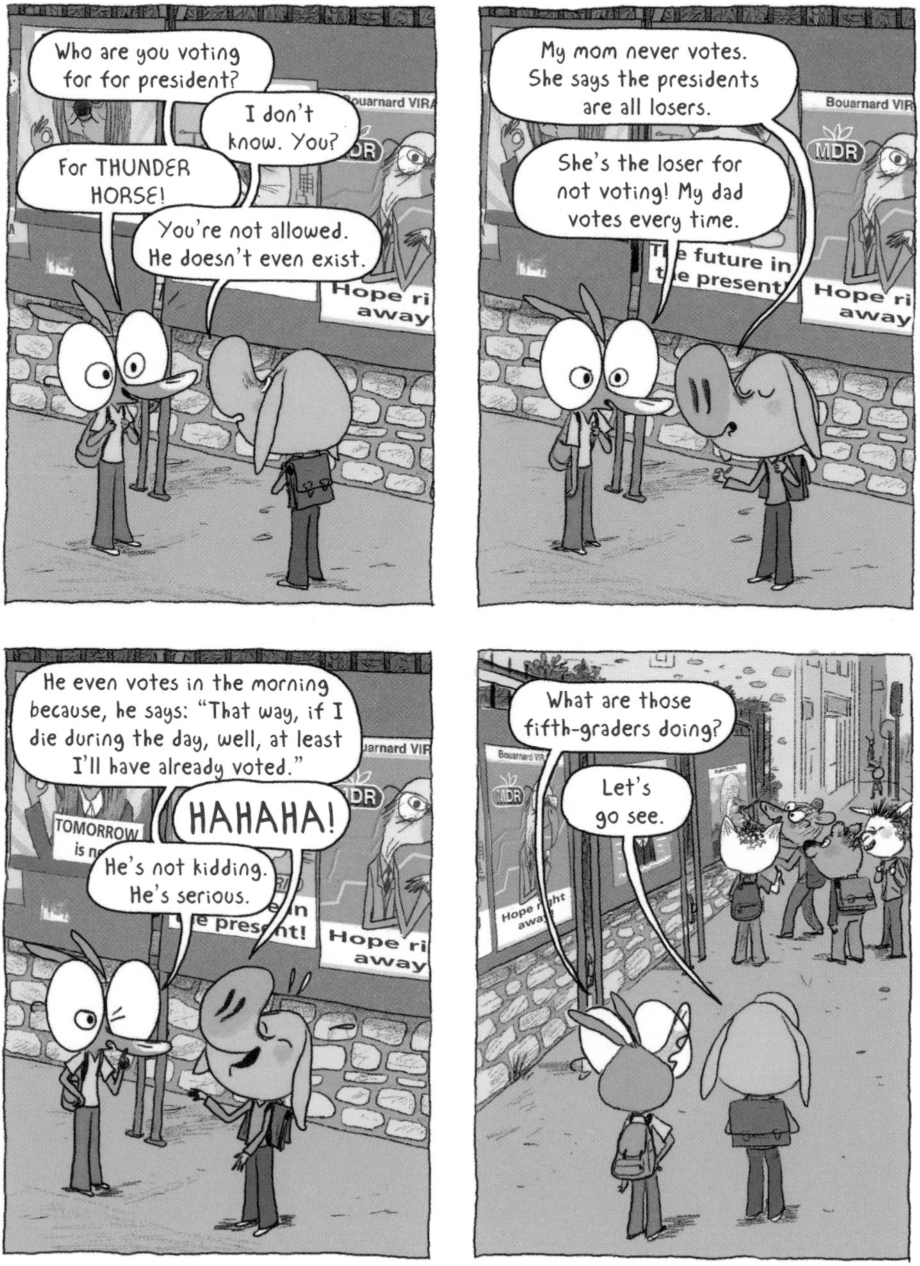
Who are you voting for for president?
I don't know. You?
For THUNDER HORSE!
You're not allowed. He doesn't even exist.
Bouarnard VIRA
MDR
Hope ri away
My mom never votes. She says the presidents are all losers.
She's the loser for not voting! My dad votes every time.
The future in the present!
He even votes in the morning because, he says: "That way, if I die during the day, well, at least I'll have already voted."
HAHAHA!
He's not kidding. He's serious.
TOMORROW
What are those fifth-graders doing?
Let's go see.

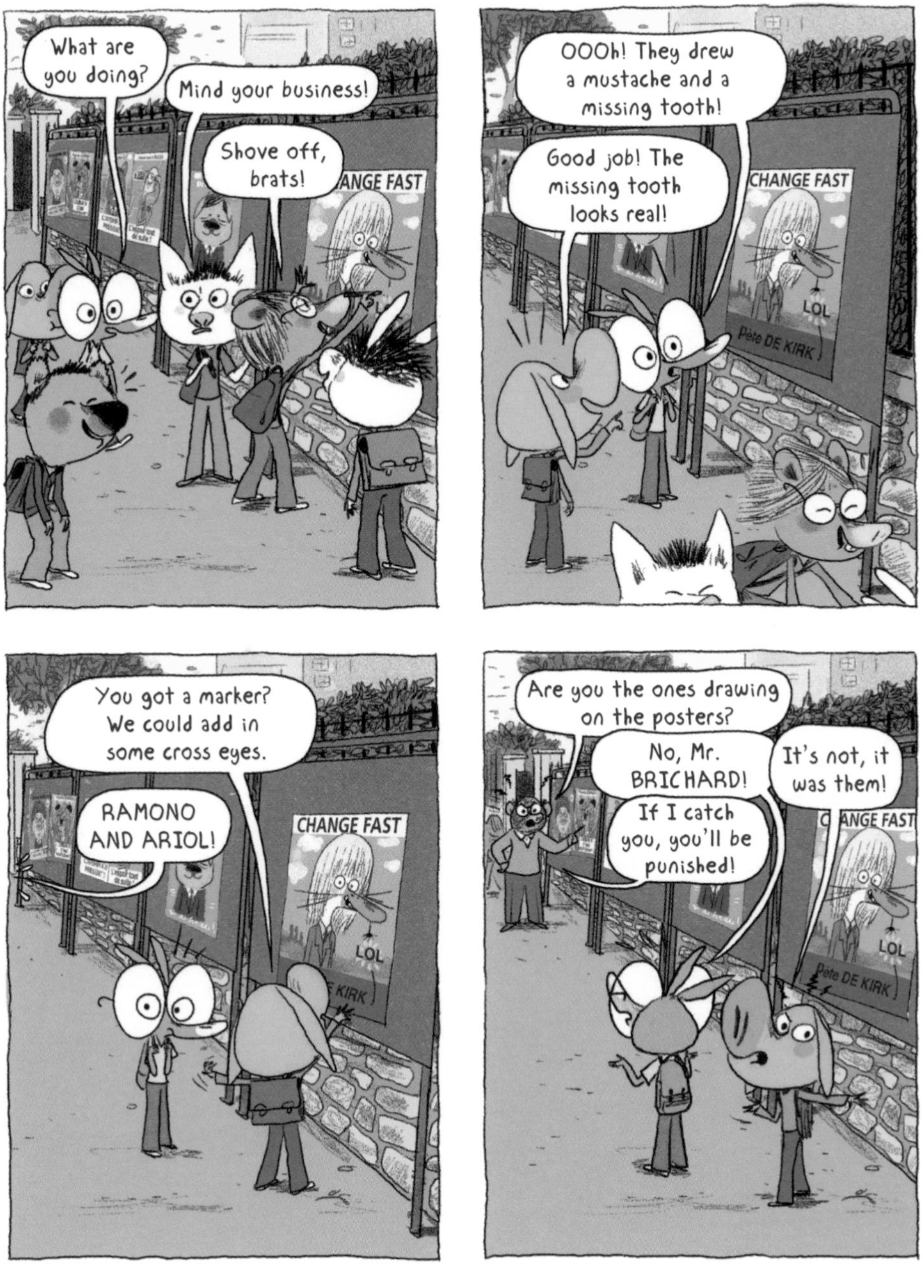
What are you doing?
Mind your business!
Shove off, brats!
CHANGE FAST
OOOh! They drew a mustache and a missing tooth!
Good job! The missing tooth looks real!
CHANGE FAST
LOL
Pete DE KIRK
You got a marker? We could add in some cross eyes.
RAMONO AND ARIOL!
CHANGE FAST
LOL
Are you the ones drawing on the posters?
No, Mr. BRICHARD!
It's not, it was them!
If I catch you, you'll be punished!
LOL
Pete DE KIRK

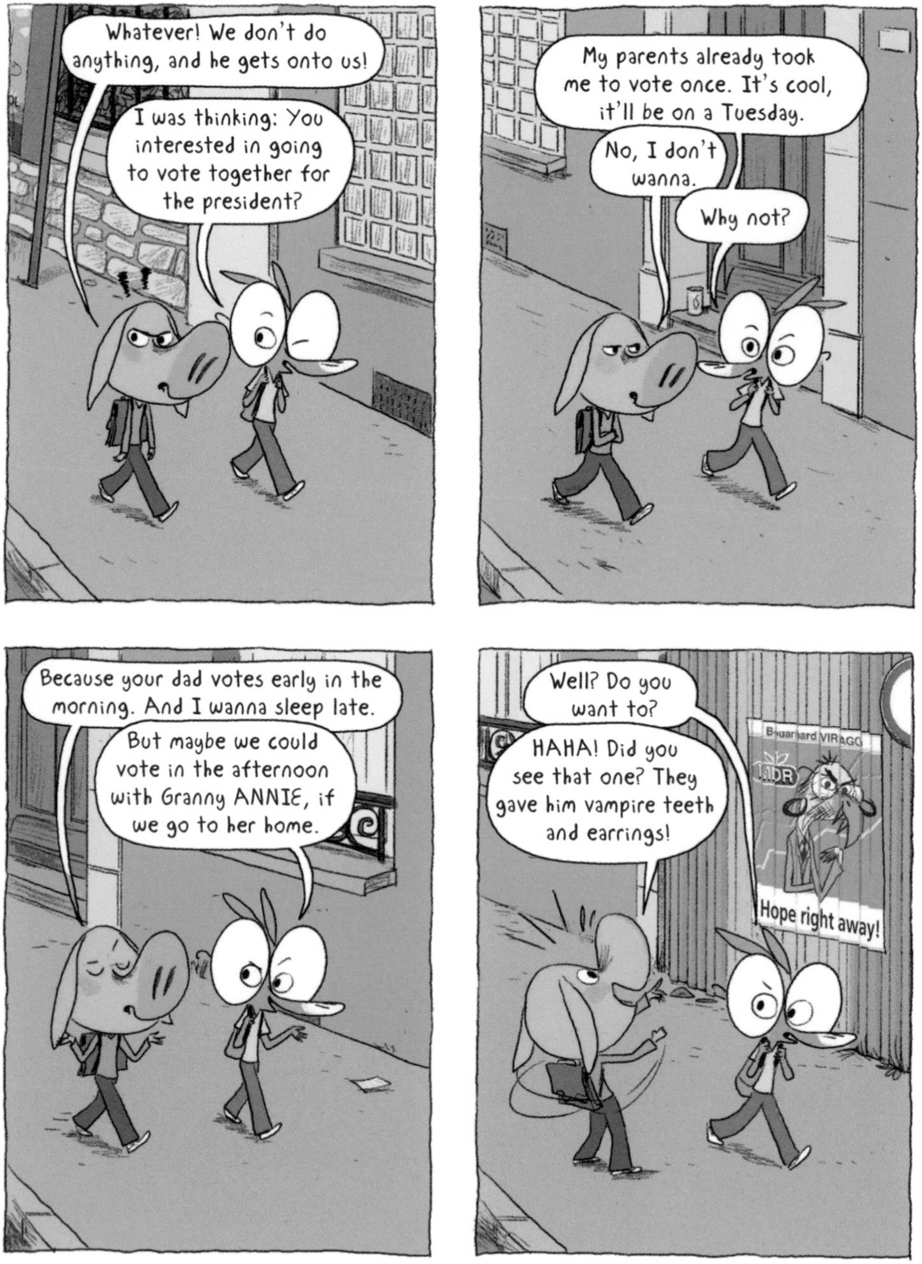
Whatever! We don't do anything, and he gets onto us!
I was thinking: You interested in going to vote together for the president?
My parents already took me to vote once. It's cool, it'll be on a Tuesday.
No, I don't wanna.
Why not?
Because your dad votes early in the morning. And I wanna sleep late.
But maybe we could vote in the afternoon with Granny ANNIE, if we go to her home.
Well? Do you want to?
HAHA! Did you see that one? They gave him vampire teeth and earrings!
VIRAGO
Hope right away!

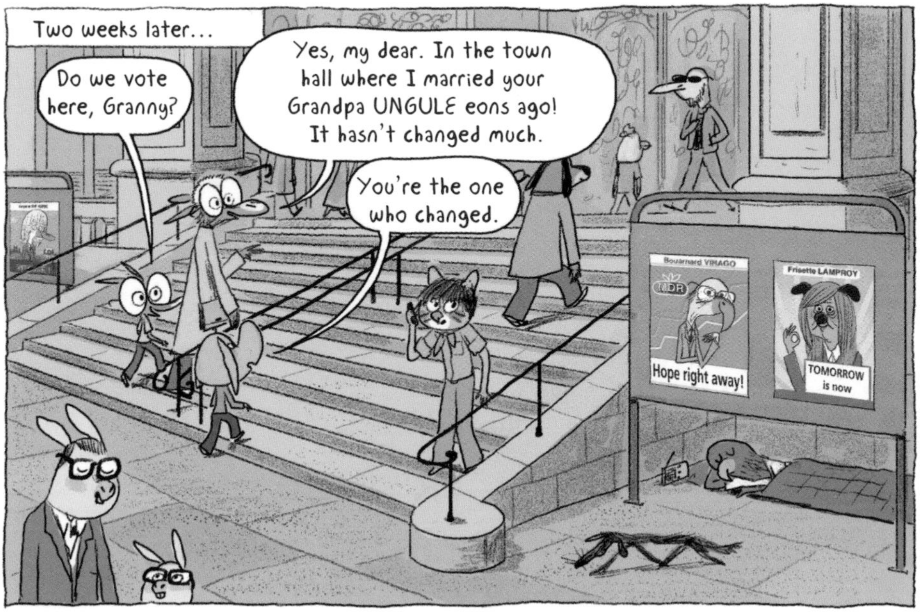
Two weeks later...
Do we vote here, Granny?
Yes, my dear. In the town hall where I married your Grandpa UNGULE eons ago! It hasn't changed much.
You're the one who changed.
Bouarnard VIRAGO
MDR
Hope right away!
Frisette LAMPROY
TOMORROW is now

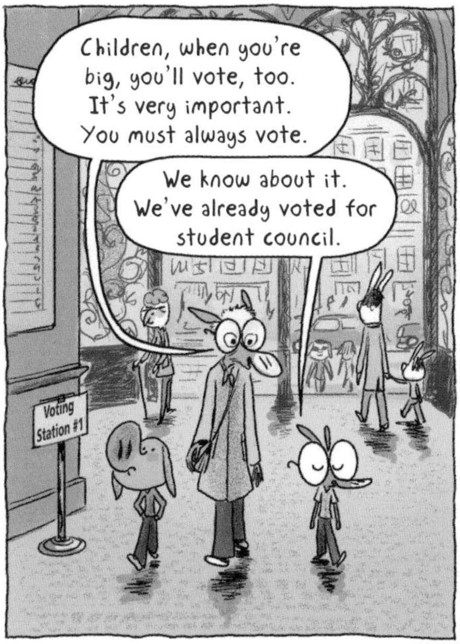
Children, when you're big, you'll vote, too. It's very important. You must always vote.
We know about it. We've already voted for student council.
Voting Station #1

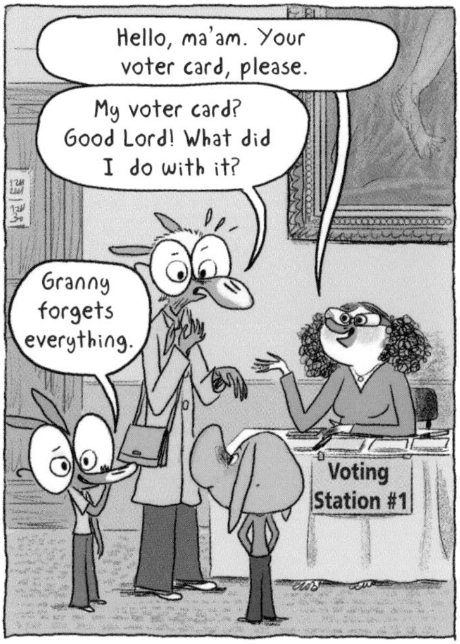
Hello, ma'am. Your voter card, please.
My voter card? Good Lord! What did I do with it?
Granny forgets everything.
Voting Station #1

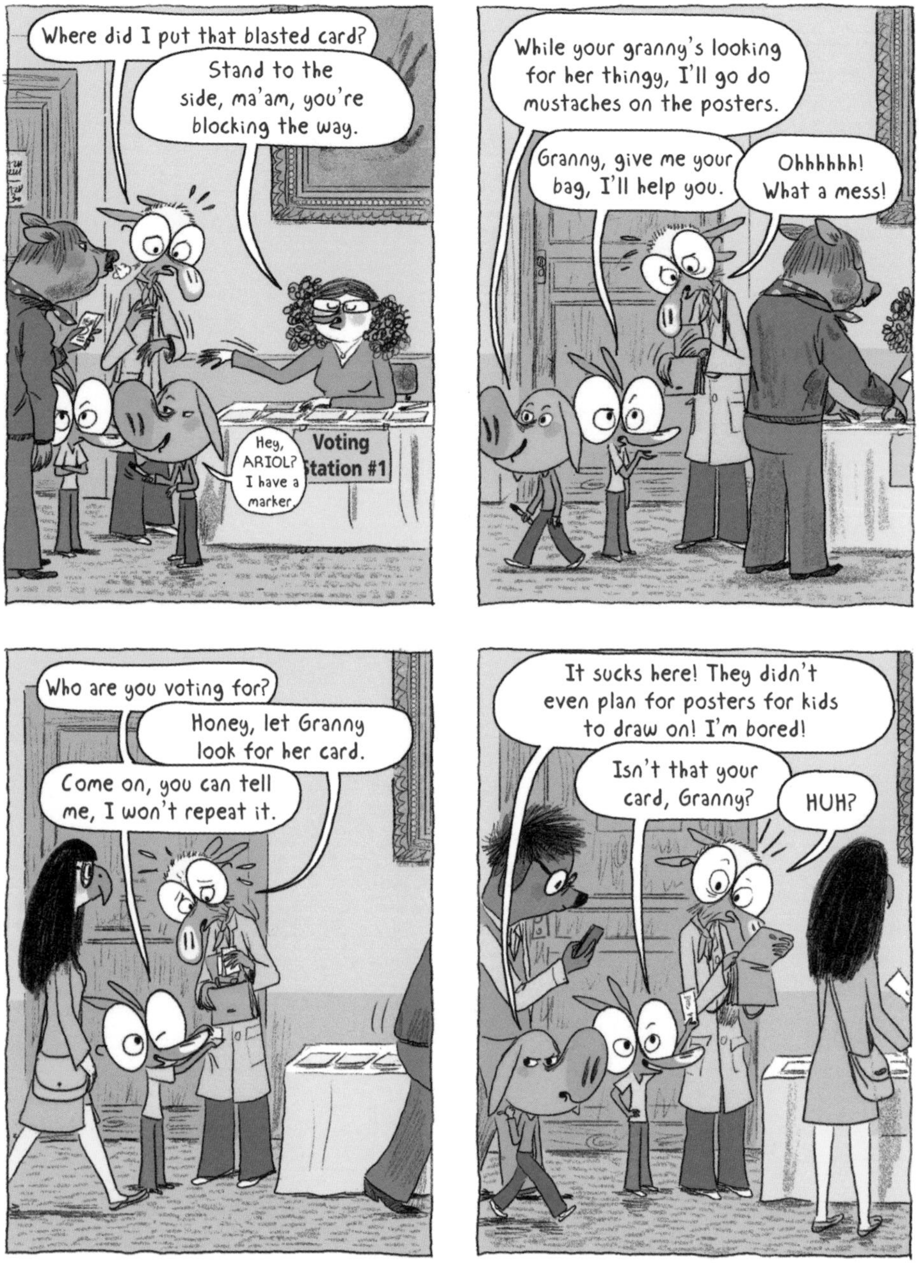
Where did I put that blasted card?
Stand to the side, ma'am, you're blocking the way.
Hey, ARIOL? I have a marker.
Voting Station #1
While your granny's looking for her thingy, I'll go do mustaches on the posters.
Granny, give me your bag, I'll help you.
Ohhhhhh! What a mess!
Who are you voting for?
Honey, let Granny look for her card.
Come on, you can tell me, I won't repeat it.
It sucks here! They didn't even plan for posters for kids to draw on! I'm bored!
Isn't that your card, Granny?
HUH?

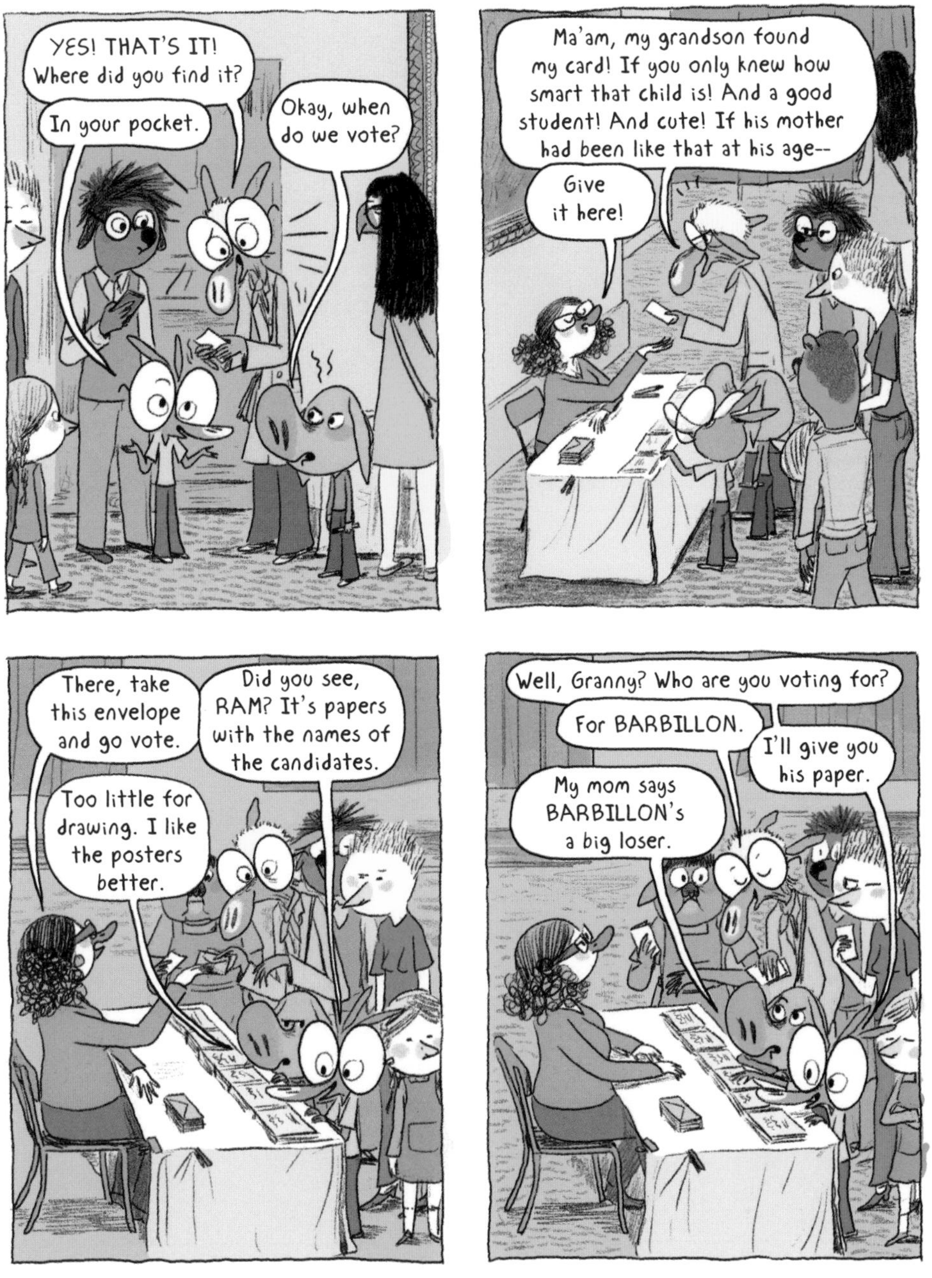
YES! THAT'S IT! Where did you find it?
In your pocket.
Okay, when do we vote?
Ma'am, my grandson found my card! If you only knew how smart that child is! And a good student! And cute! If his mother had been like that at his age--
Give it here!
There, take this envelope and go vote.
Did you see, RAM? It's papers with the names of the candidates.
Too little for drawing. I like the posters better.
Well, Granny? Who are you voting for?
For BARBILLON.
I'll give you his paper.
My mom says BARBILLON's a big loser.

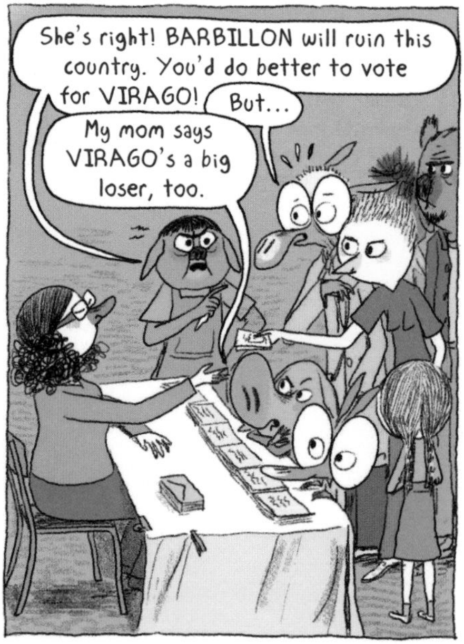
She's right! BARBILLON will ruin this country. You'd do better to vote for VIRAGO!
But...
My mom says VIRAGO's a big loser, too.

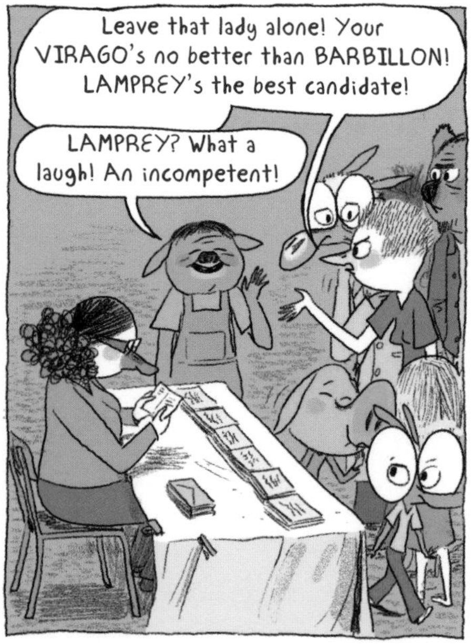
Leave that lady alone! Your VIRAGO's no better than BARBILLON! LAMPREY's the best candidate!
LAMPREY? What a laugh! An incompetent!

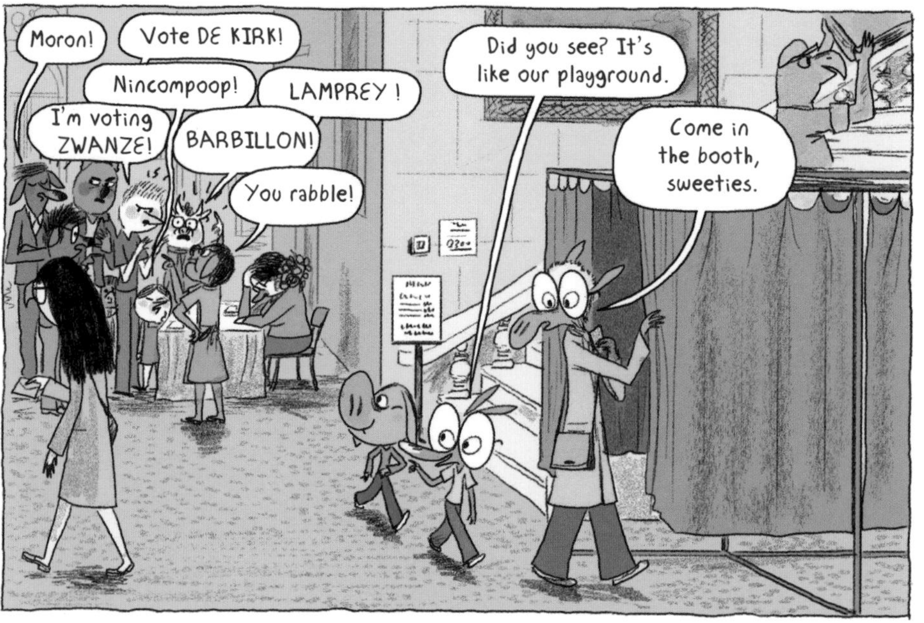
Moron!
Vote DE KIRK!
Nincompoop!
LAMPREY!
I'm voting ZWANZE!
BARBILLON!
You rabble!
Did you see? It's like our playground.
Come in the booth, sweeties.

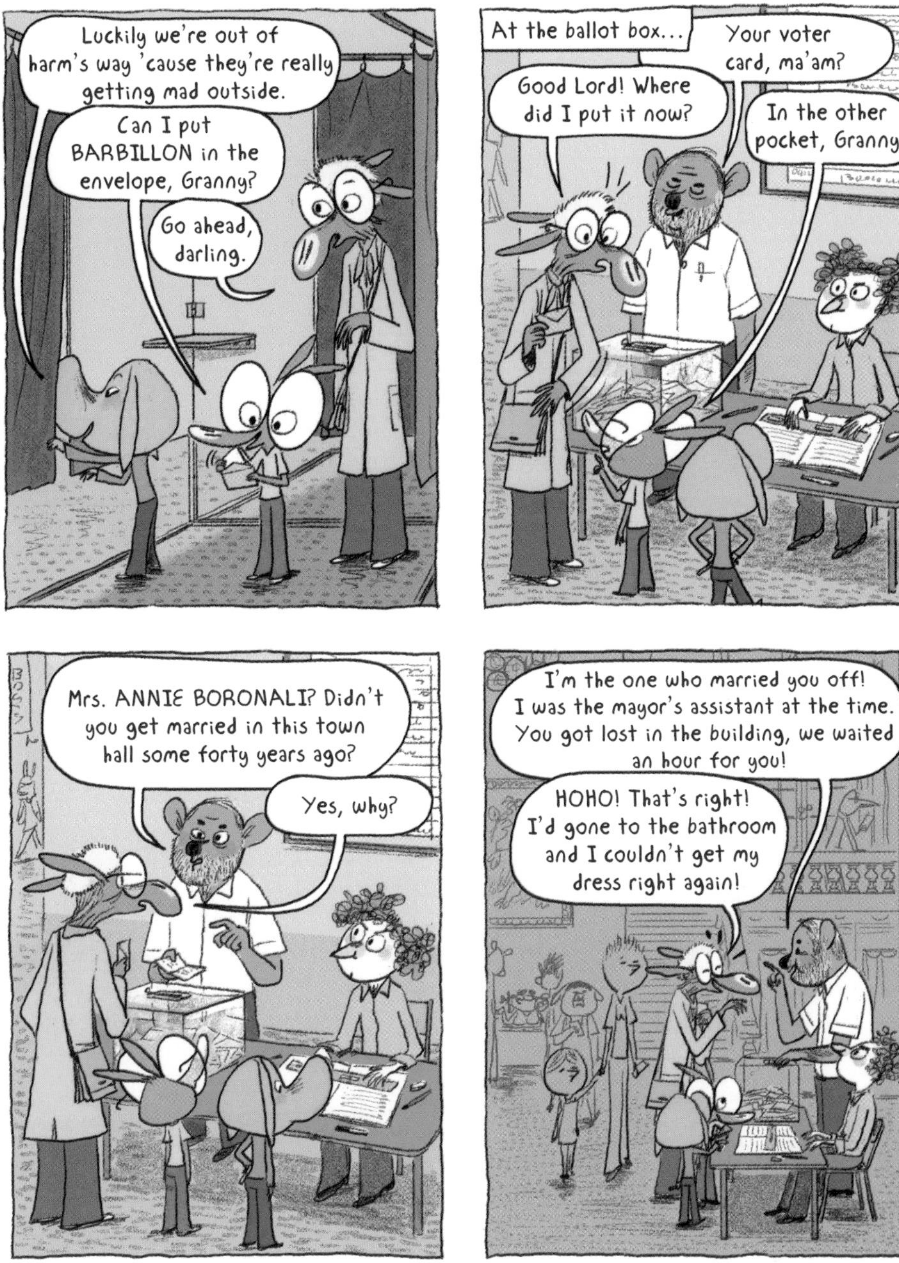
Luckily we're out of harm's way 'cause they're really getting mad outside.
Can I put BARBILLON in the envelope, Granny?
Go ahead, darling.
At the ballot box...
Your voter card, ma'am?
Good Lord! Where did I put it now?
In the other pocket, Granny.
Mrs. ANNIE BORONALI? Didn't you get married in this town hall some forty years ago?
Yes, why?
I'm the one who married you off! I was the mayor's assistant at the time. You got lost in the building, we waited an hour for you!
HOHO! That's right! I'd gone to the bathroom and I couldn't get my dress right again!

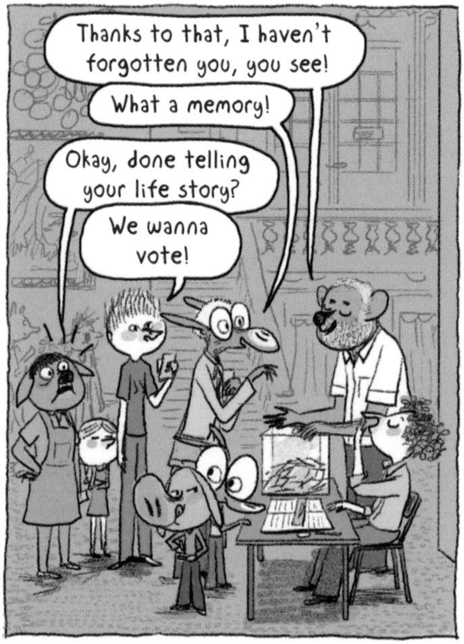
Thanks to that, I haven't forgotten you, you see!
What a memory!
Okay, done telling your life story?
We wanna vote!

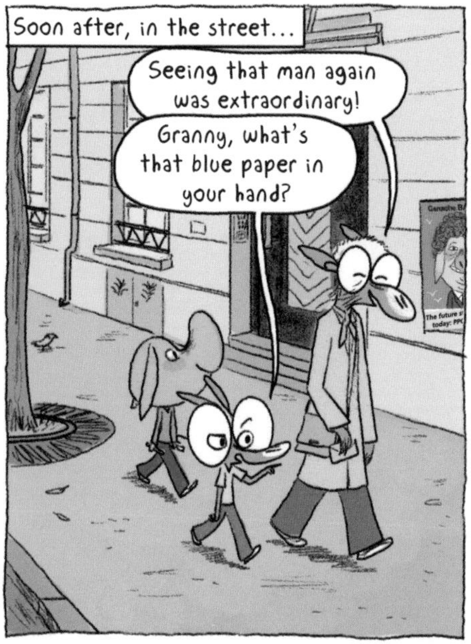
Soon after, in the street...
Seeing that man again was extraordinary!
Granny, what's that blue paper in your hand?

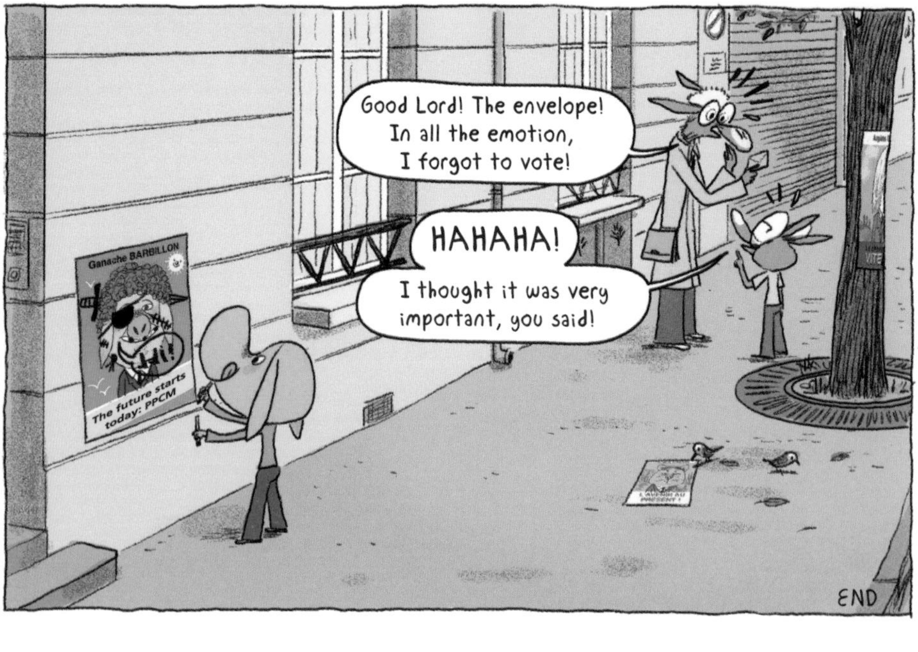
Good Lord! The envelope! In all the emotion, I forgot to vote!
HAHAHA!
I thought it was very important, you said!
Ganache BARBILLON
The future starts today: PPCM
END

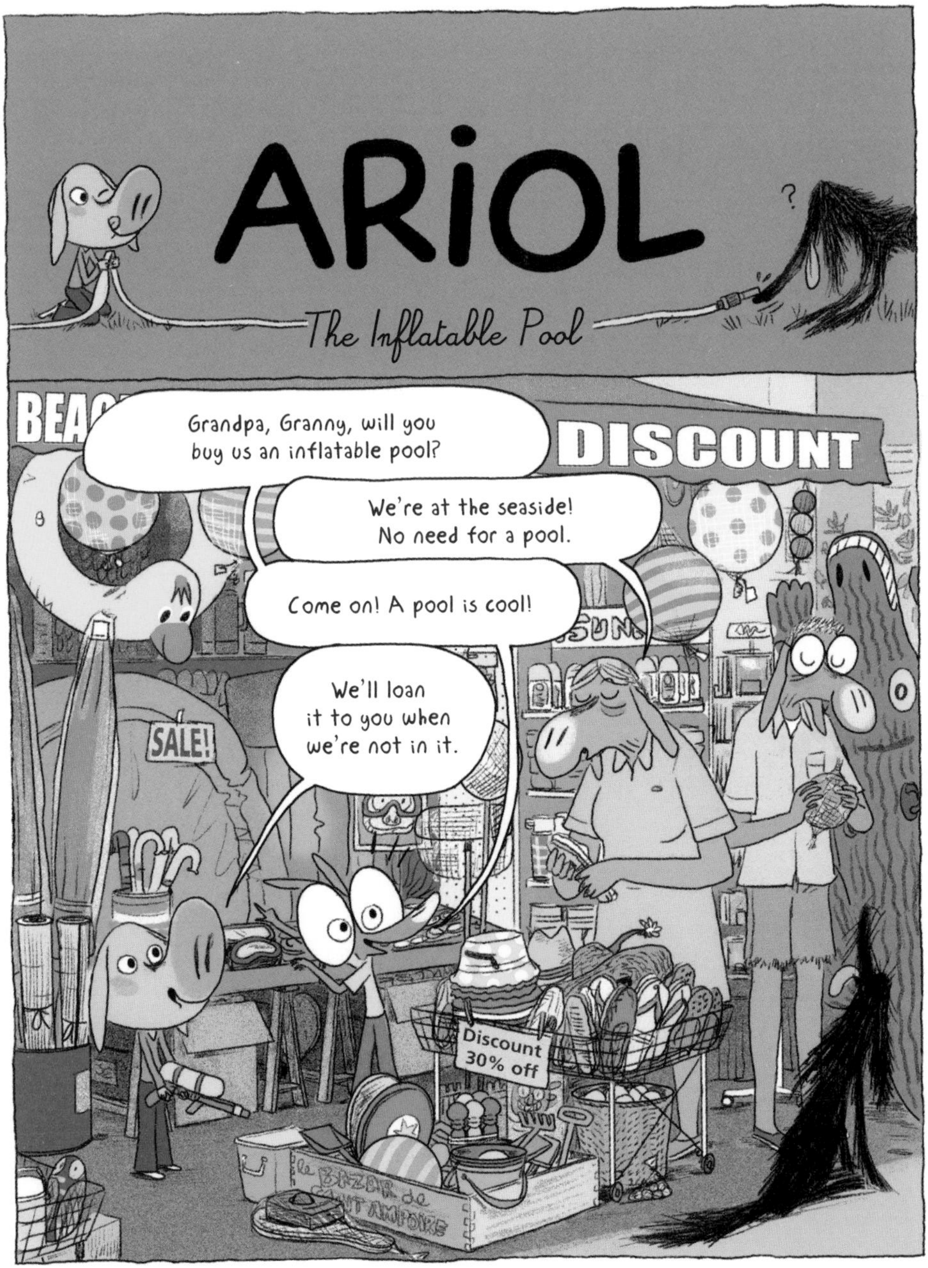
ARiOL
?
The Inflatable Pool
DISCOUNT
Grandpa, Granny, will you buy us an inflatable pool?
We're at the seaside! No need for a pool.
Come on! A pool is cool!
We'll loan it to you when we're not in it.
SALE!
Discount 30% off

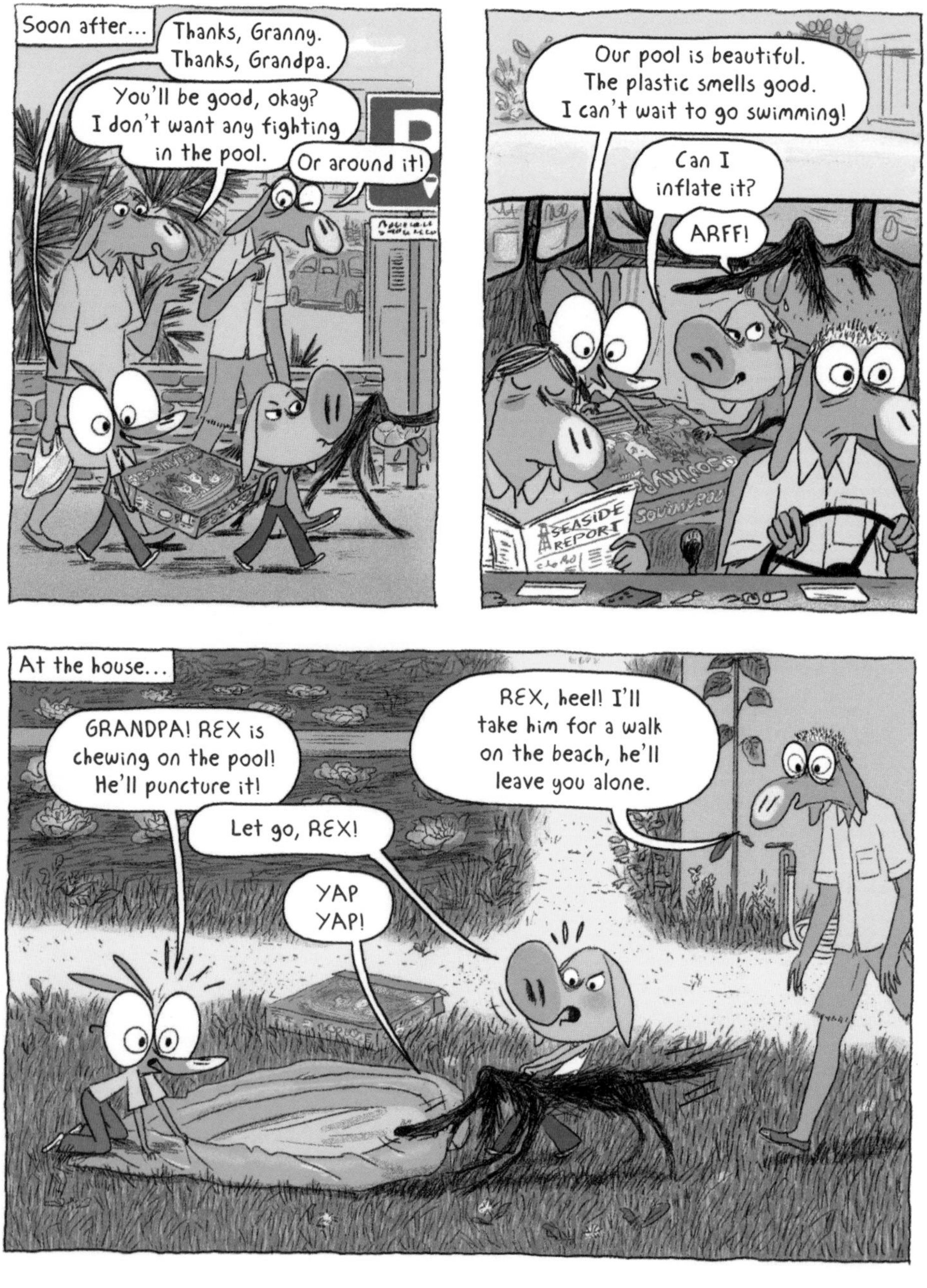
Soon after...
Thanks, Granny. Thanks, Grandpa.
You'll be good, okay? I don't want any fighting in the pool.
Or around it!
Our pool is beautiful. The plastic smells good. I can't wait to go swimming!
Can I inflate it?
ARFF!
SEASIDE REPORT
At the house...
GRANDPA! REX is chewing on the pool! He'll puncture it!
Let go, REX!
YAP YAP!
REX, heel! I'll take him for a walk on the beach, he'll leave you alone.

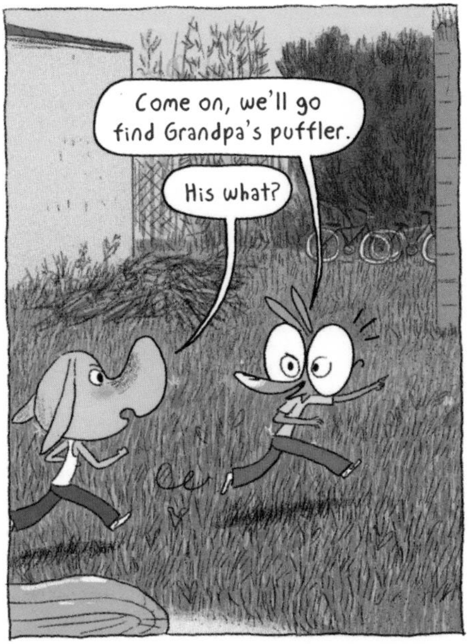
Come on, we'll go find Grandpa's puffler.
His what?

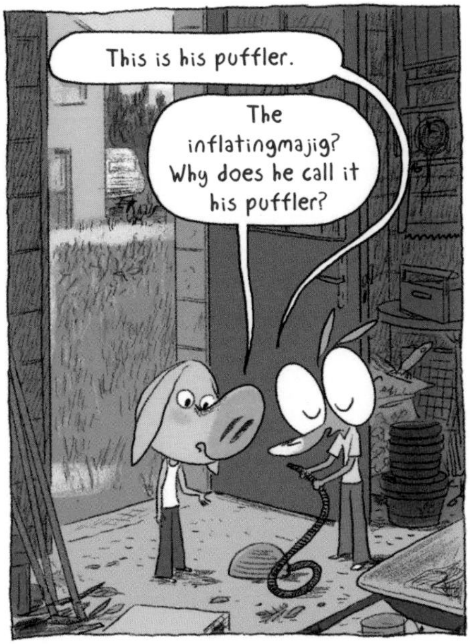
This is his puffler.
The inflatingmajig? Why does he call it his puffler?

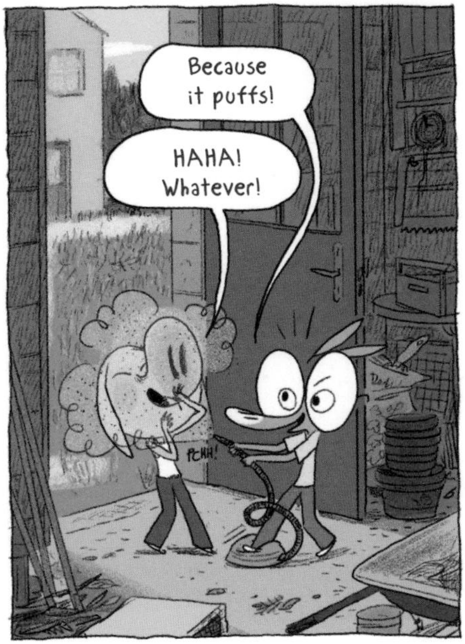
Because it puffs!
HAHA! Whatever!
PCHH!

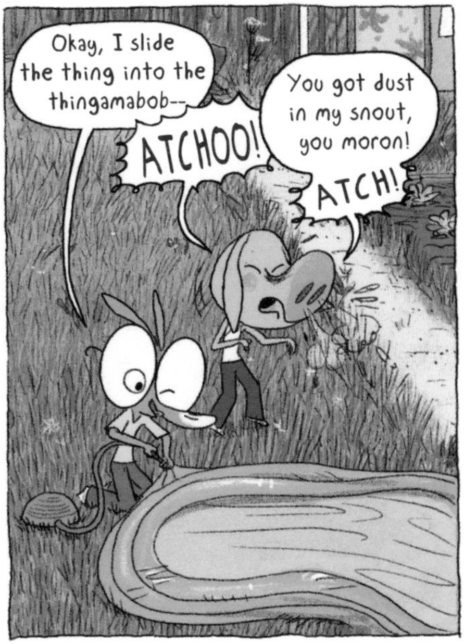
Okay, I slide the thing into the thingamabob--
ATCHOO!
You got dust in my snout, you moron!
ATCH!

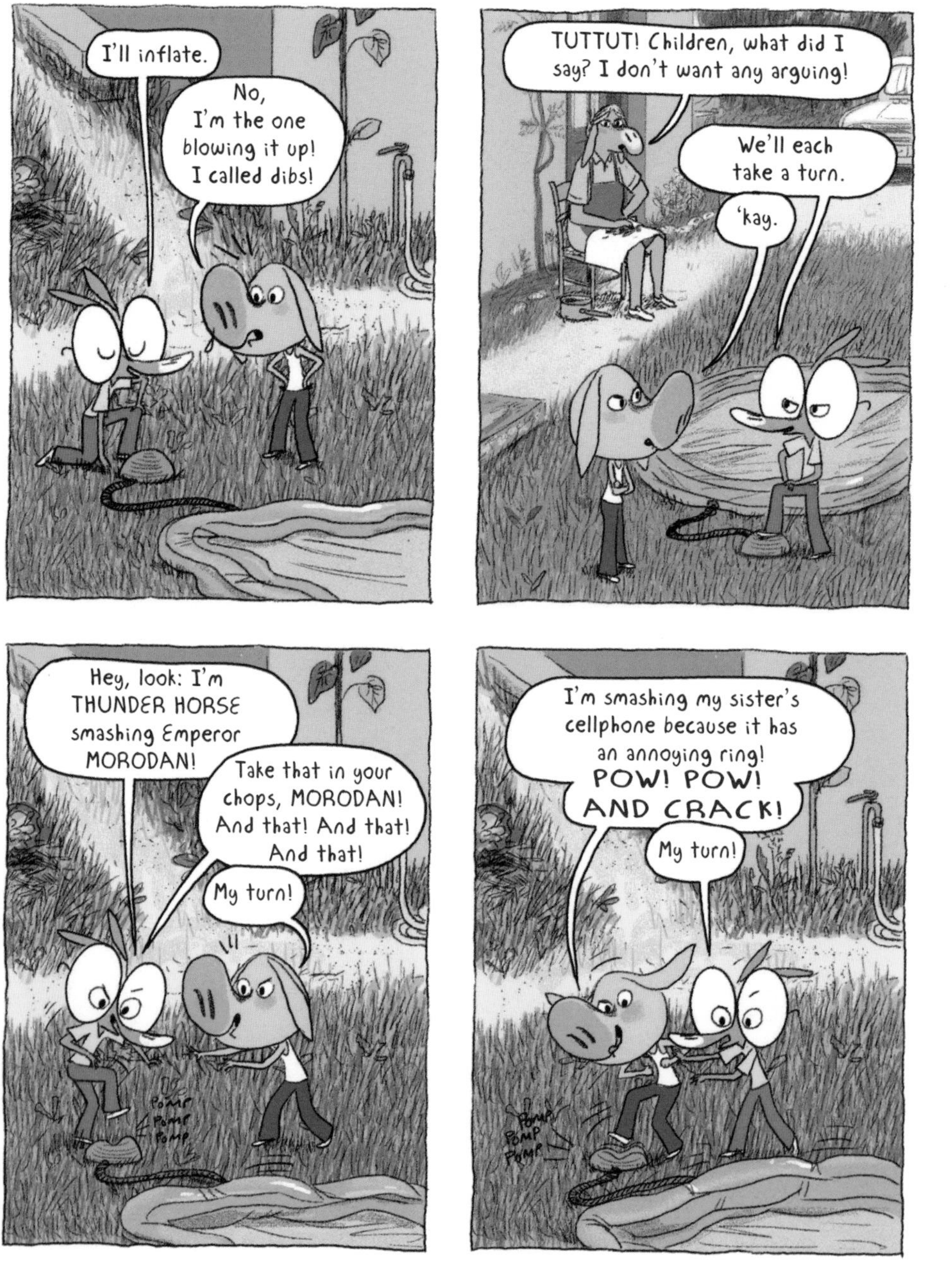
I'll inflate.
No, I'm the one blowing it up! I called dibs!
TUTTUT! Children, what did I say? I don't want any arguing!
We'll each take a turn.
'kay.
Hey, look: I'm THUNDER HORSE smashing Emperor MORODAN!
Take that in your chops, MORODAN! And that! And that! And that!
My turn!
POMP POMP POMP
I'm smashing my sister's cellphone because it has an annoying ring! POW! POW! AND CRACK!
My turn!
POMP POMP POMP

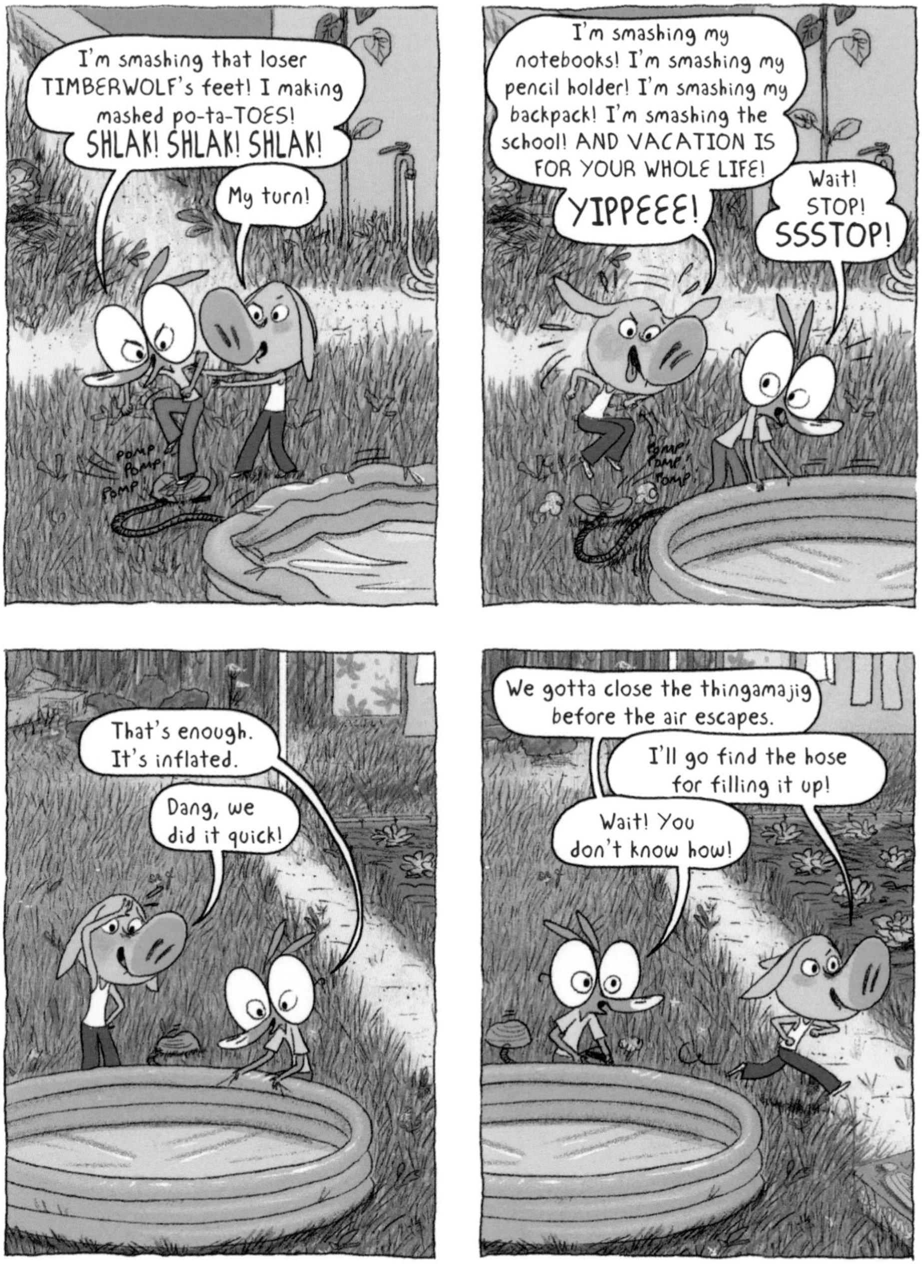
I'm smashing that loser TIMBERWOLF's feet! I making mashed po-ta-TOES! SHLAK! SHLAK! SHLAK!
My turn!
POMP POMP POMP
I'm smashing my notebooks! I'm smashing my pencil holder! I'm smashing my backpack! I'm smashing the school! AND VACATION IS FOR YOUR WHOLE LIFE!
YIPPEEE!
Wait! STOP! SSSTOP!
POMP POMP POMP
That's enough. It's inflated.
Dang, we did it quick!
We gotta close the thingamajig before the air escapes.
I'll go find the hose for filling it up!
Wait! You don't know how!

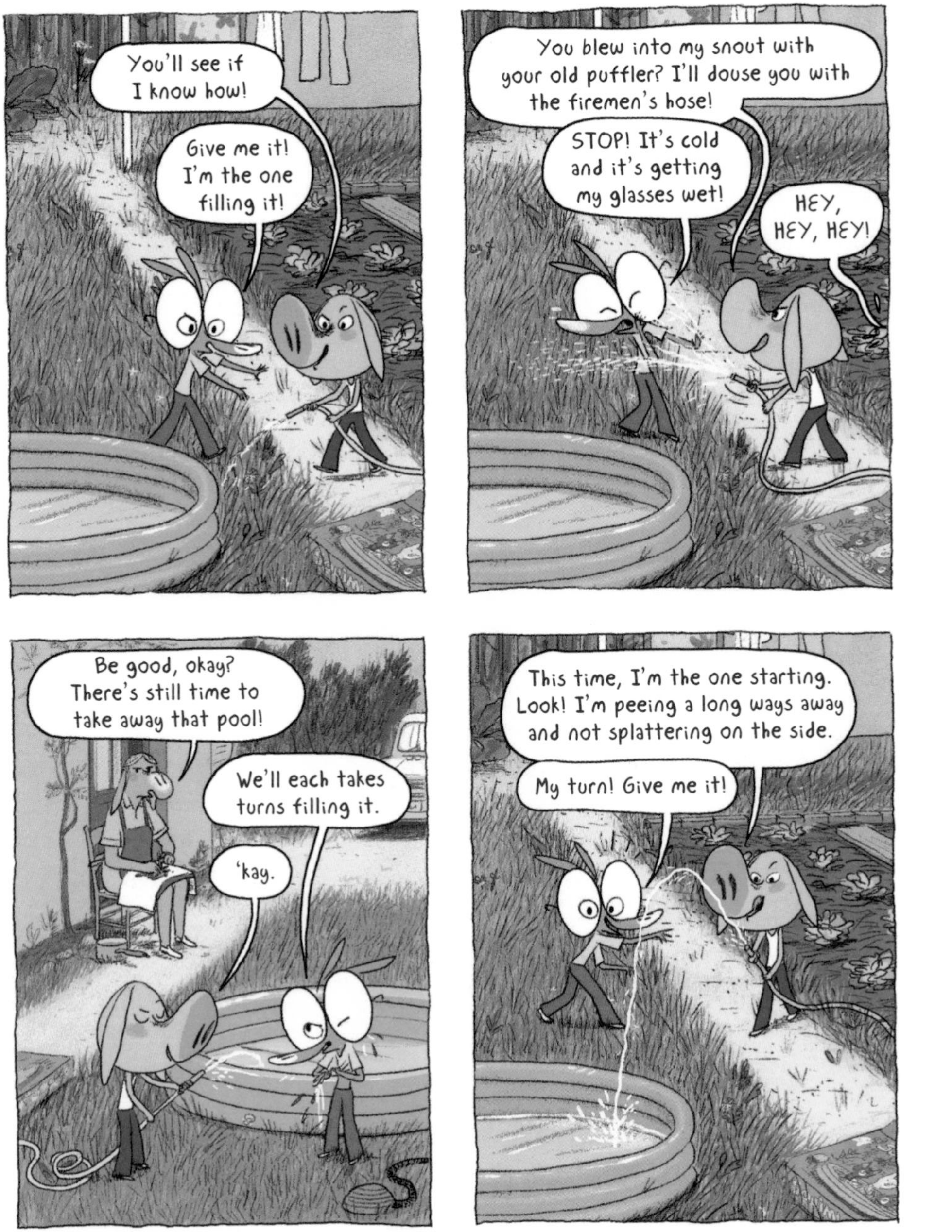
You'll see if I know how!
Give me it! I'm the one filling it!
You blew into my snout with your old puffler? I'll douse you with the firemen's hose!
STOP! It's cold and it's getting my glasses wet!
HEY, HEY, HEY!
Be good, okay? There's still time to take away that pool!
We'll each takes turns filling it.
'kay.
This time, I'm the one starting. Look! I'm peeing a long ways away and not splattering on the side.
My turn! Give me it!

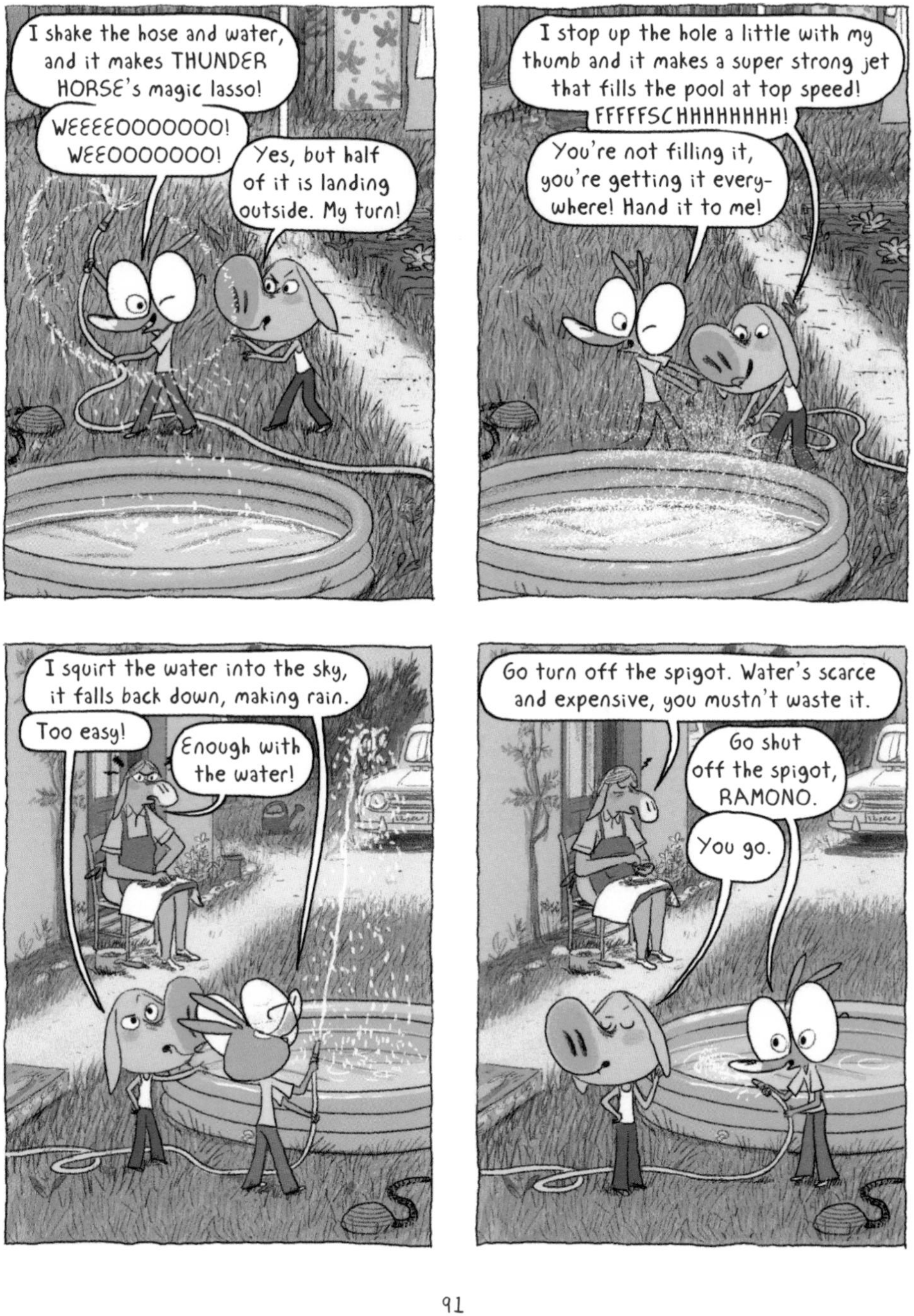
I shake the hose and water, and it makes THUNDER HORSE's magic lasso!
WEEEEOOOOOOO! WEEOOOOOOO!
Yes, but half of it is landing outside. My turn!
I stop up the hole a little with my thumb and it makes a super strong jet that fills the pool at top speed!
FFFFFSCHHHHHHHH!
You're not filling it, you're getting it every-where! Hand it to me!
I squirt the water into the sky, it falls back down, making rain.
Too easy!
Enough with the water!
Go turn off the spigot. Water's scarce and expensive, you mustn't waste it.
Go shut off the spigot, RAMONO.
You go.

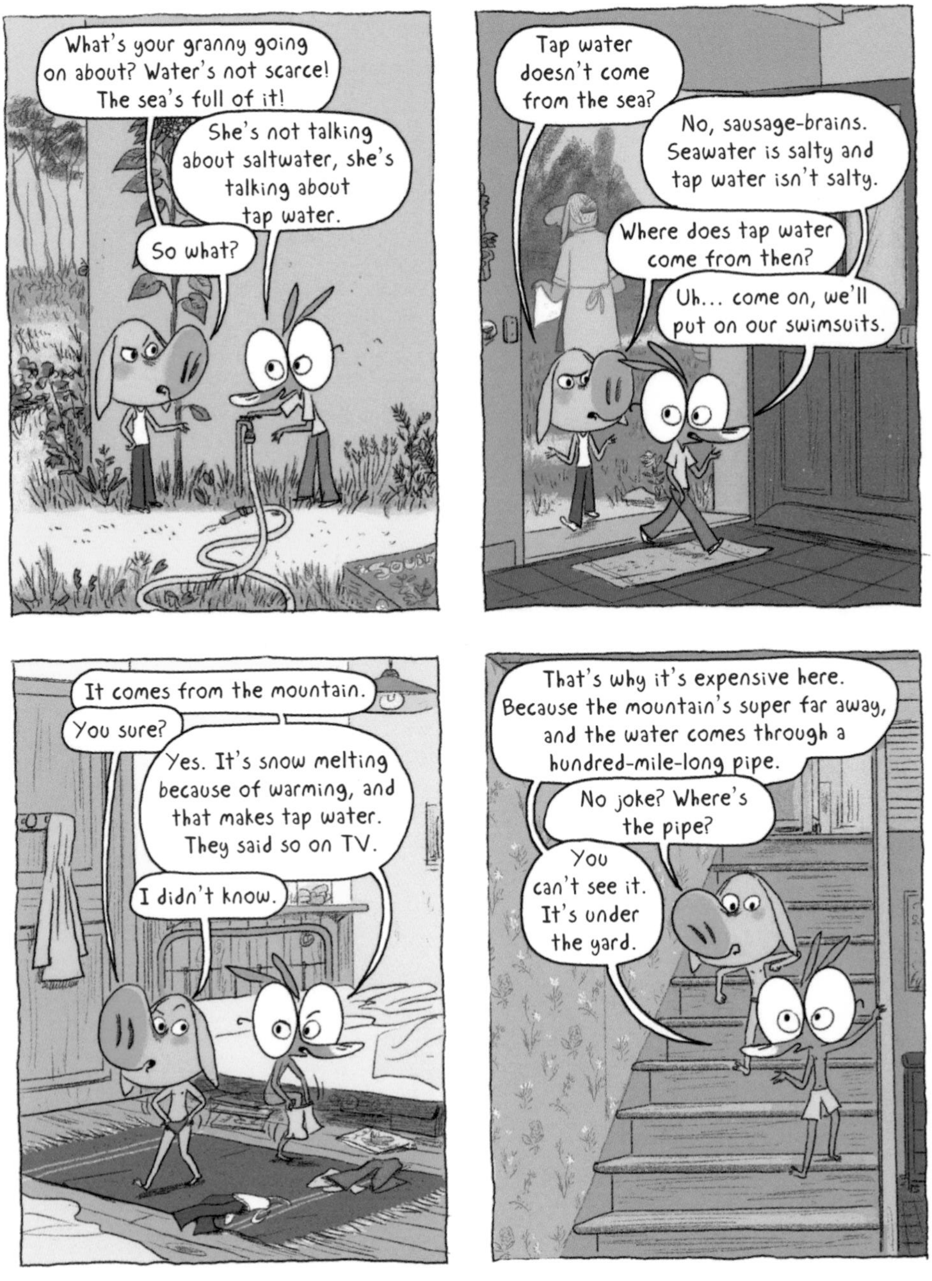
What's your granny going on about? Water's not scarce! The sea's full of it!
She's not talking about saltwater, she's talking about tap water.
So what?
Tap water doesn't come from the sea?
No, sausage-brains. Seawater is salty and tap water isn't salty.
Where does tap water come from then?
Uh... come on, we'll put on our swimsuits.
It comes from the mountain.
You sure?
Yes. It's snow melting because of warming, and that makes tap water. They said so on TV.
I didn't know.
That's why it's expensive here. Because the mountain's super far away, and the water comes through a hundred-mile-long pipe.
No joke? Where's the pipe?
You can't see it. It's under the yard.

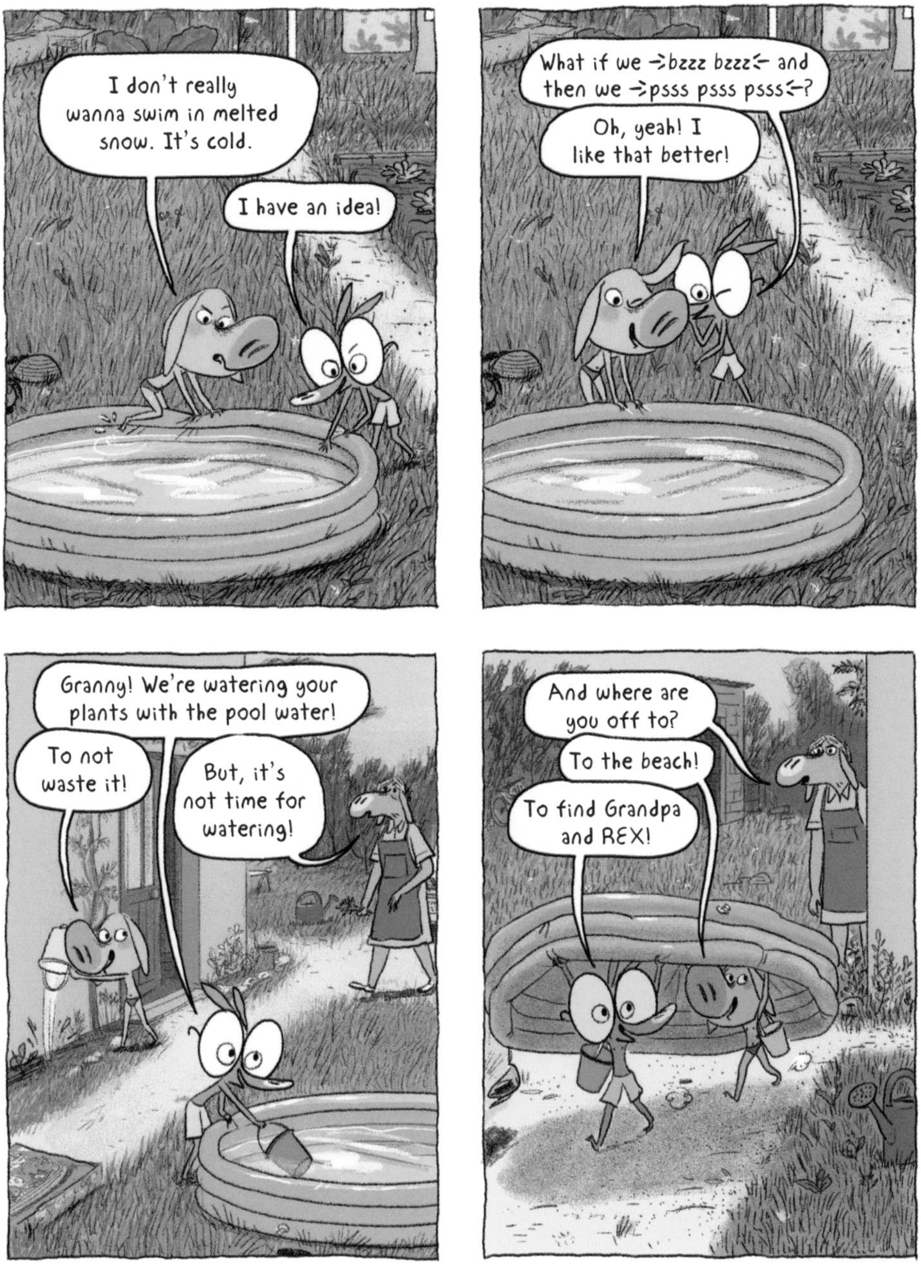

I don't really wanna swim in melted snow. It's cold.
I have an idea!
What if we ->bzzz bzzz<- and then we ->psss psss psss<-?
Oh, yeah! I like that better!
Granny! We're watering your plants with the pool water!
To not waste it!
But, it's not time for watering!
And where are you off to?
To the beach!
To find Grandpa and REX!

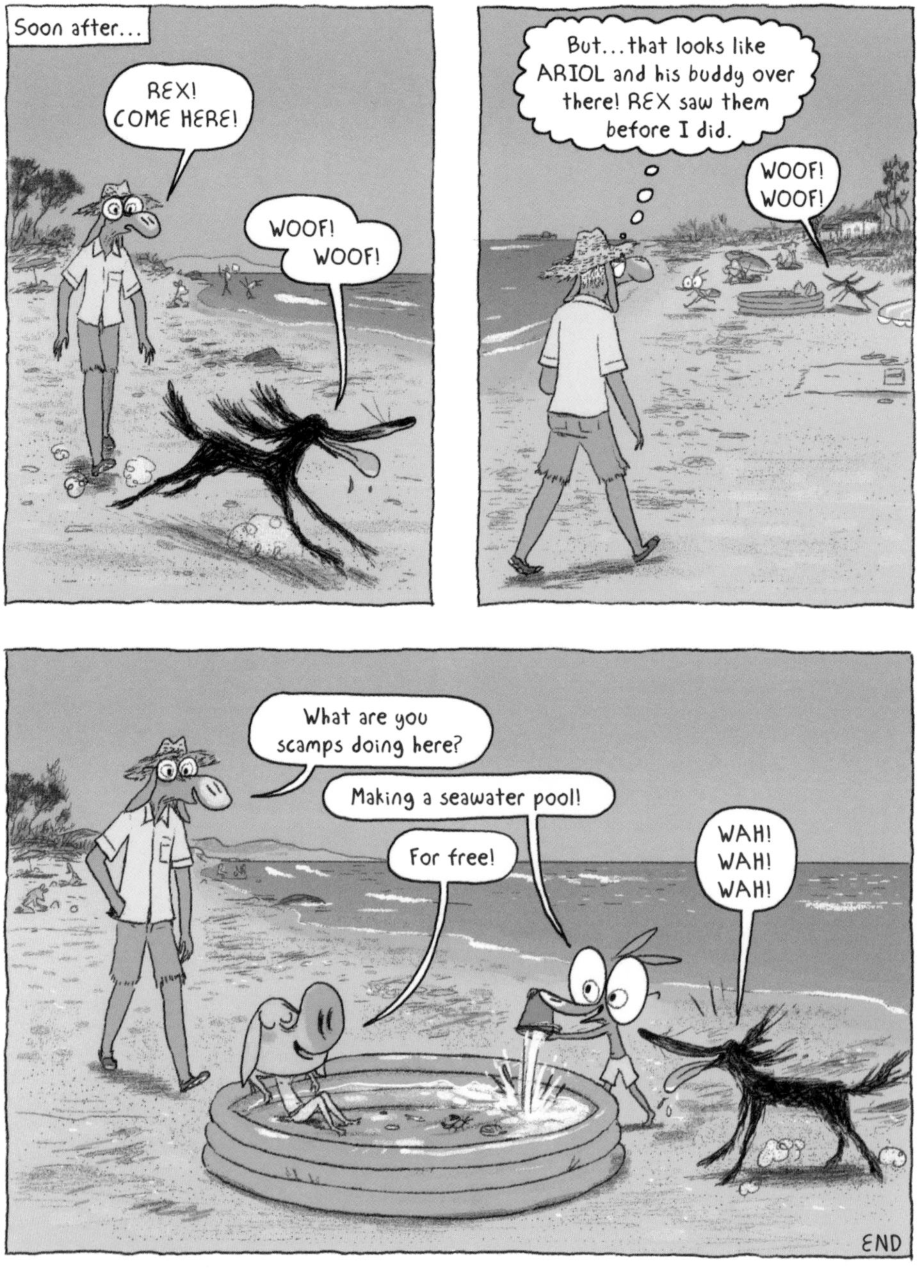
Soon after...
REX! COME HERE!
WOOF! WOOF!
But...that looks like ARIOL and his buddy over there! REX saw them before I did.
WOOF! WOOF!
What are you scamps doing here?
Making a seawater pool!
For free!
WAH! WAH! WAH!
END

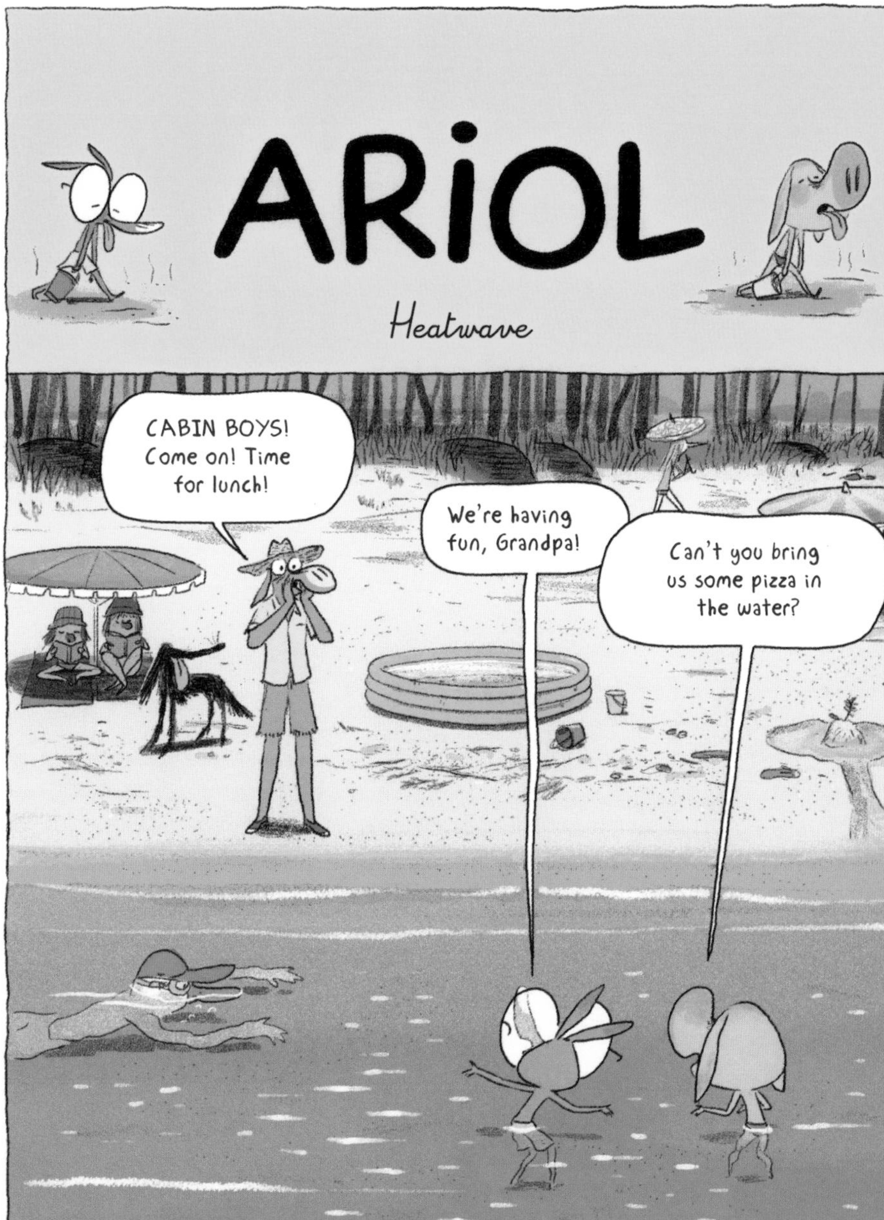
ARiOL
Heatwave
CABIN BOYS! Come on! Time for lunch!
We're having fun, Grandpa!
Can't you bring us some pizza in the water?

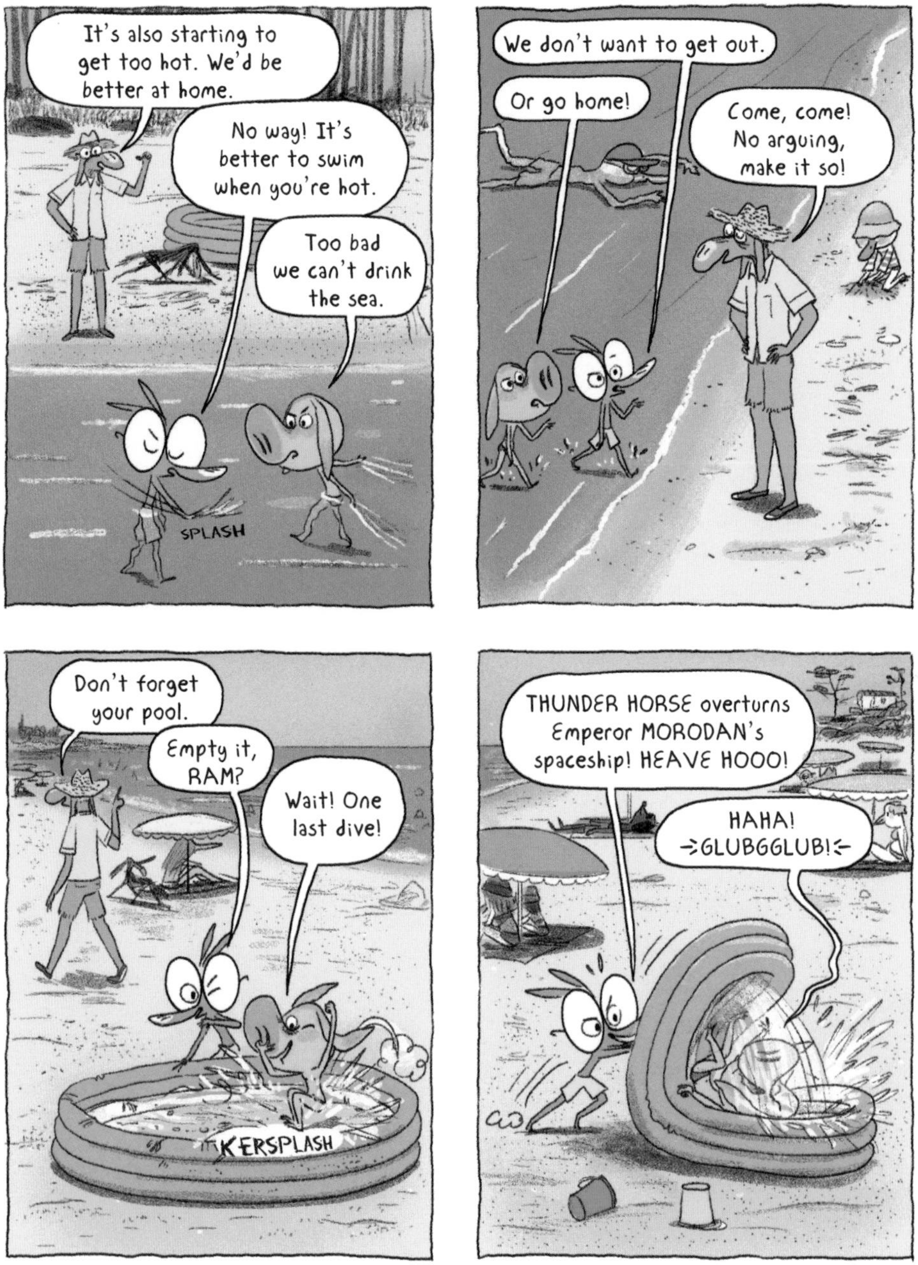
It's also starting to get too hot. We'd be better at home.
No way! It's better to swim when you're hot.
Too bad we can't drink the sea.
SPLASH
We don't want to get out.
Or go home!
Come, come! No arguing, make it so!
Don't forget your pool.
Empty it, RAM?
Wait! One last dive!
KERSPLASH
THUNDER HORSE overturns Emperor MORODAN's spaceship! HEAVE HOOO!
HAHA! GLUBGGLUB!

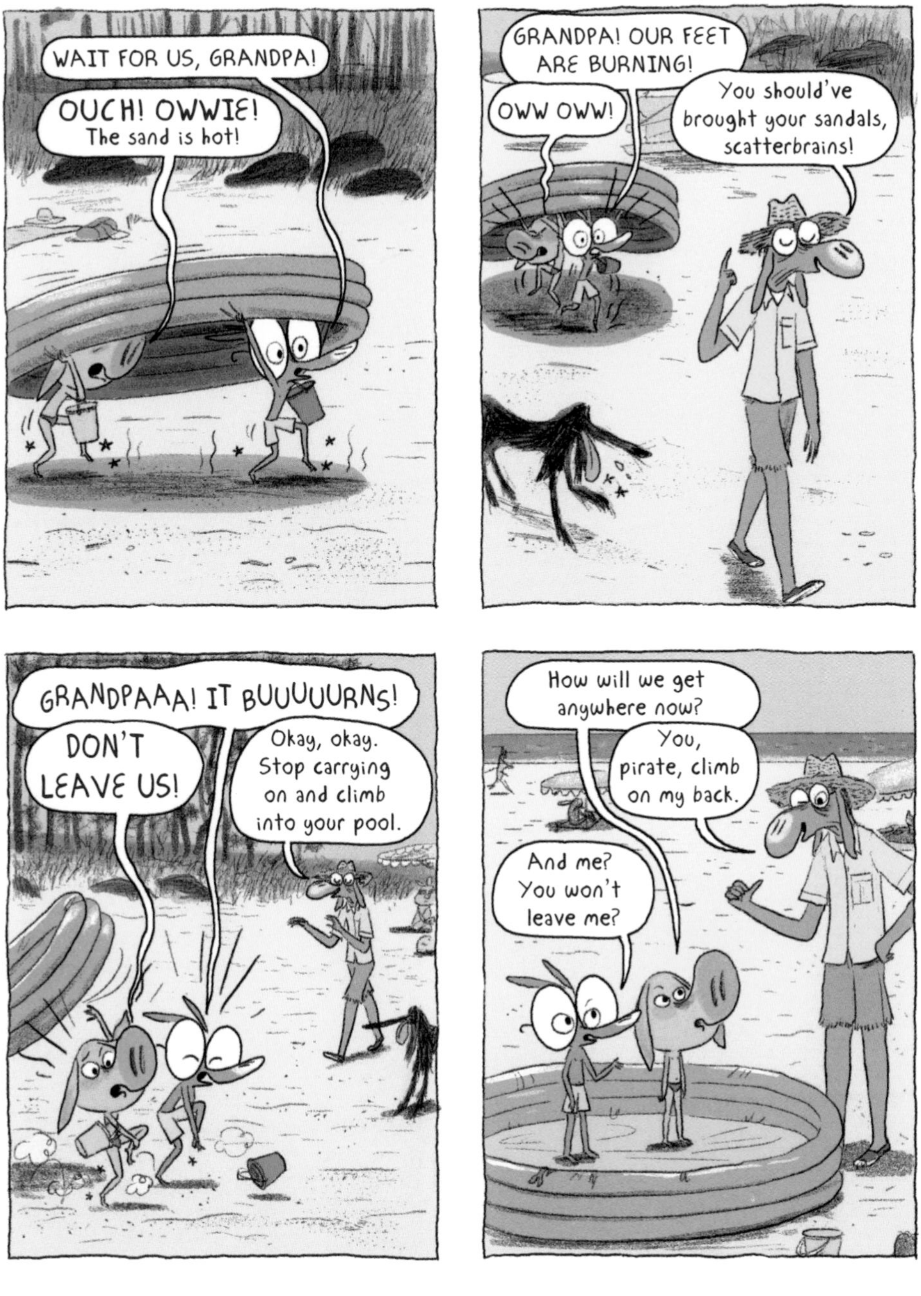
WAIT FOR US, GRANDPA!
OUCH! OWWIE! The sand is hot!
GRANDPA! OUR FEET ARE BURNING!
OWW OWW!
You should've brought your sandals, scatterbrains!
GRANDPAAA! IT BUUUUURNS!
DON'T LEAVE US!
Okay, okay. Stop carrying on and climb into your pool.
How will we get anywhere now?
You, pirate, climb on my back.
And me? You won't leave me?

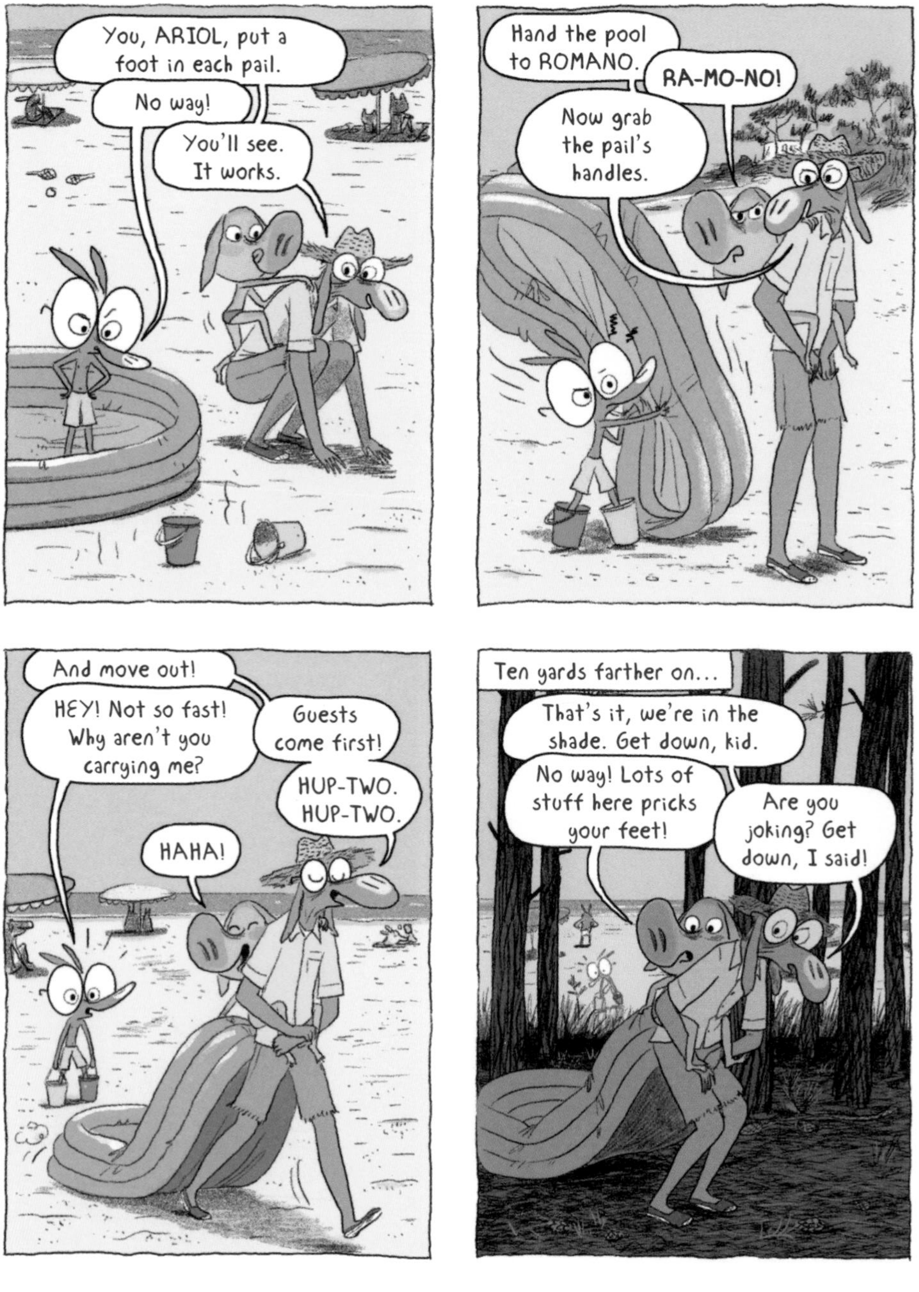
You, ARIOL, put a foot in each pail.
No way!
You'll see. It works.
Hand the pool to ROMANO.
RA-MO-NO!
Now grab the pail's handles.
And move out!
HEY! Not so fast! Why aren't you carrying me?
Guests come first!
HUP-TWO. HUP-TWO.
HAHA!
Ten yards farther on...
That's it, we're in the shade. Get down, kid.
No way! Lots of stuff here pricks your feet!
Are you joking? Get down, I said!

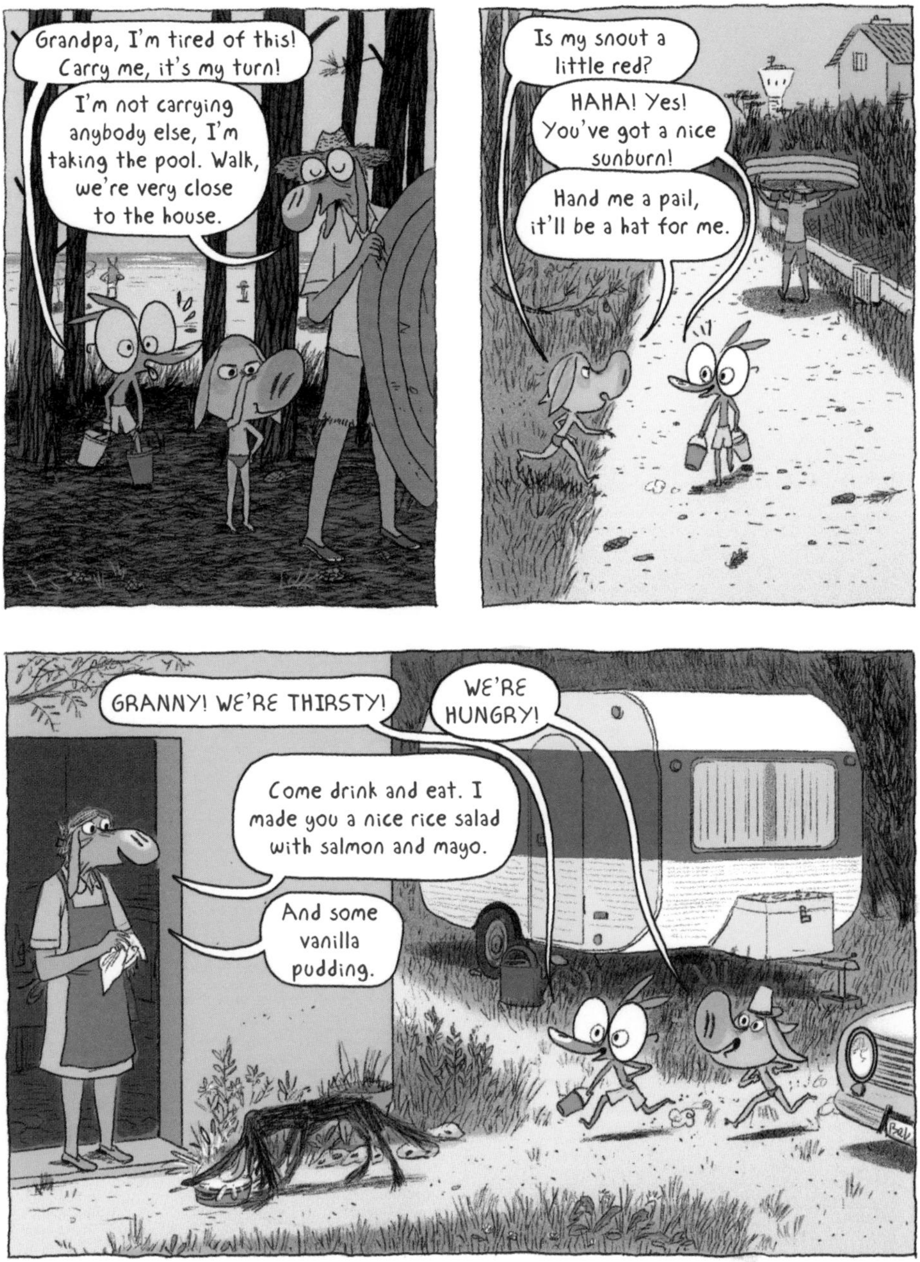
Grandpa, I'm tired of this! Carry me, it's my turn!
I'm not carrying anybody else, I'm taking the pool. Walk, we're very close to the house.
Is my snout a little red?
HAHA! Yes! You've got a nice sunburn!
Hand me a pail, it'll be a hat for me.
GRANNY! WE'RE THIRSTY!
WE'RE HUNGRY!
Come drink and eat. I made you a nice rice salad with salmon and mayo.
And some vanilla pudding.

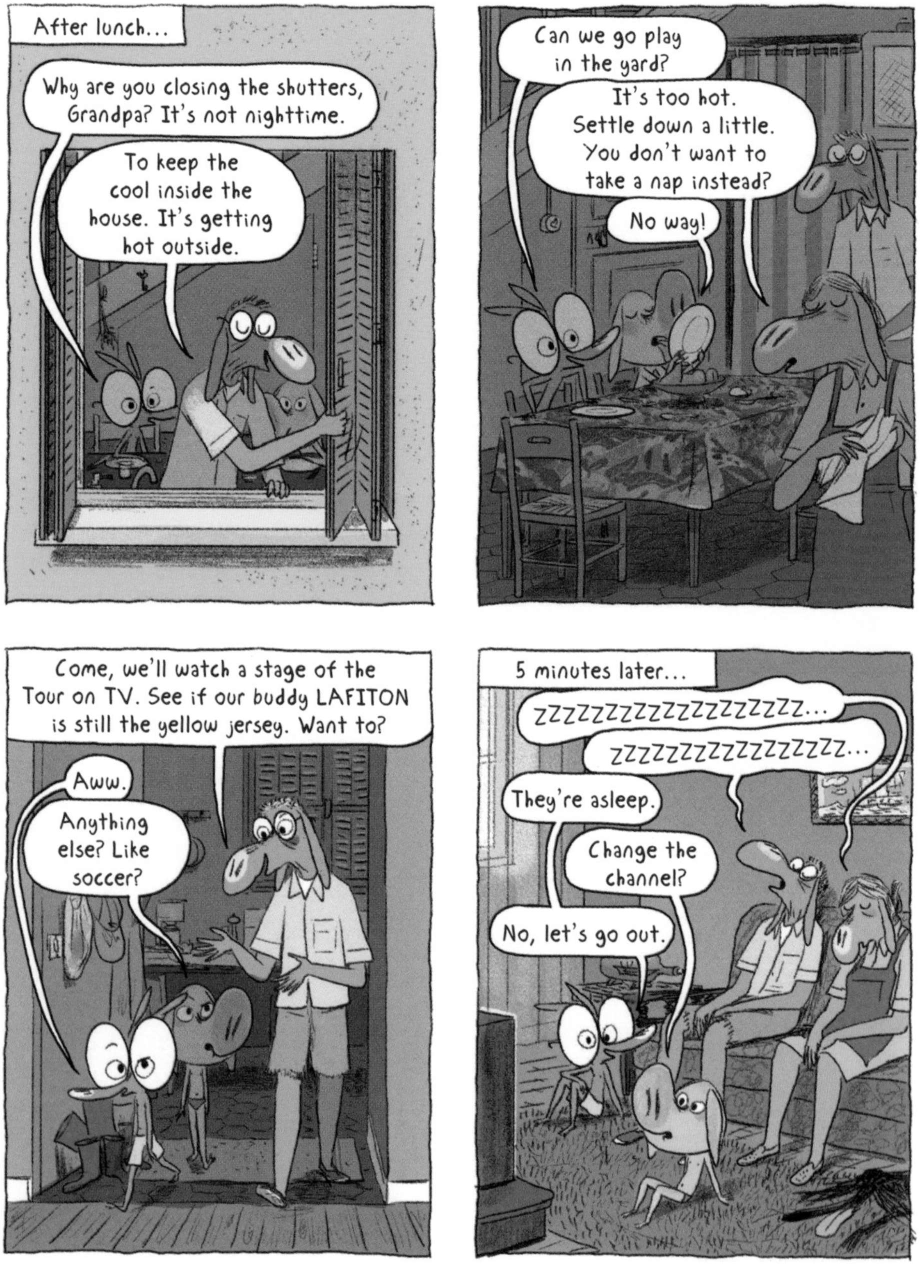
After lunch...
Why are you closing the shutters, Grandpa? It's not nighttime.
To keep the cool inside the house. It's getting hot outside.
Can we go play in the yard?
It's too hot. Settle down a little. You don't want to take a nap instead?
No way!
Come, we'll watch a stage of the Tour on TV. See if our buddy LAFITON is still the yellow jersey. Want to?
Aww.
Anything else? Like soccer?
5 minutes later...
ZZZZZZZZZZZZZZZZZZZZ...
ZZZZZZZZZZZZZZZZZZ...
They're asleep.
Change the channel?
No, let's go out.

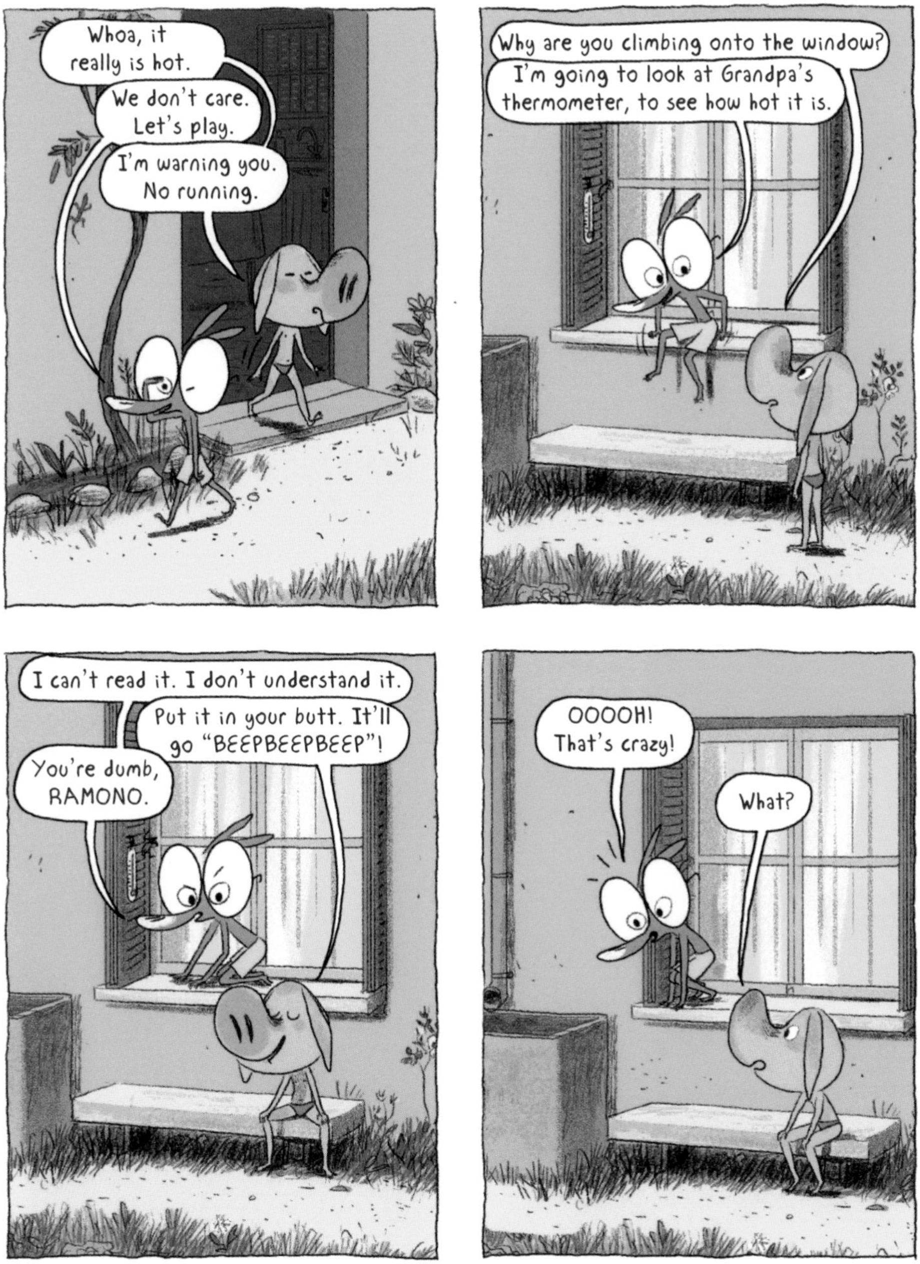
Whoa, it really is hot.
We don't care. Let's play.
I'm warning you. No running.
Why are you climbing onto the window?
I'm going to look at Grandpa's thermometer, to see how hot it is.
I can't read it. I don't understand it.
Put it in your butt. It'll go "BEEPBEEPBEEP"!
You're dumb, RAMONO.
OOOOH! That's crazy!
What?

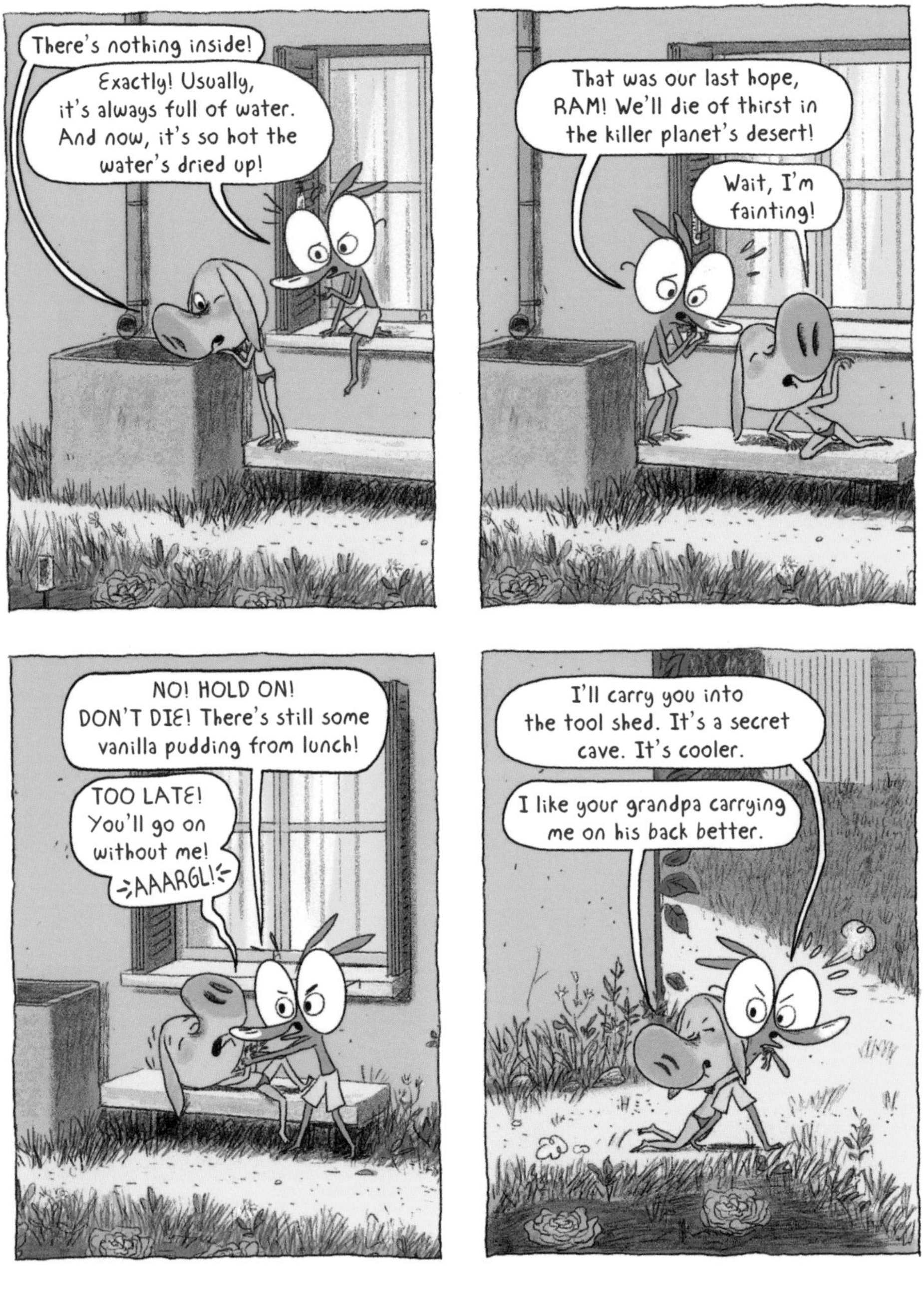
There's nothing inside!
Exactly! Usually, it's always full of water. And now, it's so hot the water's dried up!
That was our last hope, RAM! We'll die of thirst in the killer planet's desert!
Wait, I'm fainting!
NO! HOLD ON! DON'T DIE! There's still some vanilla pudding from lunch!
TOO LATE! You'll go on without me! AAARGL!
I'll carry you into the tool shed. It's a secret cave. It's cooler.
I like your grandpa carrying me on his back better.

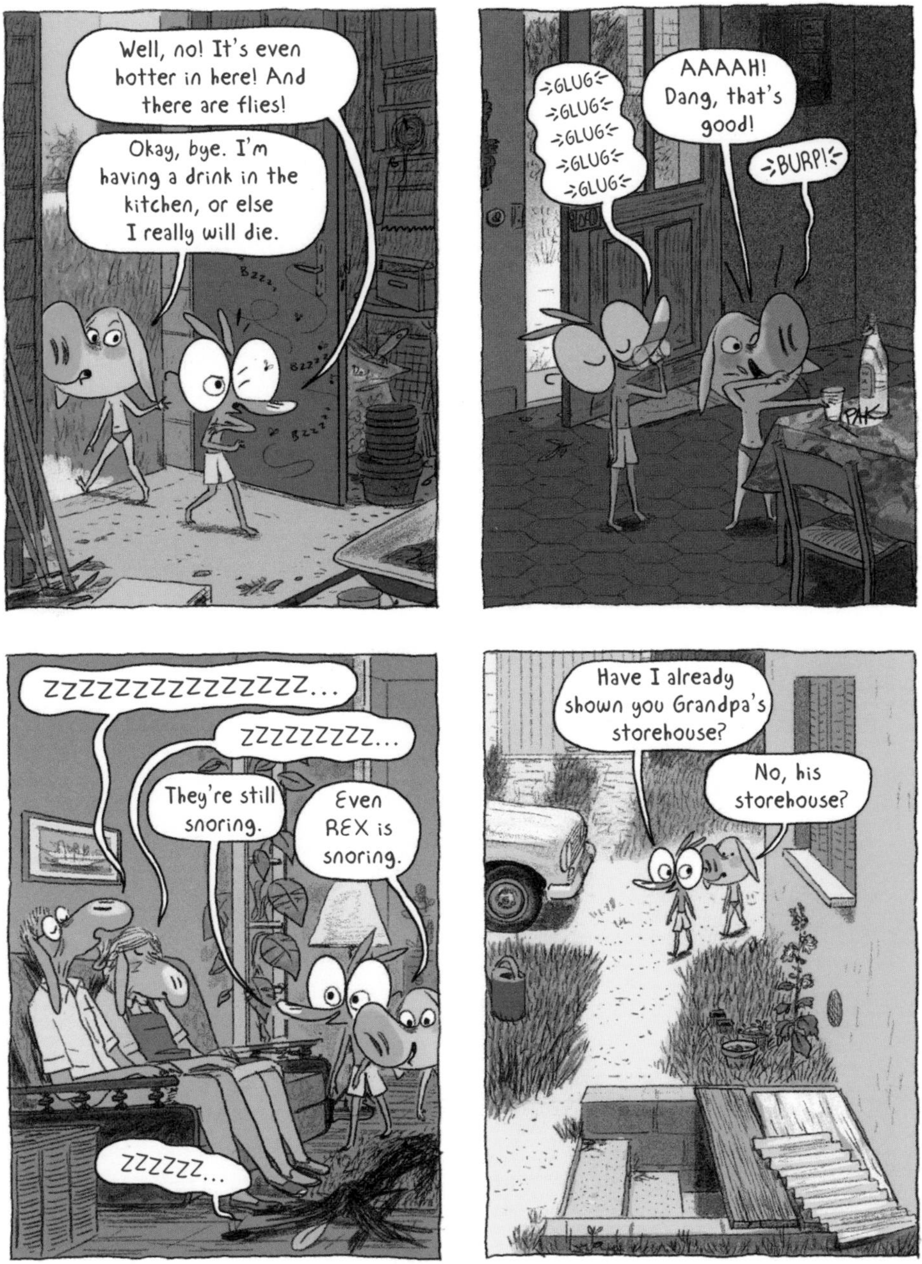
Well, no! It's even hotter in here! And there are flies!
Okay, bye. I'm having a drink in the kitchen, or else I really will die.
Bzzz
Bzzz
Bzzz
GLUG GLUG GLUG GLUG GLUG
AAAAH! Dang, that's good!
BURP!
PAK
ZZZZZZZZZZZZZZZ...
ZZZZZZZZZ...
They're still snoring.
Even REX is snoring.
ZZZZZZ...
Have I already shown you Grandpa's storehouse?
No, his storehouse?

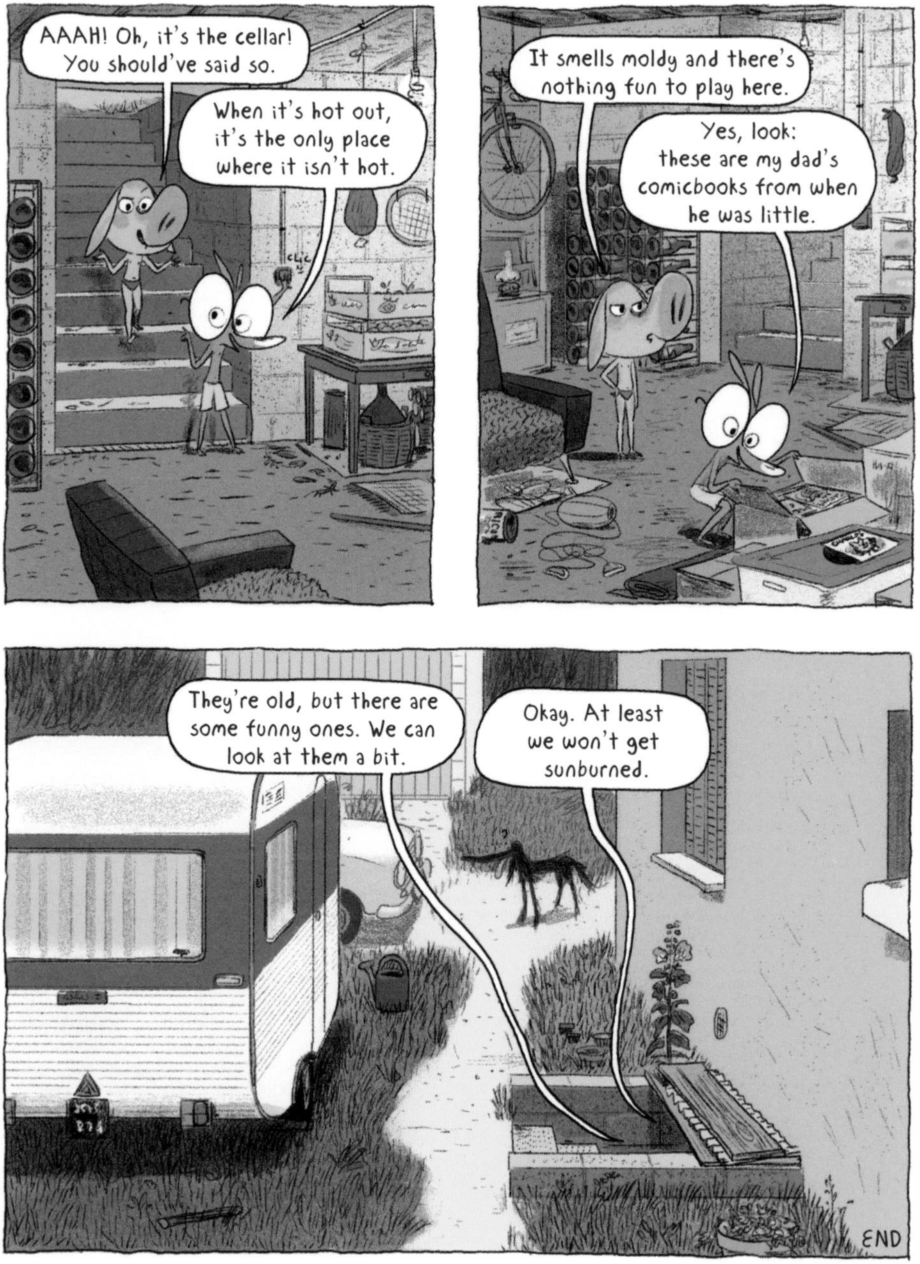
AAAH! Oh, it's the cellar! You should've said so.
When it's hot out, it's the only place where it isn't hot.
CLIC
It smells moldy and there's nothing fun to play here.
Yes, look: these are my dad's comicbooks from when he was little.
They're old, but there are some funny ones. We can look at them a bit.
Okay. At least we won't get sunburned.
END

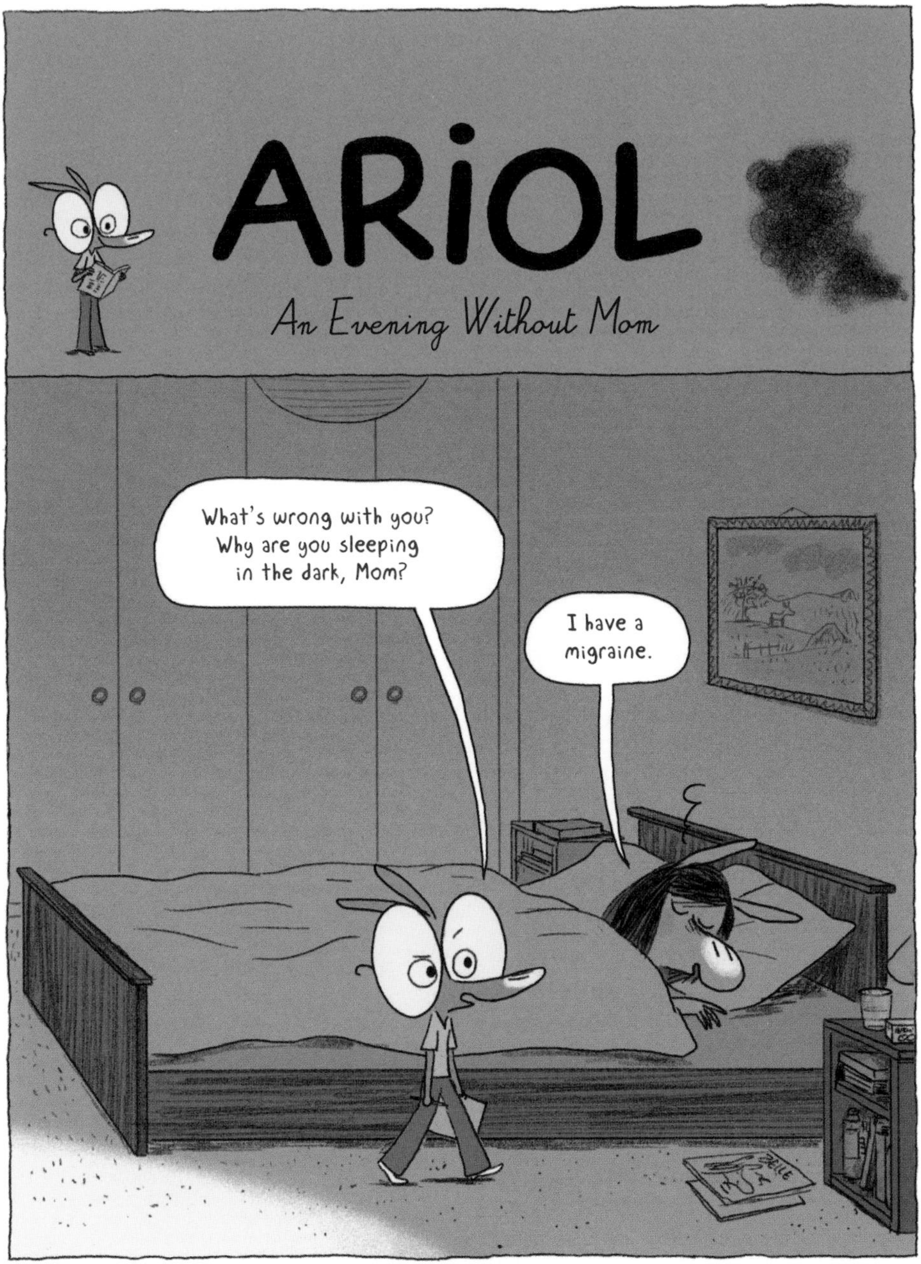
ARiOL
An Evening Without Mom
What's wrong with you? Why are you sleeping in the dark, Mom?
I have a migraine.

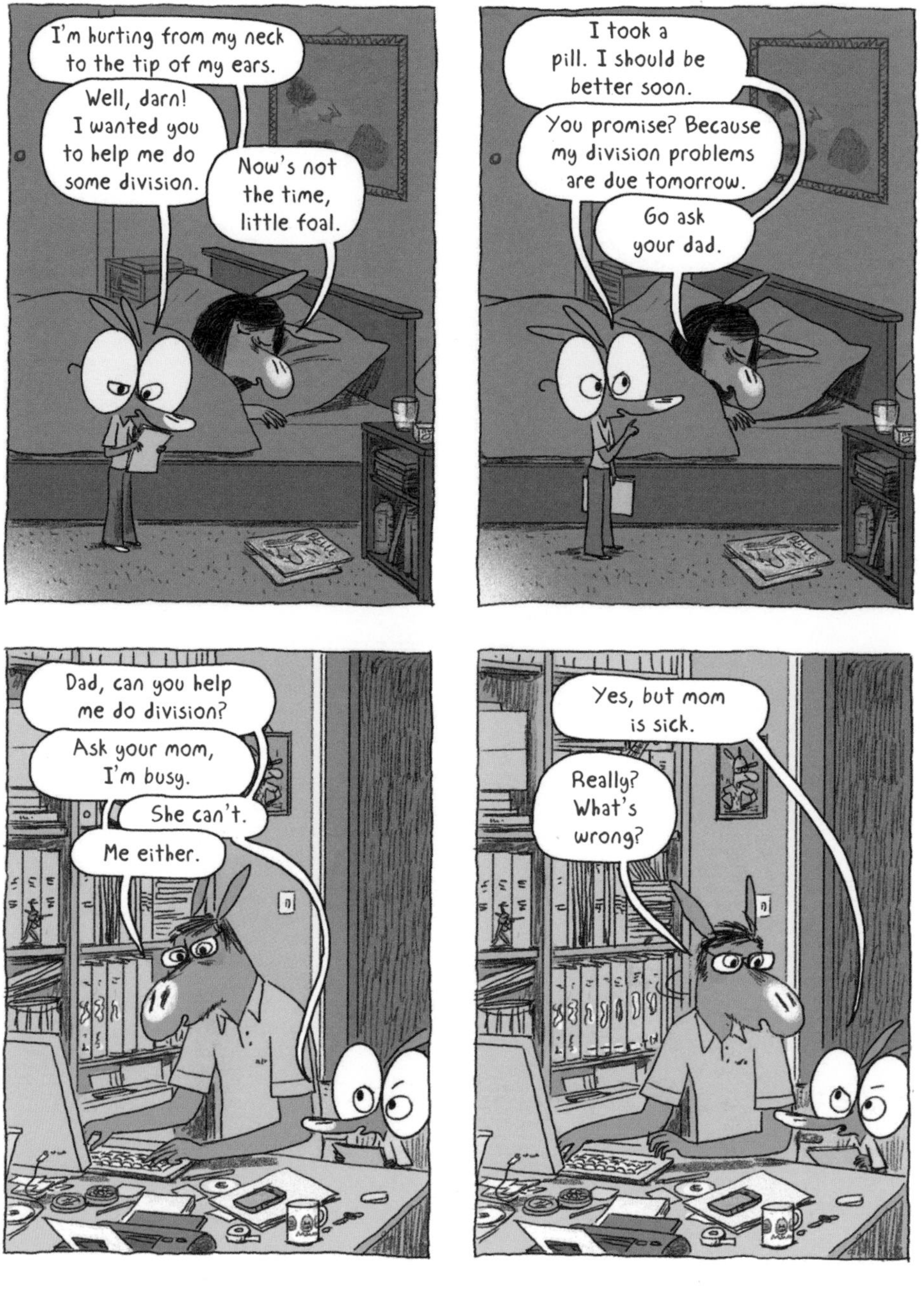
I'm hurting from my neck to the tip of my ears.
Well, darn! I wanted you to help me do some division.
Now's not the time, little foal.
I took a pill. I should be better soon.
You promise? Because my division problems are due tomorrow.
Go ask your dad.
Dad, can you help me do division?
Ask your mom, I'm busy.
She can't.
Me either.
Yes, but mom is sick.
Really? What's wrong?

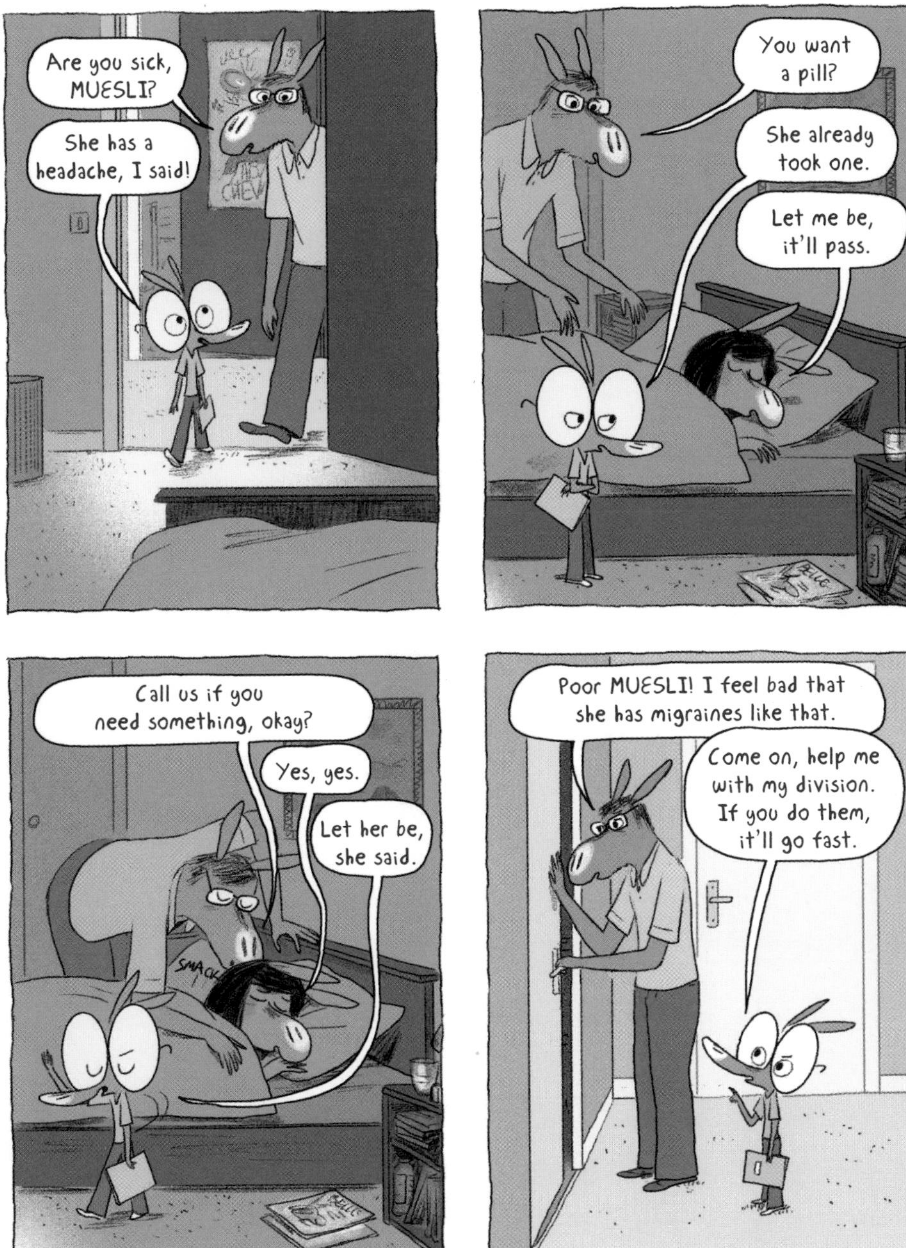
Are you sick, MUESLI?
She has a headache, I said!
You want a pill?
She already took one.
Let me be, it'll pass.
Call us if you need something, okay?
Yes, yes.
Let her be, she said.
SMACK
Poor MUESLI! I feel bad that she has migraines like that.
Come on, help me with my division. If you do them, it'll go fast.

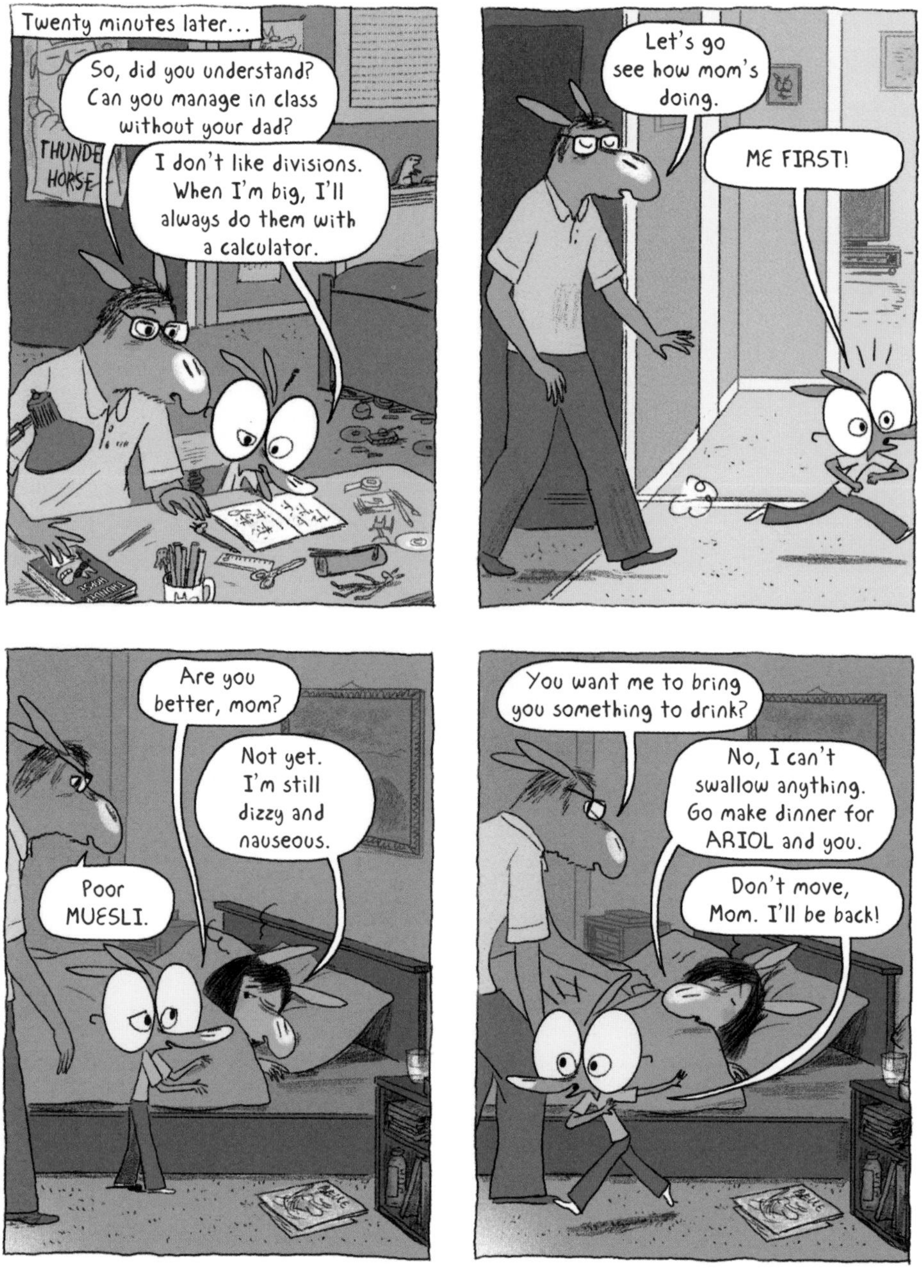
Twenty minutes later...
So, did you understand? Can you manage in class without your dad?
I don't like divisions. When I'm big, I'll always do them with a calculator.
THUNDE HORSE
Let's go see how mom's doing.
ME FIRST!
Are you better, mom?
Not yet. I'm still dizzy and nauseous.
Poor MUESLI.
You want me to bring you something to drink?
No, I can't swallow anything. Go make dinner for ARIOL and you.
Don't move, Mom. I'll be back!

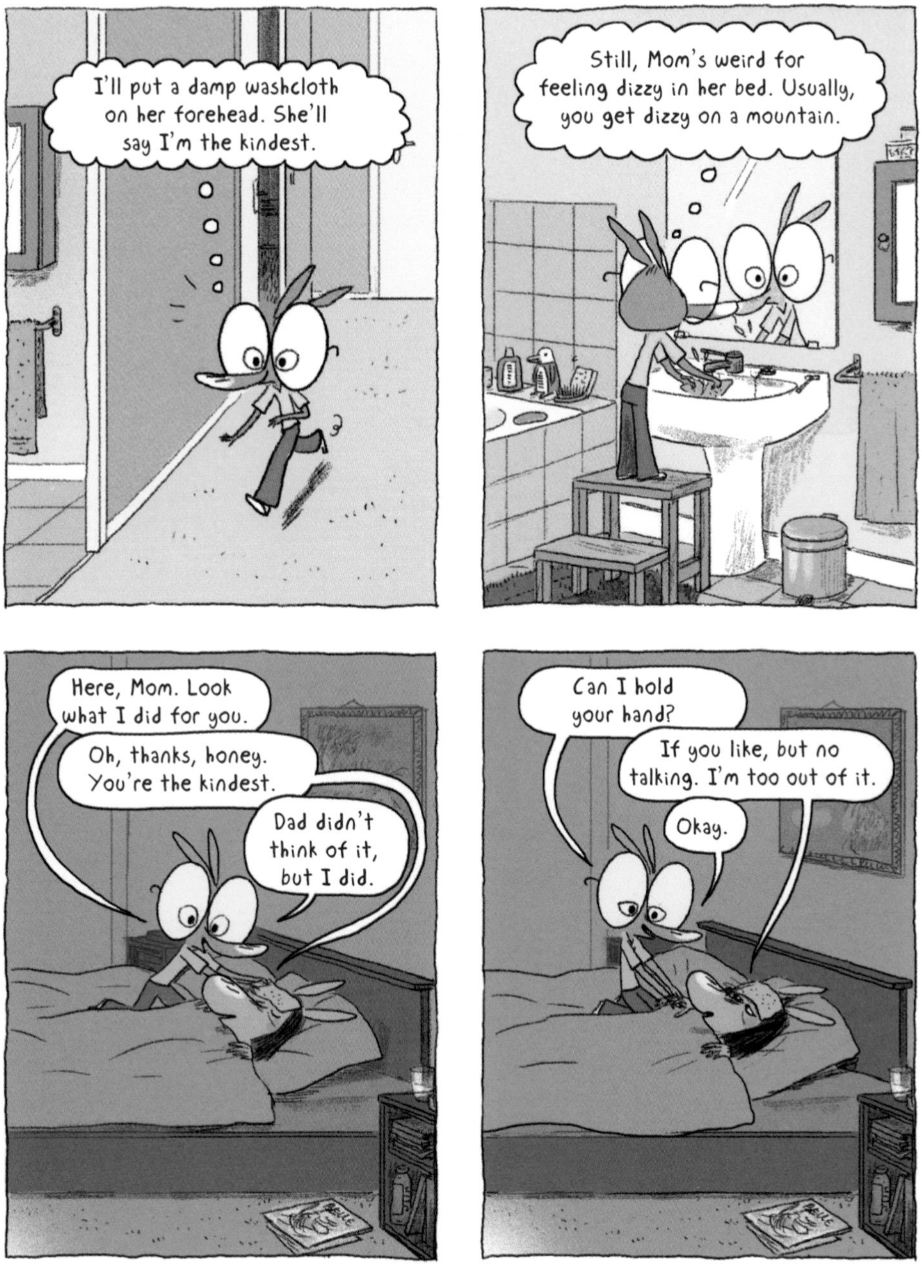
I'll put a damp washcloth on her forehead. She'll say I'm the kindest.
Still, Mom's weird for feeling dizzy in her bed. Usually, you get dizzy on a mountain.
Here, Mom. Look what I did for you.
Oh, thanks, honey. You're the kindest.
Dad didn't think of it, but I did.
Can I hold your hand?
If you like, but no talking. I'm too out of it.
Okay.

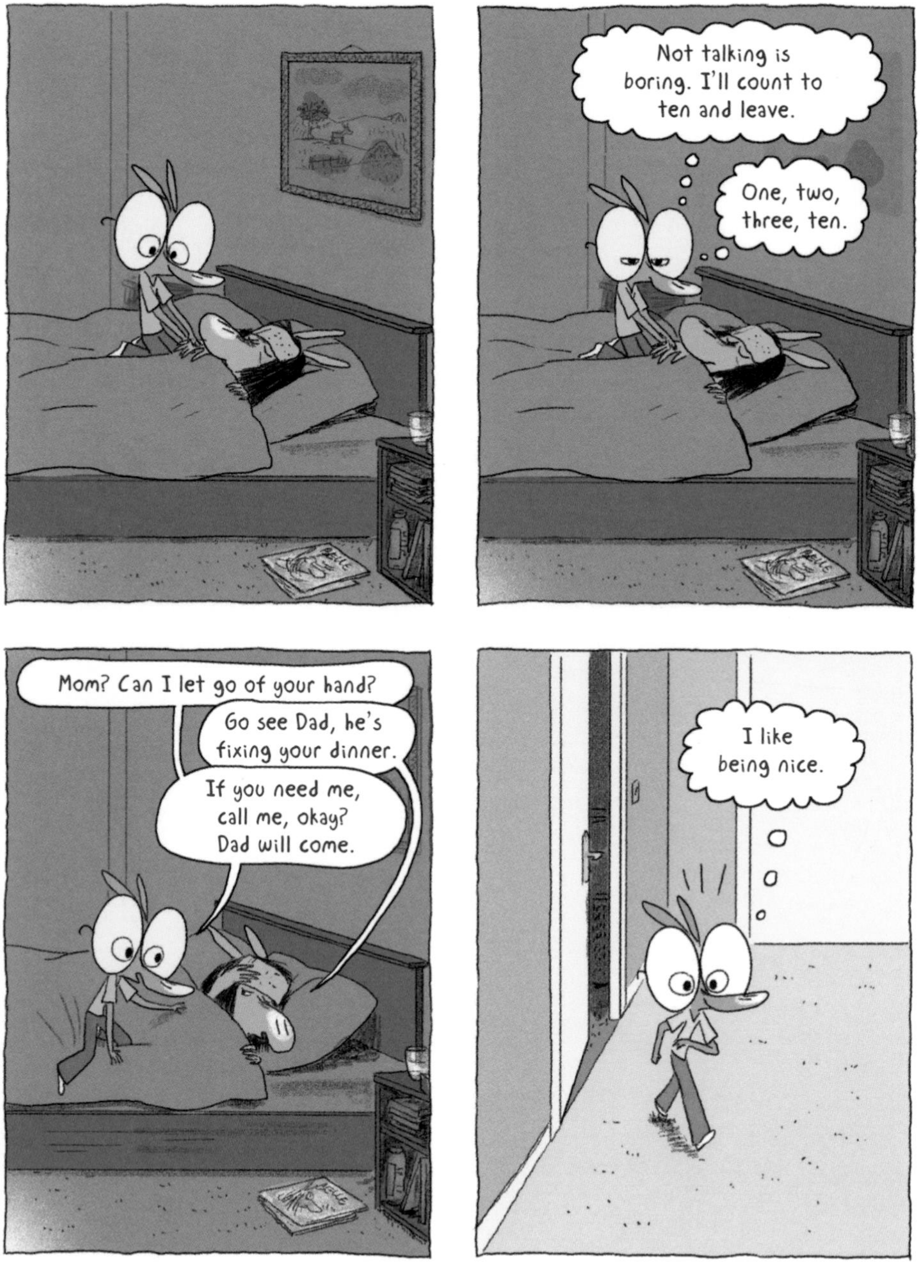
Not talking is boring. I'll count to ten and leave.
One, two, three, ten.
Mom? Can I let go of your hand?
Go see Dad, he's fixing your dinner.
If you need me, call me, okay? Dad will come.
I like being nice.

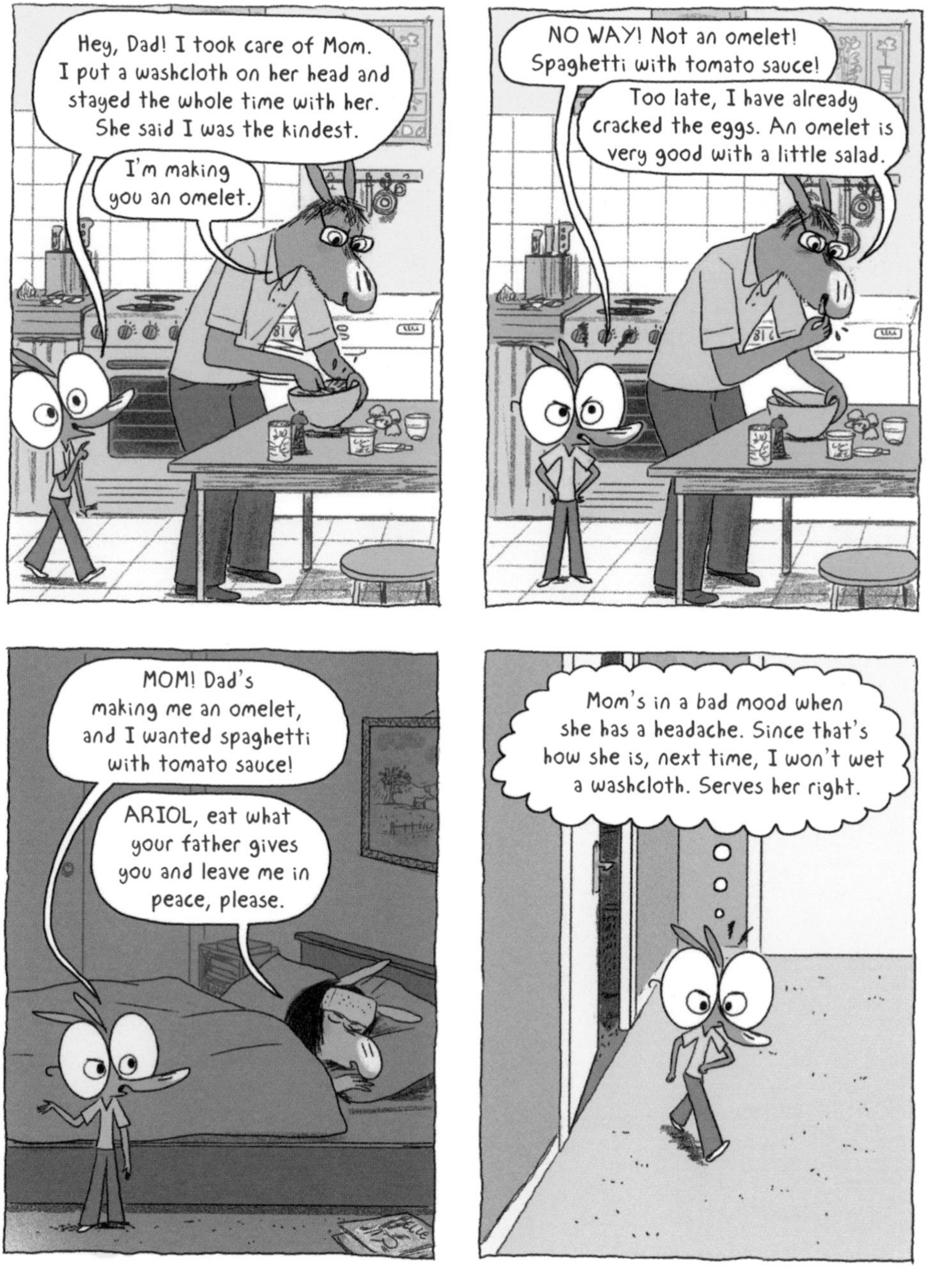
Hey, Dad! I took care of Mom. I put a washcloth on her head and stayed the whole time with her. She said I was the kindest.
I'm making you an omelet.
NO WAY! Not an omelet! Spaghetti with tomato sauce!
Too late, I have already cracked the eggs. An omelet is very good with a little salad.
MOM! Dad's making me an omelet, and I wanted spaghetti with tomato sauce!
ARIOL, eat what your father gives you and leave me in peace, please.
Mom's in a bad mood when she has a headache. Since that's how she is, next time, I won't wet a washcloth. Serves her right.

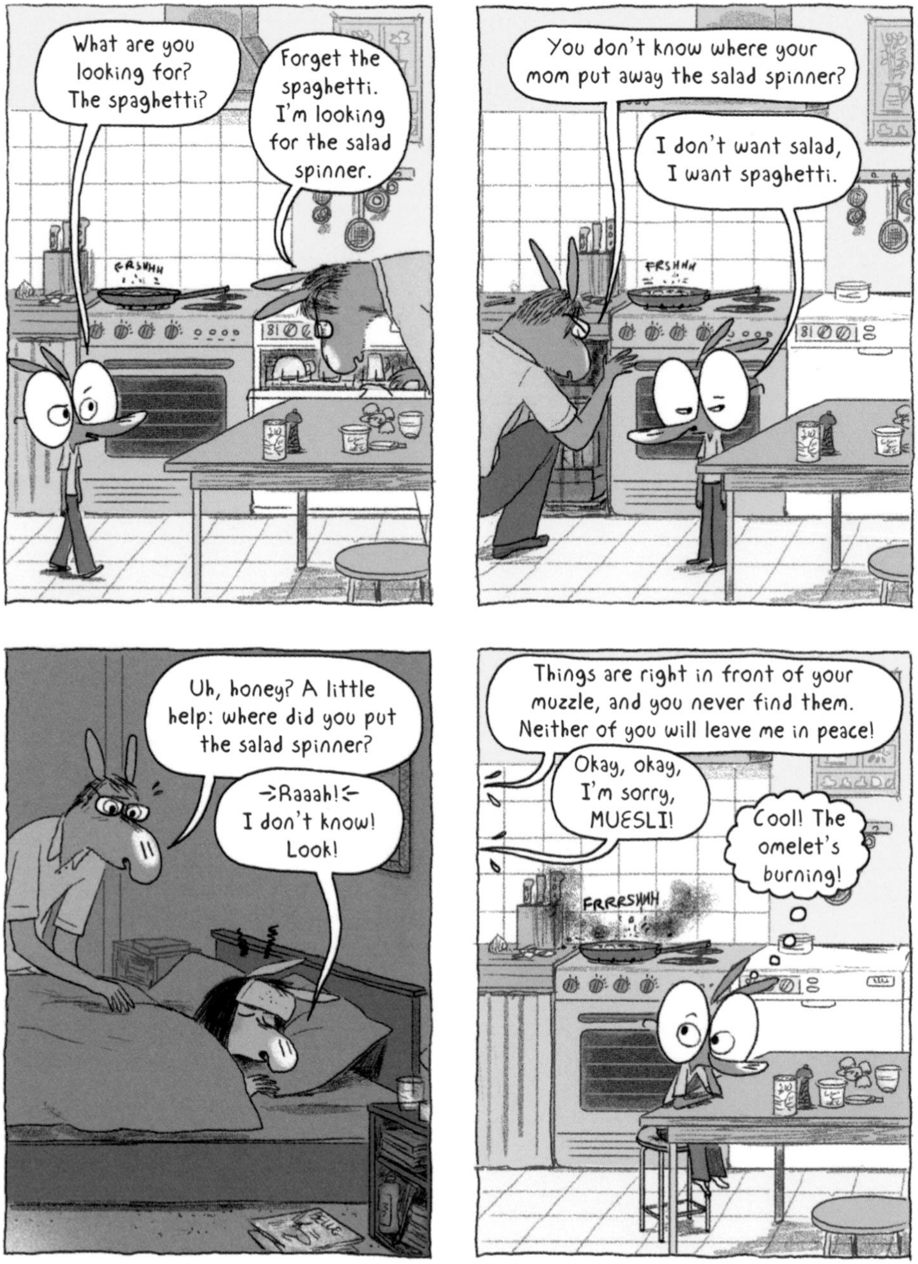
What are you looking for? The spaghetti?
Forget the spaghetti. I'm looking for the salad spinner.
FRSHHH
You don't know where your mom put away the salad spinner?
I don't want salad, I want spaghetti.
FRSHHH
Uh, honey? A little help: where did you put the salad spinner?
Raaah! I don't know! Look!
Things are right in front of your muzzle, and you never find them. Neither of you will leave me in peace!
Okay, okay, I'm sorry, MUESLI!
Cool! The omelet's burning!
FRRRSHHH

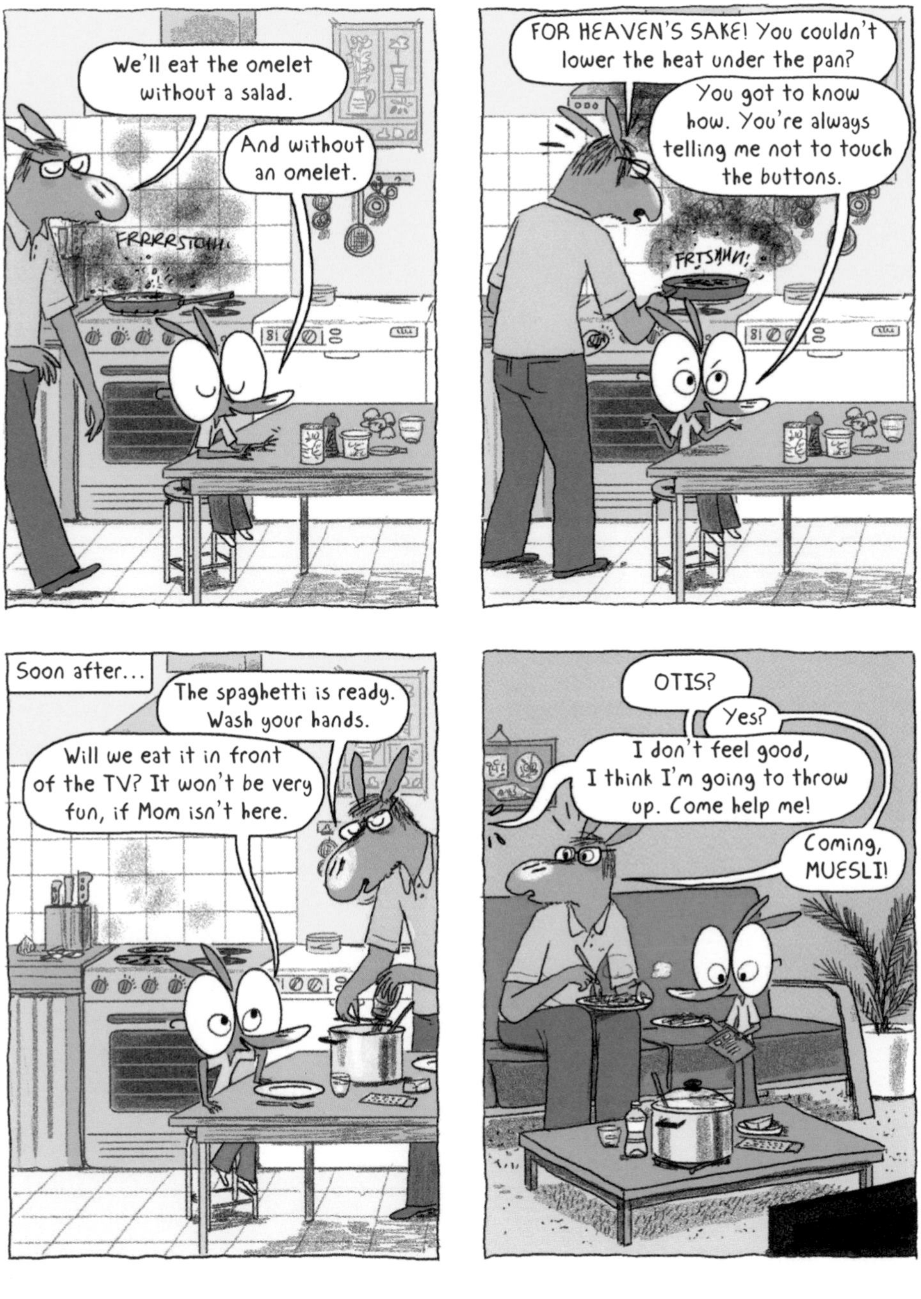
We'll eat the omelet without a salad.
And without an omelet.
FRRRRSTCHH!
FOR HEAVEN'S SAKE! You couldn't lower the heat under the pan?
You got to know how. You're always telling me not to touch the buttons.
FRTSHHN!
Soon after...
The spaghetti is ready. Wash your hands.
Will we eat it in front of the TV? It won't be very fun, if Mom isn't here.
OTIS?
Yes?
I don't feel good, I think I'm going to throw up. Come help me!
Coming, MUESLI!

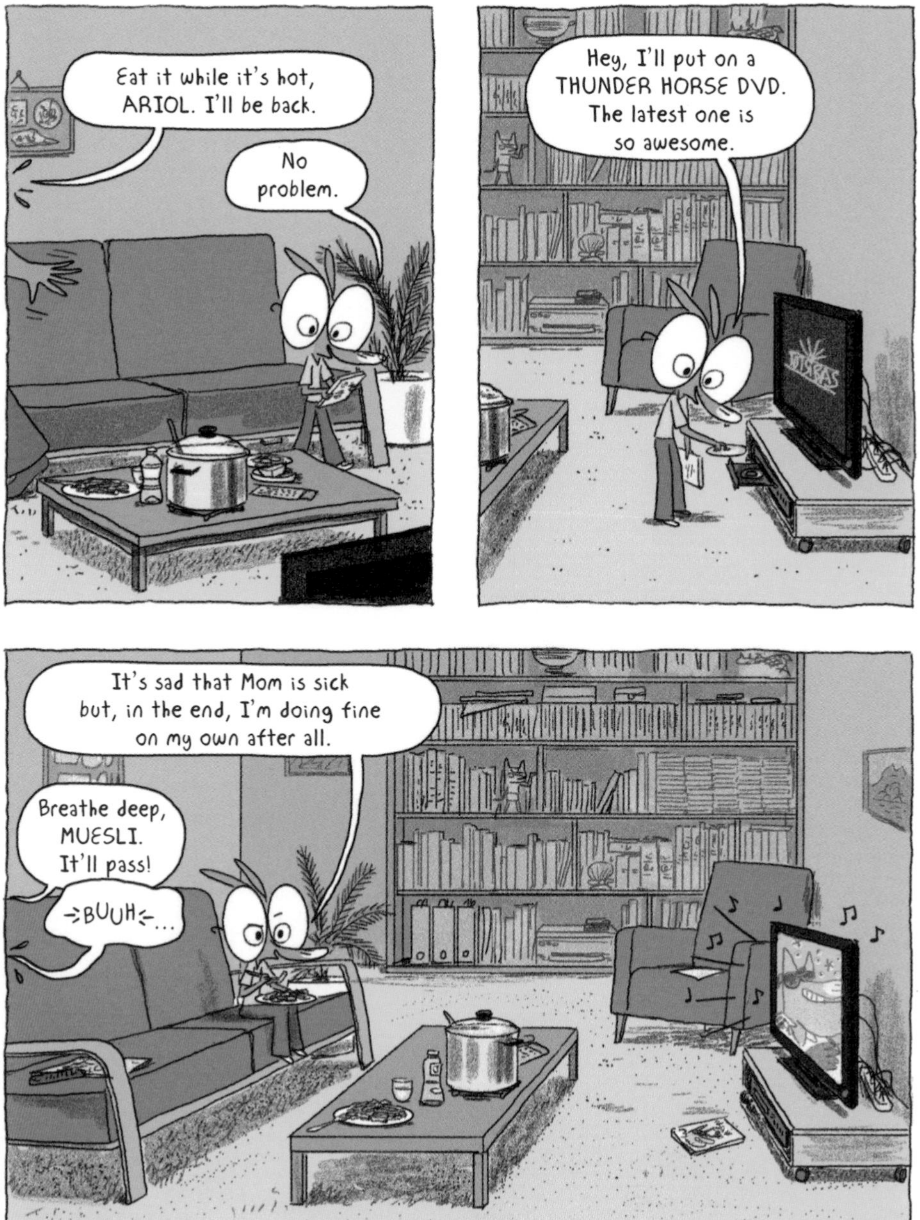
Eat it while it's hot, ARIOL. I'll be back.
No problem.
Hey, I'll put on a THUNDER HORSE DVD. The latest one is so awesome.
It's sad that Mom is sick but, in the end, I'm doing fine on my own after all.
Breathe deep, MUESLI. It'll pass!
BUUH...
End

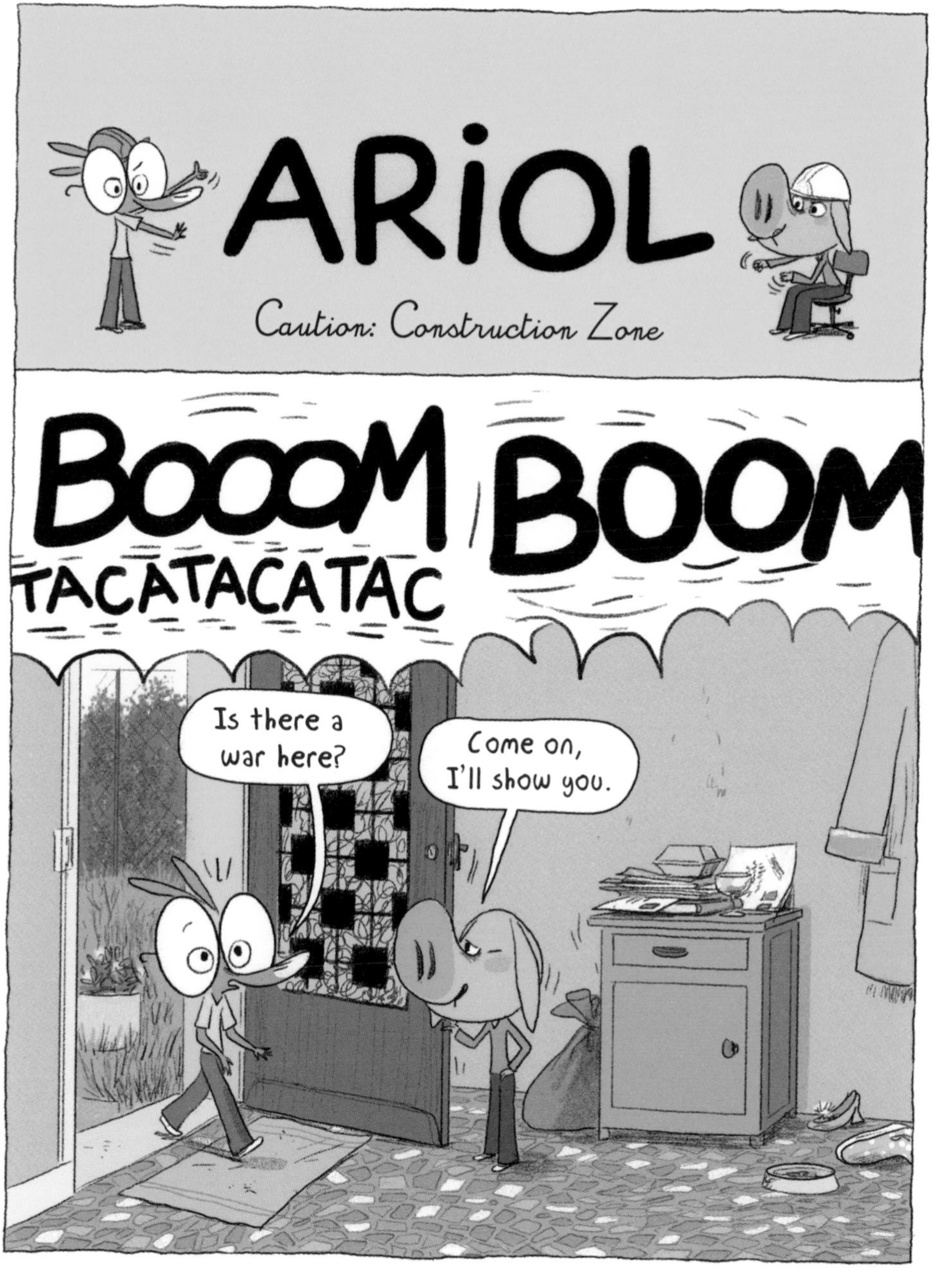
ARIOL
Caution: Construction Zone
BOOOM BOOM
TACATACATAC
Is there a war here?
Come on, I'll show you.

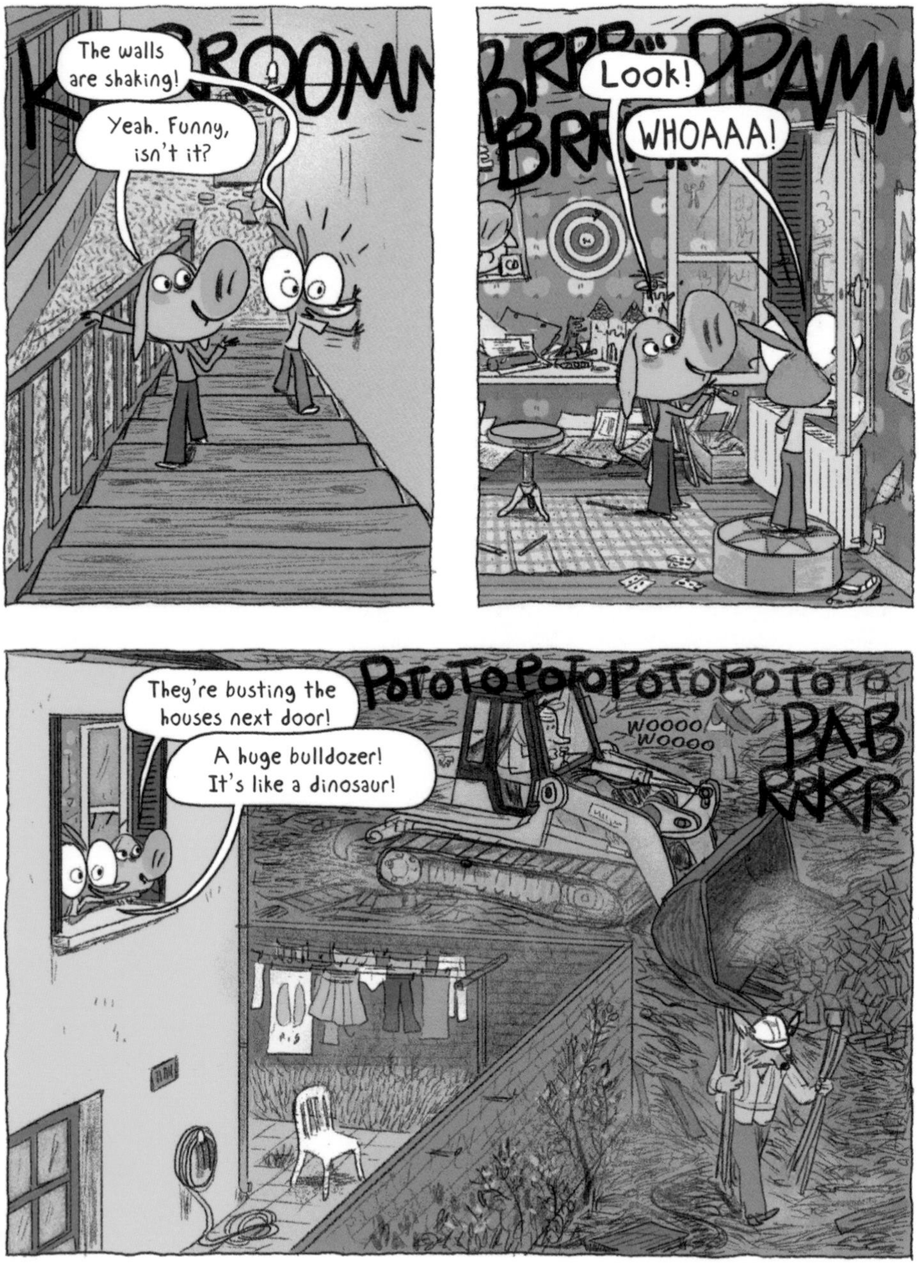
The walls are shaking!
Yeah. Funny, isn't it?
Look!
WHOAAA!
POTOTOPOTOPOTOPOTOPOTOTO
WOOOO WOOOO
PAB
They're busting the houses next door!
A huge bulldozer! It's like a dinosaur!

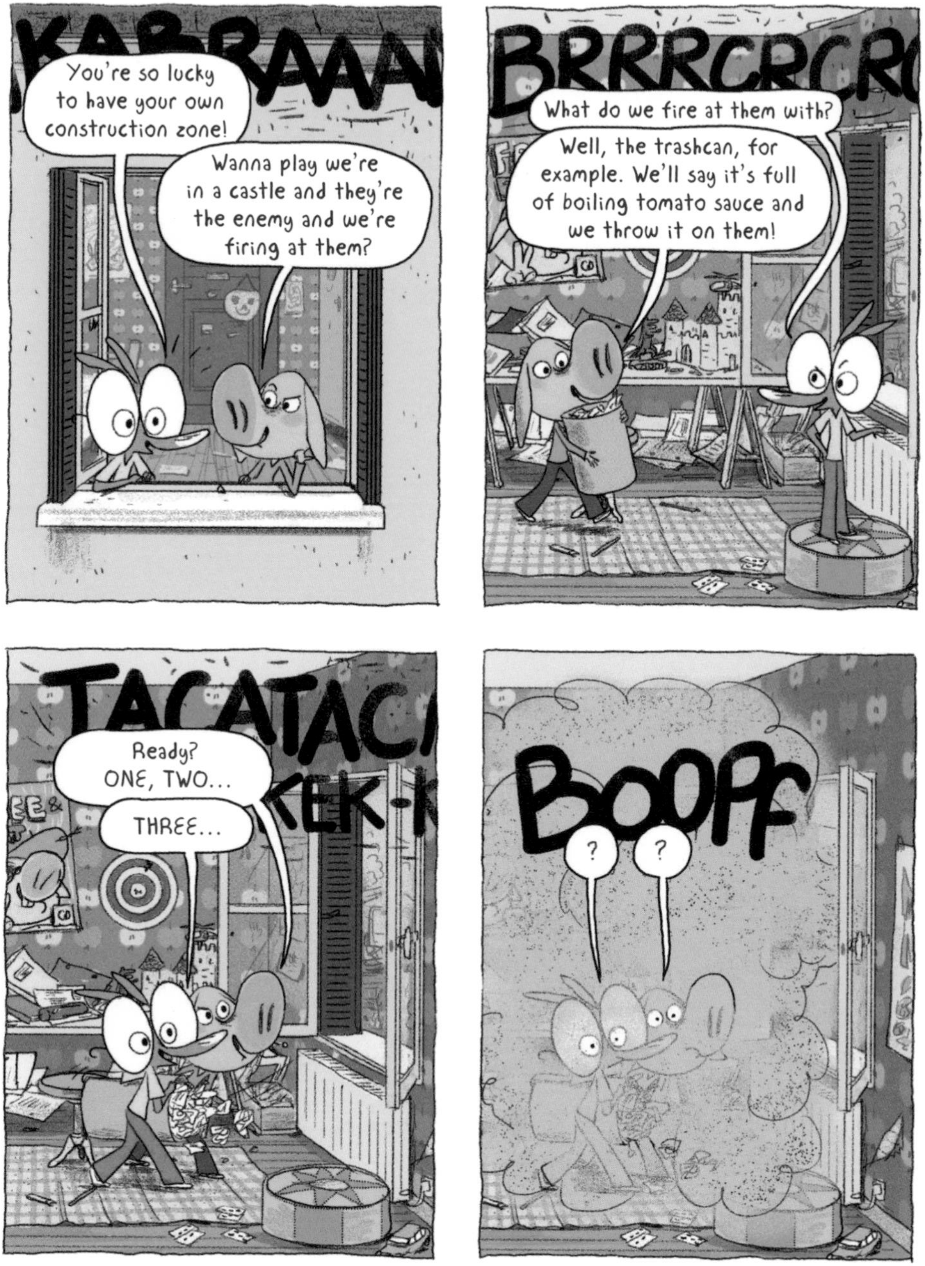
KABRAAA
You're so lucky to have your own construction zone!
Wanna play we're in a castle and they're the enemy and we're firing at them?
BRRRCRCRC
What do we fire at them with?
Well, the trashcan, for example. We'll say it's full of boiling tomato sauce and we throw it on them!
TACATACA
KEK-K
Ready? ONE, TWO...
THREE...
BOOPF
?
?

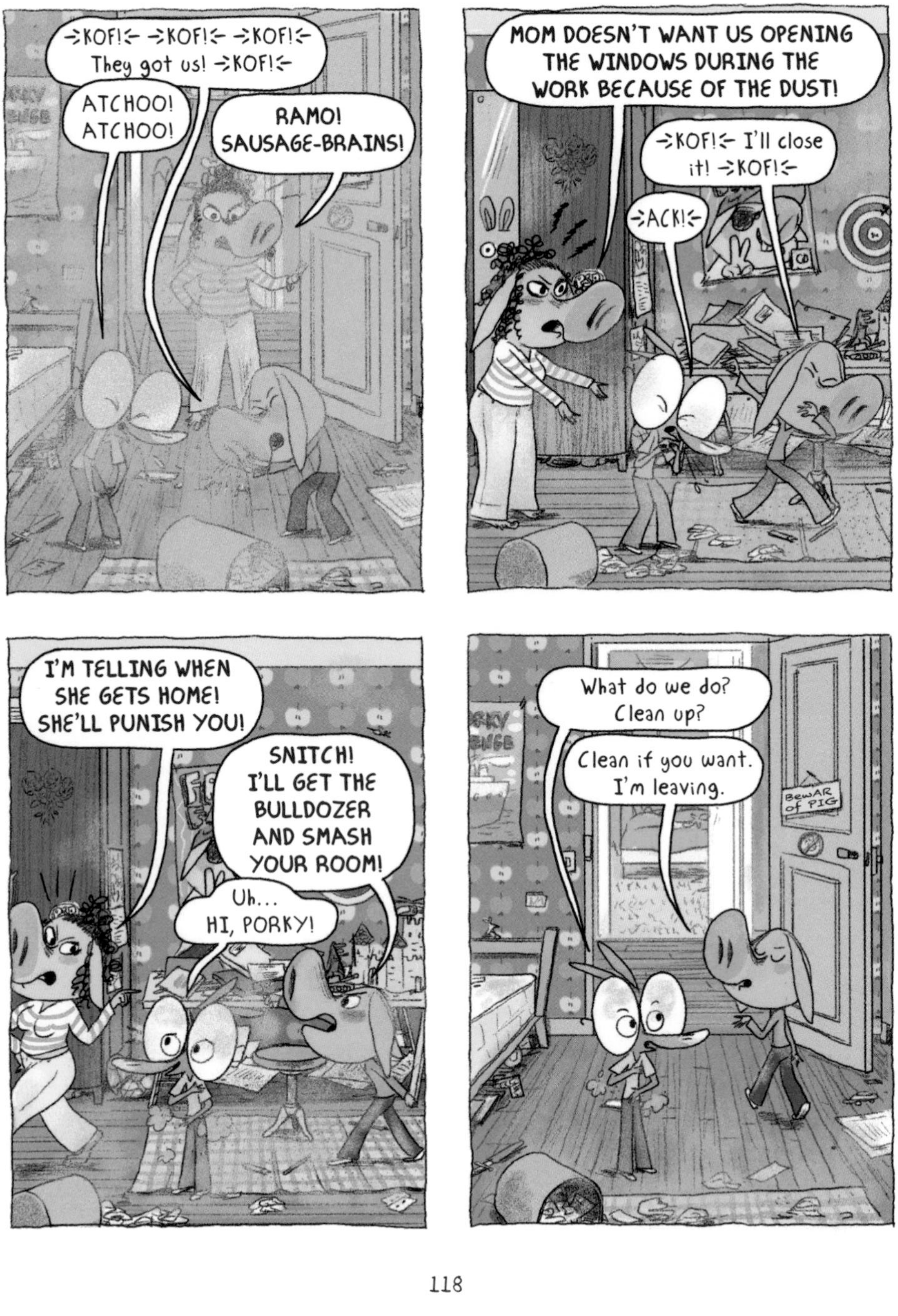

KOF! KOF! KOF! They got us! KOF!
ATCHOO! ATCHOO!
RAMO! SAUSAGE-BRAINS!
MOM DOESN'T WANT US OPENING THE WINDOWS DURING THE WORK BECAUSE OF THE DUST!
KOF! I'll close it! KOF!
ACK!
I'M TELLING WHEN SHE GETS HOME! SHE'LL PUNISH YOU!
SNITCH! I'LL GET THE BULLDOZER AND SMASH YOUR ROOM!
Uh... HI, PORKY!
What do we do? Clean up?
Clean if you want. I'm leaving.
BEWARE of PIG

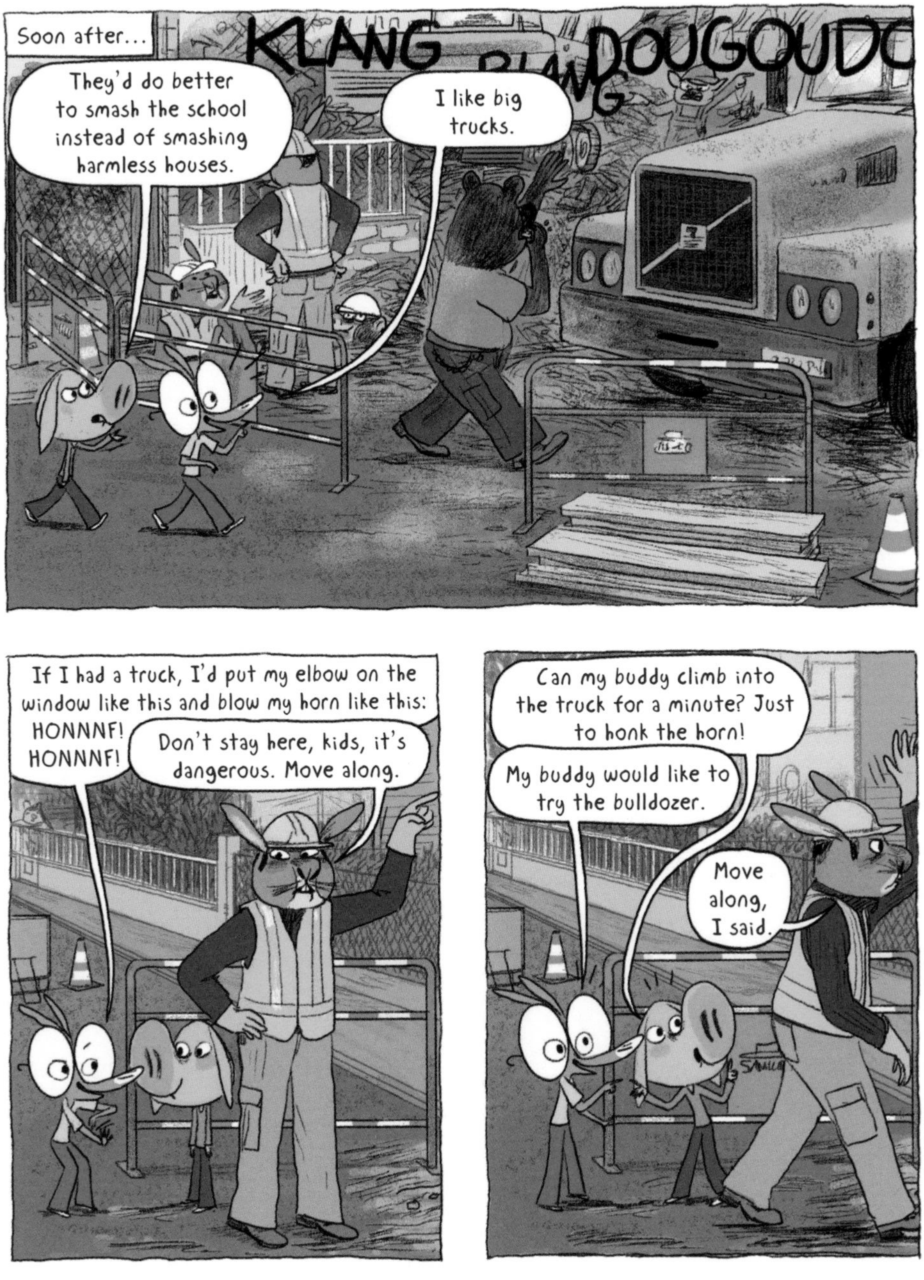

Soon after...
KLANG
BLANG
DOUGOUDO
They'd do better to smash the school instead of smashing harmless houses.
I like big trucks.
If I had a truck, I'd put my elbow on the window like this and blow my horn like this: HONNNF! HONNNF!
Don't stay here, kids, it's dangerous. Move along.
Can my buddy climb into the truck for a minute? Just to honk the horn!
My buddy would like to try the bulldozer.
Move along, I said.

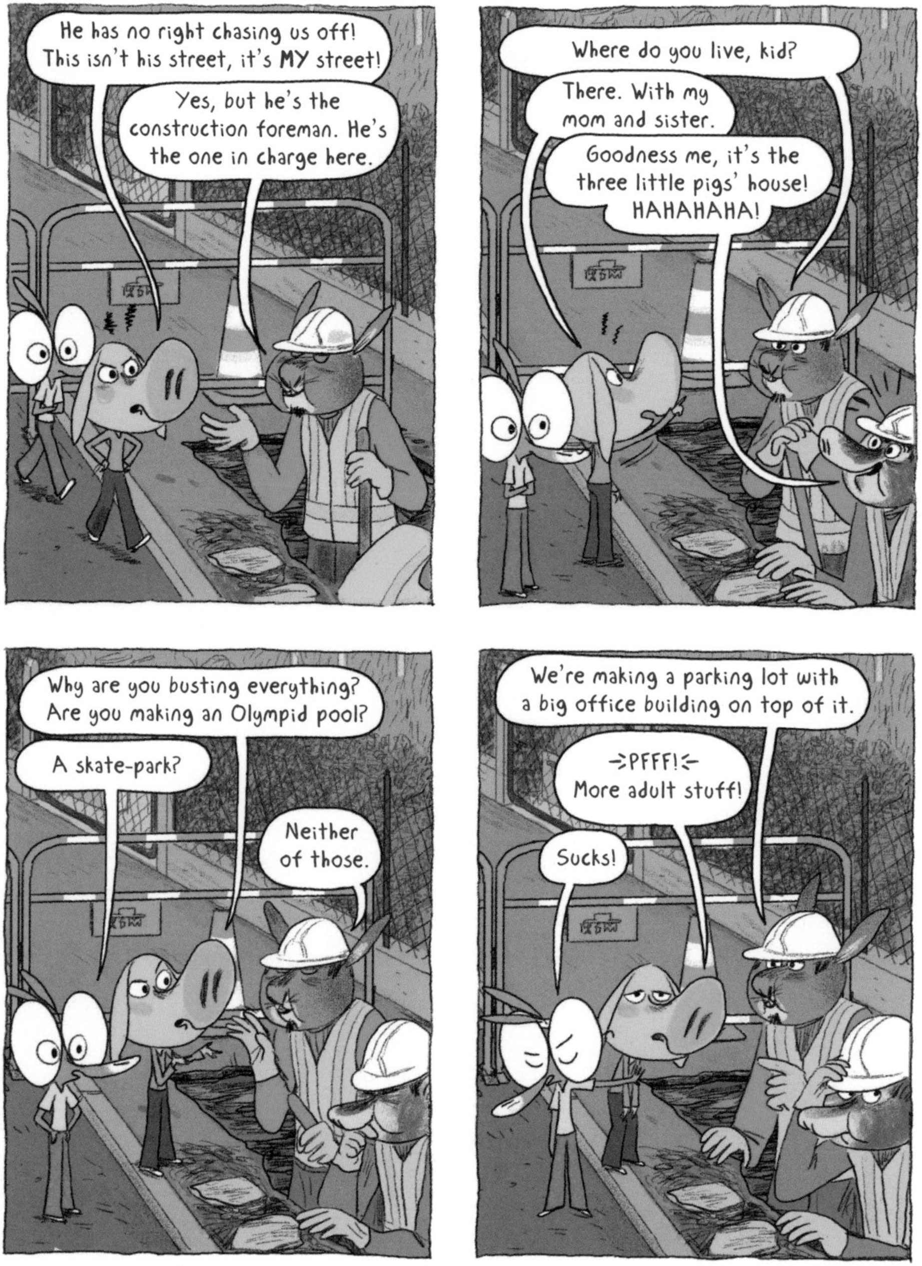
He has no right chasing us off! This isn't his street, it's MY street!
Yes, but he's the construction foreman. He's the one in charge here.
Where do you live, kid?
There. With my mom and sister.
Goodness me, it's the three little pigs' house! HAHAHAHA!
Why are you busting everything? Are you making an Olympid pool?
A skate-park?
Neither of those.
We're making a parking lot with a big office building on top of it.
PFFF! More adult stuff!
Sucks!

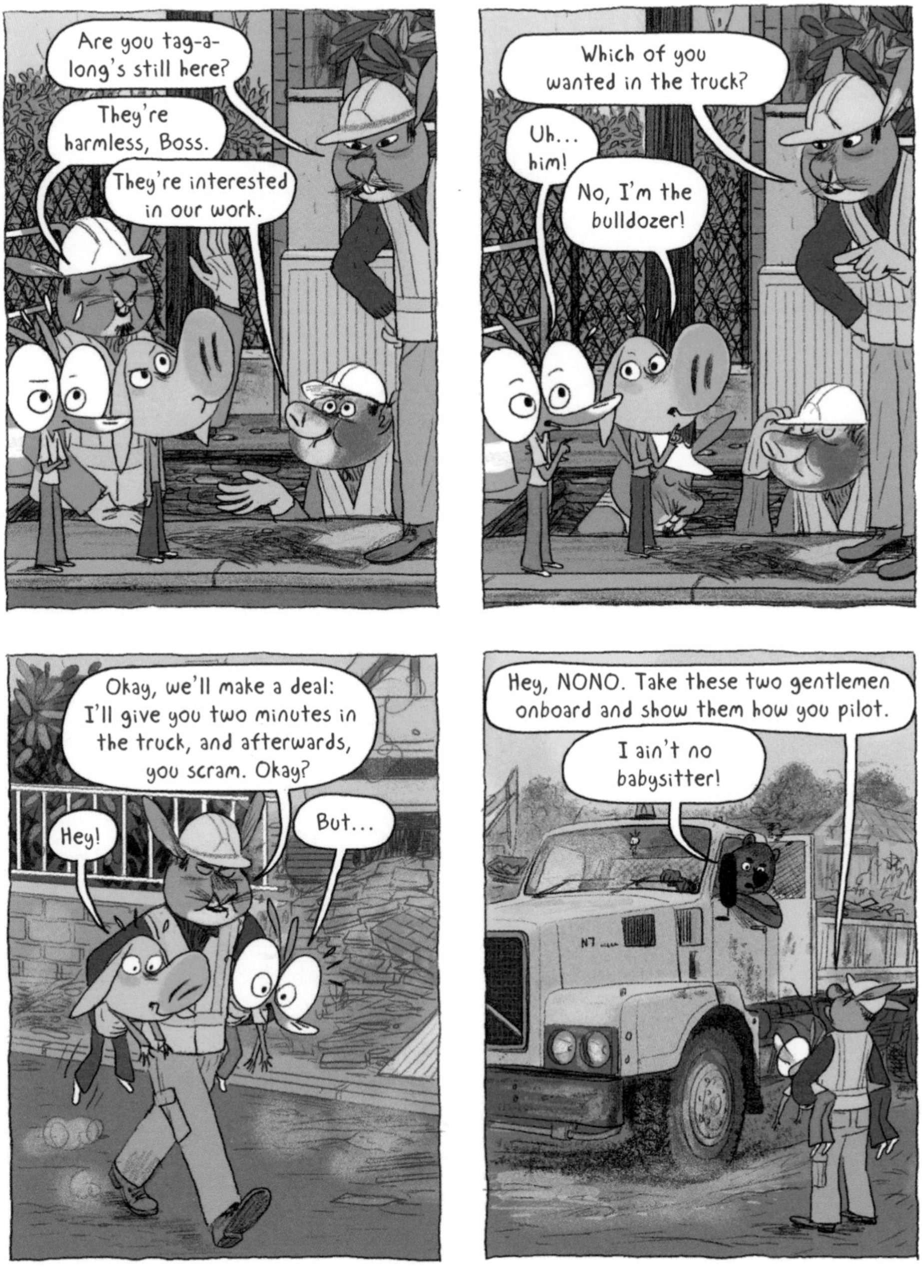
Are you tag-a-long's still here?
They're harmless, Boss.
They're interested in our work.
Which of you wanted in the truck?
Uh... him!
No, I'm the bulldozer!
Okay, we'll make a deal: I'll give you two minutes in the truck, and afterwards, you scram. Okay?
Hey!
But...
Hey, NONO. Take these two gentlemen onboard and show them how you pilot.
I ain't no babysitter!

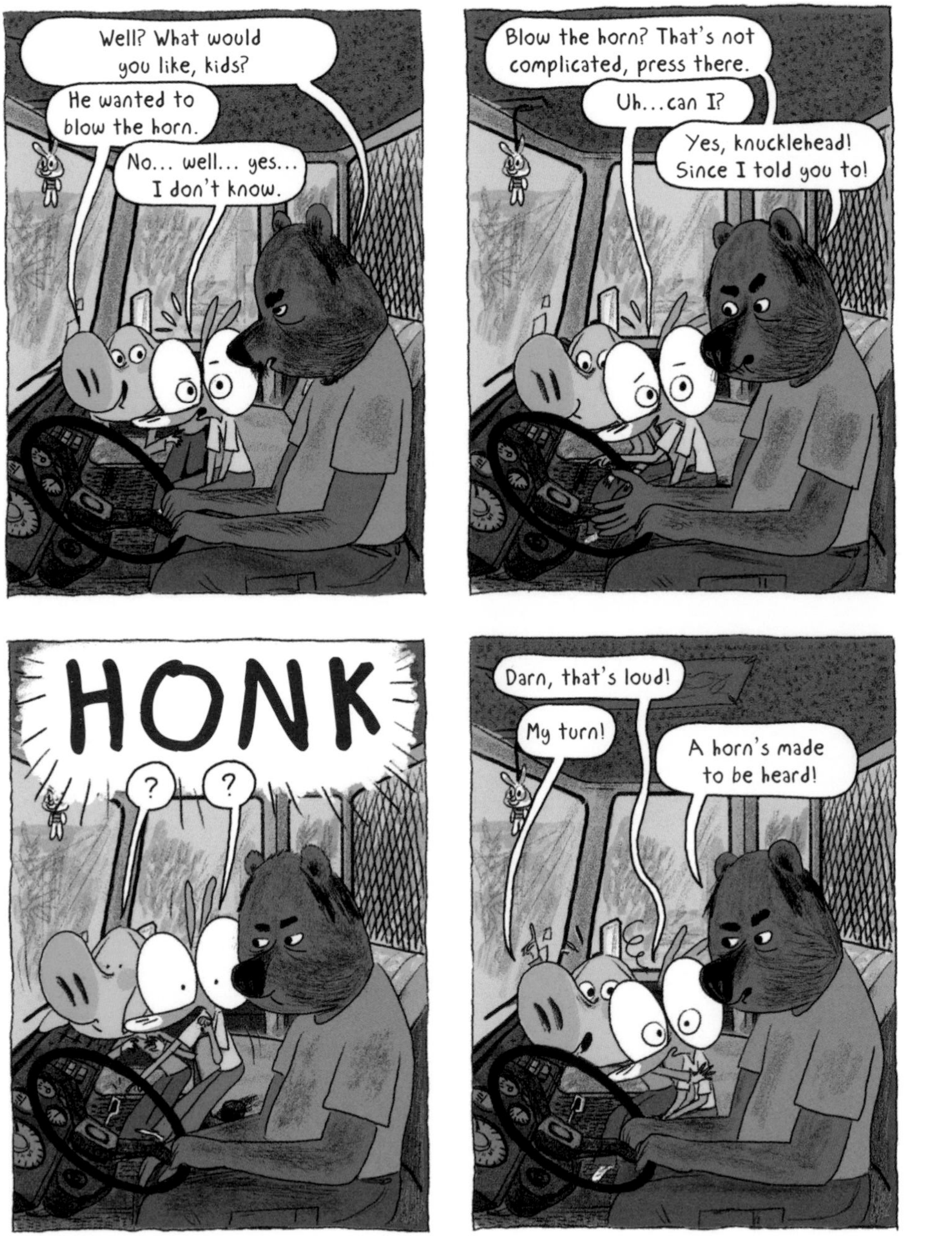
Well? What would you like, kids?
He wanted to blow the horn.
No... well... yes... I don't know.
Blow the horn? That's not complicated, press there.
Uh...can I?
Yes, knucklehead! Since I told you to!
HONK
?
?
Darn, that's loud!
My turn!
A horn's made to be heard!

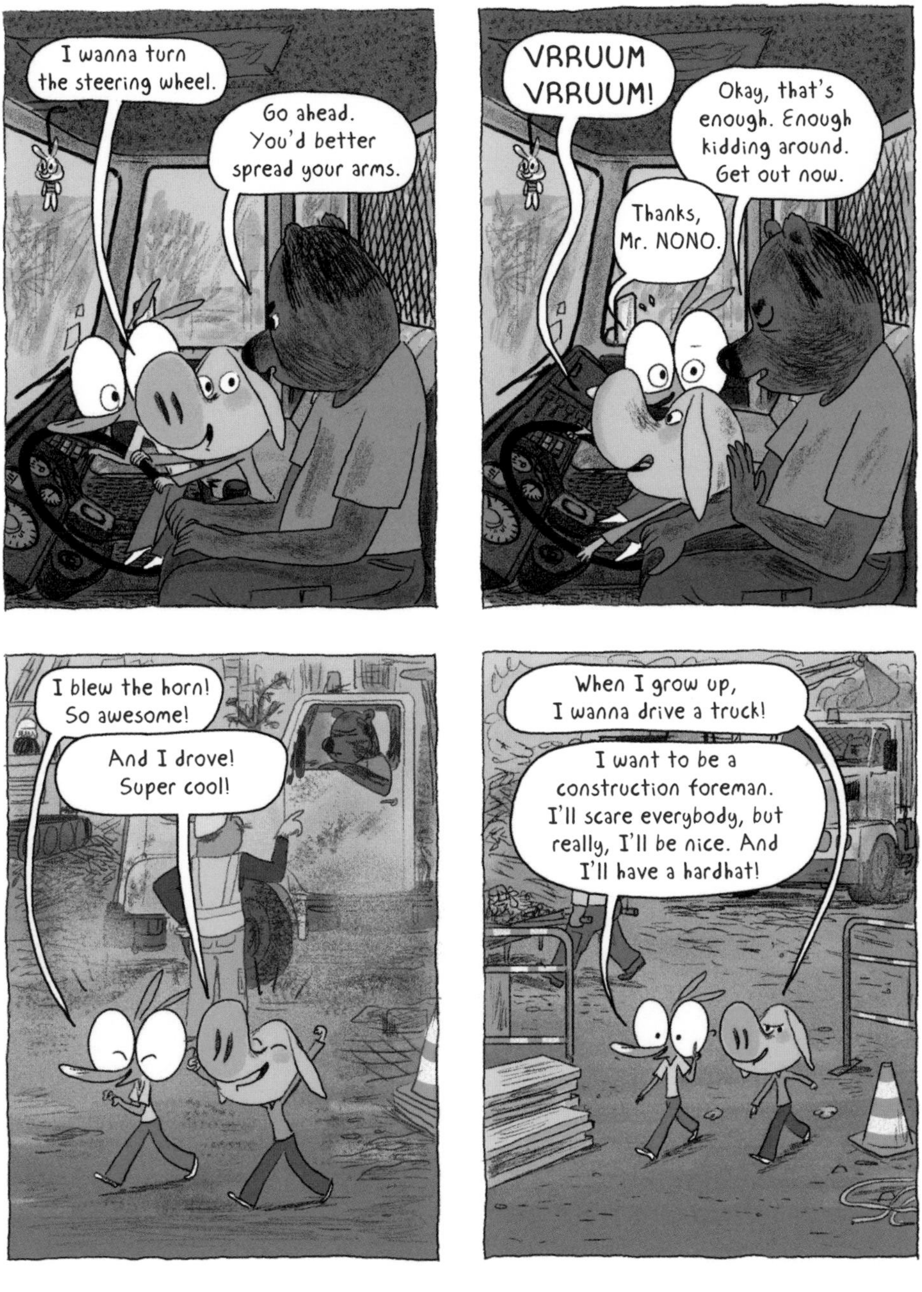
I wanna turn the steering wheel.
Go ahead. You'd better spread your arms.
VRRUUM VRRUUM!
Okay, that's enough. Enough kidding around. Get out now.
Thanks, Mr. NONO.
I blew the horn! So awesome!
And I drove! Super cool!
When I grow up, I wanna drive a truck!
I want to be a construction foreman. I'll scare everybody, but really, I'll be nice. And I'll have a hardhat!

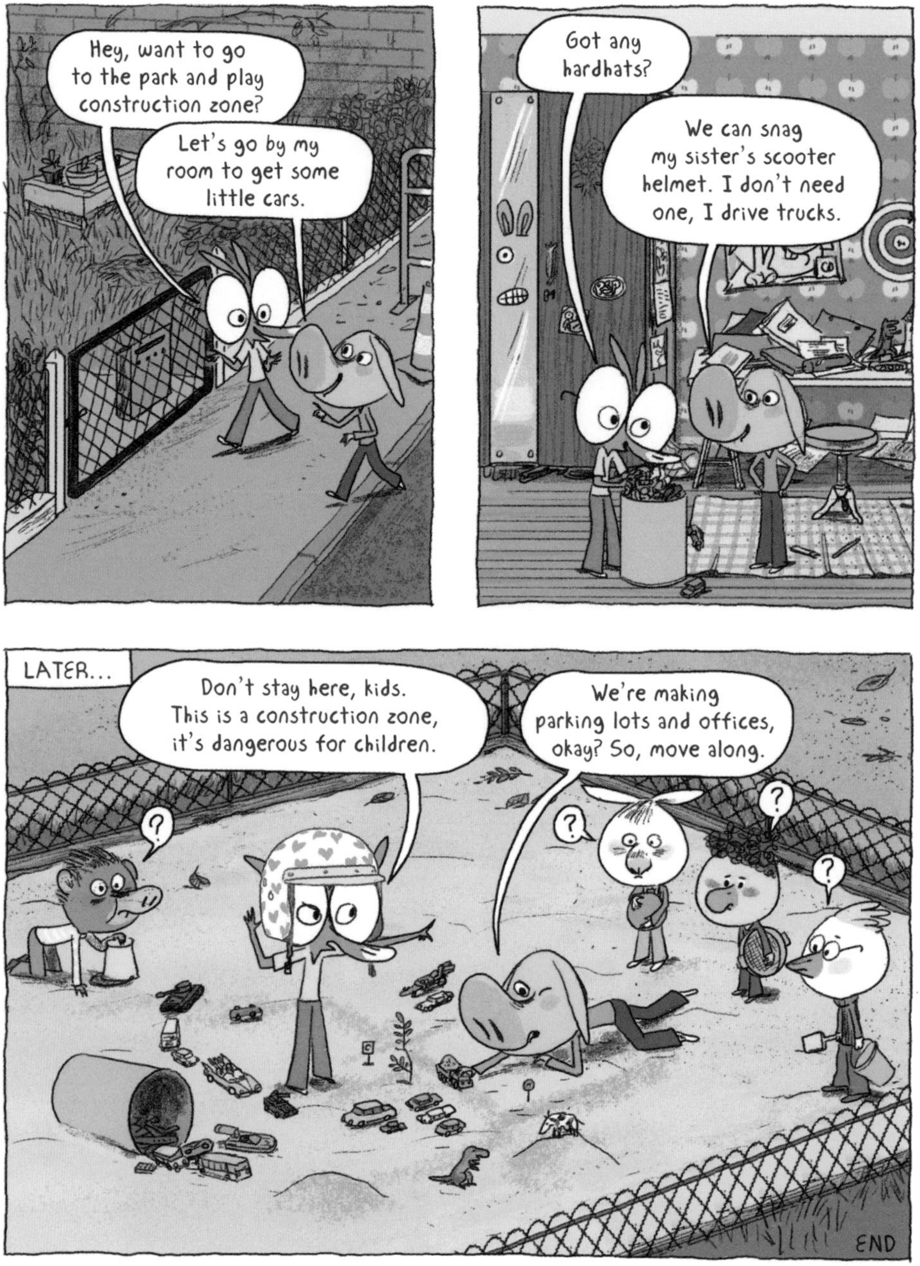
Hey, want to go to the park and play construction zone?
Let's go by my room to get some little cars.
Got any hardhats?
We can snag my sister's scooter helmet. I don't need one, I drive trucks.
LATER...
Don't stay here, kids. This is a construction zone, it's dangerous for children.
We're making parking lots and offices, okay? So, move along.
?
?
?
?
END

WATCH OUT FOR PAPERCUTZ ™

Welcome to the booty-shaking, THUNDER HORSE-approved, tenth ARIOL graphic novel, by Emmanuel Guibert and Marc Boutavant, from Papercutz – those tantrum-throwing, thick-skinned-types dedicated to publishing great graphic novels for all ages. I'm Jim Salicrup, Editor-in-Chief and part-time Comics Professor, and I'm here to offer a few personal reflections regarding ARIOL. To be clear, Emmanuel Guibert is the writer of ARIOL, but his stories sometimes echo events from my childhood –– which Emmanuel can't possibly know about –– so it's kinda spooky. Maybe it's not just me. Do any of you find events in ARIOL that seem like something that happened to you? Without further ado, here are some examples of art imitating (my) life…

In "Stinky Cheese," Ariol's dad argues that "there are things you hate as a kid that you like later on." This has certainly turned out to be true for me, but I still don't like stinky cheese. Maybe I'm still not old enough?

In "Shall We Dance?," we meet Yakima, who tries to teach Ariol's class to dance. As I've written in DANCE CLASS, another great Papercutz graphic novel series, I've been a dance student forever and I love it! If Ariol wants to get closer to Petula, dance is certainly one way to do it! It worked in this story!

"Photomate" features one of those photobooths that I love. There's even a graphic novel by Meags Fitzgerald called "Photobooth: A Biography" that I also love. (And it's not even published by Papercutz!)

"At the Street Market" really hits home for me. I had that toy garage as a boy and I loved it too!

While I may not have agonized about "A Burdensome Secret" as much as Ariol, I did grapple with the same problem when I was his age.

"At Landard's" presents the problem of a child being exposed to an adult behaving badly. These things happen, and I don't think the younger me handled it as well as Ariol and his dad.

One of my best friends growing up was Stefan Petrucha, who has written many Papercutz graphic novels over the years. When we were kids we were always working on creating our own comics, and one of the key lessons we had to learn, like Ariol and Ramono in "A Story in Six Lines," is learning to "write them down."

Is it me, or does candidate Frisette Lamproy in "Voted" look a little like Noodles in "At Landard's"? Not only is Ariol's Granny Annie as forgetful as my mother was, now I'm becoming that forgetful! (I almost forgot to mention that!)

I've already told the story in another Papercutz graphic novel of how Stefan Petrucha saved my life when we were staying at a summer house on a lake in New Jersey. "The Inflatable Pool" reminds me of the inflatable raft that almost lead to my demise. While the blazing hot sand that confronts Ariol and Ramono in "Heatwave," is another reason I'm not that wild about going to the beach.

"An Evening without Mom" is a painful reminder of how helpless I would feel when my dad would get migraine headaches. It's never fun to see the people you love suffer.

Finally, "Caution: Construction Zone" is a little too close to our current reality at the palatial Papercutz offices –– there's construction going on in both the floors above and below us. We thought we left such worries behind when we left our old office, where construction workers were literally blasting through the Manhattan's bedrock to lay the foundation for another skyscraper. Every time we heard a whistle blow, we'd hear another explosion! BOOM!

Upon further reflection I realize that Emmanuel Guibert is simply a brilliant writer, and his stories, so beautifully drawn by Marc Boutavant, attain a level of verisimilitude that totally pulls me into Ariol's world, to such a degree that I begin to believe that I'm seeing my own life in the pages of ARIOL! That shouldn't really surprise me. After all, aren't we all, Ariol included, "Just a Donkey Like You and Me"?

Thanks,

Jim

STAY IN TOUCH!

EMAIL: salicrup@papercutz.com
WEB: papercutz.com
TWITTER: @papercutzgn
INSTAGRAM: @papercutzgn
FACEBOOK: PAPERCUTZGRAPHICNOVELS
REGULAR MAIL: Papercutz, 160 Broadway,
                Suite 700, East Wing, New York, NY 10038

Other Great Titles From PAPERCUTZ™

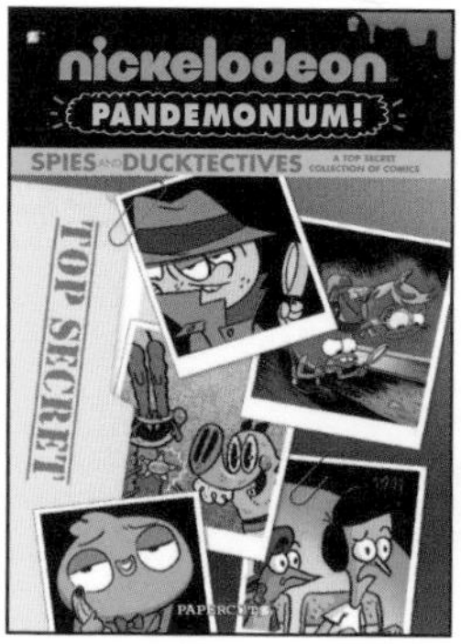
nickelodeon
PANDEMONIUM!
SPIES AND DUCKTECTIVES
A TOP SECRET COLLECTION OF COMICS
TOP SECRET
PAPERCUTZ

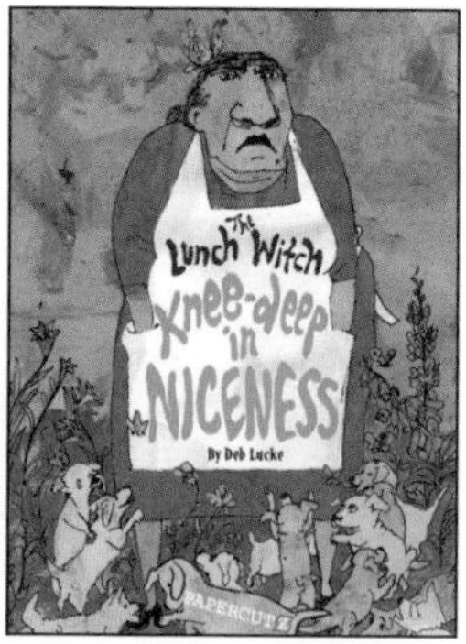
The Lunch Witch
Knee-deep in NICENESS
By Deb Lucke
PAPERCUTZ

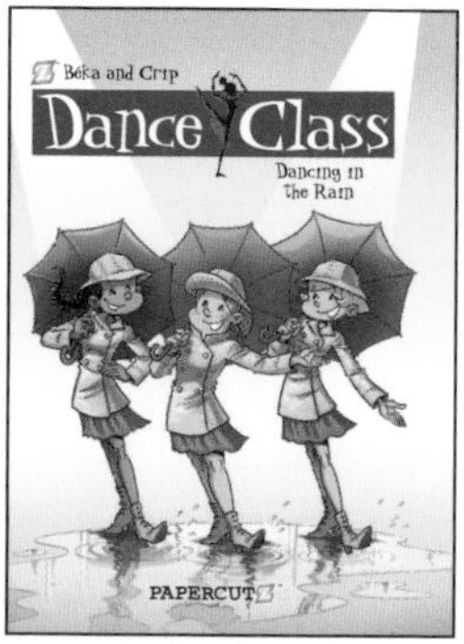
Béka and Crip
Dance Class
Dancing in the Rain
PAPERCUTZ

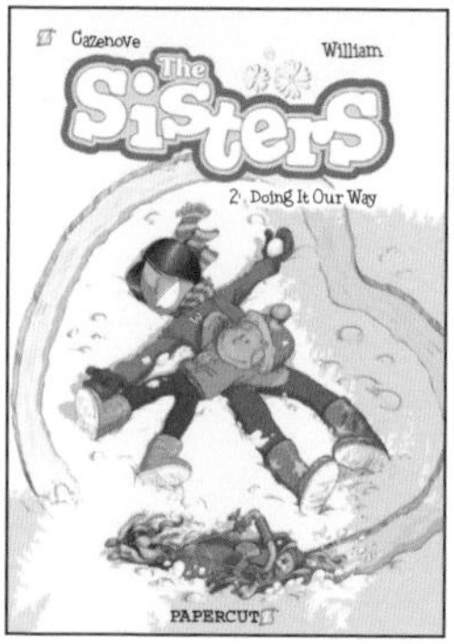
Cazenove
William
The Sisters
2 Doing It Our Way
PAPERCUTZ

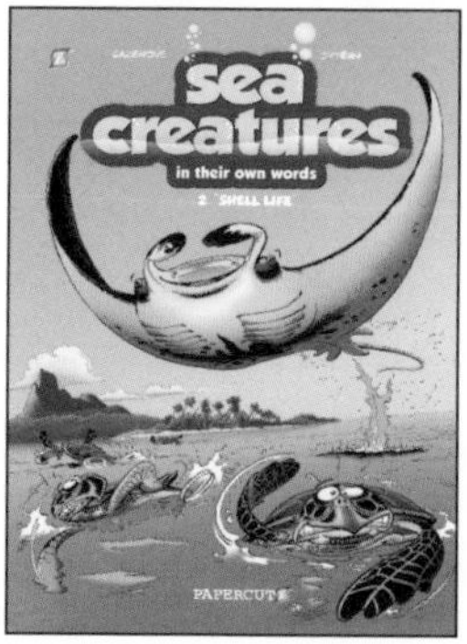
sea creatures
in their own words
2 SHELL LIFE
PAPERCUTZ

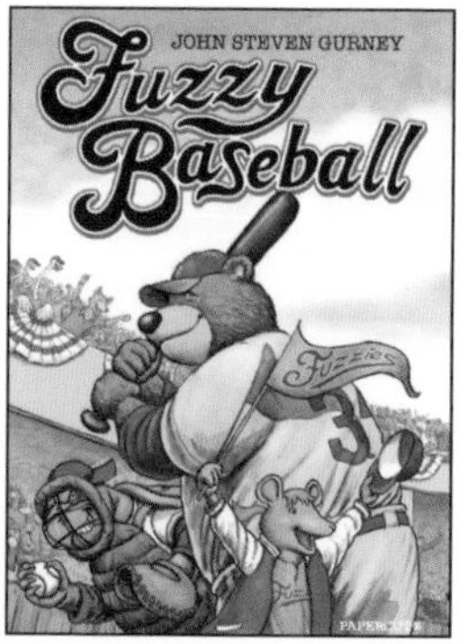
JOHN STEVEN GURNEY
Fuzzy Baseball
FUZZIES

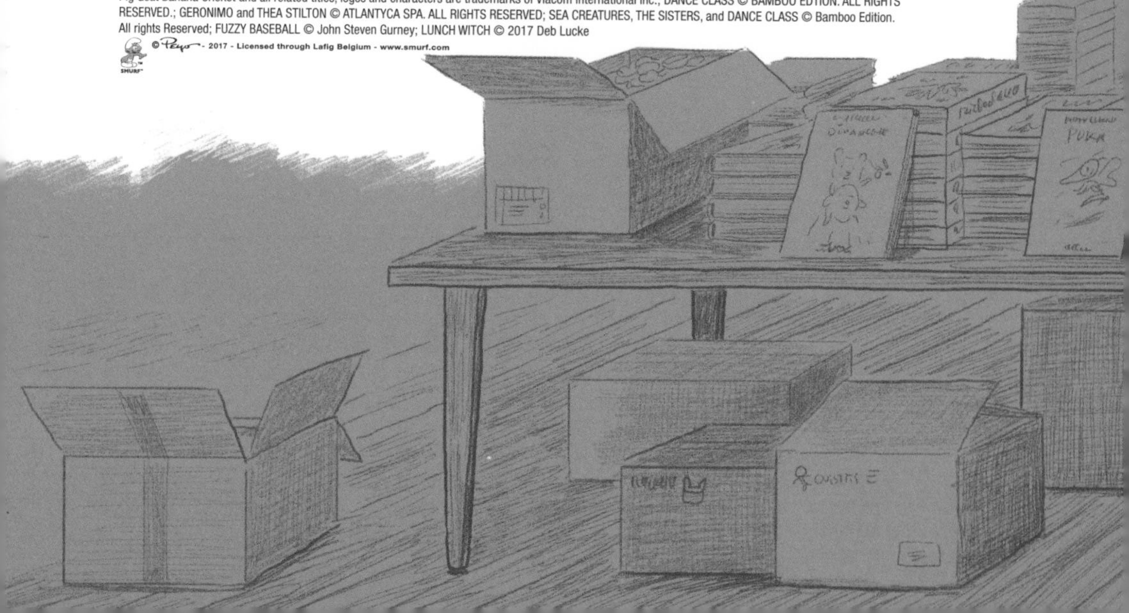